Silent Coup

Silent Coup

Joan Francis

Lobathian Publishers

Silent Coup

Lobathian Publishers

For information address:
Lobthian Publishers
LobathianPubs@aol.com

ISBN: 978-0-9821370-0-0

Printed in the United States of America

In memory of Reg and Gladys Whitlock.

Diana

1

"Otto Brehm—Attorney at Law" was written in fading gold letters on the second-story window. At least the office was real. The car Brehm had promised would pick me up at the airport had never materialized and my repeated calls to him went unanswered. After an hour I had given up and hired a cab. Was Brehm even here? Why would he send me a first class plane ticket from California to North Carolina and not bother to be in when I arrived.

I had been summoned because I was an heir of my great-uncle Bennett. Why, I couldn't imagine. I had only met the man twice when I was a child. He had lived rather like a hermit on a five-acre farm somewhere near the Smoky Mountains. No one ever mentioned why, at least not to me. I had heard that Bennett and his father, Zeb made some money with Prohibition moonshine and that Bennett had a pension from some firm he had worked for, but he had been retired since the mid 1960s. Born in 1911 and retired for decades, there probably wasn't enough left in the estate to justify the cost of my plane fare.

I was hoping my dad would be one of the other persons summoned to North Carolina. I hadn't seen him in over two years and wasn't even sure where he was at the moment. The last letter he wrote two months ago came from Kazakhstan, where he was looking at a barite mine.

My cab had taken a highway from the Tri-cities airport in Tennessee but quickly left it and followed small, winding roads through the scenic Smoky Mountain country bordering the two states. The driver stopped at the address I had been given in Thomasville, a town no more than a mile wide and two miles long. Seemingly caught in a time capsule, this town could double for a movie set of the twenties or thirties with no changes needed. I paid the driver, collected my fanny pack and small suitcase and stepped out onto the sidewalk.

The ground floor of Brehm's building was occupied by a tourist shop. Artfully displayed in the large front windows were handmade arts and crafts, antiques and collectibles, as well as tourist trap items that would probably be stamped "made in China." I entered the door just to the left of the shop which offered a separate entry to the upstairs offices. On the wall just inside the door were six mailboxes. Only three of them in use.

I climbed the narrow, creaking stairs, which were covered in threadbare paisley carpet, each step, like the depression of an atomizer, disturbing the age-old contents and puffing musty odors into the air. The stairs leading to the third floor had been crudely boarded off with one by eight planks. If this lawyer was misusing client money, he either had poor clients or put his money into something besides swank offices.

His office door stood open about six inches, and I let myself in. No one sat at the reception desk, but I could hear angry voices coming from the inner office. I was debating knocking on the inner door when a male voice behind me spoke next to my ear.

"You Diana Hunter?"

I turned to face him and found he was well within my eighteen inches of personal space and the odor of a heavy aftershave was overwhelming. He was about five foot ten, muscular to the point of stressing the seams of his jacket, had buzzed dark hair, a weapon bulging in a shoulder holster, neck mike and ear phone. He took hold of my upper arm, none too gently and I felt a surge of adrenaline and consciously slowed my breathing.

"You're wanted in the lawyer's office, Ms. Hunter."

He tried to push me toward the inner office. I stood my ground, looking first at his beady brown eyes, then at his meaty, short-fingered hand on my arm.

My voice was low and controlled as I said, "Kindly remove your hand from my arm."

Slowly he withdrew his hand. Without another word, I turned and walked to the office door and gave it two short raps. Immediately the door opened, revealing two other agent clones standing, and a slender old man, whom I assumed to be Brehm, seated behind a desk. The contents of drawers and file cabinets were strewn in piles around the floor. The door to a wall safe hung limply from one hinge and blast marks showed it had been blown open. There were also signs of maliciousness that served no purpose. A beautiful old clock carved from many natural woods lay crumpled on the floor. The carved gray-brown bird that had been nested on the top of the clock now sat with wings outspread protectively over the broken wood and tangled clock springs. Beside it lay an old meerschaum pipe carved like the head of a cavalier with a curly beard and floppy hat. Its stem had been crushed. Records and a record player lay in a heap in another corner. All the books had been razored and thrown on the floor.

The shock of seeing the attorney's office dismantled was doubled because it was all too familiar. Just two days before I had returned from a case in Costa Rica to find my apartment similarly destroyed. The anger I felt over my own apartment coupled with the adrenaline rush I was already feeling made me less cautious than I should have been.

"What the hell's going on here? Who are you people?"

A gravely voice asked, "Diana Hunter?" The question came from the one agent of the trio who had a decent haircut and an expensive suit.

"You got it, Dick Tracy. Now who are you? What possible legal justification could you have to go through an attorney's files like this? These are privileged files!"

He responded in a tone of absolute authority. "Sit down, Hunter, and don't give me any of that civil liberties crap. This is a national security matter. Now we will ask the questions. You'll answer them."

Instead of sitting, I walked over to Mr. Brehm. "Did they have any ID or warrant or anything?" As I leaned with my hands on his desk, I could see the tattered end of the phone cord laying on the floor. No wonder he didn't answer his phone.

His old blue eyes were clear, his expression calm, but his voice high and urgent. He kept one hand on his left cheek, even when he spoke. "Ms. Hunter. I have already discussed with these . . . these gentlemen, their authority in this matter. Due to certain expanded provisions of current national security efforts, they are allowed, ah, . . . an unprecedented latitude. I would strongly suggest that you sit down and give them your full cooperation."

I hesitated. "Maybe we should call and verify . . ."

With his free hand, he patted my hand gently and said, "It won't make any difference, my dear, and if you just answer their questions, it may help us get through this more quickly."

Weakly, I allowed myself to be shoved backwards to a chair. While the agent shuffled through a file, I studied Mr Brehm. Tall, very thin, probably in his eighties, outwardly appearing calm but revealing his inner stress in the short, shallow breaths he took.

Years of bumping around the world with my dad, plus a good natural ear for accents, has provided me with an excellent tool for silently and discreetly evaluating a subject's background. Brehm's accent was interesting, a North Carolina drawl with an undertone of his native tongue, German. Some of his pronunciations hinted that he had learned English in Britain.

The two agents leaned their backsides on the front edge of Mr. Brehm's desktop. The one who had shoved me into the chair was about six foot four, thin, and hollow cheeked. He folded his arms across his chest while the guy in the expensive suit questioned me.

"So, Ms. Hunter, your uncle was Bennett Lloyd Hunter?"

So that's what connected the dots. Bennett. I looked from Brehm to the agent and back to Brehm. The old man blinked his eyes in an expression unseen by the agents facing me, but to me, it substituted for a nod of the head.

"Great-uncle," I replied. "Say, would it endanger national security for you to tell me your name and show me some evidence of your authority?"

He pulled out a leather folder and opened it to show me a picture ID with the name Carl Hedgeman and a shield emblazoned with the letters SICC.

"SICC. Don't think I have heard of that particular alphabet soup. Is that SICC as in 'go sic 'em' or perhaps 'this really makes me sick'?

I saw Brehm wince, but couldn't stop myself. "Or maybe the bibliographic 'sic,' as in, we know this is wrong but we're just quoting some other ignorant slob?"

Hedgeman snapped back the folder. "That's Security and Intelligence Crimes Commission."

"Ah, that makes sense. This scene certainly looks like the commission of a security and intelligence crime." Mr. Brehm blinked again, but this time he made a barely perceptible movement of his head in a definite negative signal.

Hedgeman put his hands on the arms of the chair, brought his face nose to nose with mine, and quite literally spit out his words.

"Ms. Hunter, you are one smart ass crack away from arrest in a national security investigation, and if I arrest you under the powers I have, it could be a year before anyone even finds out what hole I've dumped you in, and five more years before any of your leftist legal eagles figure out how to bail your ass out."

He straightened up and returned to his half seated position at the desk. In a tone of finality he said, "Now you have one chance to answer my questions, all of my questions, without one more bit of resistance or evasion. Are you clear on that?"

I could see Brehm's blue eyes pleading with me. He removed his hand from his cheek so that I could see the bright red mark where he had been hit. By nightfall, the old man's cheek and eye would be black and blue. I wasn't sure whether that proved these guys were phony feds or simply demonstrated that their powers placed them above the law. I searched my memory for any information I had ever heard about Bennett. Nothing I could remember in any way explained the presence of Hedgeman and company in Brehm's office on a national security case. I would have to try to call Dad and see if he had any idea about Bennett's past that would explain this. At the moment, however, it was clear that I had no choice. I sat up straight in the chair and answered, "Yes, sir. Completely clear, sir."

Bennett, 1932

2

Ten hawsers snugged the *S. S. Bremen* to her pier in Brooklyn while six gangways surged with travelers dressed to the nines: hats, gloves, and furs. Though Bennett occasionally rubbed shoulders with some of New York's upper crust, he had never traveled in luxury like this.

He gazed around the cavernous pier. Like a live bait tank, it was filled cheek to jowl with both ticketed travelers and curious visitors hoping to snag a pass to board and view the ship before she set sail. A smile spread across his face. He, a moonshiner kid from backwoods North Carolina, was actually going to sail on her to Germany.

The country boy in him stood gawking up at the ten-story-high craft. From her black hull to her white superstructure and her two ochre-colored funnels, the *Bremen* gleamed, reflecting the many lights that lit her berth. This new queen of the North German Lloyd Line was not as elegant or streamlined as her British, American, and French cousins, but her pudginess was well engineered German muscle. On her maiden voyage she made the Atlantic crossing from the Cherbourg Breakwater to the Ambrose Lightship in a new record time of four days, seventeen hours, and forty-two minutes. She then had the audacity to turn around and break her own record on the return trip. Speed was not her only virtue. In addition to her luxury appointments, her broad beam held her steadier in the water, providing her passengers with a smoother ride.

"Hey, mister," yelled the cab driver, "you going to pay me and take your luggage, or does it ride back to Yorkville with me?"

"Oh, sorry there, bub. You want to give me a hand with this steamer trunk?"

"Not particularly," grumbled the driver, but he helped Bennett set the steamer trunk out and left Bennett to unload the two suitcases.

No sooner had the second bag hit the ground than a stocky young German wearing a maritime uniform and pushing a luggage cart materialized at Bennett's side. The boy tossed the trunk and cases on the cart like they were hat boxes, then escorted Bennett and his luggage to check in. As Bennett stood in the long line he had time to reflect on the huge change that was taking place in his life.

Just a few short weeks ago he had been playing hide and seek with Deputy Parks and loading up what turned out to be the last delivery of whiskey he would take from North Carolina to New York. Deputy Parks' patrol car had been hidden behind the brush on Skunk Ridge overlooking the farm but that was no problem. Bennett and his dad, Zeb simply left the house through the trap door in the bedroom and made their way through the tunnel to the cave. Bennett hated every cold, dark step he was forced to take underground. His back ached from walking stooped over through the long tunnel and he was certain that one day the thing would cave in and bury them both.

Bennett climbed down the long rope ladder to the cave floor and used a hoist to lift the bottles to the tunnel level. Then he and Zeb hauled them in a small wagon back through the tunnel to a trap door in the floor of the corn crib. Zeb handed the wrapped bottles of aged malted corn whiskey up through the opening and Bennett loaded them into the various specially constructed hiding places he and his friend Doug Duffy had built into his new 1931 Packard. Every nook and cranny of the long, luxurious Cabriolet had been crafted like storage in a fine yacht: seats, floorboards, doors, and car body. Once the booze was stowed, he again filled the backseat with the boxes of clocks that he carried and sold as cover for his booze runs to North Caroline.

Bennett had remained uncharacteristically quiet while he and Zeb worked and continued silent as they walked into the house. As he put the kettle on to heat water for his bath he finally turned to Zeb and said, "Daddy, got some bad news I got to tell you." Bennett could never call Zeb "Dad" or "Pop" the way the city kids did. It wasn't proper hill folk way. In fact, at Zeb's home, Bennett's whole speech reverted to the hill country accent and word usage of his youth.

"Well, I could tell you been chewing on something. Spit it out."

Bennett picked up the newspaper he had brought with him from New York and handed it to Zeb. "Says there that Rockefeller will change his mind on Prohibition and support repeal. I don't understand why he would do such a thing. He's a teetotaler, and I know that for a fact. I talk with his house staff. Says here that if he goes along with it, the government will do it. They'll repeal Prohibition. Then what the hell will we do? Our business will be through."

Zeb put on his glasses and took the paper. While Zeb read, Bennett poured the kettle of hot water into the corrugated wash tub and added cold water. He shed his work clothes, climbed into the tepid water and scrubbed his lean, firm and well muscled body. After soaping his blond hair he climbed out to rinse it under the faucet.

As Bennett dressed in his city suit Zeb said, "Answer to your question is right there in the next story. See here. Rockefellers and Duponts are tired of paying the income tax the government set up to pay for the Great War. They want liquor legal so they can tax it instead."

"Damn, is that it?" Bennett took the paper.

As Bennett read, Zeb said, "Yeah, you always got to watch what the rich folk are doing 'cause you never know when some millionaire's going to put a bump in your road."

Bennett tossed down the paper and put on his tie.

"But don't worry, Ben. We'll still have business. Most moon shiners have gone to making stuff with potash and car batteries, stuff that'll kill a person. There'll always be folk who'll want the real thing."

Bennett slammed his open hand against the door jam. "Like who? Hill folk who got no money? Our city customers are rich family folk who don't want to get poisoned or deal with gangsters. But as soon as it's legal they won't need us any more. They'll be able to get all the quality booze they want at the corner store."

Zeb took off his glasses and pointed at Bennett with them. "I don't know what you did with your share a cash, but mine's safe put up. I grow my own food and put it up for winter, raise my own hogs. If I sell a bit a shine to the locals and a few hogs and goats, I'll do just fine. Course, I can see that just plain living might not agree with you no more."

Bennett closed his eyes and shook his head. There was nothing left to say to that. Without even a goodbye, he turned on his heel strode out to the car, and headed back to New York.

As Bennett reached the first check point his suitcases were sent to his room and his steamer trunk marked for the cargo deck. A long line snaked around to the documents window and Bennett fingered his passport wondering if there was any chance his false identification could be discovered here. He doubted it. He had held documents in the name Sizemore since he was fourteen and used a dead cousin's birth certificate to get a driver's license. At fourteen, however, dodging and outrunning the law was an exciting game, a time he called his "pirate years." This was different.

His thoughts drifted to the unpredictability of life. Pirate time had ended suddenly when cousin Henry came to visit. Henry was on Zeb's German side. While Zeb's great grandmother had married an Irishman and moved west, Henry's had remained in the Yorkville district of New York City. He was a clockmaker and jeweler who found the Roaring Twenties to be very good to him financially. His shop became one of the places the "good people" of New York, the very rich and the newly rich, all came for high-priced trinkets.

On a trip to North Carolina cousin Henry had stopped off at Zeb's farm to pay a family visit. After biscuits and a pot of Brunswick stew, Henry, Zeb and Bennett started sipping on a bottle of Hunter's best corn whiskey. As the level of the bottle went down, one thing led to another. By the time they all went to bed, it had been decided that Henry would take the sixteen-year-old Bennett as an apprentice in his clock shop. Under this cover he would make sure Bennett met people who would appreciate quality whiskey and pay well. Overnight Bennett found himself on the way to a whole new life in the wildest city during the wildest time in history. With the repeal of Prohibition, and the stunt Marabella pulled, life was changing again.

Diana

3

"So, Bennett Lloyd Hunter was your great-uncle? Is that correct, Ms. Hunter?"

"Yes."

"Your father's uncle?"

"Yes."

"When was the last time you heard from him?"

"I never have."

"I warned you, Ms. Hunter."

"And I am telling you, Mr. Hedgeman, I have never heard from my great-uncle in my adult life."

Hedgeman glared at me. I wasn't sure whether he thought I was lying or was afraid I was telling the truth. "You're his sole heir and you never heard from him in any way, letter, phone, email, nothing?"

"Sole heir?" I looked at Brehm for verification, but he was studiously examining the pen holder attached to his desk and wouldn't meet my eyes.

"Why should that surprise you? He has no children and you're his only niece. Somehow I find it hard to believe you haven't heard from him at all."

"He was sort of a hermit and kept to himself."

"So you never knew him?"

"I met him twice, once when I was about five and again when I was about nine. My dad and I came here for a couple of visits. That's it. That's all I know about him other than the fact that he was a very old man and had been retired for many years. Why, . . . please tell me why your commission would have such interest in this old man or his estate. By now he must have been living on nothing but Social Security. What the hell is this all about?"

Hedgeman held me in his gaze for a long time as if weighing possible answers, then with a dismissive wave of his arm said, "Sorry you made this trip for nothing, Hunter. You're right. There's nothing left in his estate but a broken down old house and a shed full of homemade hootch, both of which have been seized by the government for illegal activities and back taxes. Don't try to go out to the property. You would be trespassing, and that could be an unsafe thing to do."

Hootch and back taxes? Then why were SICC agents here? Why not the ATF and the IRS? And the property had already been seized? What happened to due process of law? Brehm silently implored me to be still, even venturing a barely discernible hand signal, warning off any response or argument.

I look down and shook my head, giving myself time to force down the outrage and find some appropriate response. Finally, I laughed to clear my throat and gain control over my voice. "Well, looks like Grandpa was right about old Uncle Bennett. He did end up no good. Hell! I've been traveling since early morning. Mr. Brehm, I don't suppose that hotel room is still available? My ticket back isn't until tomorrow."

"The room is prepaid. I am sorry your trip was a wasted effort. Please have dinner at the hotel dining room as my guest."

"Thanks, but that's not necessary. It's not your fault if Uncle Bennett was a deadbeat." Under the watchful Mr. Hedgeman, I picked up my fanny pack and suitcase and left without another word.

I checked in, locked myself in my room and tried to make sense of the last three days. After a sleepless thirteen hour flight from Costa Rica I had returned to Bluff Beach to find someone had literally taken apart everything in my loft. They had razored the covers off every book, removed the frames from every photo, taken apart the overstuffed furniture, and even dismantled the legs on the dinning room chairs and table. The insides of my TV lay on the floor. Every drawer and cupboard had been dumped. My computer was gone. It hadn't been a burglary. The only things missing were the computer and an old family photograph of me, my Dad and Uncle Bennett. The theft of that photo made little sense until this morning. Fortunately, the computer was an old one that I only used to surf the web. I kept the real information on my laptop that was hidden in the secret room built for me by my friend Sam Dehany.

Sam had built in a long narrow room which ran the length of my loft. The real purpose of the room was to hide Yeabot, a robot Sam had made for me with robotic technology he had hidden from his past employer, the U.S. Government. His first question when he saw the disaster was, "Did they get Yeabot?"

To answer his question I had simply pushed a button on the side of the watch he had given me and a door that had been invisible a moment before slid silently open. Nothing in the secret room had been disturbed.

"At least they couldn't find your secret room, Sam."

He had looked around my loft and said, "Only because they weren't looking. These guys were pros, but this place faked them out. They took one look at this dilapidated loft and never considered the possibility."

Ignoring his snide remark about my home, I thankfully retrieved my laptop computer, Yeabot and an Arthur C. Clark quote I put up in honor of Sam and the secret room. It read, "Any sufficiently advanced technology is indistinguishable from magic."

The real mystery, however, was my mail. I had gone to the post office to collect mail which had been on hold for three weeks only to be told someone else had picked it up. When I demanded to talk to the Postmaster, the man seemed frightened and had said the most baffling thing. He said he was forbidden by law to talk to me about who took my mail. He wouldn't even tell me what law.

Brehm's package with the tickets and summons arrived by special messenger as I was clearing out my apartment or I wouldn't have gotten that either. Was that the purpose of the mail theft? Had SICC searched my loft and seized my mail so I wouldn't show up here? Nothing made any sense.

Exhausted, I decided on a hot shower to clear my brain. The shower was running cold by the time the phone rang or I might not have bothered to answer. I was too deep in my thoughts to want to be distracted. As it continued to ring, I wrapped a towel around me, walked to the bedside table, and picked up the receiver.

"Yes?"

"Well, hello there, Beautiful. How's North Carolina?"

It was Sam, but I didn't want to say too much from this telephone. I had noticed as I checked in that the phone system here at the hotel was an antique switchboard with a real person running it. Eavesdropping would be easy.

"Don't have time for details now, but it's a mess here. By the time I arrived, the feds were in Brehm's office and had seized Uncle Bennett's estate for some sort of unspecified illegal activities and back taxes."

"Unspecified?"

"That's right. Well, they did say he had a shed full of moonshine, but since they were here on something to do with national security, I suspect they're after more than booze."

"What agency?"

"Their badges said SICC. Security and Intelligence Crimes Commission. The guy in charge is a Carl Hedgeman."

"They detain you?"

"Only long enough to find out I didn't know anything about Bennett and tell me I had no inheritance."

"You going to take a look at the old homestead before you come back?"

"No. Agent Hedgeman said to stay away, and you know me and the rules."

"Right. Well, I'll pick up your mail. Check in later and I'll let you know if there is anything other than bills and junk mail."

"Thanks, Sam." From that comment, I figured he must have learned something about my missing mail, and I knew he would also be checking up on SICC and Agent Hedgeman. And of course he would know that there was no way in hell I would stay away from Uncle Bennett's property. With nothing but a rural route number, the trick was going to be figuring out just where that was. Asking openly was out of the question.

I dried my hair, dressed, and went down for a late lunch in the hotel dining room. One of the agents, the tall slender one, was sitting in the lobby. He followed me to the dining room and took a table across from me.

The lone waitress in the place was a plump woman who looked to be in her thirties, wearing blue jeans, a white blouse and an apron. Her name, Bonnie Sue, was on a name tag pinned just above her left breast. It was artfully displayed on a flared hanky that looked right out of the movie *Alice Doesn't Live Here Anymore*. I chatted with her in a quiet conversational voice, barely loud enough to be heard by the agent. I wanted my shadow to hear, but I didn't want him to get the impression that I was broadcasting.

"Bonnie Sue, my name is Diana Hunter. I'm in town for just the day and I would like to see if I could find any Hunters on this branch of the of the family. You know any Hunters in town?"

"The only one I know is old Ben, but he just passed, ya know. Was he one of your folks?"

"Yes, he was my great-uncle."

"Gee, I don't think he had no other folk here. Any Hunters left in these parts is over at Newberry or Cranbury. Sorry."

"That's okay. I saw a county building when I came into town. Maybe I'll just do a little genealogy research there."

When I finished eating I headed for the Thomas County government offices. As expected, my shadow followed but waited for me on a bench at the entrance. As he chain-smoked out front, I located and copied property records and plot maps showing Uncle Bennett's place. Now I just needed to overlay those on some local maps.

I headed back up Commerce Street, stopping in at the little tourist shop on the ground floor of Brehm's building. My shadow waited for me on the other side of the street and two doors down.

The proprietress greeted me from a curtained doorway at the back of the shop. Through the gap in the curtain, I glimpsed a small sitting area. "Afternoon," she drawled. "Let me know if you need help; otherwise, look all you want." She was a short old lady whose shape reminded me of those plump little Russian dolls that stack inside each other, but her face was more like the wrinkled, pink-cheeked apple-face dolls she sold in her shop.

"Thank you. Looks like you have some lovely things." Small paper labels identified the local artisan who had created the apple dolls, wooden trains, trucks and cars, quilts, place mats, doll-clothes, baby clothes, oil paintings, wooden salad bowls and napkin rings. With an apple doll in hand I worked my way around to the local maps and selected one topographical hiker's map and one county road map. As I picked up the second map, a male voice behind me said, "Miss Hunter." It took the greatest control not to jump. I knew my shadow was still in place across the street, and I knew no one else had come in the front door. I turned slowly to see an old man with a tripod cane. He must have come from the living area behind the shop.

"Hello, Mr. . . ."

"You can just call me Ned, Miss Hunter. That there is my wife, Emma. No time now for chitchat. I have a message for you. Otto would like a private word with you this evening about ten o'clock, but it's best you not be seen going in. If you make your way down a few blocks, you can slip between a couple shops and into the alley and come up behind our building. You'll see some stairs. The second floor door will be unlocked. Understand?"

"Understood, and thank you, Ned."

He nodded, then hesitated. "You know, don't you, that Fed feller has been following you around all afternoon?"

I smiled. "He would be pretty hard to miss, Ned, but not too hard to lose."

He nodded again and held me long in his gaze. "Ben said you was the only one to leave things to." He paused, still studying me. "I hope for everyone's sake he knew what he was doing." With that doubtful appraisal, he turned and walked to the back of the shop and disappeared behind the curtained door.

Curious statement. Leave what to me? I bought my doll and maps, leaving the doll unwrapped, and securing the maps in the interior of my fanny pack. I thanked Emma and went back out on the street.

I took a roundabout route back, walking through the parking lot behind the hotel to verify there was a fire escape. My shadow followed me into the hotel, watched me climb the staircase to the second floor, then flopped into an overstuffed chair in the lobby. As I rounded the corner to my room, I saw him take out his cell phone to make his report.

By evening there had been a changing of the guard. The other of Hedgeman's goons, the short, muscular one, was in the lobby. He made a call on his cell and by the time he and I were served, the other two agents had joined Muscles for a quick supper break. I wondered if Mr Brehm was getting to eat too.

When I finished dinner, Muscles followed me to the lobby and watched as I went to the desk and rented two nice, romantic chick flicks for the VCR in my room. As I headed upstairs, the other agents left the hotel and Muscles settled into a lobby chair behind the pages of an Elmore Leonard novel.

As soon as it was dark I would go see Brehm and find out what the heck

Uncle Bennett had been up to. Prohibition was long over. What in his life besides moonshine could possible have led to a national security investigation? I vaguely remembered hearing that he had worked on something secret in Europe during World War II but that was sixty years ago. How I wished I had asked more questions about the family.

Bennett

4

Using the printed deck plan, Bennett began the game of finding his way through the maze of decks, halls, and stairways to his stateroom. He was shouldering his way through the crowd, heading for the main passenger elevator when he spotted her. Marabella and Police Commissioner Whalen stood not twenty-five paces from him talking to a young ship's officer. "Damn, how could she possibly know?"

Bennett turned and walked the other way, not daring to look back until he had the shelter of a ship's portal. He watched as the officer carefully examined a document the Commissioner was holding, then took the document and searched the boarding manifest. The question was, what name was he searching for, Bennett Hunter or Bennett Sizemore? Bennett held his breath. Only when the officer shook his head and handed the paper back did Bennett begin to breath again. He watched from his hiding place as Marabella and Whalen retraced their steps and descended the gangway to the dock. Damn, was she checking every ship leaving New York or had she gotten a tip? Any doubts he might have had about his decision to blow town evaporated. It wasn't right. It wasn't fair. He had done a lot of illegal things in his life but in this case he had done nothing wrong and this one had unleashed a full manhunt for him. "Damn you Marabella!" He seethed as he thought back to the day she pulled the last and loathsome stunt.

It was the day he had delivered his last load of booze to the Myerhoffer estate that he had gotten his first hint that there was trouble. Charles, the head butler, asked, "Have you seen Miss Marabella yet, Mr. Hunter?"

He spoke in an unnecessarily loud voice, obviously intended to be heard by the the kitchen staff. All talking ceased. Most work stopped, and everyone in earshot waited for Bennett's answer. Alerted, but not yet alarmed, Bennett answered casually, "No, she in?"

"No, sir. I believe she has plans for this evening."

A giggle escaped from Holly, the young girl who had recently arrived from Germany. That triggered a snort from Sandra, who sat with Holly creating pastry tarts.

Bennett set the last bottles on the pantry shelf, gave the staff a nonchalant smile and said, "Okay, have a great party this weekend." As he turned and walked to his car, he heard Charles's voice but could not hear what he said. Whatever it was, it drew a huge burst of laughter.

Bennett was never comfortable at the Myerhoffers' because he didn't belong either upstairs or downstairs. When Marabella insisted he attend family parties he was often treated with suspicion and curt superiority by the extended family. The exception to that was Fritz Myerhoffer, Marabella's father. He was a self-made man, the richest and most successful of the clan, and also the only true democrat in the whole group. The domestic staff treated Bennett even more rudely, openly displaying their disapproval of his consorting with the family.

The strange reception at the house gave Bennett some forewarning; so he was not too surprised when he entered his Manhattan apartment to find Marabella there and halfway through her process of dressing and putting on makeup.

He had moved into her luxury apartment when he and Marabella were "close," and for various reasons neither of them had felt it necessary that he move out. Now, however, it was primarily Bennett's private quarters. Marabella stayed at her family's large estate on the Hudson or, when in the city, in a suite at the Waldorf Astoria. It was a handy arrangement. She had Bennett available when she needed an escort and he could maintain an apartment at a prestigious location at no cost to himself. This arrangement didn't stop either one of them from carrying on intimate trysts with other people in the apartment. They were very open minded about such things. Sometimes they were together, and sometimes they were with someone else. Life in swinging New York City was an open buffet.

She looked up from her makeup mirror. "Hello, darling."

Bennett removed his coat, and as he hung it up replied in a tone mocking hers, "Well, hello, Bella."

She stood and gave him a warm embrace and lingering kiss. Rather than the arousal she intended, Bennett felt the hair stand up on the nape of his neck. Over the last two years he had learned that a sweet Bella was a devious and dangerous Bella.

As she returned to her dressing table, he folded his arms, leaned against the wall and studied her. Marabella Myerhoffer was one of the foremost beauties of New York's high society, and in addition to her physical beauty, she carried herself with the supreme self-confidence of one born to privilege. When she first ensnared him he had been hopelessly in love with her. Even after the hurt, after his mind had given her up, the sight of her was still magnetic. Though Bennett had liked her long curly red hair better, he still found her breathtaking with her hair cut to a short flapper style and dyed black. As always, she dressed to reveal her ample bosom, but tonight her gown was not the usual skintight style. It flowed loosely from her bust to the floor and looked quite elegant. Was she finally developing a little modesty? She looked up at him with a disarming smile, the one he had learned to fear.

"You had better shower and dress quickly. We are due at Papa's in two hours."

"Tonight? I thought the shindig was tomorrow night."

"Oh, the big party for Ingrid is, but we can't invite the teetotalers and enforcers to a party with booze, nor can we snub important people. Tonight is the dry party."

Her tone of voice held not a trace of the shrew, and she stood and gave him another tender kiss. On full alert now, Bennett headed for the shower with trepidation.

To Bennett, their arrival was perfectly timed: too late for small talk and hors d'oeuvres but in time to quickly dump their wraps with the butler and casually shuffle into the elegant dining room with the other guests. Bennett recognized the usual members of the dry side of the family as well as a few of New York's moderately well-to-do and upper-level politicians. On rare occasions, the Myerhoffers might entertain some of the truly grand members of society, but most often they hosted the millionaires, not the multi-millionaires.

In well-learned habit, Bennett proceeded to Marabella's normal place of honor on Fritz Myerhoffer's left and pulled out the chair for her. To his consternation, she stopped at the other end of the table and picked up place cards for Mr. And Mrs. Colin Bruce. These she set at hers and Bennett's seats and carried their cards to the far end of the table and seated them one on each side of the guest of honor, Police Commissioner Grover Whalen.

Through the first two courses she went out of her way to utter loving and considerate words to him, sounding as if they were the most devoted of couples. The seating arrangement made it necessary to utter these words around and across the good police commissioner.

Life was always some sort of elaborate game to Marabella, and she never announced the name of the game, much less the rules. She simply dropped her victims, unarmed, into the middle of her own private arena and opened the chutes. The person she cast as the Christian for her lions was forced to simply watch in a three hundred and sixty degree radius to see what sort of beast she would unleash upon him. Tonight, Bennett knew he was to be her victim, but he hadn't a clue as to why.

Over the entree Marabella began quizzing Whalen about last year's acquittal of two big-time thugs known as Legs Diamond and Charlie Green, suspects in the Hotsy Totsy Club murders. The Hotsy Totsy was the first speakeasy to be set up as a cafe and become famous and popular. All the big-stage stars, writers, and underworld figures came there to dine, dance, and drink. On July 13, 1929, a drunken brawl had erupted in the bar of the Hotsy Totsy, and before it was over, twenty-four slugs had been fired and two men lay dead. It was an open secret that Legs Diamond and Charlie Green were the shooters—at least they were the ones that walked away—but for some reason, New York's Finest had been unable to catch them. When they had finally given themselves up, the DA had been unable to convict them. In a great New York scandal, they walked.

Marabella started her inquest innocently enough, but as she continued to needle the commissioner on this infamous case, he became more and more defensive. Finally he responded hotly, "Why couldn't we convict them? Because in a club filled with people that night, no one saw anything. As they say on the street, nobody knew but nothin."

"There had to be other witnesses," challenged Marabella. "Why didn't the DA call them?"

"Other witnesses, right. Like the cashier, Thomas Ribler, disappeared and reportedly dead. Same with the waiter, Volst. The bartender, William Wolgast, was found murdered in Bordentown. Even Hymie Cohen. Can't find his body, but the stool pigeons say he was murdered too."

"But I thought the papers said Cohen was Legs's partner and best friend. He would never have talked, would he? Why would Legs kill him?"

The commissioner took a deep breath and let it out slowly. Other conversations around the table had quieted, and many of their fellow diners were bending an ear toward Marabella and Whalen. He looked around the circle of expectant faces and shrugged. Marabella had been peppering him with the same questions everyone was asking. Legs and Green had both since been murdered by other unknown bad guys. What difference did it make to tell her about Cohen now?

"Oh yeah, great friends, honor among thieves and all that. We hear that in honor of that great friendship, Legs shot Cohen clean and easy, didn't burn him or torture him first. But he had to kill him. Cohen was a junkie. Friendship or no, if we had gotten hold of Cohen, we could just have put him on ice until he was ready to talk. Legs knew it. Altogether, we think ten people died over the last couple years, just because they were in that club that night. That's what comes of these God . . . Garsh darn booze clubs."

"So is this the best we can hope for, Commissioner? We can't rely on our police ? We have to wait for some other thug to murder the murderer? Why, then, is our family supporting your administration?"

The commissioner's face slowly turned crimson. Fritz stopped his conversation mid-sentence and rounded on his daughter "Marabella! That is quite enough."

Marabella's face took on an innocent expression. "Oh, no, please. I never meant that it was your fault, Commissioner. I am so sorry that it came out that way."

By now the entire table was silent. All faces were turned toward Marabella. She had center stage and a hushed audience waiting for her next words. In this silence she faced Commissioner Whalen. Her eyes darted for a second or two to Bennett, checking her victim. He braced for impact.

"I was simply thinking about the terrible influence these liquor salesmen have had on our society. It worries good people. Especially if they are thinking of raising children." She produced her best coy smile and even managed a manufactured blush. "Perhaps it worries me more now that Ben and I are looking to settle down and raise a family in the city."

With that insinuated announcement, she reached her left hand across the table in front of the commissioner. To Bennett's amazement, a huge diamond engagement ring now sparkled on her finger, reflecting the light from the table candelabra. With a loving smile, she took Bennett's hand in hers. "We just don't want any of those nasty old rum runners to harm our children's future, do we, darling? If we knew any booze runners, we would help the commissioner find them, wouldn't we, dear?"

Bennett had braced himself for almost anything, but not for this. He sat staring at Marabella, speechless.

Fritz was no less surprised by his daughter's announcement but was quick to understand the significance of her statement and the implied blackmail. Either Bennett accepted Marabella's sudden rush toward marital bliss or she would expose him as a purveyor of whiskey. That would be unfortunate not only for Bennett but for Fritz, who was one of his best customers. Whatever her motives, she was finally doing what Fritz had wanted for the last two years. Looking around the table at the stunned and expectant expressions of his guests, Fritz leaped into the breach.

"Hear, hear," he said as he stood and raised his wine glass filed with apple juice. "I am delighted you two have at last made it public. Beautiful ring, Bennett. Your cousin Henry does get the best diamonds in the city. Marabella, my dear, I'm happy for you. Ladies and gentlemen, a toast to Marabella and Bennett." The guests all lifted their glasses, sipped, and mumbled appropriate words, then waited.

With his right hand firmly in Marabella's grasp, Bennett lowered his head and ran the fingers of his left hand through his hair. While his face was hidden from view he took a long deep breath, and looked up. Everyone looked back, not only the family and dinner guests, but all the staff who could find any excuse to be in the dining room. Fritz's face held an appropriate look of pride and joy while his eyes beseeched Bennett's acceptance. Gertrude Myerhoffer, Marabella's mother, tried to display an expression of pride and acceptance, but conflict contorted her face. Charles stood at the door to the dining room. In his hands was a covered terrine, on his face an undisguised sneer. Holly was unable to hide her awe and envy, while

Sandra was choking down a laugh. Ingrid, on the eve of her great coming-out party, saw she had been upstaged once again by her older sister. As she looked from Bennett to Marabella, anger vied with tears. When tears won out, she rose and left the table without a word.

Having had a brief moment to regain his balance, Bennett turned toward his newly betrothed, the smile on his face indistinguishable from the real thing. Marabella was so taken by the apparent joy on Bennett's face that some of the catlike pleasure disappeared from her smile. Bennett raised their joined hands up over the police commissioner, stood, and pulled Marabella to him. He wrapped his arms around her, bent her backward, and kissed her passionately. It was far more of a display than was respectful, even on such an occasion. The kiss took her breath away and ended only when applause and hoots arose from around the table. Looking into her eyes, Bennett declared with perverse truthfulness, "Marabella, I thought you would never be mine." He was delighted to see that it was now Marabella who was at a complete loss.

Bennett

5

Marabella kept Bennett playing his role by inviting Mark and Karen to ride back to town in Bennett's Packard. By the time they reached the outskirts of the city Marabella had instigated an impromptu celebration of their engagement which began at Jack Kriendler and Charlie Berns new Club 21. The posh speak had tables set with fine linens and china, walls hung with fine art, and live music filled the place with infectious dixieland jazz. Regulars Dorothy Parker, Robert Benchley, and their whole crowd held court at the most prominent table while Charlie Chaplin and a gorgeous blond reigned at another. The rest of the room was filled with a glittering array of well-dressed politicians, socialites, writers, actors, and other denizens of New York's classier speakeasy nightlife.

From there they elected to go to the Stork Club but found it so crowded that they had to split up, which was fine with Bennett. Mark and Karen garnered chairs at a friend's table and Marabella and Ben were given a small table at the side of the bar.

For the first time since her grand announcement, Marabella was alone with Bennett. As they sat down he was no longer smiling and she did not meet his eyes. Looking around for distraction, she said, "Oh, look, there's Hal Lindy. I'll just say a quick hi and—"

He took both of her hands, circling her slender wrists with his thumb and forefinger.

"No, you won't, Bella. You'll stay right here and tell me what the hell game you think you're playing tonight."

She met his cold glare. For just a moment she faltered, her eyes drifted to her drink, and a look of childlike vulnerability washed briefly across her face. It was so fleeting Bennett wasn't sure he had really seen it. Even if he had read the look correctly, he had learned that she played so many roles and had so many layers of deception that he now doubted anything about her could be genuine.

Looking back up at him she smiled her lopsided sarcastic smile, the one she saved for suckers, losers, and anyone dumb enough to fawn at her feet. "Very good, Ben. I have to admit you played the role well. For a while there you almost had me convinced you really wanted the little heiress and all of Daddy's kingdom." Any glimpse of the child was gone.

"Why, Bella? I can't believe you could be so jealous of Ingrid that . . ."

"Jealous of Ingrid? Don't make me laugh. Her pissy little debut is coincidence, that's all.

He leaned forward and said through clenched teeth, "Then why?"

"What's the matter, Ben, don't you want to marry Bella?"

He sat silent, waiting for a more responsive answer. In his impatience, he failed to realize he was squeezing harder on her wrists.

"Ouch, you're hurting me, Ben."

He loosened his grip slightly and waited for an answer.

She shrugged. "I just have a little problem, Ben; and I am afraid, like it or not, we need to be married."

"What kind of little problem?"

Slowly she drew his hand to her belly. "You may not have looked closely enough lately to notice, but I am beginning to lose my girlish figure and get a bit thick around the middle."

Bennett's brow wrinkled. Was Bella suddenly afraid of getting old and fat? Seeing his confusion, she offered a further hint, "Just around the middle. Get it?"

Still he looked bewildered. She shook her head. "I guess I have to spell it out for you. I'm pregnant, Ben."

His hand came off her belly as if he had touched something hot. Neither spoke as Bennett took a moment to digest what she had said.

"So why didn't you just tell me? You think I am the type of man who would have to be trapped into . . . who wouldn't be man enough to accept his responsibilities? Is that how little you think of me?"

She didn't answer. She gave him the same look she did when they played charades, the superior look that demanded he work out the answer himself. She wasn't about to help him.

"What changed your mind? The first time, you went to that doctor and took care of it. And that time we were actually in love . . . or at least I was. Why have this one?"

"It's too late. The doctor won't do it this time."

"Too late? How far along are you?"

"Four and a half months."

Slowly he made the mental calculations. "Four and a half months ago . . . while you were in Europe. So . . . it's not even mine. You killed mine and any feeling I might have had for you, and now you expect me to take care of some other guy's bastard?" He pushed away from the table, distancing himself from her even if only by a few inches.

She looked down at her drink, and once again Bennett thought he glimpsed the vulnerable girl. Quickly she replaced that look with a sophisticated, ugly sneer. "Don't worry, Ben. His father is a real German baron. Unfortunately a married one, but our little bastard will have blue blood in his veins."

"You mean your little bastard, Bella. I'll not have anything to do with it."

Ignoring his declaration, she continued in a matter-of-fact tone, as if she were planning a day at the beach. "This won't in any way inconvenience you or change our basic arrangement. Oh, we'll have to buy a proper house in a good neighborhood, but we can keep the apartment. The kid, the nurse, and I can live in the house, and you can continue in the apartment and make appearances as the doting husband and father when our social life demands it. We can continue our independent life. Just be discreet."

"Why me, Bella? You have your choice of New York's finest. You have half of them in love with you. Why not pick one with real money and social position? Even if Prohibition continued, I could never buy you that 'proper house' or support you in the style your father does. And Prohibition's going to end soon. I won't even be able to support myself."

"Of course you will, Ben. For some reason I could never understand, you're Daddy's favorite. I've dated princes and dukes, oil tycoons, the scions of New York's finest families; but to Daddy, you were the only one who was good enough for me: a nameless, homeless, booze peddler from . . . You know, I never have known where the hell you lived before New York."

"No, I don't buy that. You're not doing this for Fritz. You never do anything for anyone but yourself."

She shrugged. "Just think how convenient it will be, dear. Daddy's approval of you guarantees that you will have an excellent job with his company, and we can continue a lifestyle we already enjoy. Everyone already knows we live together, sort of, and we already have worked out an excellent arrangement regarding our separate lives." She sipped her drink. "If I picked anyone else, I'd have to retrain him like a new puppy that shits on the rug."

She may have added that last line out of wounded ego because he was balking at her deal, or she may have just been unable to break the habit of cruel superiority. For whatever reason she said it, it was the mistake of a lifetime. Handled properly, Bennett might have come around to some form of accommodation, at least for the short term; but that phrase was a knife that slashed the last thread of love or whatever it was that Bennett had once felt for Marabella.

In the next few moments of silence, Bennett's thoughts raced though all that needed to be done. First, he needed her game plan. Subtly he switched gears.

"I could keep the apartment?"

"Of course."

"What kind of a job do you think Fritz will give me?"

"Whatever it is, within a year, you will be a VP in his firm."

Carefully he asked, "What if I refuse?"

"You don't even want to consider that, Ben. I have friends with the ability and the will to have you put in prison as a lowdown booze runner, and I know enough to make sure you would have company. How long do you think your cousin's little clock shop will stay in business once they arrest him for all the beer he brews? How many of New York's finest would continue to buy their expensive trinkets there if that news got out?"

"Well, let's see now. I could be a jailbird or a high paid VP. You make quite an attractive proposition, Bella."

"So we've reached an understanding?"

"Absolutely. We have reached complete understanding."

"Good, then I can go show off this diamond to a few friends and put a bug in Winchell's ear. We'll be celebrities when his column appears tomorrow."

He watched Marabella walk over to Winchell's table, and mumbled under his breath, "Oh, no, please, don't do that. It might embarrass you tomorrow." As Marabella displayed the huge diamond on her left hand, Bennett smiled, his first genuine smile of the evening.

Otto

6

Otto Brem sat looking out his second story office window, not really seeing the dirty streaks on the glass or the street scene beyond. His vision was focused inward, his mind embracing each note of Beethoven's *Moonlight Sonata* as the music's melancholy touched his soul. The record had a few new scratches when he pulled it from the rubble, but he was just thankful it still played. He knew his life was about to end and there was no more fitting music for his final song. Ironic, he thought, to survive the Third Reich and die here, in the land of freedom. It wasn't the prospect of death that troubled him, however. He was ready for life to end. It was the fear that he would not be able to fulfill his final promise to Ben.

He had known Ben for over seventy years, a lifetime. Sometimes those earlier years when they had first met in Germany seemed like a dream or like stories told to him by another person. He could only remember isolated events. Much of his childhood was simply gone. Memory erased. Maybe this is what death would be like. Maybe memory of this life would be that vague, partial memory, no real sense of loss because you would be living in a new time and place. Or, maybe there was nothing after. Maybe all supposition about the soul and afterlife was wishful thinking.

The last few notes dropped like silver as Rudolf Serkin drew from the piano keys the soul-deep passion of Beethoven's sonata. Then the arm lifted the needle from the groove and the turntable clicked off, releasing the old lawyer from its spell.

As they had planned things out Otto was to have time . . . time to tell Diana what she would need to know, time to prepare her to survive the life she was about to be dropped into. Of course, no information had been kept in Otto's office. Bennett was far too security minded for that. But all the codes and keys of a lifetime were in Otto's keeping in one way or another. If tonight's meeting failed there had to be some backup, some message, some key he could leave in a safe place for Diana. It had to be something he could do with Hedgeman watching and something that would endanger no one else. One idea came to him, but would he have time before they came back.

Diana

7

About nine p.m. I stuck in a movie and turned up the volume on the TV. Then I opened my small suitcase and pulled out my Walther .32. Sam, seeming to know more than he told, had insisted I bring it. I had packed the unloaded Walther and two full clips with my PI license and my CCW attached, and checked the suitcase at the airport. That permit to carry a concealed weapon wouldn't really save me if someone found the gun and decided to prosecute. It was only good in one California county, and last time I checked, federal regulations required you to declare a weapon even if it was packed in checked luggage. Since the Walther made it here with me, inspection techniques must not have changed too much. I loaded one clip and put the Walther and extra clip into my fanny pack.

Dressed for stealth in dark jeans, black blouse, socks, and tennis shoes I slipped out of the room to keep my appointment with Mr. Brehm. A peek into the lobby told me that Muscles was still there. Hedgeman and Hollow Cheeks could be anywhere. Climbing the back stairs to the rooftop exit, I went out to the fire escape landing and allowed my eyes to adjust to the dark while I listened to the evening sounds and watched for the watchers.

Other than the crickets, which filled the night with their music, the little town was amazingly quiet. There was no traffic, no human voice, and only an occasional dog bark. Faintly, I heard the television in a room to the left of the fire escape. A whisper of sound in the distance may have been the murmur of the river that flowed through town or perhaps just the wind in the trees. The light breeze carried odors of cooking food. I surveyed the buildings, cars and shadows but saw no sign of anyone watching back.

Quietly, I descended the fire escape and jumped the last few feet to the ground. Then, stepping carefully to avoid any noise that would disturb neighborhood dogs, I made my way down the alley for two blocks, crossed

Commerce Street, and slipped into the alley on the other side. Making my way to the back entrance of Brehm's office building, I looked up and was puzzled to see lights on the third floor but not on the second. The inside stairwell to the third floor had been boarded off and the outside stair stopped at the second floor.

The old wooden stairs creaked as I tiptoed up. Carefully I turned the handle on the back door, but found it locked. Above me I could hear muffled sounds of voices and some sort of pounding or thumping. Stepping back to the edge of the landing, I could occasionally see silhouettes as people moved past the third floor windows. I didn't like the image they were creating. It looked like a fight, or worse, like a beating. Confirming my fear, a man's scream shattered the quiet of the night, then was suddenly cut off. Picturing frail old Otto Brehm, I ran down the stairs and around to the front of the building.

As I reached the sidewalk, I heard the shattering of glass above me. Looking up, I saw Brehm's body, shards of broken glass and bits of splintered wood all in the air just below the shattered third story window. I think I screamed "No" as he fell, but it was all too surreal for me to be sure whether I screamed or just thought it. I heard the sickening sound of his body smacking onto the cement. Falling bits of glass tinkled to the sidewalk all around him.

For a moment I stood motionless, my mind paralyzed by the horror. Then I turned it off. I don't know why or how this happens. Minor emotions like embarrassment are capable of rendering my mind useless, but in any real emergency, my emotions are simply turned off. My mind takes quiet, unimpassioned control.

I walked to Brehm's body and knelt down to check his pulse and respiration. I was fairly certain, however, that he'd already been dead when he came out of the window. His head had been at such an unnatural angle, I was sure his neck was broken. His body had fallen limp, lifeless and silent. At least he must have gone quickly.

A night breeze fluttered bits of paper that drifted down from the window, then a large pane of glass crashed to the sidewalk. I looked up, and my eyes met Hedgeman's as he leaned out the window to view the street. When recognition dawned on his face, he pointed down at me and said something to Hollow Cheeks. They would be on me in moments.

Backing away from Brehm's body, I debated the best escape route. Looking down the side of the building I saw a car pull quietly to a stop in the alley. Inside were two people, their features concealed beneath sweatshirt hoods. I was about to run the other way when the driver turned toward me and I could see that it was Ned. Reaching back over the driver's seat, he opened the back door and motioned me to the car. I looked around the darkened street, weighed the odds, and ran for the car.

Diana

8

Ned spoke slowly and without undue emotion. "Lay down on the floor, Miss Hunter. We are going to pull down the alley a ways here. Emma's got a blanket and some decorations from the church on the seat, and she's going to spread them out and cover you up. Get comfy because we'll be a whiles before you can come out again. And be very quiet. We're gonna to come back and stop at the shop so the Feds won't wonder what happened to us and come looking. Okay?"

"Yes." With my claustrophobia, being buried in this cramped space wasn't exactly "comfy," but under the circumstances, I wasn't going to complain.

When he pulled to the curb in front of his gift shop, he and Emma stepped out of the car. I could hear them and several other voices. Evidently, it didn't take long to draw a crowd.

"Oh, My Lord, Sheriff Tumey, what's happened here?"

There was a long pause, and when the sheriff answered, he and Ned must have been standing right next to the car. Tumey spoke in a low confidential tone. "Looks like Otto came outta the third-story window up there and broke his scrawny old neck. Those federal agents over there say they saw Ben Hunter's niece running away from the scene, and they want me to issue a warrant for her arrest. What do you think of that, Ned?"

"Otto looks like he took a hell of a beating before he come out that window. Now Ben's niece looks sturdy enough for a woman, but I reckon it would take someone a mite more powerful built to inflict that kind of damage."

"I was thinking along them same lines myself. Don't suppose it makes no matter what I do, those feds'll get them a federal warrant anyways. Ben's niece is most likely gonna end up on the FBI's most wanted."

A familiar gravely voice intruded, farther from the car but approaching. "Who's this, Sheriff?"

"Agent Hedgeman, this here is Ned and Emma Holt. They run that gift store on the bottom floor of Mr. Brehm's building.

"Mr. Holt, were you in the gift shop this evening?"

"Not since we closed up at five o'clock."

"Where were you?"

"We was over to the church potluck and social."

"The entire evening?"

"Well, pert near. After the social ended we made a stop up the street at the drugstore and saw all the commotion and come down to the shop to see what was happening."

"We're searching for a suspect in the death of Mr. Brehm. Her name is Diana Hunter. She was here to see Mr. Brehm about her uncle Bennett Hunter's will this morning and evidently didn't like what he told her. Have you seen her?"

"Well, I think she was in the store sometime, wasn't she, Emma?"

"Yes. It was after lunch, maybe 2:30 or 3:00, I recon."

"You haven't seen her this evening?"

"No, sir."

"Will you be in the building tonight?"

"Hell, no. We'll go home. Be back here tomorrow morning about ten o'clock."

"All right. If you see or hear anything of the suspect, call the sheriff."

"Will do. Night, Sheriff. Gentlemen. C'mon, Emma. Let's get home."

The Holts climbed back into the car, and as we drove away Ned said, "Okay, Miss Hunter, hang on just a bit and it will be safe for you to climb out of there."

About ten minutes later I felt the car leave the pavement and bump down a rutted dirt road. The dust and gas fumes that seeped through loose door fittings aggravated my claustrophobia, and I tried to lift the pile of stuff Emma had covered me with so I could get a breath of air. When it caught on something and I couldn't get it off, I hit the panic button. "Ned, get me out of here. Now."

Ned brought the car to a stop, opened the door, and lifted the decorations.

I crawled out and took some deep breaths of night air. The ripple of a nearby stream and the smells of damp earth and moldy vegetation were, by comparison, a welcome relief.

"Getting a little close in there?"

"Yeah, never have liked tight spaces."

We were stopped in the middle of a narrow dirt road that followed the hilly contours of the Smoky Mountain foothills. In the headlights of the car I could see that thick woods and dense underbrush grew right up to the edge of the road. The crickets were almost deafening.

"Sorry, I imagine it was a little stuffy in there, Miss Hunter."

"Sorry? You saved my neck! Thanks. And, Ned, I hope you don't think I had anything to do with Otto's death. I was just coming to meet him whe—"

"Now, Miss Hunter, I may be old, but I'm not stupid."

"Nonetheless, I heard what the sheriff said, and I think you better get clear of me as soon as possible. If you're found with me—"

"Yes, ma'am, I suspect Emma is thinking along the same lines, after what happened to Otto and all, but you see, I'm pert near the last one left. There's one thing I promised Ben I'd do after he was gone, and now that Otto's gone, I got to also try to help with his part and show you what your Uncle left to you." He paused and looked at his watch in the headlights. "We really should get going. You feel up to driving on? I'll move this stuff aside and you can sit in the backseat now."

"Oh, of course."

As Ned put the car in gear, he continued, "You see there is a lot more to your uncle Ben than you or anyone knew. In fact Otto was about the only one who could of told you what you're gonna need to know. Well, there may be one more, but I don't know . . . I don't know the business stuff that Otto knew. Best I can do is show you Ben's place, and after that I'm afraid you're on your own. I reckon most of what you will need to know will be somewheres at Ben's."

"But, Ned, none of this makes sense. Do you have any idea why federal agents would swoop down on the property of an old man like Bennett?"

He took a breath as if to speak but Emma reached out and touched his arm. He looked at me in the rearview mirror and said, "I'm sorry, but I was never in on the business end of this thing." He looked back to the road and I knew I should ask no more questions of these people who were already risking their lives for me.

We drove for about thirty minutes on a series of dirt roads, then Ned pulled off and stopped. He picked up a bag from the floor of the car, then signaled for silence. With dome light off, he opened our car doors for us, shut them quietly, and guided us single file along a footpath. When we came in sight of the farm, he signaled for Emma and me to wait. Opening the bag he had taken from the car, he made his way slowly and cautiously toward a small house that looked vaguely familiar.

As we waited for Ned I surveyed the place by moonlight and eventually picked out the garden wall, the tool shed, the barn, and the corn cribs. Gradually this tiny derelict acreage, seen now in shadowed silhouettes, began to conform to my childhood memories of Uncle Bennett's great green farm. The memories flooded back.

On the east side of the wall there had been a huge field of corn that lived in my memory as an almost mythical place. Uncle Bennett had taken me into the field and taught me to pick out corn ears for dinner by looking at the color of the silk, not too pale green and not too brown. We carefully chose the young ears with small kernels and pushed our thumb nails into the kernel to see if it squirted milk or was already too dry to eat. He showed me how to chew the inner green leaves and suck the sweet flavor out before spitting them onto the ground. "Better than chewing gum," he had declared. The next day I had ventured back into that field on my own and wandered among the rows of corn, listening to the breeze blowing through the plants and hearing the rasping sound as the grooved leaves grated against each other. To my delight I found an empty space where, for some reason, the corn had not come up. It became my hideout, my cool shaded fort, carved out of a great jungle of sweet-smelling corn.

Though he spoke in a whisper, Ned's voice was sufficient to recall me from my secret childhood hiding place, back into the adult hazards of this bizarre night. "There's no one at Ben's place now, but we have to hurry cause we don't know when those boys will be back out here trying to find what they couldn't get from Otto."

He was carrying a pair of military issue night-vision binoculars, and carefully replaced them in the bag he had taken from the car. I had to think a minute to realize why that came as such a surprise. It was my own California bias. Ned and Emma lived in some sort of backwater Mayberry, and my mind had cast them as characters out of the past. They weren't supposed to be sophisticated enough to have such tools. It's embarrassing when we come face to face with our own prejudice.

"Come on, and quiet now," he whispered.

We entered the house through the back kitchen door. All the blinds were pulled, but still Ned dared only a small penlight pointed down at the floor to guide Emma and me through the house. Even in that dim glow I could make out enough to know that this house was much smaller than the one of childhood memory: a good size kitchen, very modest living room, and a closet size bathroom with the luxurious addition of a small stall shower.

When I had visited, baths were taken in the kitchen because it was the warmest room. Water was heated in a kettle and poured into a corrugated tub to be mixed with cold water. Even with the wood-burning cook stove going, the kitchen was cold and there was never enough water in that kettle to have a hot bath. Growing up in mining camps all over the world, I experienced many places like this with few modern conveniences. As a result, to this day I take showers and baths so hot they turn my skin pink.

Then there was the bedroom, which held a mystery that had remained vivid through all my years of growing up. Something happened in this room that made Uncle Bennett one of the most fascinating people I had ever met; but it was secret, a secret I had kept even from my dad. Sometimes my grown-up mind wondered if it really happened or if it was just part of my pretending, like all the adventures I had in the cornfield. I wasn't sure what Ned wanted to show me here, but I knew I had just a few moments to learn if that old secret was real.

Intent on finding the answer, I dismissed all other concerns and reached out and borrowed Ned's penlight. I shined it on the dresser against the far wall, a five-drawer highboy with a red-brown finish and two small round wooden handles on each drawer. It matched my memory of it perfectly. I held the light in my mouth so I could have both hands free to slide the dresser aside and out from the wall. When I shined the penlight on the floor I couldn't help letting out a quiet laugh. There it was, Uncle Ben's secret trapdoor. I bent down and opened the door, letting it fall back against the wall. Even the narrow beam of the penlight revealed that the tunnel below was not only there, but was, unlike the house, much bigger than I remembered.

"Wow," I whispered. "It's real and it's huge!" I turned back to say something to Emma and Ned and found both of them staring open mouthed. They looked almost fearful, as if the demons of hell would rise up out of the tunnel. "What?" Neither of them spoke. "Ned, Emma, what's the matter?"

"How . . . how did you know about that? Did you talk to Otto?"

I laughed, relieved that this was his only concern. "No, I learned about this years ago. I was over there in that corner playing when Uncle Bennett came in the bedroom, didn't see me, and went over and moved that dresser out. When he seemed to disappear into the floor, I went over to see where he went. I, I think, if I remember correctly, that the tunnel was smaller then, because he couldn't walk upright. He was walking back up the tunnel carrying two bottles, but he was bent over, and didn't see me until he started back up the little ladder. I never thought to hide because I didn't know it was a secret. We met eye to eye. At first I thought he was going to get mad at me, but instead he smiled and said, 'Diana, I think you're going to grow up to be a person who is very good with secrets. This is going to be your first big test. This tunnel is our little secret and you must never tell anyone, not even your daddy. Promise?' I promised and never told a soul until this moment."

Ned stared at me another moment then said, "Maybe old Ben knew what he was doing about you. But of course your daddy knew full well about this . . ."

A cell phone was ringing. Emma reached inside her pocket and put the phone to her ear. Again I marveled at how anachronistic it seemed. This little old woman with her apple doll face, her flowered house dress, and a sweat jacket, standing in a home that must have been old when I was born. We seemed to be in the middle of nowhere, and her cell phone rings. Of course, we were in the Twenty-First Century, and cell phone repeaters are everywhere.

She said "Yes?" and "Okay," and hung up. "The feds just passed Sizemore's place. If they don't get lost on the back roads, they could be here in forty-five minutes."

"Well, let's get moving. Miss Hunter, please don't get upset with what I'm about to do. Your uncle made me swear I would do it without fail. Understand?"

I nodded and watched silently as Ned took a kerosene can from the closet and walked toward the kitchen. With gentle reassurance, Emma nudged me to the trapdoor and the two of us descended the ladder.

Diana

9

By the time Ned joined us in the tunnel and slammed the trapdoor shut, flames were crackling through the tinder-dry house boards like the place was so much kindling. Though most of the smoke rose skyward, some was beginning to seep into the tunnel.

From a shelf just below the trapdoor, Ned picked up three yellow hardhats, each mounted with a miner's lamp, placed them on our heads, and turned on the lights. "Hurry now, ladies," he said and led the way down the well-timbered tunnel.

As I walked behind Emma, I realized that Ned used no cane and Emma had to work to keep up with him. Dozens of questions raced through my mind, and I tried to sort for ones I could safely ask them.

"Ned, you said that what I needed to know would be somewhere at Bennett's. You just burned his place down. How am I . . ."

"No, I didn't. That hasn't been Ben's place for fifty years. It's just sort of a front. I'll show you Ben's shortly. Be patient now and keep up. You okay, Emma?"

"Yeah, I'll make it to the end."

The tunnel, which had been descending gradually, took a sharp turn to the left and began to climb. We stopped just before reaching the bend, and Ned moved his head, searching the wall with his miner's lamp until he located a three-foot-wide gray utility box on the wall. Inside was a large round iron wheel with six spokes. Without a word, he and Emma each took one side of the wheel and began to turn it. As they moved the wheel, Diana heard the crunching and clunking of an array of gears of various sizes. As the gears meshed and turned like a clock's works, a huge boulder that had looked like part of the tunnel wall began to slide sideways, creating an opening to the outside. Through a narrow crack I glimpsed a star-filled sky, and warm fragrant air rushed in.

I moved in closer to inspect the mechanism. The boulder rested on partly recessed wheels that moved along a narrow set of mine rails on the tunnel floor. Each turn of the iron wheel moved the giant boulder another inch. As the apparatus moved the boulder, a pawl clicked down the notched teeth of a ratchet wheel and prevented the rock from moving backward.

"Ned, did Uncle Bennett build all this?"

"Nope. I did. Well, Ben's daddy Zeb started it all, and Ben figured out the gears and works for this here boulder but I enlarged and timbered the tunnel and constructed this contraption."

He paused briefly, wiped sweat from his brow, then continued turning the wheel. "You see, first it was just a cellar under the house to store his whiskey, but old Zeb saved one barrel every year starting from nineteen and twelve. So next he made a tunnel to the corn crib and put in a second cellar. His tunnels weren't no more than rabbit holes. It's a wonder he and Ben weren't buried alive in some cave-in."

The gears, ratchet wheel, and rails made it possible to move what must have been several tons of stone, but it was still heavy work. When the boulder was about half open, Emma held up a hand to signal for a break. I stepped in and took her place.

"But this tunnel is long. We must have walked well past the corn crib by now."

"Yeah. That's right. Zeb got real ambitious when Prohibition come in, and he extended—" Ned paused again to catch his breath. "Better get this rock open. Talk later." In silence we finished opening this amazing door, then the three of us stood there at the wall of the tunnel looking out at a narrow canyon. Mountains loomed on both sides of the door. This must have been the only place where the tunnel was not burrowing through the mountains.

When his breathing slowed, Ned turned to Emma. His tone of voice sounded as if he expected an argument from her. "Now, Emma, there's no need for you to be in here for this. You wait out yonder on the little knoll."

"Oh, I'll go out all right," she answered, "but I'm not sitting around here while you do all the work. I'll go get the car and bring it up the canyon trail."

"No, you're not going to be wandering around these hills in the dark. You just wait for me, and we'll go get the car together."

"Ned Holt, I was hunting possum at night in these hills before you ever even saw this country." He started to draw a breath to answer but she cut him off. "No, I won't brook no argument from you on this. You know well enough we can't take a chance on the feds finding our car by Hunter's burned-out farm. I'll be waiting just outside, in the car, when you're done in here."

With that she turned on her little heel and marched out the door. Ned started to call after her, but gave up, shaking his head. "Nobody ever warned me that quiet little woman was actually half mule. Well, come on, Miss Hunter, we better get moving and I'll show you your uncle's secret lair."

We followed the tunnel around the bend to the left and then began a steep climb. The further we went, the danker it smelled. I shined the miner's lamp on the walls and ceiling, noticing that we were no longer in a manmade tunnel. In this section the tunnel was much wider and the roof higher and there was no timbering.

"Are we in a cave?"

"Yes, ma'am. This here is part of the original cave." Ned took hold of my arm. "Here." He was breathing heavy after the climb and took a moment before continuing. "We're real close to the edge here." Again he searched the wall with his miner's lamp until he located a smaller utility box. This one held a light switch, which he flicked on. Before us was a cavernous opening in the earth, so large that the darkness absorbed the light long before it reached the other side.

I sucked in my breath, and though we were not near enough to the edge to require it, I stepped back as if the precipice might pull me over. Ned took my hand and walked me carefully to the edge. I couldn't see the bottom. We stood near the uprights of what would normally be the headframe over the entrance to a mine shaft. I had seen a lot of them in my travels with my dad. This headframe, however, was anchored to the rock at the rim of the giant cavern. Attached to it was a metal ladder that descended into the black pit below.

"That there is your uncle's hidey hole. Think you can manage that one?"

I looked at him questioningly.

"It's about two hundred feet to the bottom. You think you can safely climb down there?"

"Ah, yes, but why should I? What's down there?"

"Everything your Uncle Ben's been hiding for over fifty years." He studied my face and I knew my apprehension and doubts were showing. "Now don't be afraid. It ain't no snake pit down there. Fact is, my home should be so well fit out."

I couldn't answer and simply studied his face trying to make sense of what he was telling me. He grew uncomfortable under my steady gaze, looked away and rearranged his hardhat over his gray hair.

"Now, as soon as you get to the bottom you look to your right and you will see a box with a set of light switches. You flip them and you'll light up that place like Yankee Stadium. As to learning all Ben's secrets, I truly can't help you, but Otto says it's all there. Here is one more thing I can tell you. On the other side of that cave is a short little piece of tunnel, recessed only about six feet. I know this cause your daddy introduced me to Ben years ago so I could enlarge this here tunnel and build Ben the new one and see they was shored up safe and proper."

"You know my dad?"

"Sure. Knew you too. But you was a little bit of a thing then. Maybe three or four. I mined with your daddy in a place called Montaña Roja in Colombia."

My guts clenched at the name and the dark memories it stirred.

"Your daddy respected my mining, and when Ben needed someone who knew what he was doing mining-wise and could keep his mouth shut, your daddy called on me. That's when I moved here. Ben pretty well saw to it I never wanted for nothing again. Now, I got to keep my last promise to him. I got to make the tunnel between the Hunter's old farm and the cave disappear before the feds get to looking too close."

"How in the hell are you going to accomplish that? You may have only about fifteen or twenty minutes before the feds get to the house."

"When I enlarged this tunnel, I rigged it for this night and checked it every year since. Course we didn't know when this night would get here. You best get down that ladder. Hang on tight on the way down. When you flip on the lights, I'll know you're safe and I can collapse the tunnel."

"Collapse the tunnel? How will you get out?"

"There will be a few seconds' delay. I'll go out that bolt hole that Emma went out. Once I release that pawl on the ratchet wheel, the boulder will close by itself. Then, if all goes as planned, the tunnel will collapse from the trapdoor to where the tunnel takes a sharp turn. Shouldn't be no damage down your way, but it might be a good idea to wait at the entrance to the other tunnel on the far side."

"How do I get out?"

He smiled. "The other tunnel has—"

"Where could a six-foot tunnel take me?"

"To an elevator."

For a moment I was overcome by paranoia. A man who was really no more than a total stranger was asking me to climb down in a bottomless pit in the middle of the earth and wait for him to blow up my only known exit.

"Oh, sure, I just take the elevator to the first floor. Look, Mr. Holt. I really don't know you from a hole in the ground . . . that may not have been the best expression to use, but having to pull answers out of you is not really helping my faith in what you're telling me. Where the hell does that elevator go, and why do you want me to go down into that black pit? And if it's all so safe, why aren't you and Emma coming with me? Maybe I should be coming with you."

Ned looked around in all directions as if he might find an answer lying about somewhere. "I understand, I mean, of course you would, . . . look, Miss. Hunter, this wasn't supposed to happen like this. Otto was supposed to take you over to Ben's big place, in through the security, and show you the house and the cave from the other side. I was supposed to have time to blow this end before you or anyone even knew it was here. And me and Emma, honey, we couldn't make it down that ladder. Now I understand why you have no reason to trust me, and if you want, you can come back with me and out the bolt hole; but if you do, we got to worry about the Feds, and I don't know how we would ever get you into the big house. And, if I leave that tunnel much longer, the Feds is sure to find the hole to it at Ben's burned-out place. Now I got to keep my promise to Ben and go close that tunnel. You can go to the cave or come with me, whatever you choose. I can't waste no more time."

We stared at each other, both waiting for me to make up my mind. "If it helps any," he said quietly, "I helped your daddy burry your momma at Montaña Roja. He called her secret burial place El Corazón Verde."

My eyes stung with tears. I thought that no one knew that name. After a moment I nodded, unable to speak, and turned toward the ladder. Ned touched my arm, holding me back. "The charges are all small and rigged to go in sequence, but to be safe, stay back from this edge, hear?"

I nodded again and shook his hand. "Thanks, Ned." Firmly I grasped the cold iron of the headframe and began my descent.

Bennett

10

Once again Bennett headed toward his stateroom. Seeing Marabella and Whalen had shaken him and he mentally went over all the precautions he had taken to cover his tracks and to protect both his cousin Henry and his dad, Zeb. He had always kept Zeb's home a secret because of the whiskey and he had warned Henry to clean out all the beer and told him about Marabella.

Finally he had returned to the farm so he could hide his great Packard in the only place he could think of. He had timed his return for dusk, giving himself just an hour of light and parked in a small hollow far off the road where he wouldn't be heard. Carefully he removed fenders, running boards, mirrors, and spare tire, making his Packard as narrow as possible. When all the parts had been loaded inside the car, Bennett settled down in the driver's seat and drove toward the cave. He pulled to a stop and sat a moment looking across the creek to the waterfall.

When he was fourteen years old he had avoided capture by old Sheriff Williams by driving his wreck of a Model T Ford through the waterfall and into the cave. For chancing the exposure of their secret cave, Bennett received the worse beating Zeb had ever given him. Memory of that gave him pause, even years later, but he had to hide the car. Packard had only made this luxury car one year and Marabella's dogs would be watching for it.

Bennett made a hard right and drove off the road. He coaxed the Packard through the tangle of brambles, wincing at the scratching noises, slogged it across the sandbar and into the stream. Then clunking over the river stone, he drove right up the streambed to the waterfall. He got out to make sure the Packard would clear the sides of the cave entrance, then climbed back in and drove her through.

When Zeb came down the tunnel to the cave the next morning he went out the waterfall entrance and inspected Ben's job of covering his tracks. He made no critical comments and listened politely as Ben explained his problems. Zeb was also uncharacteristically understanding about Ben's trouble with Marabella.

Surprised and pleased, Bennett said, "Thank you for understanding, Daddy."

After a long silence, Zeb said, "I guess its only fair to warn you. I plan to close up that door you drove that car through this morning."

Bennett stared at him blankly. "Close what door?"

Zeb had that sly, horse-trader grin on his face. "Did you notice the hoist and them boulders over there by the entrance?"

"Yeah, why?"

"Well, that there is my next improvement on our cave. I'm fixing to cement them boulders over that hole so nobody else can come along and find our cave behind them falls. From outside it will just look like part of the mountain. If you're gone for long, I reckon there will be no way for you to get that fancy car outta here."

Zeb's grin turned into a full self satisfied smile. This was Bennett's comeuppance for daring to flout his father's order about never driving a car through the falls again.

Bennett looked at his Packard up on blocks and then back at Zeb. He shrugged. "Well, if that's what you got to do . . . I can't do nothing about it now. Guess I'll face that problem when I get back."

Zeb nodded, the smile no longer on his face. "What you planning to do now?"

"Well, there's this guy who comes into the shop to buy watches and such for his company's employee dinners. He's been trying to hire Henry's boys and me because we can speak German and have what he calls "engineering skills." He thinks being watchmakers qualifies us to work on some machine his company makes. It'll mean some travel. In fact I'll be in Germany for at least a year."

Zeb nodded.. "Not many companies hiring these days. What's the company?"

"The American company is Information Storage Service, calls itself ISS. I'll be heading for Germany to work for their subsidiary there, Deutsche Information Storage Service, DISS."

Zeb nodded again. "I know you always wanted to travel and see the world, but I'll miss you come harvest time."

Diana

11

The metal rails of the ladder were so cold, and I had clung to them so tightly that my hands felt numb, but even when I took that last step I was reluctant to let go.

I searched the wall to the right—no light switches. I took a deep breath and expelled it slowly to calm the rising panic, then searched the wall to the left. There was a gray metal utility box on the wall. "It's on your other right, Ned," I mumbled. I checked the floor with the miner's lamp as if the solid floor might be only an illusion and a misstep would suddenly plunge me into an abyss. Assuring myself that the floor was level, I took one step to the left but still clung to that ladder with one hand. With the other I opened the box and flipped on the five switches inside.

As Ned had promised, the lights lit up the place like Yankee Stadium, revealing an enormous cavern. The main room was a roughly circular space irregular around the edges but flat floored in the middle. That central floor was filled with such an array of cabinets, cars, and furniture that it looked as if it had been inhabited for decades by a whole colony of modern-day cave dwellers.

Like streetlight standards shining downward, the bright lights did not reveal how high the cave was, and I couldn't see up to the headframe. Looking to the edges of the light, I could see just enough to show me that the cave did not end with this great room. A solid but irregular cave wall circled behind me, to my right and on to the far side of the room. On the left there was no wall, and the darkness of the farther cave swallowed the light like a great black hole. From that blackness came a faint movement of air and dank odors from the bowels of the earth.

In several places, stalactites and stalagmites had been lit with small spotlights like fine pieces of art. The natural beauty of some appeared to have been enhanced by the hand of man, sculpted here, polished there. To the right was a space where cave wall was replaced by solid cement. I wondered if that opening had once led to another tunnel.

Two cars stood in the center of the room, completely encased in transparent boxes like models in a kid's toy collection. These, however, were not toys. One I recognized as a Ford Model T; the other was a long luxurious classic, but I didn't know what make or model. Both were polished and gleaming, as if they had just come from the showroom floor. Walking up close I could see the boxes were hermetically sealed cases and the cars were labeled. The luxury model was a 1931 Packard Cabriolet Custom Sedan Limousine. It was magnificent, with gleaming white body, black top, four doors, whitewall tires, spare on the running board just in front of the door, shiny hood ornament, and perfect leather upholstery. I looked up from the car and around at its home in the cave and laughed aloud. "That's one hell of a bat mobile, Uncle Bennett. What on earth were you up to in here?"

My voice echoed slightly, then was lost in the expanse of the cave. Another sound rumbled from the tunnel above. Like distant thunder, the blasts exploded in synchronized relays. From the ordered sound of the blasts, Ned's rigging must have gone off as planned. I could visualize them because I had watched my dad set aboveground blasts. It had always bugged me, however, that he would never take me underground in any mine. I had so wanted to see what it was like, but Dad refused my repeated requests for two reasons: one, it was dangerous, and two, many of the miners who worked for him were as superstitious about women underground, as sailors used to be about women on board ship.

The sounds did come closer, but nothing, not even dust, made it to the great cavern. Ned knew his stuff, but then if Dad had recommended him, he would have to be good. I assumed that the tunnel was closed as planned and hoped that Ned and Emma would get home safely.

I walked across the great central room that was filled with office furniture: file cabinets, desks with computers, worktables, and great racks of electronic equipment that I couldn't identify. Everything that could be corroded by the damp air was maintained in cases similar to the ones the cars were in.

In the far back of the cave I could make out two pieces of equipment I recognized from photographs as large copper stills. I was wondering if Uncle Bennett still made booze like the old days when I noticed the wooden cabinets built along the far wall. Like polished walnut lockers with leaded glass windows, each liquor-filled cabinet was labeled with a year, the earliest being 1912, the latest being this year. Not much doubt that my uncle Bennett made illegal hooch. But did that explain those three men with the SICC badges?

In the center of the wall of cabinets was the other tunnel. Peering in through the opening, I flicked on the light switch. This was not a natural tunnel but a great hallway cut out of solid rock and polished like marble. And there, just as Ned had tried to tell me, was an elevator.

Such an improbable object in such a preposterous place beckoned irresistibly. I walked toward it and was startled as the door opened. Had someone opened it or was it motion sensitive? I peered in cautiously and saw an elevator box big enough to hold the Cabriolet. Perhaps that's how he got it down here, but why on earth would he want to?

I looked back at the cavern. There was so much to check out, but I had to see where the hell the elevator went. I pulled my Walther from my fanny pack, chambered a round, and stepped into the elevator. The only button on the wall read "Up." Not wanting to give myself time for second thoughts, I touched the button. The door to the cave closed, and the elevator began to rise.

Diana

12

The large elevator rose slowly and must have climbed at least three stories by the time it came to a stop. There were doors at each end of the large box, and I waited to see which one would open. Several seconds passed and neither door opened. Nervously I noted that were no "open door" buttons in this elevator. The lighted panel on the door to the cave now read "Down." The door on the far side had a single lighted panel that simply said "Key." Nuts! Would I need a key to get in? If I didn't have one, would I be marooned in that damn cave until I died?

As I turned to walk back to the cave door, the key light started to blink, and in time with the blinking there was a musical ding, ding, ding. It was like the idiot alarm in a car that berates you when you leave your keys in the ignition or your headlights on. As a test I pushed the down button. The dinging stopped and the box obediently descended. When it reached the cave floor level, the door opened. Okay, I needed a key to get into wherever this elevator went but not back into the cave. Maybe the key was somewhere in the cave. I stood on the threshold of the open elevator door staring out at the huge room, trying to guess how long it might take me to search this cavern and find the right key.

Wait a minute, right key? I didn't remember seeing a keyhole. How . . .

I stepped back into the elevator, and the button now read "Up." My nervous chuckle echoed around the silent tunnel. Like Alice down the rabbit hole, trying to eat just the right amount of whichever food would make me the right size to get the heck out of here. I pushed the up button, and back up the elevator went.

On the way, I thought I figured out the key button; but if I was right, I could be in real difficulty. On my old apartment door in Bluff Beach, Sam had installed a thumb print, biometric scanner that looked like a lighted doorbell. All I had to do was place my thumb on the scanner and all the locks and deadbolts he had installed would automatically unlock and the door opened. The problem was, if the key was also biometric, whose print would it be keyed for? Not mine.

When the box stopped and the key button lit up, I tried my theory by pushing on the button with my thumb. A quiet electronic hum emanated from the door. A small drawer appeared just under the button and slid open. A moment before there had been no line, no crack in the wall, no indication that there could possibly be a compartment in that door.

I jumped as a pleasant male voice with a crisp British accent spoke from unseen speakers in the elevator wall.

"Welcome, Ms. Hunter. Please take the watch with the remote key button from the drawer."

Looking in the drawer, I retrieved a watch with a small push button on the outside of the case. It looked suspiciously like the one Sam had made to open and close the hidden room in my Bluff Beach apartment. The elevator door opened, but I stood facing a wall. In the wall was a wide-angle video monitor showing a huge garage with several automobiles. I examined the screen carefully, assuming it was showing me what was on the far side of the wall. No one appeared to be in the garage. Where, I wondered, was the owner of the disembodied British voice?

If it hadn't been for my friendship with Sam Dehany, this whole experience would be enough to convince me I was having a really bizarre dream; but because of Sam, this all had a familiar feel to it. I pushed the button on the watch and the wall slid open.

I fastened the watch around my wrist and stepped cautiously into the garage. A second push on the watch button and the garage wall slid silently closed, leaving no trace of the opening. "Magic," I mumbled, but what I felt was a terrible confusion bordering on a fear of betrayal. The similarity to Sam's work added whole new layers to my already overtaxed analytical capacities.

When I have too much input my mind tries to go in many directions at once. I feel as if there is a whole committee inside, a sort of board of directors, each member trying to approach the problem from her own point of view. I have learned to identify a few of my internal board members so I can hear their different voices without chaos. Today's events were definitely enough to summon my board members.

The trained investigator tried to take in all the objects in the garage. This takes more concentration and effort than it might for others. When God handed out my skills, one She deprived me of was visual memory. My brain works like a video camcorder with no tape. My eyes may take in a scene, but once I look away, the picture is gone. If I want to remember details, I must change what my eyes see to words and remember the words.

There were six cars and a windowless van, all clean and polished. There were cabinets with closed doors, and a few tools hanging on the walls; but this was a formal car barn, not your run-of-the-mill suburban garage. In fact, I had seen car barns like this only in movies about very rich people. How on earth did that jibe with my poor old hillbilly uncle living out his days on Social Security? The analyst on my board tried to reconcile the disparity between Uncle Bennett's old broken-down farmhouse and this. I wondered fleetingly if illegal whiskey really paid that well these days.

The mother on the board who is always afraid for me, wondered what was outside, and if "it" or "they" were deadly. All the large garage doors were closed. There was one small people-door at the end of the building. Gun at ready, I started for the small door.

As I walked past the cars, my investigator tried to add detail to my observations, checking the makes and models: a Lincoln town car, a Chevy Lumina, a Ford Taurus, and a Toyota Prius. Neither the van nor the small red sports car had any make or model visible. I was looking in the window of the sports car when I heard the click of a door latch. I crouched at the side of the sports car, rested my hands with the Walther on the hood, and aimed at the door.

The door, which had begun to open, stopped when it was only cracked an inch or two. The same voice I had heard in the elevator emanated from behind the door.

"Please do not fire, Ms. Hunter. You are quite safe here. I am Robert James, Mr. Hunter's butler and property custodian."

He must have a monitor outside the garage door. Guess the ball was in my court.

"Okay, I won't shoot. Show yourself, hands first."

The door edged open and two wrinkled hands appeared, followed by a tall slender older man dressed in pajamas, robe, and slippers. He didn't really seem concerned that I would shoot. His words and actions were protocol, not fear. Despite his age, I doubted that there would be much of anything he would fear. From his thinning gray hair to his slippered feet, he appeared eminently sure of himself and stood before my gun with erect bearing and confident demeanor. I stood, lowered gun, and walked around the sports car toward him.

"How do you do, Ms. Hunter. I am happy to finally meet you and glad you made the journey safely." He smiled and held out one hand. I didn't offer him mine. He withdrew his hand, smiled again, and nodded.

I nodded back and replied formally. "How do you do, Mr. James."

"Ms. Hunter, my full name is Robert James Westerman, and though I know it is a mouthful, I am rather accustomed to being called Robert James."

"Okay, Robert James."

"We shall be better acquainted soon. I, of course, have known of you for many years now, but you won't have heard of me. We shall remedy that. Your method of arrival is curious, but I imagine you are tired and hungry after your trip, so I won't burden you with questions now. If you would like to follow me to the house, I shall prepare you a bit of a snack while you freshen up. Then, after you have eaten, we shall talk a bit if you feel up to it. If not, it will wait until morning."

He turned, holding the door so I could exit. Weirder and weirder. With my Walther still ready, I said, "Why don't you lead the way."

My caution seemed to amuse him, but he answered, "Certainly."

As we stepped outside the garage door, the sound of a nearby waterfall filled the air. He led me along a gravel path that was edged with green vines and flowers and was lighted dimly by small solar lights. The path skirted the outer edge of the mountain that contained the cavern and the farther we went the louder the roar of the falls became. At the falls a small footbridge spanned a great rent in the hillside, and as we crossed the bridge the air was damp with mist. The water tumbled down the rock-covered mountain, rumbled underneath the bridge and cascaded into the dark night beyond.

If I hadn't totally lost my sense of direction in the depths of the cave, the waterfall would be approximately where the cement wall was inside. So much for my extra tunnel theory. No cement could be seen from the outside, just the rock and shrubbery of the mountainside. The tourist on my internal board wanted to take in the beauty of it, while my ever practical manager wondered what time it was and how long it had been since I'd seen Mr. Brehm fall from the third-story window. Ever since Robert James mentioned "tired and hungry," my body had been demanding that I stop ignoring it and acknowledge that I was, indeed, exhausted. My day had started at four in the morning when I got up to drive to LAX and the events of the last twenty-four hours had been enough to wipe me out emotionally even if I wasn't in need of sleep. I wondered where my guide was leading me, who he really was, and if it was going to be safe to go to sleep, or if closing my eyes would be fatal.

Bennett

13

Bennett made his way through the SS Bremen soaking up the luxury and feeling quite pleased that he had made it through the training and been hired for this job. His first night when he was taken to meet Mr. Thaddius Williams at the Waldorf Astoria it had seemed doubtful that his lifestyle would be able to conform to the corporate demands.

At the hotel he had been rushed into the ballroom as soon as he arrived and was surprised to find the room so highly decorated for a business meeting. Rows of tables gleamed with white linens, china, and silver service, and at each place was a name card designating assigned seating. The balcony boxes around the edges were obviously set for guests of honor and hung with great swaths of silk. The dais had more than a dozen place settings and was dressed with enough flowers to fill a church. Behind the dais was a great banner that read, "BELIEVE."

Salesmen seated at the tables were dressed so uniformly in dark suits and starched white shirts that they reminded Bennett more of a costumed chorus line than a meeting of businessmen. In addition to dressing alike, they each displayed the same look of attentiveness and enthusiasm, but modulated so that they didn't appear boisterous. Almost without exception each had a wife beside him trying to look supportive, decorative, and obedient.

Don Janeway, the tall handsome ISS manager who had recruited Bennett, explained the purpose of the occasion. "Tonight honors the employees who achieved 100 percent of their sales quota for the year. They and their wives are invited to New York, expenses paid, for a full week of dinners, pep sessions, speeches, and awards. Each man is given an award, like a check, a gold watch, or sets of candlesticks, and each is given three minutes to make his own speech."

Bennett looked around the huge ballroom and tried to calculate how long it would take for all the men to give their three-minute speeches. He pulled out his

Camels and was about to light up when Janeway grabbed the package from his hand.

"No," he said urgently. "Mr. Williams doesn't approve of smoking. Hide those and don't even let him see you have them. While we're on the subject, there are a few other things you ought to know if you're going to work for Mr. Williams. Never have any liquor. If he hears that you have been in a place that serves liquor or beer, you will be fired on the spot."

Bennett kept a straight face but wondered what sort of outfit this was.

"Same goes for the ladies, unless of course you're married. And for the most part Mr. Williams prefers that you get married. In fact, if I don't agree to marriage soon this appointment to Europe will be my final promotion."

Bennett was astounded to hear that so much of his personal life would be subject to oversight by Mr. Williams. "Is this guy a businessman or a preacher?"

Janeway laughed, choosing not to hear the derisive tone in Bennett's voice. "A little of both, I guess. Most of us figure he could probably walk on water. He's already created the miracle of the bread and fishes. Look how many men are out of work, how many businesses shut down, but every year ISS makes more money and expands to more countries around the world."

The orchestra struck up a familiar anthem and everyone in the room leaped to their feet singing like a church congregation. Janeway pulled Bennett up, handed him a small songbook opened it to the appropriate page. By the second verse Bennett managed to find his place and join in, but his eyes drifted around the room. To his astonishment he saw that everyone in the hall was giving full throated praise to the virtues of ISS.

When the song ended, Bennett was about to take his seat, but Janeway nudged him to keep standing. A man walked in from the wings, tall, lean, straight as a Puritan on Sunday, and strode toward the center chair on the dais. The orchestra struck the first chords of a new song and Janeway changed Bennett's songbook to the appropriate page. As he did he whispered, "That's Mr. Williams." The assemblage once again burst into song, this time in praise of Mr. Williams, accompanied by loud enthusiastic clapping.

Williams was followed by a diminutive Mrs. Williams, then Vice President David Morreson and his wife, then the rest of the lesser company dignitaries. There was sustained applause and song until all had entered, then a hush fell over the room and a minister offered a prayer. At the "amen" they all took their seats with a great scuffle of chairs.

After an excellent steak dinner, a luxury in the middle of the Depression, came the payment: four hours of awards and speeches including a sermon by Williams in which Hell's fire was reserved for those who failed to work hard and be loyal to ISS. As the evening droned on, Bennett made a mental note never to make his sales quota.

When Williams's speech ended Bennett tried to leave, but the orchestra struck up the first chords and the room filled with voices singing the ISS anthem. As the final verse concluded, Janeway led Bennett to a long line of the faithful waiting to be presented to the great man. When his turn came, Williams shook Bennett's hand and immediately turned him over to a colleague, who began speaking in rapid-fire German. Recognizing a test, Bennett answered carefully and fully.

When they finished, the man turned to Williams and reported, "He speaks the language perfectly, complete with the idiomatic phrases and without a hint of an American accent. I would have taken him for a native German."

Williams gave Bennett a warm, approving smile, and Bennett found that this acceptance and approval was disturbingly pleasant. He had held himself aloof from the sermon, just as he had done as a boy in church, but when Williams's power and charismatic charm shone directly on him, he couldn't resist its warm glow.

"You appear to be a fine young man, and I know you will succeed," Williams intoned. "I want to give you just two pieces of advice as you begin your new life with us. First, remember that joining a company is an act that calls for absolute loyalty. Second, never feel satisfied. Always strive for more."

Diana

14

The blackout drapes were very efficient at keeping out the rising sun until it reached a certain point in its morning arc. Then the gap between the drapes admitted a slender streak of light that shone like a laser right in my eyes. Despite being exhausted, I couldn't sleep through that solar wake-up call.

At first I hadn't a clue where I was. Sleep had left my morning memory peacefully blank. The chair I had wedged against the door was the first memory jogger. Then the entire bizarre trip from California to North Carolina to Uncle Bennett's farm, tunnel, and cave came rushing back. The horrifying vision of poor old Brehm falling to the pavement came vividly to mind.

I got up and pulled open the drapes and in the morning light began exploring the room. It was actually a lovely suite that included a pleasant sitting room with windows that looked out on the surrounding woods.

When I had first entered it last night, I had been startled to find the walls covered with pictures of me at all ages. Robert James explained that this room had always been kept for me. I was too exhausted to examine the photos then, but I did find them reassuring. I didn't think I would be murdered in my bed in a room that appeared to have been waiting for me my entire life. Nonetheless, caution had dictated that I at least make sure all windows and doors were locked and my Walther was within reach.

Examining the photo gallery on the wall, I found my life passing before me, moments of my existence caught at the click of a camera shutter. Arranged around the sitting room in chronological order were my first baby picture, school class pictures, snapshots from the two visits to Uncle Bennett's farm, and many other photos that Dad had taken as I grew up in various places around the world. The people, places and critters I was photographed with certainly did accentuate the exotic nature of my young life.

Looking at this collection, I felt a sudden sadness. This uncle I had only met twice and didn't really know had obviously taken a great interest in me. Now he was gone and I would never get to know him. The only one left in my direct family line was my dad, and I seldom saw him. At times like this I was forced to consider the fact that mine had not been what you would call a normal family life. Family Christmas meant Dad and me getting together with the rest of the mine workers in the cook shack to sing carols and dine on wildebeest or iguana or whatever exotic fare was at hand. Most of that life, however, I had throughly enjoyed the adventure and hadn't noticed the loneliness.

When I came to the last photo on the wall my mood changed abruptly. It was a picture of me reading and sunbathing on Sam's boat. It wasn't from the latest visit, but it had been taken only two months before. Only one person could have taken that picture–Sam. I looked back a few pictures, and with shock realized that at least four other photos were probably shot by Sam over the last three years. The thumb print sensor, the watch, the secret panel, and now photos. Sam's fingerprints were all over this place. How long had he known Bennett? When I first met Sam and agreed to help him with his retirement problem, had he really hired me because of my reputation, or had Bennett put him up to it? Was he really my friend, or was he Bennett's spy?

And what was it that Ned had said about the tunnel? He had started to tell me that my dad knew all about the tunnel. What kind of friendly conspiracy was going on here? The sooner I had a talk with Robert James, the sooner I could get some answers.

My small suitcase was back in Thomasville, and the clothes I had worn reeked from wear, sweat, and fear. I craved a shower. I opened one of the closet doors to find a small but well-selected wardrobe that looked to be my size. "The surprises just keep coming, Uncle Bennett."

The bathroom had a garden shower, a jetted hot tub, and a spacious dressing room. I laughed out loud when I saw the photo on the bathroom wall. It was me at about age five taking a bath in the corrugated tub in the kitchen at Uncle Bennett's old farmhouse. I was frowning and looking cold and miserable.

As I stepped into the shower, lights came on revealing that the entire outer wall of the shower was one large curved window. Surrounding the window was an opaque hothouse filled with orchids of every size and color imaginable, rosy pink petals with deep red centers, orange and yellow with persimmon centers, ivory brushed with golden yellow, solid lavender. There was even one with a tiny red checked pattern like a piece of gingham. The super star, which bloomed in the center of the garden, was more than four inches across. It was a bright butter yellow with one dazzling crimson petal that was tightly ruffled around the edges like a lacy scarf. As I showered, the steam vented into the hothouse and kissed the orchids with mist.

It was the most delightful shower I had ever had. Mesmerized by the orchids, I stayed in there much longer than I had planned. Finally pulling away from the exotic beauty, I climbed out and wrapped myself in the soft butter-yellow robe that hung from a bathroom peg. I was delighted when I raised the hood of the robe and saw that it was crimson, colors precisely copying the star orchid in the garden.

I selected a pair of jeans and a loose-fitting sweatshirt from the closet and was in the middle of dressing when there was a knock at the door.

"Yes?"

"The coffee is on, Ms. Hunter. Breakfast will be ready in about five minutes."

"I'll be right out."

"Very good. Do you prefer breakfast in the kitchen, the dining room, or on the patio?"

"The patio sounds nice. I trust you plan on joining me. We need to talk."

"Yes, Ms. Hunter, I shall."

I simply followed my nose to the kitchen, guided by the pleasant aroma of fresh ground coffee, frying bacon, baked omelet, and something with cinnamon and sugar. As I entered the white and stainless steel kitchen, Robert James was just removing a skillet omelet from the oven. He greeted me with a cheery, "Good morning," and a nod of his head. "Out this way, Ms. Hunter," he said and led me through open French doors to a patio set on a small flat terrace.

As he set out our breakfast I walked to the far edge of the terrace to look back at the house. It was perched on a hill that jutted out from the mountain above and was landscaped with three scalloped terraces that dropped away sharply to a ravine below. From the patio I looked right out into the tops of trees that grew downhill. It was like living in a tree house, designed out of the lazy summer dreams of my childhood. The surrounding land, as far as I could see, was filled with green woods. There was no sign of any other human inhabitants.

I turned to catch Robert James watching me. "I'm glad to see you like it, Ms. Hunter. Bennett would be pleased. Our breakfast is ready. Let's not let it get cold."

His statement raised a question: Was this magical place now mine or was it too under federal seizure? Or did it belong to Robert James or someone I didn't even know about? As we sat down to eat, I would love to have blurted out the question but put that off for the moment. "Thank you for the lovely breakfast."

"It's my pleasure. It's rather lonely cooking for one. Bennett traveled a great deal in the early years, but as he got older, he was home most of the time. Living as isolated as we do here, we settled into a comfortable routine and . . ."

In the pause as he considered his words he rolled the cuffs of his starched white shirt to just below the elbow. That, I suspected, was as casual as he got.

"It seems rather like he is just away on business now. He was healthy right up until the end, you know. Never spent a day in the hospital and was . . . I'm sorry to rattle on. I am sure you have many questions."

This morning as he served breakfast, Robert James seemed like a friendly, lonely old butler, but last night I had glimpsed another side to him. I decided to give him his head and see where this went.

"No, I like hearing about him. How come he never . . . that room, created for me, why didn't he invite me here when I could have gotten to know him?"

Robert James smiled as he considered the question, but there was a sadness in his eyes. It looked genuine but I didn't know him well enough to read him with certainty.

"He always intended to, Diana, but there was always one more. . . . His work was sometimes dangerous. He wanted you protected from that . . . and yet contradictorily, he chose you for his heir a long time ago."

He chewed his small bite of egg thoroughly, then dunked a torn strip of cinnamon roll into his coffee.

"He was so proud when you became a private investigator and showed such promise. It proved he had been right about you, that you were the one to leave his life's work to. He was always torn though. He knew what a burden it would be, and toward the end he considered blowing up the whole cave so that you would never be drawn into the life, never have to deal with . . . but I get ahead of myself.

"Let's dispense with the practical matters first. I assume Otto explained that you are Bennett's sole heir and that—"

"Otto never had a chance to tell me anything. Three thugs with some sort of federal badges beat him, broke his neck, and tossed him out of the third-story window of his office building."

Robert James blanched and looked so shaken that I wished I had stated the facts in some gentler and less tactless manner. Then he put down his fork, wiped his mouth with a napkin, and his entire countenance changed again. Chameleon. The steely, capable man I had glimpsed last night returned.

"So it begins." Even his voice had changed. "Perhaps, Diana, you had better tell me everything that happened yesterday. Please do not omit any details."

He listened attentively as I gave him the blow-by-blow description of events. He nodded approvingly when I told him about Ned setting fire to the house and blowing up the tunnel.

"Now I understand why you showed up in the cave rather than coming around the road."

"A road? If there's a road, why did Ned drag me though that tunnel?"

"Ned doesn't know how to get through the security. Only four, no, with Bennett and Otto gone, only two people have the codes to get in here. This house sits in the middle of a full section of land, six hundred and forty acres, and a real expert set up the security around the perimeter. I can see now that Ned had little time. He had to get you to safety and get to the farm to collapse the tunnel before the gentlemen from SICC got there. He did well. I will have to call and make sure he and Emma are all right."

Leaving his breakfast, he stood abruptly. "Please excuse me, Diana."

"Wait, please. One other question. What about this house? Will the SICC guys show up here to seize this place next?"

He smiled, this time with genuine humor. "Not very damn likely. This house and all of your uncle's fortune are so well hidden in a series of interlocking partnerships and corporations that they could never be traced to this estate or to its true owner." He turned to go into the house.

"What true owner?"

He looked back. "Why you, of course, Diana. You are a very wealthy woman, but don't worry about showing up on the wealthiest women list. One thing Bennett and Otto learned from the fascists in Germany was how to hide the money from public scrutiny. Excuse me, won't you? Feel free to explore the house. It's yours."

I tried to eat the rest of my breakfast but could only think about what he had said. I was a very wealthy woman and this wonderful house was mine. How could Bennett have hidden so much for so long?

Something else nagged at me, intruding even on this astounding revelation. The few answers Robert James had given hadn't cleared up anything but rather had added layers to the mystery. What did Bennett and Otto have to do with German fascists, and what had Bennett been doing that was so dangerous he considered blowing it up? Why had Robert James made such a sudden departure? I felt rather like I had been patted on the head and told to go out and play. Whatever he was up to, I was sure he had more on his mind than a phone call.

I put down my coffee and went looking for him. My bedroom with its orchid garden was on the east. I wandered through the other rooms on the ground floor, the kitchen, dining room, and living room. He wasn't there. Each ground-floor room had a door that led to a utility room in the back of the house. All the controls—electrical, plumbing, and so on—seemed to be housed together in this long, narrow oval, which ran the length of the house. A staircase as well as an elevator were also in this oval room. It was a design I had never seen before. The second floor consisted of three bedrooms, each with its own bath. One was obviously Robert James's room; a second was Bennett's. The walls in Bennett's room were covered with photos, but I didn't take time to look at them. The third bedroom appeared to be unused, perhaps a guest room. No sign of Robert James. The third floor was a huge open rectangular room, well lit, with windows filling the outer wall and floor-to-ceiling bookcases filling the inner wall. There was a desk at one end and a worktable at the other and various comfortable-looking chairs positioned for reading or viewing the surrounding land. No sign of my new friend.

One more flight of stairs led to an outdoor sundeck adorned with potted plants and trees, but no Robert James.

I walked back downstairs, took the path to the car barn and the elevator down to the cave. As the door opened I could see Robert James sitting at one of the computer consoles, clicking away on the keys. With his eyes concentrating on the screen and headphones over his ears, he didn't hear me approach.

"What are you finding there?"

With a click of the mouse he minimized the screen but not before I got a glimpse of the subject he had been studying.

"Diana! You startled me."

I folded my arms across my chest and waited for him to answer.

"Did you finish your breakfast? Have you had a look around the house? Sorry to run out on you, but I did want to check in with Ned. By the way, he and Emma are fine. They got back home last night with no further incident and are busy minding the store this morning."

I still held him in my gaze, making no response.

"Ned had a private chat with the sheriff this morning. Seems your SICC agents did eventually find their way to the farm after being lost on back roads for a couple of hours. By the time they got there, it was nothing but charcoal, and they were livid. Woke the sheriff to . . . ah, express their displeasure, forcefully."

During his performance his face seemed innocently transparent, and thus could be convincingly deceptive. As he had chattered on, he looked every bit the elderly butler: friendly, charming, guileless. His British accent was skillfully modulated for that role.

"Our sheriff is a very patient man, but I guess they pushed him too far. He came back at them with both barrels, and this morning—"

"Robert James, who are you? I mean, what are you? What did you do for my uncle? What was your relationship with him? What is your position now that . . . he . . . he's no longer here?"

The kindly old retainer act disappeared. He sighed deeply and set the headphones down on the console. The expression he now wore raised his apparent IQ at least forty points. His body language also changed as he straightened his shoulders and back. Even through his shirt I could see that the musculature of his arms and upper body were still quite firm. Overall, the change in him added a hint of danger, a feeling that behind those penetrating brown eyes was a keen mind that might already be three steps ahead of me. If he had at that moment answered my questions with the words "Bond, James Bond," it would have seemed perfectly in character.

"Yes, of course," he said. "I knew we needed to have this conversation. I just underestimated the speed with which . . . but then you are of Bennett's blood. I should have known."

He stood and pulled another chair up in front of the console. "Won't you join me? You have already seen part of what I do. Sort of a jack of all trades. I helped Bennett with his work and was his butler, cook, housekeeper, property manager, chauffeur, security officer, et cetera. I began by helping him with a case that grew out of . . . well, out of some work we had done together a long time ago. I stayed here with him on a temporary basis at first, but Bennett needed complete privacy and could not chance a full staff. Whatever he needed, I was it, or he was."

Robert James chuckled. "He was quite egalitarian about the duties, actually. One week I would vacuum and he would wash the cars; the next week we would rotate work details. What I shall be now or whether I shall even stay on is entirely up to you."

"And what I shall do depends on the answers I get from you. Why did you hide the screen when I came up?"

He took a long time before he came up with an answer. "You may never know the extremes Bennett went to trying to protect you. It is a habit hard to break."

"Protect me from what?"

"Ironically, from the same information he spent his life collecting, the information he planned for you to inherit."

He clicked the mouse, and on the screen was the image I had glimpsed when I walked up. It was a full-face view of SICC agent Carl Hedgeman with a long list of aliases and a complete dossier.

"Dangerous information. Information men like this would willingly kill to find and destroy. Diana, you were never meant to come in through the cave, never expected to be exposed to all this before you were seasoned to it. Bennett never dared marry, didn't even dare to see you or your father. He lived his life by secrecy, disguise and hiding. He had a huge fortune, yet he was a prisoner of this estate.

Take time to enjoy your inheritance and learn about—"

"And the man there on the screen, the one who beat Otto to death. What about him?"

"Even if you could bring him to some kind of justice, there are hundreds more waiting to take his place. It's an endless job, Diana. You really must learn more of your uncle's life before you leap blindly into affairs you are in no way trained to handle."

Diana

15

He tapped keys and the file on Hedgeman disappeared.

"Please pull that back up. I want to read it."

"Not now, Diana. Come up to the house and I'll show you your uncle's diaries. He wanted you to start at the beginning so you could understand his life."

Our conversation went downhill from there. No matter what approach, what logic I used, no matter how forceful I was, even using my authority as new owner of Bennett's possessions, Robert James would not pull up that file or divulge any more information. He just kept insisting I take time to read Bennett's private diaries before I learned more about the database in the cave. When neither of us would move past this impasse he stood and headed for the house.

"I'll find Hedgeman's file for myself," I called out to his back.

He turned, shrugged and said, "Help yourself."

I knew Hedgeman was in this database. His face with aliases had stared out at me from the computer screen. I had been a librarian and a PI and certainly knew my way around filing systems, both paper and digital. But despite my considerable skill, I could not pull up Hedgeman's file no matter what I tried. I couldn't discern the organization of Bennett's system, and when I did manage to pull up something at random, it was meaningless without context. It was like going into library stacks and reading a few paragraphs without knowing which book or even which shelf they came from. After two hours I left the cave defeated and went back up to the house.

The frustration and failure left me a tad testy and as Robert James and I sat down to lunch, I crammed the salad into my mouth and chewed in seething silence.

He read my mood, and after one attempt at polite conversation concentrated on his lunch and the morning paper. Finally, after verifying that it was today's paper, my curiosity overcame anger. "How did you get that paper?"

He looked surprised by the question. "I picked it up at the mailbox"

"You get mail delivery out here?"

"Oh my, no. We keep a box at the post office in town, not in Bennett's name of course. I drove in while you were . . . busy in the cave."

"Busy in the cave? Damn it! You knew I wouldn't be able to figure out Bennett's system. What is the matter with you? Why don't you help me? Otto Brehm is dead! Hedgeman murdered him. Don't you get it? Don't you care?"

Slowly, silently, he folded the paper, giving himself time before speaking. He laid it on the table and his eyes focused on me with cold, controlled furry. Tossing down his napkin, he said through clenched teeth, enunciating each word, "Of course I care. In just a few days I have lost the only two friends I had in the world. The *only* friends. I am the last dinosaur. I also care about the work the three of us gave our lives to. I care that this work has been turned over to a dangerously inexperienced young woman who could destroy it all in one false move."

"Ah! The light dawns. He should have left it all to you, huh?"

"Good God no, girl! I'm too old. Don't you understand what I tried to tell you this morning? You are into something that is beyond your experience and abilities. You can't just run out and play cops and robbers with Hedgeman. You will be killed! And if you are, I must carry out Bennett's last wish. I shall have to destroy everything he dedicated his life to."

He looked away from me and mumbled more to himself than to me. "That may be all that is left anyway. His was always a quixotic cause, which may already have failed ." Looking back at me, he added, "But I am not ready to surrender yet. I want to believe there is hope. You are the hope. He should have brought you in before, trained you himself, but —"

"So quit being mysterious and tell me about Hedgeman, or at least tell me how I can find his file."

"First I would have to teach you sixty years of history and not the version you get in school. Instead of jumping right into the files, go upstairs and read that history in Bennett's diaries.

Without further attempt at conversation I left the table and went to my room. Beyond anger, I was confused, stymied, and alone. So alone. I no longer feared Robert James or this place, I feared what was happening to my life. In response to his words I considered how few friends I had and tried to call Sam on my cell phone. No signal. Using the extension on the night stand I tried both his home and his cell and got no answer. Who else could I call? A father who was always out of cell range? Jenny, my friend who now had a husband and two children and no longer wanted to be exposed to the danger inherent in my investigations?

No wonder Sam and I had grown close over the last three years. We were as alone as Robert James and Bennett. Sam had retired from a career with U.S. military intelligence. High-tech toys were his area of expertise and he had spent his last four years in service developing advanced robotics technology. When disillusionment and disgust replaced duty and patriotism, Sam decided he didn't want his technology put to the uses the military had planned for it. With my own brand of deception, I helped Sam leave the service with his secrets. He lives quietly in San Pedro, no wife, no children and few friends. He can never again use his skills openly and I have been the lucky recipient of any new toys he comes up with. We have been each other's closest confidants. No wonder his secret association with Bennett seemed like such a betrayal.

I turned on the TV and listened to the early news to see if there was anything more about Otto's death. The local anchor flashed Otto's picture and promised more details later.

There was a knock at my bedroom door. "Diana?"

With the TV going it was hard to pretend to be asleep. I got up and opened the door. "Yes, Robert James?"

"I am sorry we got off on the wrong foot at lunch. This is a hard time for me, and I was unnecessarily gruff. I hope you can understand."

"I, uh, I was a bit testy myself."

"There is something I can tell you about the files downstairs and in fact about everything Bennett did. He was the most secretive man I have ever known, and he encoded everything. He lived by the 'need to know' principle, and even I, his closest associate, was never given all his codes and keys. Much of what you were supposed to have learned died with Otto."

"But you didn't have any trouble finding Hedgeman."

Ignoring my comment, he handed me a small worn book. "Here is the first of Bennett's diaries. He left them for you." He started to say something else, then thought better of it and simply said he would have supper for us at seven. I turned off the TV and curled up on the bed. I didn't open the book. I just lay there trying to analyze the information I had been hit with in the last two days. What it boiled down to was that old Uncle Ben, the moonshiner, was really some kind of super avenger complete with bat cave and a 1931 Packard batmobile. What did that make me, Batgirl? I began to giggle. Alarmingly, the giggling became almost hysterical. If I hadn't brought it under control it would probably have developed into a good cry. This whole trip was too bizarre, and I was simply too wiped out emotionally and physically to be able to deal with it. I needed much more than the three hours' sleep I'd had, and after sleep, I needed some serious think time. At least in this isolated home I seemed to have time and safety for both. I set the diary on the night stand, unopened, closed my eyes and slept without even waking for supper.

I awoke at 2:15 a.m., stretched, and turned on the lamp. On the night stand was a bottle of tomato juice in a small silver ice bucket engraved with the North German Lloyd logo and the name S.S. Bremen. Nestled in the ice beside it was a chicken sandwich in a plastic bag.

I realized I was hungry and smiled, both at his thoughtfulness and at the elegant silver bucket. As I sat there munching my sandwich, I also picked up the diary. I was now quite rested and figured I might as well learn something of Bennett's life. Maybe I would also get some clue as to what SICC wanted with his estate and why it was worth murdering poor old Otto Brehm.

Bennett

16

The door to his cabin was open. He checked the number and looked into the small tourist class room. His bags were waiting for him and to his shock, so was Don Janeway, newly appointed to the head office in Europe, the big boss. Bennett felt his stomach clinch.

Janeway was six foot four, had a slim torso with broad shoulders, movie star good looks and was dressed in the ISS uniform, dark suit, bright white shirt, highly polished shoes, and a hat.

"Mr. Janeway, what a surprise."

"Glad to see you made it Sizemore." Janeway was seated on one of the two small bunks and waved Bennett to the other one. "Come on in and sit down."

Bennett sat on the other bunk, wondering what the boss was doing here.

"I walked down here from first class to tell you something and I find this arrangement will never do. Your accommodations in tourist are just a matter of false economy. I need you much closer so we can use those language skills of yours. I'll talk to the chief steward and have you moved immediately. I'm sure there's space in first class."

Bennett's heart sank. Any hope of a few days' enjoyment on this cruise had just been dashed. He said, "Yes, sir. That will work better, I guess."

"Yes, and I need you at a breakfast meeting tomorrow morning. Of those three fellows from the German subsidiary, only one speaks much English. The three of them are always talking in German, and then one translates what he wants to. I need you to sit in on our discussions. Don't let on that you know German but just listen and see if that guy is giving me a true translation. Okay?"

Bennett said, "Okay," but he was thinking, "Oh shit." Not only would he be in first class, he would be sitting in on every meeting Janeway took with DISS.

"Good man." said Janeway as he stood up. "See you at eight in the main diningroom." As he turned to leave he added one last instruction. "Oh, and Bennnett, take care of those shoes."

Bennett looked at his highly polished shoes. They were so shiny he could use them for a mirror. "What's wrong with them?"

"Sitting on that bed with your leg crossed, and I can see a hole worn clear through the half sole, big as a silver dollar. Can't have our ISS men looking shabby, now can we?"

"No, sir. I'll take care of that as soon as we get to port."

"Port? No, I need you at the breakfast meeting. Take care of it right now and show up tomorrow looking sharp."

Bennett looked blank. "Uh, yes, sir, but how can I do that when we're due to sail in less than twenty minutes? I'll never get off and back on the ship; and besides, no shoe shop will be open at this hour of the night."

Janeway gave his underling a quizzical look, then began to laugh. "You've never sailed before, have you? Believe me there is no service you might need on shore that the *Bremen* can't provide. They'll have at least one cobbler on board, maybe more."

"Oh, okay, I'll, . . . I'll take care of it right away."

"Good man. When you're done, check with the assistant steward for first class. He'll have your bags moved and can tell you where your new stateroom is. You lucky dog, you. Took me years to work up to where I could go first class."

"Yes, sir. Thank you, sir." As Janeway strode away, Bennett closed the cabin door and mumbled under his breath, "Can't believe my stinking luck."

Bennett

17

If Bennett had been a seasoned traveler, he would have known that one did not hunt down a cobbler aboard a luxury liner. A passenger simply spoke to his steward and all his needs would be immediately attended to. But for all his surface polish, his apparent New York style and sophistication, he was still a provincial backwoods boy in terms of international travel.

His deck plan had no notation for shoe shop so he took the elevator from his C deck room up to the shopping arcade on the promenade deck. Checking every shop, he found no shoe repair. A fellow passenger suggested that it might be back down on B deck with the first-class barber and beauty shops. After a few wrong turns he found the barber but no shoe repair. When a waiter emerged from a nearby elevator carrying a covered tray of food, Bennett stopped him and asked in English, "Can you tell me how to find the cobbler?"

The man looked puzzled, which made Bennett doubt that a cobbler existed.

"You want to go down to the cobbler?" the man asked in accented English.

Bennett thought that perhaps the misunderstanding was a language problem, so he switched to German. "Yes, does the ship have a cobbler?"

The man's eyes widened. He looked first at Bennett's face, then glanced quickly at his coat lapel and back to his face. His expression revealed more than puzzlement. He seemed suspicious and almost fearful, which unnerved Bennett.

The waiter drew himself to attention, held the heavy tray in his left hand, and with his right gave the straight-armed Roman salute Bennett had seen the Nazis use in news reels. The waiter answered in German, "Crew deck, sir. Just astern of the sleeping quarters."

The salute startled Bennett, but unsure how to respond, he simply looked down at his deck plan to find the crew deck. It only showed the public sections of the ship, however, and didn't provide the answer. He looked back up to ask the waiter, but the man had rushed on down the corridor.

Bennett pushed the call button for the elevator that had disgorged the waiter, but when the door opened found that there was no elevator operator. He stepped in and pushed a small black button on the wall panel and the elevator began its descent. He marveled at the German technology. He had heard of self-guided elevators, but not even in New York City had he ridden in one.

When the box stopped and the door opened. Bennett peered out into a wide white-walled and carpeted corridor. A small plaque identified it as deck F. The door across the hall was partly open and had a sign that translated as Chief Storekeeper. Bennett peeked in seeing a neat office painted nautical white and furnished in mahogany. It contained brass scales, record books, and a bank of pilot lights, but no person who could help him. Bennett checked a few of the rooms and found white doors, locked and barred. Over each door was a sign indicating the type of provisions stored there and the proper temperature for each item written in centigrade: potatoes +8, game -3, fish - 5, ice -6, white wine 0, and so forth.

He hurried back to the elevator to try again. When the door opened on deck G, it took only a brief glance to see that this floor also held an entire corridor of storage rooms. He marveled at how much room it took to store food for this liner. The last button down took him to deck H, a cavernous space filled with cars and stacks of stored steamer trunks. This time as the elevator closed, a uniformed guard shouted something Bennett didn't quite catch. However the tone was sufficient to confirm his growing apprehension that prowling around below decks was not exactly the proper thing for a passenger to do.

On deck E he found not one kitchen but a labyrinth of many kitchens, each with blackboards mounted over their serving windows listing their specialty: grilled meats, sandwiches, special diets, cold dishes, soups, dairy, roasts, toast, fish, foul, potatoes, ice cream, salads, etc. This floor was as busy as the storerooms had been quiet. Even at this late hour, stewards moved efficiently from window to window, picking up the components to fill their passengers' orders. Most seemed too busy to give Bennett more than a passing glance of surprise, but behind him he heard an undeniable voice of authority saying, "Halt! You, in the suit, what are you doing in the kitchen?"

Bennett turned and saw a large red-faced man who wore a chef's hat over his curly brown hair. Speaking German had gotten such a strange reaction from the waiter that Bennett tried English. He held out his deck plan like an apologetic note to the teacher and began explaining that he was hunting for the cobbler.

The chef cut him off. "You are a passenger? You have no business in the kitchens. If you want cobbler, ask your steward. Our kitchen has three flavors."

Bennett was momentarily confused. "Three flavors? Oh! Oh, no, sir, you see, I need a shoe cobbler, that is a shoe maker."

"What?

Bennett held up the bottom of his shoe to show the hole in the sole. Exasperation replaced the chef's confusion, and he ordered two crewmen to escort Bennett back to the passenger decks and see to it that he kept out of the kitchen.

Bennett went docilely with the crewmen and was taken to an elevator at the forward end of the ship. Instead of being quiet and empty, this one was filled with many crewmen changing shifts. As they left the elevator and headed for their bunks, Bennett finally found out where the crew deck was and which button he must press to get there. His escort, however, would tolerate no detours. He was deposited unceremoniously on the promenade deck.

At ISS, failure was not considered an option. He returned to the first elevator at the stern of the ship and took it to the crew deck. Peeking out he saw no one in the hall. To his left, at the very stern of the ship, he could hear voices and read a sign that translated as Passenger Laundry.

He walked toward the bow slowly, listening for other voices, not wanting to get caught and kicked out again. He passed a tailor's shop. That was hopeful. Where there is a tailor, perhaps there is also a cobbler. The next room was a very large print shop, with presses rumbling. Stacks of menus and of the ship's daily newspaper, the *Lloyd Post,* were stacked in the hall. He passed three doors that were locked and barred and had no identification. Then he heard the elevator door open and at the same time heard voices from both ends of the hall. Just ahead of him was an open door and he slipped through it. Looking around him to see where he had taken refuge, he saw a long counter about waist high. In the backroom he could hear the clatter of a telegraph tapping out morse code. Radio room, he concluded.

Voices converged from both ends of the hall, but more disturbing were the two voices he heard coming from the back room. One spoke quietly, secretively, and

Bennett heard only a low mumble, catching a word or two here and there. The other man, however, spoke in a distinctive high, whiny voice, at a volume that seemed indiscreet considering what he had to say. As the meaning of their conversation became apparent, Bennett crouched down and moved to the cover of the counter where the men in back couldn't see him.

"No," said the high, whiny voice. "That is not for you to know. The Fliegerzentrale must have the parts, and to hell with Versailles. The Abwehr has had a man here since early 1927. He buys under the counter anything the Americans won't sell on the open market and steals what he can't buy, and he is very successful."

A mumbled question.

"You don't need to know that, either. Besides, he changes his identification frequently. He will not know who you are, either. It's safer that way. He knows who on this ship is a courier, and he will get the message to that man. The courier will deliver it to you. Once a week the purser will bring you the coded radiogram with the storekeeper's list of provisions, which you will radio to our offices in either New York or Bremerhaven. The five hundred food items are coded from 100 to 600, and each number followed by two digits indicating the amount. The messages our man in America will be sending will be numbered 900 to 999, followed by two digits which convey information you do not need to know. You simply insert the coded messages in the end of your food list."

Another mumble.

"Don't worry how it's done. You just do your part."

Bennett cursed mentally, not daring to even whisper. If he was seen by the people in the hall, he would be taken back up to promenade deck, but if he was caught in here listening to this conversation, he might get tossed to the sharks.

Waiting barely enough time for the people in the hall to pass, he crept to the door and looked out. Empty. He left the radio room and walked rapidly until he came to the shoemaker's shop. The night duty cobbler sat as his bench, working on a pair of high heels. He was somewhat surprised to see a passenger, but when Bennett explained his problem, the man simply shrugged and agreed to repair the shoes while Bennett waited.

As the man worked, Bennett took out his business notebook and began making a few notes. Substituting Albert for Abwehr and Fritz for the Fliegerzentral, he worded it all so that it looked like notes on a sales call. He wasn't sure what the Abwehr was but he could guess that the Fliegerzentrale was an aviation bureau and that someone was in America secretly buying airplane parts that the United States refused to sell openly. Or stealing them. All, evidently, in opposition to the Treaty of Versailles, which prohibited Germany from rearming itself after the Great War. So the parts in question must be for military airplanes instead of commercial planes. That sounded like information someone in the U.S. government ought to know, but who? And how the hell was he going to explain how he came by this highly secret information? Well, that problem could wait. His problem now was to find his new cabin, get some sleep, and be prepared to "look sharp" tomorrow morning.

Diana

18

I stood, stretched, and flipped off the light. Seven in the morning. I had read the rest of the night away and the sun shone brightly in my bedroom windows. I turned the small volume over in my hand. It was entertaining and informative, giving me a chance to learn about my uncle, but there was something else about it that was curious. On the first page Bennett had doodled some lines, dots and squares. I noted them, but only with annoyance that he would deface his diary in that way. On a later page I found another doodle scribbled, a tic-tac-toe game, but not with *Os* and *Xs*. The first square on the upper left corner had an *A,* and a *B* was in the next square. I/J was in the lower right corner. The rest were blank. A few pages on I spotted another tic-tac-toe with *K* and *L* in the positions *A* and *B* had occupied, but with two dots under the letters. I flipped back to the first tic-tac-toe and realized each letter had one dot under it that I had failed to notice. The original diary was written with a fine-pointed ink pen, giving the writing a spidery look, but the doodles were written in a heavy, easily smeared ballpoint pen. I turned back to the doodle on the first page. Now I could see that it was squares or partial squares with one dot, two dots, or no dots. The pattern registered. Each tic-tac-toe square, except the center one, was incomplete in a different way. The *A* square had only two sides, like a backward *L*. The *B* square had three sides, like a *U*. The *K* had the same number of sides as the *A* but had two dots instead of one.

I grabbed a pen from my fanny pack and on the paper napkin from my midnight supper, and wrote out three tic-tac-toe hatch marks and created the full key.

A. |B. |C.   K..|L..|M..   T |U |V
D. |E. |F.   N..|O..|P..   W| X| Y
G. |H. |I/J.   Q..|R..|S..   Z |

With this key I decoded the message on the first page. The first letter was represented by a three-sided square like an upside down *U* with one dot. That had to be *H*. The second was a full four-sided square with one dot. That was an *E*. When finished, I had a message: "HELLO DIANA WELCOME TO MY WORLD." I chuckled and at first was delighted at having solved the puzzle. Then I realized how truly useless this was. It was no more than a parlor game. Then I considered the fact that he had to give me three clues before I recognized his doodles as a message. I guess he knew he would have to begin my education with the cryptologist's equivalent of kindergarten.

I considered running down and telling Robert James what I had discovered but checked that idea. Instead, I picked up the bedside phone and dialed Sam. I really needed to talk with him. I needed to get his analysis of the whole SICC thing, needed to learn what he had found out about Hedgeman and my mail. For the last three years, we had discussed every case, and he had generously helped me analyze and work them, teaching me things most private investigators never learn. As the phone rang with no answer I realized I needed him for more than case analysis and I really needed to know what sort of duplicity was going on here. When and why had he been here at Bennett's? Was he the friend I believed him to be or was he just on Bennett's payroll? Ten rings. He wasn't there or wasn't going to answer. I set the phone down in the cradle.

I blocked the thoughts, opened an airmail letter tucked into Bennett's diary, and read on.

Bennett

19

Dear Daddy,

I've tried several times to find a way to tell you about the school for ISS training == Frankly nothing sums it up better than this photograph I'm sending you. The rules for us trainees are stricter than Bible school: no smoking, no drinking, no women, and despite the fact that everywhere you look there are signs that say "BELIEVE," they are pretty particular about *what* you believe. If the Depression wasn't so bad, and if this job wasn't so good, I'm not sure I would stick it out. So far, I'm top of the class, and if I make it I go to Germany, all expenses paid.

The guys you see behind the fence, all done up in suits and starched collars, are my classmates. See me, fourth from the right.

The lucky bastards you see marching down the street are the workers from the Johnson shoe plant across town. They're mostly Catholic immigrants and have their own churches, music, and folk dances. Almost every other week they're holding some festival or parade or party, all well lubricated by grape and dandelion wine and home brew beer. If we even get caught near such an event, we're fired.

They have great fun telling us ISS guys what pricks we are. Here they're marching past the school. You can see our "BELIEVE" sign over the door.

Then note the sign they got. In case you can't read it in this picture, it says, "While you're believin', we're drinkin'." The expressions on the faces of men in both groups pretty well sum up what it's like here.

Better mail this before some jerk in the student hotel tattles on me.

Ben

Diana

20

I now looked with suspicion at every mark Bennett made, and carefully examined a postcard tucked between the next two pages. The innocent-looking card was written in plain text, but I noticed that it was not addressed or stamped, and though written with an ink pen, it was not the same ink pen used in the journal. It read, "Have I told you when I will be able to return to the USA? Expect me sometime in December."

The hidden message was now familiar, so not hard to spot. Some of the letters were slightly darker, as if the pen had leaked or the writer had to go over them twice to correct them. The first dark letter was the *H* in "Have," the second, the *I,* and the third was the *d* in "told." The rest of the message popped out at me as if it were the only thing on the page. It read, "Hi Diana." The *ber* in "December" was also written over, and the *r* written to look like an *n.* Ben. Again, a nice little puzzle, but nothing that was going to help me with the database.

I went back and reread Bennett's letter to his dad. It was authentic, the crinkly old blue airmail paper, address, postmark and all. I reread carefully. Sometimes, instead of formal punctuation, a letter writer will draw a line or two to indicate a pause or an emphasis. At first reading that's what it looked like Bennett had done. However, I now saw those lines as an equals sign after "ISS training" and an underline beneath "photograph." The sentence read, "I've tried several times to find a way to tell you about the school for ISS training == frankly nothing sums it up better than this photograph."

Quietly, I made my way upstairs. I could hear Robert James's softly purring snore as I tiptoed past his room and into Bennett's room. Either Bennett was very neat or Robert James had cleaned his room. The only thing lying out was a plastic sack on the dresser. I looked in it and found it was his personal belongings from the hospital, including his billfold. I closed the sack again. I would deal with that later.

His walls were filled with photographs collected over a lifetime, but they were in chronological order so it wasn't hard to find the photo he had described. The expressions on the men's faces made me laugh out loud. The men in the ISS line had expressions ranging from pious disdain to open envy, while the marchers looked joyous and exuberant, taking obvious delight in their taunt.

I took the photo off the wall and turned it over. With a fingernail file from Bennett's dresser, I loosened the screws and turned the keepers to free the photo from the frame. There on the inside of the cardboard backing was written an alphabet, then the word "photograph" with a line crossing out any letter that occurred twice. Beneath that was written, "codeword = photgra." Beneath that was an alphabetic key.

A B C D E F G H I J K L M N O P Q R S T U V W X Y Z
P H O T G R A B C D E F I J K L M N Q S U V W X Y Z

Below was a message: AKKT WKNE TCPJC. It was a simple substitution code using the keyword "photograph." The message read, GOOD WORK DIANA.

With hope, I headed for the cave. Seated at the computer, I pressed my thumb to the lighted button on the CPU and was instantly logged in and greeted by a little voice: "Good Morning, Diana. Would you like voice or keyboard activation?" I have always loved the anthropomorphic intimacy of machines that talk to me, but in this case I wanted to type in my coded request. "Can I do both?"

As the words scrolled a little voice said, "Yes. How may I help you?"

I typed in "Find File: CQQ SNPCJCJA." The screen went blank, then opened with a title page: "My Time in ISS School, the Uncensored Version." I was inordinately pleased with myself. I had finally found something in the database. I spent more than an hour skimming through this version of Bennett's diary, finding detailed bios of his teachers, technical details on the machines, descriptions of students he met, girls he sneaked out to date, as well as the tricks he used to have an occasional cigarette or drink. When my stomach began to growl, I decided it was time for coffee and breakfast. Before leaving, I checked to see if this codeword would also work for Hedgeman. The computer replied, "File not found." I didn't expect anything else but still it depressed me.

In Bennett's room I had seen a bookshelf filled with small diary volumes.

There must have been thirty or forty of them. If I had nothing better to do this would be great fun, but a life had been taken, and mine was in danger. This wasn't the time for games. I hoped Robert James wouldn't make me read all the volumes before he picked up his sword. What was he waiting for?

Bennett

21

Showered, shaved, pressed, dressed, shined, and half soled, Bennett
appeared fifteen minutes early for his breakfast meeting with the Janeway and the
DISS men. From a platform half a story above the dining room, Bennett was
escorted down an elegant staircase to the grand salon. The first one at Janeway's
table, Bennett had time to admire the high-ceilinged, luxuriously appointed hall.

As he waited for Janeway, he alternately people-watched and read the
menu. Astounded by the variety of dishes, he was deep into making his choices
when steward appeared at the table and offered a mimosa, Bloody Mary, or
champagne. Janeway walked up behind the steward, declined for both of them and
asked for American coffee.

By the time the steward returned with the coffee pot, the three DISS men
had arrived, and despite Janeway's glare of disapproval, the Germans defiantly
ordered mimosas.

Bennett got his first indication of his duties when one of the Germans said
in German, "I love to see the expression he gets when we drink. Do you suppose it's
really disapproval or envy?" The other two chuckled, and the one who spoke
English translated the conversation as, "Erhardt would like to know who your new
man is."

As Bennett was introduced to Alfred Kordt, Erhardt Leidler, and Franz
Fischer, he put on his best country boy manner and poker face. This breakfast was
not going to be easy.

The next hour and a half was indeed a test for Bennett, not only of his
poker face but also of his memory. He had no background to peg conversation on,
which made it very difficult to keep straight the names of people he didn't know and
comments on business activities he didn't understand. In addition he had to listen to
two conversations at once. As Franz would translate for Janeway, Bennett would

have to listen for the translation while also keeping an ear to the side conversation between Alfred and Erhardt.

His dilemma was, what should he tell Janeway? For instance, was it important for Janeway to know the snide and insulting little comments, like the one about the alcohol, or did he need to have information pertaining only to business? Did Bennett have the right to make that decision or should he simply tell Janeway every word he heard? If Janeway got angry, would some of that anger be taken out on the messenger?

When breakfast was finished and the DISS men had excused themselves, Janeway handed Bennett an expensive cigar and suggested they walk to the deck rail and have a smoke. Well, so much for Mr. Williams's admonition against smoking. They strolled casually to a spot on the deck where they were alone and could not be overheard. "Well," said Janeway. "Did you hear them say anything they didn't translate accurately?"

Bennett had made up his mind that he would start with the business stuff and see how Janeway took it and what kind of information he seemed to want most.

"Yes, sir, I did. Quite a bit. I just didn't understand all of it because I'm not sure who or what they are talking about. For instance, who is Hartzman?"

"Wilhelm Hartzman is the fellow who founded DISS back in 1910. He brought the whole punch card technology to Germany, by lease agreement with our company, of course."

"Does he still own it?'

"He . . . still holds an interest in it, yes. Why? What did they say?"

"Erhardt seemed to think that Mr. Williams stole the company from Mr. Hartzman."

"He said that?"

"Well, not in so many words, but I got that impression. What exactly did happen?"

Janeway took a puff from his cigar and let the smoke stream aft. "In 1922 when Germany was having terrible inflation, Hartzman was in big trouble. He owed ISS over a hundred thousand dollars in royalties and couldn't pay it. So Mr. Williams helped him out by taking a percentage of DISS in exchange for the debt."

Unable to stop his tongue, Bennett asked, "How big a percentage?"

Janeway couldn't help a sly smile. He took another puff, and as he blew out the smoke, replied, "Ninety percent."

After a startled pause, Bennett replied, "I see." Then hearing his own tone of voice, he quickly changed the subject."Well, they also mentioned that they weren't too crazy about Prohibition while they were in the States."

Janeway laughed. "I don't need a translator for that piece of information. Anything else?" Bennett nodded. "What is the NSDAP?"

"That's Hitler's political party, the National Socialist German Worker's Party."

"Hitler's a socialist? I thought he was a Nazi."

"He is. Nazi is sort of a nickname for the NSDAP. The party started out as socialist, but under Hitler's leadership, it gave up that commie crap. Hitler is now the biggest backer of big business. He knows what it takes to get a job done and make a profit. What were these guys saying about the Nazis?"

"That business would really take off once the Nazis were in power. They believe that is just about to happen. And . . . and the part that seemed significant was that this Hartzman fellow is working secretly to get in tight with the NSDAP. He thinks that the company would be more, well, Alfred used the word 'volk' or 'volkish,' meaning it would be more German. What did they mean by that? Could that hurt our business? How does Mr. Williams feel about Hitler?"

Janeway looked at Bennett a moment, then patted him on the shoulder. "You did a good job, Bennett. Even knowing you knew German, I never caught a thing that would give you away. You should have been an actor . . . or maybe a spy." Don Janeway laughed, but Bennett felt a chill down his spine. "Tonight we'll have a dinner meeting in the Continental restaurant on the sundeck. This is the crème de la crème, way above even the first-class dining room. You'll love it. Be there in formal attire at eight sharp."

"Yes, sir. Sounds interesting."

Bennett stayed at the deck rail, thinking about the first day of his new life. So far he had been forced by circumstances to be false in some way to every person he had met. This wasn't exactly how he'd envisioned it would be. He hoped this wasn't an indication of things to come.

Bennett

22

Orders had arrived by wire from DISS that Bennett was to report to Berlin and spend his first two weeks inspecting all the DISS offices. It was like orders to take an all-expense-paid vacation.

Too excited about his future to enjoy his last day on the ship, he packed his bags, made arrangements for the steward to put them aboard the train for Berlin, then strolled aimlessly around the ship. From the railing he watched the harbor at Bremerhaven come slowly into view. A complex of military, merchant marine, and passenger docks were sprawled along the coast, but the somber looking town was no match for the New York City skyline. Except for one tall church steeple silhouetted against an overcast sky, Bremerhaven's buildings looked no more than two to four stories high. As the ship drew closer to the Columbus Quay, Bennett could see the *Bremen's* twin sister, *Europa*, docked and ready to depart for New York.

The *Bremen* engine compartment was so well muffled that the sounds of the thunderous engines were not heard anywhere on the passenger decks. Bennett more sensed than heard the engines come down to dead slow in the water and saw the bow wave sink to a placid ripple. The *Bremen* stopped instream and waited for the tugs to slowly maneuver her in and warp her to the pier. As she quietly slid in close, there was a sharp pistol shot from the stern as the rocket pistol shot a line to the dockmen. Within twenty minutes the ship was snugged to the dock by ten eight-inch hawsers.

When the gangplanks were lowered, Bennett was first in line with his passport, papers, and his new book, waiting as anxiously as a two-year-old thoroughbred at his first race. Once processed through customs, he walked directly across the narrow dock to the two-story Columbus Bahnhof to catch the train to Berlin.

Disappointed to find he would have a two-hour wait, he stood trying to decide whether lunch in the Bahnhof cafeteria or a walk would be more beneficial. Then a nearby conversation caught his attention and one of the voices totally swept away his travel fatigue. It was without doubt the same high, whiny voice he had heard below decks in the ship's radio room.

Slowly, casually, he looked in the direction of the voice and saw a short, dark-haired man with narrow shoulders standing at the ticket counter. Bennett turned to an oblique angle, opened a time schedule and appeared to study it while he observed the man with peripheral vision.

An overcoat hung across his left arm and on the floor at his side was a black leather valise. As he turned he was looking down, putting his money and ticket away in a long thin wallet, which he deposited in the breast pocket of his uniform jacket. Bennett recognized the braid on the sleeves ranking the man as an assistant purser on the *Bremen*. He had a small round face with dark eyes, small nose and mouth. His face was marred by two scars, one on his chin and one just under his right eye. Before picking up the valise, he put on his overcoat. Gleaming from the lapel of his coat was a swastika pin. He picked up the bag, walked to the newsstand, bought two copies of the Nazi paper, *Völkischer Beobachter,* and walked out of the Bahnhof.

Without conscious effort or decision, Bennett found his feet were moving him out the door in the wake of the purser. When the man hopped aboard the nearby street car, Bennett climbed on and took a seat four rows back. It was not reasoned thought that had provoked this action, simply irresistible curiosity. As the streetcar started up and carried them into the heart of Bremerhaven, Bennett listened to the click-clack of the wheels, the hiss of the overhead electric catenary, and the pounding of his heart. What was he doing?

Surreptitiously he watched the purser open the valise on his lap, put one copy of the *Beobachter* into the case, then casually remove an envelope from the case and lay it on the other copy. He then closed the case, folded the newspaper with the envelope inside it, and sat quietly for several blocks. He got off the streetcar on a street Bennett would recognize in any city of the world. The sidewalks were filled with sailors, the majority of businesses were bars, and every corner was decorated with both women and men of doubtful virtue. He watched the purser to see which door he entered and debated following him. By the time he finished the debate, the streetcar had started up again. Impulsively Bennett jumped up, pulled the cord, and got off one block up the street. As he walked toward the brew house where the purser had entered, a boy of about fourteen held out a copy of the *Völkischer Beobachter,* practically shoving it against Bennett's chest to stop him. The boy wore a brown shirt and on his arm was a band with the Nazi swastika.

"Do you have your volk news today?" The tone of the boy's question was demanding and insolent, and he gave Bennett a smug stare. With his other hand he held out a can and shook it, rattling the coins inside.

Bennett found the boy's sales technique less than winning but dug out a coin and took the paper. As he started to move on, the boy again stopped him, this time with the coin can against his chest. "Contribution to the NSDAP." It was not a request but a cocky demand.

Bennett gave him a slight smile, grabbed his wrist and pushed his arm aside, saying, "Not today, son."

The boy became rigid at Bennett's touch, and the smug look on his face turned to anger. His eyes darted up and down the street, and Bennett knew that if he had spotted any confederates close by to aid him, he would have taken Bennett on.

Bennett entered the brew house and walked directly to an empty corner table, without looking around. A barmaid appeared at Bennett's table and asked for his order. He was so distracted that he ordered a beer and a ham sandwich without a second thought.

Once his eyes had adjusted to the darkened interior, he pulled his hat brim down to partly cover his eyes and looked for the purser. He spotted him by the narrow shoulders, sitting with his back to Bennett, kitty-corner across the room. The folded newspaper lay on the table between him and a tall, paunchy man with receding blond hair and eyebrows so highly arched they gave the impression of trying to fill the bald spot.

The barmaid returned quickly with the beer, saying his sandwich would be out soon. Bennett thanked her absentmindedly and took the first sip of beer he'd had in months. The taste of cool, tangy brew startled him. He looked down at the glass stein, then quickly looked around the room, as if Janeway might suddenly appear in this sailors' bar on a back street of Bremerhaven and fire him on the spot. Then full realization of his new freedom dawned on him. No Prohibition, no teetotaling bosses. He smiled and sucked down half the stein.

Over the rim of the stein he watched the two men across the room. They spoke quietly for only a minute or two more, then the purser stood and walked out, leaving the newspaper lying on the table. The blond man sat for five minutes, finished his beer, picked up the paper, and left.

Bennett ordered a second beer to go with his sandwich. He was sure that a German spy had just handed off some secret information that he or one of his confederates had obtained in America. The adult within Bennett tried to caution against the soaring adrenaline rush he was feeling, but the kid in him, the pirate of his youth, was thrilled that a whole new adventure was starting. He would find out who he could give this information to.

He finished his sandwich, drained the last of his beer, and smiled as he leaned back in his chair. He was to have a legal job that paid well, new places to see, new people to meet, and in Germany he anticipated a wonderful new freedom. His mood soared on optimism, adventure, adrenaline, and a very good bock beer. He was sure that Germany in 1932 was going to be a wonderful place to live.

Diana

23

As I entered the house all was quiet, but I could smell the coffee, so knew Robert James must be up. Not finding him, I assumed he had driven into town for the mail and newspaper.

In Bennett's room I put the first diary back, picked up the next one, and sat down in a soft upholstered swivel rocker in front of the window. A few minutes later, I heard the door open downstairs, and then heard the elevator. I wondered why the old boy didn't take the stairs. A few moments later a slightly mechanical voice behind me said, "Good morning, Mother. You have many messages. Would you like to hear your messages now?"

I swivelled around to see my robot, Yeabot, rolling toward me on his all-terrain wheels. Yeabot is about three feet high. His little body is made of molded white plastic, giving him a look that is somewhere between R2D2 and the Pillsbury Dough Boy. He performs useful tasks, like searching Internet databases, being the perfect secretary and providing me with a roving security guard armed with Taser darts. But he also does fun things like pour my evening scotch, answer me when I talk to myself, and satisfy my penchant for fantasy.

The last time I had seen Yeabot was in Sam's car when he dropped me off at the airport. I was, therefore, not too surprised to see Sam follow the little robot into Bennett's bedroom.

"Hello, Beautiful," he said as he strode in, a broad grin on his face.

I was so delighted to see him that I ran across the room, threw my arms around him, and hung on in one long bear hug. Startled and a little discomforted, he held me a moment, then gently pushed me back so he could look at my face.

"Whoa, are you all right, Diana?"

Unexpectedly, tears started rolling down my cheeks, and I pulled him back, hugged him, and held on. "I felt so alone here. I am so glad to see you."

He patted my shoulder. "Well, you've done a pretty good job of hiding your feelings. Robert James was afraid you were too blasé. He really hurried me back here to make sure you didn't go out and do something stupid."

"I'm not sure I even knew what I was feeling until you walked in." Changing mood abruptly, I pulled back. "Hey!" I poked my finger in his chest. "How long have you known Bennett? You did that elevator, and the watch, and. . . . Who are you, really? You secretly sent Bennett photos of me. Did you really hire me or was that just a setup so you could spy on me, and—"

He laughed and playfully stifled my tirade with one finger to my lips. "And I'm happy to see you too, Diana. RJ will have breakfast ready in a bit. Why don't we go to the terrace, have some coffee, and I'll see if I can answer some of your questions?"

Yeabot understands the spoken word and is not programmed to wait until he is spoken to before joining in a conversation. As we turned to go out the door, Yeabot beat us through it, asking, "Would Mother and Uncle Sam like a coffee?"

As we walked toward the patio, Sam's words registered. "RJ? He was quite specific with me about wanting to be called Robert James."

"Yes, and if you tried RJ he'd make you pay for it, but we go way back. I knew the old fart before he turned into such a stuffed shirt."

From the kitchen we heard, "With that spare tire you're carrying around under yours these days, I wouldn't talk about stuffing shirts if I were you."

Sam grimaced. "Nothing wrong with the old boy's hearing, anyway."

With fresh coffees, we settled into comfortable cushions on the wicker chairs, and Sam began the explanation I so needed.

"I met Bennett just a bit before I hired you. RJ and I had known and worked with each other years before, but I had totally lost track of him. He called me when Bennett developed some security issues they wanted me to work on.

"The perimeter security? You're the expert that Robert James mentioned."

He nodded. "Among other things, yes. As we worked on the place here, I got to know and admire your uncle, and he became aware of my 'retirement' problem. Eventually he suggested I hire you. He wanted something in return, however. He wanted me to keep a protective eye on you. He also made me promise to keep all of this secret until after his death. The rest, you know."

"I see." I had guessed something like this, but there was something else I need to know. Nothing on his face told me the answer.

He saw my plea but shrugged. "I would have told you if I could, Diana, but Bennett was more concerned about protecting you than anything else."

Still I tried to read him. If I asked him, would he tell me the truth? Whatever the truth was, I needed to know it. I said, "And our friendship. . . ?"

He understood immediately. With a tender smile he answered, "My God, Diana, you have to know the answer to that." He sounded hurt that I should doubt him. He stood and came over to my chair, pulled me up and held me close. "Our friendship is absolutely genuine. The best bonus I could have gotten from the deal."

I started to cry again. "Thank you. When I realized you must have known Bennett, I was afraid. . . ."

Robert James walked out to set the breakfast tray on the table but stopped short, staring at us. We let go our embrace and I wiped the tears from my eyes. The three of us were silent. Robert James was the first to recover. Setting the tray on the table, he protested, "I don't care what tale she's been tattling to you, I have not been beating her. Breakfast is served."

We sat down to another lovely breakfast, but I hungered more for information. Maybe it was the reassurance of Sam being there, maybe I had just had enough. As they picked up forks to attack the eggs and bacon, I decided to firmly establish the morning's agenda.

"Okay, fellas, my apartment in Bluff Beach was tossed by pros, my mail was taken from a U.S. Post Office, and the postmaster was afraid to tell me why. Otto Brehm, who was supposed to explain my inheritance, was murdered and the men who killed him have a federal warrant for me for the murder. I think it's well past time for you secret warriors tell me what the hell kind of a double life Bennett led and what agent Hedgeman is after."

Robert James concentrated on his eggs and Sam sat back and sipped his coffee. Without meeting my eyes.

"Well?" I pushed my breakfast back, folded my arms across my chest, waited silently for answers.

"My assumption," began Robert James, "would be that they are after something in Bennett's files or assets. They may hope that with him gone, they can find what they're after, or may fear that his death will trigger release of information to the public. They obviously believed that Otto Brehm knew the hiding place."

In exasperation, my temper flared. "No shit! I figured that much out myself. What the hell is in Bennett's files?"

He hesitated. "It's almost impossible to know where to begin. Diana, how much of Bennett's diaries have you read by now and how—"

"No, no, no! We're no longer going to play that game. Just tell me what's down there and what those bastards want?"

Robert James turned to Sam, eyebrows raised, a slight grimace on his face.

Sam nodded. "Diana, as to what's down there, it's a huge data base and all in code. Bennett began his files during the years when he worked as a spy in Europe and he's been adding to it ever since."

"My uncle Bennett was a spy? I never knew that."

"Ah!" Robert James put his fork down, sat back, and interlaced his fingers over his lap. "That is just the beginning of what you don't know and what you might have been learning from his diaries. Bennett was the most successful spy we ever had there. He spoke the language like a native and had lived and traveled in Germany for seven years before the war. He could move throughout the country with impunity. Before the war, he spied on the German military and arms industry for a spy master at the American embassy. He also worked with the German underground to save lives and undermine the Nazis anyway he could. When the war in Europe began, he worked for Britain's MI-6, and when the U.S. entered the war, he worked for American Army Intelligence. He even worked for Wilhelm Canaris who was head of the German Abwehr but was also a secret member of the resistance against Hitler."

"Damn! I never heard a hint of that from the family."

Sam set down his coffee. "No, for many reasons Bennett made sure you never knew. For one thing, his work didn't stop when the war ended. The problem is that none of us know what this is about and much of the information we needed to find out was lost when Otto died without being able to give you the keys and codes to Bennett's database. For now you're safe here and we have time for the three of us to try to find some answers and figure out someway to get the bastards who killed Otto. So eat your breakfast and today we will begin the search for answers."

Bennett

24

Bennett entered the embassy for the second time in two days. Removing his hat and taking his place in line, he was faced with a different receptionist. This receptionist was heavy set, with short brown hair, glasses, and a no-nonsense attitude. He wondered if he would have to go through the whole explanation and waiting all over again.

In his turn he stepped to her desk and waited for her to finish with the paperwork from the previous fellow. By now, not only was he wondering if his spy story was worth all this time and trouble, but he was also beginning to wonder if he had made a tactical error by calling attention to himself in this way. He was, after all, living under the alias of his dead cousin. Maybe the embassy was using this time to check him out.

She looked up with the unsmiling face of someone who is civil but all business. "Yes, may I help you?"

"Morning, ma'am. I'm Bennett Sizemore. I'm supposed to meet a fellow here this morning, but I wasn't given his name. Yesterday I spoke to a Mr. Hathaway, and he—"

"Yes, Mr. Sizemore." She picked up an envelope from the top of her desk and held it out to him. "You'll find all necessary information in here. Thank you for coming by."

Bennett took the envelope but was confused. He was about to ask her for further information but she forestalled his question with a polite but firm, "Good day, Mr. Sizemore." Then looking around him, she called, "Next."

He mumbled a thanks, replaced his hat, and left the building. On the sidewalk he found a streetcar bench and sat down to open and read what was in the envelope. The typed page inside contained detailed instructions, guiding him from the embassy by way of two streetcars and a taxi to a particular sidewalk cafe across from the Tiergarten park. There, he was to sit at a table close to the street and order an American coffee, black with four sugars. It seemed a silly damned way to meet someone, but in for a penny, in for a pound, as the saying goes.

He found the cafe and ordered the coffee as instructed, but he wasn't about to use those sugars. As he habitually did, he moved the cup from the saucer to the tablecloth. It was one of those personal idiosyncracies that would drive him nuts if someone else did it. He had found that waiters often spilled coffee into the saucer and the cup would drip on his tie or shirt. Actually, that wasn't the only reason. There was something about the sound of the cup scraping against a saucer that was to Bennett like nails scratched down a blackboard. He simply couldn't stand that sound. As he waited somewhat nervously, he considered this little mannerism of his and wondered if he would someday end up as dotty as his great-aunt Betty.

He had taken only a few sips of the coffee when a man in a gray suit and gray overcoat appeared at his side and said, "Good morning, Mr. Sizemore. Thank you for coming. Could you join me for a walk in the park across the street?"

It was more of a demand than a question. Bennett complied. As they walked, Bennett tried to size the fellow up. He was about Bennett's height, six foot one, with several more pounds on him, much of it in his middle. Curly gray hair protruded from under his hat, hinting at a full head of hair despite the fact that he must have at least twenty years on Bennett. When they reached a clear path with no one else near them, the man stopped and turned to face Bennett, his blue eyes appraising him from top knot to toe.

Under scrutiny, Bennett felt compelled to talk. "Ah, they didn't tell me your name."

"You can call me Jordan."

"How do you do, Mr. Jordan. How come we had to—"

"Not Mr., just Jordan. Not a good idea to waste too much time, Mr. Sizemore. Let's get right to it. I have the report you gave Mr. Hathaway. I just want to check a few details. On this, uh, unauthorized tour below decks on the *Bremen*, are you sure no one saw you or knew you overheard the radio room conversation?"

"Well, the shoemaker saw me in his shop, and the cooks saw me in the kitchens, but nobody saw me in the radio room or knew what I heard."

"And when you went to the bar, are you sure the purser didn't know you were following him?"

Bennett had played hide-and-seek games with the law since he was about thirteen. He knew how not to be seen, or rather, how to avoid being noticed, but he couldn't exactly explain his experience to this guy. He settled for looking him in the eye and saying, "I am positive he didn't notice me."

"Okay, now did he actually say that this drop-off was for the Abwehr?"

Bennett thought a moment, replaying the conversation in his mind. "Well, now, I don't know that he said anything about any drop-off. I didn't know anything about that until I saw it happen there in the bar." Suddenly Bennett realized his mistake. Feeling foolish he confessed, "And I guess to be honest, I didn't really see anything dropped off for sure, either. I saw the purser buy two of the Nazi newspapers in the train station. On the streetcar I saw him put one in his briefcase and leave one out. Then he took an envelope out of his case and stuck it into the folded newspaper. Then in the bar I saw a newspaper lying on the table. I never saw the envelope in it and I never saw who put that newspaper on the table. Guess it could have been the other guy's paper. I just assumed. . . ."

Looking at him sternly, Jordan said, "Quite right, Mr. Sizemore, you assumed." Instead of chastising him, however, Jordan smiled and said, "But being able to recognize the difference between fact and assumption is basic to the analytical process of investigation. Now think carefully and tell me how the conversation referred to the Abwehr and the Fliegerzentrale."

Here Bennett was a great deal more sure of himself. Not only had he committed the words to memory, he had written them down in coded form as he waited for his shoes to be repaired. "The guy I couldn't hear, and that I assume was a radio man on the *Bremen*, asked the purser something because the purser answered, 'No, that is not for you to know. The Fliegerzentrale must have the parts and to hell with Versailles.' Now I didn't know what the Fliegerzentrale was, but I figured it must be an airplane bureau, and since he said, 'to hell with Versailles,' I figured it must be military, since the Treaty forbids them to rearm."

"Umhum, and what about the Abwehr?"

"He said, 'The Abwehr has had a man here since early 1927. He buys under the counter anything the Americans won't sell on the open market and steals what he can't buy, and he is very successful.' What the heck is the Abwehr, anyway?"

"It's a German military intelligence organization, Mr. Sizemore. Spies. We knew they were trying to set up a spy ring in the United States, but frankly we had no idea they had started as early as 1927, and we were rather shocked to hear they are doing so well in procurement. I want to thank you very much for coming forward with your story. You have done your country a great service. Now are you sure they are going to send coded messages with the food orders?"

"Yes, sir, in the items between 900 and 999."

Jordan abruptly shifted gears. With a broad smile he said, "So, you're going to be working here in Germany, huh? Happy with your job?"

"Yes, sir. Very happy."

"Good, good. Well, you're a smart young fellow, and I'm sure you will do well. Say, I wonder if you would do me a favor? Once you're settled, would you call the embassy and ask for Mr. Hathaway and let him know your address, just in case I need to get hold of you again?"

With that Jordan shook Bennett's hand and departed as quickly as he had appeared, leaving Bennett to ponder why Jordan would want to get in touch. What was it Janeway had said? He would make a good actor or a good spy.

Diana

25

Like a good girl, I tried to eat but my brain just kept sorting the information. "Ok, it's a really big leap from Uncle Bennett spying on Nazis to Hedgeman but I'm not even going to try to go there. Let's deal with what we do know. Robert James knows how to open the Hedgeman file. I saw it."

"Yeah. Tell her what you found in the Hedgemam file RJ."

Robert James shrugged, took a deep breath and said, "Hedgeman is a political operative who first came to our attention during the Nixon administration. At that time he was a very junior member of the dirty tricks campaign. Bennett came across him the next time during the Reagan Iran Contra scandal. His duties had increased in importance by that time but he was still tucked away in the background and was never called before Congress. After that he popped up from time to time in election campaigns or as a lobbyist but for eight years he has been either very quiet or very well hidden. There was nothing more on him until now. We have no idea who he is working for or why. To our knowledge, he has never been involved in murder before. I suspect one of his team – ah, exceeded orders."

I sat silent for a moment, disappointed there was nothing more helpful but relieved I was at last getting some answers. But there were so many more questions. "It makes no sense that Hedgeman would want a lot of old Nazi stuff. Robert James, do you know any other reason he could have been trying to find Bennett's files."

"In general terms, maybe. To understand what is in the cave, you must understand this: *By the end of the war Bennett had spent fourteen years living for one purpose only: to end the scourge inflicted upon the world by the Nazis.* The suffering and inhumanity he saw during those years galvanized his soul. If he'd returned home at the end of the war, he might have been able to take up a normal life. But he was too valuable. The army put Bennett and Otto to work in CIC, their counterintelligence corps, and kept him in Germany for the occupation.

"Doing what?"

"Hunting down Nazi war criminals and bringing them to justice. At least that is what they were told they were doing."

Sam poured us more coffee and said. "Unfortunately, Bennett was in a position to learn the truth."

Robert James stared at his interlaced fingers, but I think it was the past he was seeing as he explained Bennett's dilemma. "Yes, that was his tragedy. You see, within two weeks after the war ended, powerful people in American intelligence had *forgiven* the Nazis and embraced them as allies. In our new war on communism the Nazis were no longer considered the enemy. They, *and their methods,* became valued assets to be employed and protected by our secret government within the government."

"I can't believe that. I've never heard of such a thing."

He took me literally and his voice rose in volume and vehemence. "Your ignorance of the facts does not make them untrue."

"I . . . I'm sorry. I didn't mean that I didn't believe you. That's just an expression."

Only partly mollified, he turned silent on me again and sipped his coffee.

Sam said, "Try to imagine how Bennett must have felt when he learned that he was actually being employed to find *assets* rather than war criminals. Fourteen years of sacrifice, fourteen years of seeing friends tortured and killed only to have a covert force within his own government embrace the enemy and accept its brutal methods. There was no way to fight it openly, so he started his files and took what action he could, when he could.

"So the cave has a list of old Nazis? Aren't most of them dead by now? I find it hard to believe . . . I don't mean I doubt your word. I just . . .how is that sufficient motive for Hedgeman's actions."

Robert James turned to Sam. "I told you, this is useless. She simply doesn't have the historical context to understand."

Sam said, "Diana, the information in the cave may have begun with Nazi war criminals, but as covert and illegal activities expanded during the cold war the database was expanded. Bennett's files contain many secrets regarding the fascist poison that oozed out of a defeated Germany and contaminated every facet of modern life from 1945 to the present. That's the problem. We're not trying to hide information from you. We really can't tell you what Hedgeman is after because we don't know who employed him.

Bennett's files contain the names and actions of men of power who hold fascist beliefs and don't want to have their decisions countermanded by democracy. His files document their efforts to use covert force to dominate our foreign policy and clandestine methods to control domestic politics. In short, it holds some of the most dangerous and disturbing secrets of the Twentieth Century. In that vile haystack you must search for the one poisonous needle that Hedgeman seeks."

Bennett

26

When Bennett stepped off the train at the little town of Kasselbronn, he was almost in the center of Germany; and for the first time in days, the constant gray clouds had cleared and he stood in bright sunshine. Snow still whitened the tops of the surrounding mountains, but the valley seemed to be under the spell of an early spring.

His tour had taken him from Berlin to the DISS offices at Dusseldorf, Frankfurt, Stuttgart and Sindelfingen for endless business meetings and his ears were tired and his brain turned off. He had seen some beautiful countryside as well as picturesque buildings, estates, and castles, but unfortunately he had seen them only through the windows of trains, streetcars, and taxis. He wanted to get away from the sterile meetings and meet some real Germans.

On the train he met a couple of British tourists, Carolyn and Margo, who sang the praises of the little medieval town set in a quiet river valley surrounded by mountains, woods, and walking paths. The kicker to their sales pitch was their description of the great local beer and the scenic beer garden. That sounded like the perfect place to spend his weekend.

"Mr. Sizemore," called Margo. "You want to share a taxi to the hotel?"

"You know, I've been riding so much the last couple weeks that I really want to stretch my legs a bit, but I would be grateful if my suitcase and overcoat could hitch a ride with you."

"Done," she replied.

He deposited his luggage in the taxi and thanked the girls, promising to join them for lunch in the hotel.

The train station was much larger than he expected for a town this size and the scheldule showed it was a major hub for rail lines running both north-south and east-west. He walked from the station enjoying the view of the wide slow-moving

river and the sensations of the early morning: the sun on his face, the musty smell of
the river and the wet earth, and some sweet-smelling, early blooming flower. They
only unpleasant intrusion was smoke and noise of the shunt engine as it worked
back and forth in the railroad yard.

The walk from the station into town took him past small, poorly maintained
workers' homes one might find by a railroad track almost anywhere. It was the
central part of town that promised new and different sights. On a rise above the
river, ruins of an ancient moat and crumbled castle walls summoned to Bennett's
mind romantic images of knights, fair damsels, and chivalrous adventure.

On the outside of the wall he could see cook fires, tents, and lean-to
shelters of various shapes and sizes, and wafting up from the fires were mouth-
watering aromas of sausages and coffee. In Bennett's mind this sight grew into a
vision of a merry Medieval fair. "What a perfect place for breakfast," he mumbled
to himself. However, as he walked closer, that fantasy evaporated like fairy rings in
the morning sun.

There were in fact a few vendors selling the sausages and coffee and a few
more peddling tobacco and chocolate smuggled in from Holland, but most of the
encampment consisted of ragged, ungroomed, hungry-looking men and a few
women and children as well. For this scene he wouldn't have had to leave Berlin or
even New York. These were not happy Medieval fair goers; these were the out-of-
work, homeless victims of the worldwide Depression. Most slept or stared vacantly.
The few who met Bennett's eyes looked either angry or so hopeless and sad that any
thought he had of having breakfast under the ancient wall vanished. He felt both
foolish and disheartened. Unbidden came his father's voice reading from the Bible.
"But now that I am grown, I've put away childish things."

He was about to continue into the town when he noticed several well-
groomed young men and boys moving among the homeless. They looked to be
between twelve and fourteen, and walked through the crowd handing out leaflets of
some sort. Unlike the pushy Nazi youth he had encountered in Berlin, these boys
walked among the people smiling and speaking quietly. One of the older boys
stopped beside a small child who looked to be about four. The pamphleteer dug into
his pocket for a few pfennigs and gave them to the child, who ran and gave them to
his mother. She quickly bought a sausage and bread, and mother and child settled

into a spot against the wall to eat.

As Bennett walked toward him the young man looked up with curiosity. After a moment of assessment, he said in German, "Good morning. You are maybe a visitor to Kasselbronn?"

The lad looked older than Bennett had estimated, maybe fifteen or sixteen. "Good morning. Yes, I am. My name is Bennett Sizemore," he answered, offering his hand.

The boy shook his hand and replied. "How do you do? I am Otto Brehm."

Pointing to the leaflets, Bennett asked, "What have you got there?"

Obligingly, Otto handed Bennett a copy of the leaflet. It was put out by a group called the Red Falcons. They warned against the "Brown Pied Pipers" and called for solidarity in the fight against the Nazis.

"What is this Red Falcon group?"

Otto looked at him with suspicion.

"I'm new here from America," Bennett explained. "Not familiar with all the German clubs and groups yet."

The boy gave him a broad smile. "Really?" He said in English. "I study in England each summer. I would never have guessed from your German that you were an American. May I practice my English with you?"

"From your English, you don't sound like you need much practice, but maybe you could use your English to educate me about German clubs."

"A good bargain. We Red Falcons are mostly sons of socialist workers, though that is not exactly my reason for joining. My father is a professor and writer, but I work with the Red Falcons against the Hitler Youth and the SA. Oh, the SA is another group to explain. We do have a great deal of them I'm afraid. There is an old saying that goes, 'Two Germans talking, a conversation; three Germans talking, a club.' Would you believe that here in this small town we have over one hundred and sixty clubs? That's about one for every sixty people."

Bennett chuckled. "I see I have a bigger job ahead of me than I figured on."

"The SA is the *Sturmabteilung*, or storm troopers of the Nazis. Some call them the Brown Shirts." He lowered his voice and said with a wry smile, "Some also call them the Brown Plague."

Bennett laughed again. "I ran into a few in Berlin. They were a rather pushy bunch of young toughs."

"Yes, especially now. They are feeling rather cocky because in the presidential election last week, their man Hitler won the second place and is now in a runoff against von Hindenburg. Hitler will never beat Hindenburg, of course, but it raises the Nazis one step closer to the seat of power."

"So why do you battle the SA among these homeless. What can they do?"

"The SA recruits the younger men from here, among other places. They offer hot meals from their field kitchens and new boots made of real leather. It's difficult to resist when you are hungry, cold, and humiliated by being unemployed."

"I can see that. How much do you suppose it would cost for those vendors there to give everyone here a hot breakfast this morning?"

Otto's mouth opened, but he paused, considering his answer. "If this is a serious offer, I could speak to the vendor and negotiate a good price."

"Good. I'm serious, but I wouldn't want to make a big announcement about it, if you get my meaning."

The boy nodded. "Would you like my Red Falcons to distribute the breakfast?"

Bennett smiled, admiring the tact with which the boy seized upon an opportunity. Good for the people, good for the Red Falcon image. "Good idea," he answered.

Bennett watched as Otto walked over to the vendor. He was almost six feet tall but still had the slender youthful build that marked him as a school-aged boy. He had straight sandy-blond hair and blue eyes and a confident demeanor.

In a few minutes Otto returned, reported the price he had negotiated, and Bennett slipped him the necessary Deutschmarks. As the Red Falcons began the distribution, Otto said, "Now, you have bought breakfast for the jobless. Please allow me to buy you breakfast at my Aunt Anna's. That will be a perfect place to teach you more about our German clubs and political parties, because at this hour representatives of many of them will be there for breakfast. And," he added with a grin, "few will understand our English. I would especially like you to teach me the American idioms that differ from the British ones."

As they walked into the walled part of town, they exchanged introductory information and Otto gave Bennett a private tour. He pointed out buildings of interest on the broad main street and supplied commentary on the residents who lived down narrow cobblestone side streets lined with half-timbered houses. Though his companion was several years his junior, Bennett realized this was the first time since he'd entered Germany that he had felt an immediate connection to anyone, and it lifted the loneliness that he had begun to feel as a stranger in a foreign land. A comfort settled over him that was hard to define or explain. Perhaps his soul guessed, even then, that this beginning under a castle wall would grow into a friendship that would last a lifetime.

Bennett

27

The aroma of freshly baked breads and pastries filled the little cafe and floated down the street on the morning air. The place was packed; tables as well as soda-counter stools were filled, and two women stood at the bakery counter to buy bread. But as soon as Anna saw Otto enter the room, she began clearing the small table that was tucked into the space between the kitchen door and the end of the soda counter. Everyone knew this was Anna's table. She used it for infrequent rest breaks, to fill condiment bottles or peel and pare vegetables, or to work on her bookkeeping. No one took that table unless she expressly invited them to.

With the table cleared, she set down two cups, filled them with coffee, and headed for the front table near the window. An arthritic hip produced a slight hobble in her gait but never slowed her rapid and efficient motion around the cafe. As she passed Otto and Bennett, she motioned them to her table, saying, "Sit, Sit."

On her next pass through from the kitchen to the dining room, she plunked down two plates piled with strudel, potatoes, and sausages. Bennett observed that the heaped plates contained far larger portions than those served at the next table. He looked from the plate to Otto. "Your aunt really takes care of you, doesn't she?"

"Well, yes, she does, but I think today she is also showing off a bit because I have a friend with me." What he didn't tell Bennett was that the extra portion also meant Aunt Anna needed a favor of some sort.

As she hurried back to the kitchen, she paused to asked, "You going to England to study again this summer, Otto?"

"Yes, Aunt Anna. But this morning I get to practice my English right here. I'd like you to meet my new friend, Herr Sizemore. He is from America and has come here to work for DISS."

"Yes, I heard your English. Good to meet you, Herr Sizemore. Welcome to Germany and to Kasselbronn." She topped off the coffee cups, which hardly needed it. "Otto, you know the Davidson girl, don't you? Juliane?"

"Yes, she's a year behind me in school."

Anna directed her next words to Bennett but her glance to Otto. "We can talk more later when it isn't so busy."

Bennett was either gifted or cursed, he had never decided which, with an ability to sense what folk meant even when they didn't put it in words. As a child he assumed everyone did this, but as an adult he had come to realize that much of what he observed in people was totally unknown and unseen by most others. He knew, for instance, that the casual conversation between Anna and Otto had conveyed much more than the literal meaning, and it aroused his curiosity.

A roar of laughter erupted from the table near the front window. Bennett looked over and Otto followed his gaze. Three of the four men there had laughed at some comment. The unsmiling man stared down the others. Under his unpleasant glare, they all stopped laughing like schoolboys caught telling a dirty joke. He was a short man with a thick square build, powerful in appearance despite his less-than-perfect physique. He had a ruddy complexion and a hardness of countenance that suggested a lifelong animosity to just about everyone and everything. His current displeasure settled on a roughly dressed farmer who wore boots caked with manure and clothing that was none too clean. "Think you are funny, Fuchs?"

Fuchs shrugged and mumbled, "Just a joke, Kurt."

"You stink. You're spoiling my breakfast. Get out of here."

"But I haven't eaten my breakfast."

Most other diners listened but pretended to pay no attention. Bennett still stared openly. Otto picked up his fork in a way that brought his hand in front of Bennett's eyes and said casually in English, "Don't let your breakfast get cold." His motion interrupted Bennett's stare, his tone of voice and focus on his own plate issued a subtle warning. With sidelong glances Bennett saw that almost no one looked directly at the front table. There was one exception to this. At a large round table in the back corner sat six men. One of these individuals was calmly smoking a cigar and openly watching the small drama. His expression was enigmatic but it was clear that this distinguished, sandy-haired fellow was one man who was not cowed by the bully at the front table.

When Fuchs failed to move, Kurt's face darkened to a deep red. There was no one in town who didn't know that danger sign. Discussion around the room was silenced, and everyone seemed intent on their own plates. It was, therefore, no great surprise to anyone except Bennett when Kurt reached over, picked up Fuchs's plate, and threw it at him. Fuchs tried to dodge but the edge of the heavy pottery hit him on the eyebrow, bursting the skin. His attempt to evade the missile succeeded only in tipping his chair backward, and he and his plate landed with a crash on the floor. Despite this compelling scene, only one man dared to watch openly as Fuchs stood, silently and sullenly, and left the cafe.

At the sound of the crash, Anna had peered out the kitchen door. With broom and dust pan she headed toward the front table. In her normal rapid motions, she righted the chair and swept up the mess.

Slowly the room returned to its normal buzz of conversation, and Bennett chuckled. "Bit of a temper. He the town bully?"

Otto pointed to the map of Germany on the wall above them, and with his face to the wall answered quietly, "Kurt Schutz." Then he continued in English, keeping both his voice tone casual as if discussing Bennett's travel plans.

"He has been a bully and a roughneck his entire life, but since he was made the local group leader for the Nazis, he has become insufferable. This morning he was just picking on one of his 'friends,' so no one interfered. All three of the men at that table are his Nazis."

"Who was that fellow who just left?"

"Fuchs. He's a right wing leader of the farmers in the valley and can be counted upon to stir up trouble and hatred against the SPD. Oh, there is another group. SPD is Social Democratic Party. They are mostly working people, like my Red Falcons, who believe passionately in our democracy and fight the Nazis to protect it."

"Let me guess, the table in the back, they SPD?"

Otto looked surprised. "Very good! How did you guess that one?"

"The fellow with the cigar was the only one in the room to openly stare at Kurt."

"Yes, that is Martin Meylin and his SPD friends. If Kurt had picked on one of them instead of Fuchs, there would have been a real fight, but not in here. Aunt Anna treats everyone with respect, even the Nazis, and her cafe is respected by all."

"I've been reading in the newspapers about a lot of fights and violence of all kinds. Is this normal in Germany?"

Otto picked at the potatoes on his plate as he considered the question, then answered thoughtfully. "The normal divisions that have existed since the establishment of the Weimar Republic have become more radicalized since the beginning of the Depression. Some are predicting a civil war; some fear a Communist *putsch*, and some a Nazi *putsch.* "

"What is a putsch?"

"Ah, how do you say in English? I think you use the French, coup or coup d'etat—anyway, an armed takeover."

Otto glanced at the front table. "I personally fear a Nazi seizure of power. They are everywhere, taking over powerful positions. That fat Nazi sitting with Kurt, the one in the dark suit, he's the manager down at the railroad yards. If you don't join the Nazi Party, you already cannot get or keep a job there."

Bennett had done a lot of watching and reading but this was the first time he had someone to explain the conflicts he was seeing in German society, and he was fascinated. "How about those three well-dressed men at the center table."

"Ah, yes. The slender one is Johann Zimmerman, owns the bookstore. He's an intellectual and was the first person in Kasselbronn to join the NSDAP. That is the Nazi party, you know. He and his two colleagues at the table are 'old Nazis' who joined in the Twenties and still believe in the party's utopian socialist ideals. He refuses to see that Hitler has become a Fascist. He believes that once Herr Hitler is in power, he will discipline the Nazi rabble like Kurt Schutz and allow Zimmerman and his intellectuals to manage the new society. I fear that if Hitler comes to power, Zimmerman will find it will be quite the other way around."

Breakfast hour was over and Anna's was emptying, but Otto seemed to be stalling. Bennett wasn't sure why. Did the young man feel obligated to stay on Bennett's account or was Bennett just his excuse for lingering?

When all the businessmen had finally left to open their shops, Aunt Anna brought a cup of coffee for herself and joined them. In paying her for their breakfast, Otto slipped in the story of Bennett's purchase of breakfast for the homeless.

Anna was very thoughtful after hearing this story. She asked a few polite but skillful questions of Bennett, and in the process learned why he was here, where he was going next, and when he would be leaving. Then she reached over and pulled at one of the buttons on Bennett's suit coat, saying. "Oh, my! Look here. That is so loose you might lose it. And what a shame to miss one button and have to replace them all on so fine a suit. Otto, you must take your friend over to Herr Dobler's tailor shop on your way to school. Introduce him as your trusted friend and make sure that button gets sewed on right away, this morning."

While Bennett tried to refuse politely, saying that wasn't necessary, Otto looked quizzically at his Aunt. "Herr Dobler, not Herr Davidson?"

"Yes, yes," she answered, standing and picking up all three coffee cups. Then almost as an unimportant aside, she informed him, "Herr Davidson's tailor shop was vandalized last night, windows smashed and clothing slashed. The family sleeps in the back, poor things. Frightened them to death. They say it was out-of-town Nazis, but of course, no one was caught."

Anna set the cups on the counter, picked up a pencil and a small piece of brown notepaper, and scribbled a quick note. Though she turned her back, Bennett was at an angle that he could see her place the note on a saucer, cover it with a paper napkin, and set a large piece of chocolate cake on top of the napkin. "Take this cake to Herr Dobler and tell him that it is a thank-you for his fine mend on my dress. Hurry now. You will already be late for school. And Herr Sizemore, you will find your trip to Dresden will be just as fast if you go to Berlin first. There are many more connections from there to Dresden."

Otto and Bennett were both quiet as they walked up the main street toward the tailor's. Otto was obviously lost in his own thoughts, and Bennett was trying to digest all he had just observed. In Germany, Bennett had expected to encounter different social customs, but the things he was bumping into here were more extraordinary than he'd anticipated. He thought about the secret conversation in the radio room of the *Bremen*; the white envelope slipped into the newspaper by the purser; hostile German factions, possibly on to the point of civil war; the code of silence observed in fear of the town bully; the tailor's family terrorized by late-night vandals; the note Anna had hidden under the piece of chocolate cake; and her instructions to Otto to introduce Bennett to Herr Dobler as a "trusted friend."

Bennett

28

Local group leader Kurt Schutz stood on a small pedestal in front of a mirror as Herr Dobler used white chalk to mark alterations in his new SA uniform. It was a testament to Dobler's skill that he was able to make a garment that flattered even Schutz's fireplug figure.

The tailor was a tall man of medium build and military bearing, who looked to be in his late forties. He was elegant, both in dress and deportment, and meticulously groomed.

As they waited in the front of the shop, Bennett noted that Dobler was able to flatter Schutz with comments that were in no way fawning but seemed to simply acknowledge his natural leadership as local group leader of the party and as a town councilman. Dobler's attitude left no doubt in Bennett's mind that this man was one more of Schutz's Nazi confederates. Confirming his suspicions, a rack in the front of the store was filled with both brown Storm Trooper and black SS uniforms. Dobler was tailor to the Nazis.

Once the fitting was completed, Schutz went behind the curtain at the back of the shop to change clothes, and Dobler turned his attention to Otto, who switched from English to German.

"Good morning, Herr Dobler."

"Good morning, Otto. How may I help you today?"

"First, I brought you a nice big slice of Aunt Anna's chocolate cake, and she says to tell you thanks for the mend in her dress."

Dobler accepted the cake with neither smile nor hesitation and set it on the counter. In a tone that seemed detached, he said, "That is very kind of her but not necessary. Did you come all the way here to bring me this?"

"I also brought my good and trusted friend. May I introduce you to Herr Bennett Sizemore? He is an American and has a button about to fall off his suit coat.

Aunt Anna said to bring him here and have it sewn back on before he must leave for Berlin on business."

One eyebrow flicked up momentarily, but Dobler's tone remained impassive. "How do you do, Herr Sizemore. Come, let me see."

He stood Bennett on the pedestal and checked not only the loose button but also the fit and hang of his suit. He picked up a piece of chalk and began making markings. "Umhum, you see here, Herr Sizemore, the way your jacket pokes up at the back of your neck? That is not a good fit. Also the sleeves are a fraction long. We will adjust that a bit and the—"

"Herr Dobler, that really isn't necessary. I have to leave early Monday morning, and here it is the weekend—"

"No problem. I will complete this small alteration this afternoon. You have a business meeting in Berlin on Monday, yes? You must look your best, and to look your best, your suit must fit."

Kurt Schutz walked out to the front of the shop, eyeing both the chocolate cake and Bennett. "Herr Sizemore, did I just hear you are an American? How come you speak such good German?"

Before Bennett could answer, Schutz turned and asked, "Herr Dobler, you don't mind if I have a bite of your cake, do you?" Then without waiting for an answer he picked up the large slice with his fingers.

Alarmed, Bennett watched as Schutz raised the cake to his mouth. The napkin stuck to the frosting and the note was exposed on the saucer. In town for only one morning, Bennett had already become aware of the caution people used in what they said, and he had witnessed Schutz's nasty temper. He had no idea what was on that note, but if Aunt Anna had gone to the trouble of concealing it, Bennett was sure it should not be seen by Schutz.

Dobler admonished him. "One moment, Herr Schutz. We can't have our councilman showing up at city hall with chocolate on his clothing." Dobler raised the saucer to the cake and napkin and aided Schutz's unwilling hand in replacing the cake on the saucer. Setting the saucer back on the counter, Dobler used his own handkerchief to remove the frosting from the group leader's pudgy hand. Picking up the spoon from his morning coffee, he handed it to Schutz, saying, "Here, I don't have a fork, but you may use my coffee spoon."

As he dug into the cake, Schutz looked to Bennett for an answer to his question. For just a second Bennett was distracted by the deftness with which Dobler had handled the situation. Whose side was he on? Then regaining his own poise, Bennett put on something close to his country boy persona and said, "Well, I was raised with my cousin Henry, and he and his folks still speak German in their home. I either learned to speak German or starved to death."

"Good, good." Schutz dug in for another huge bite of cake, and as he did he moved the napkin about the plate. The fear that he would again expose the note made it difficult for Bennett to avoid watching the saucer.

"I am glad to hear there are German volk in America who haven't forgotten their heritage. What brings you back to the Fatherland, business or vacation?"

"I'm going to be living here. I've got a job with DISS."

Schutz attitude changed from inquisitorial to surprised and almost respectful. "I know of this company. The Landstag uses some of their services in statistics, and the railroad uses them for all ticketing and scheduling. This is a very fine German invention. It was a German American like yourself who invented this wonderful technology" He spoke with his mouth full as he continued to decimate the slice of cake.

Bennett wondered how he could eat more after the breakfast he had just finished at Anna's Cafe.

"You will be living here in Kasselbronn?"

The question surprised Bennett because he hadn't considered even the possibility of selecting this small town as his residence. As he hesitated Schutz leaped to the next question with the mounting excitement of a true chamber of commerce booster. "Is there to be a DISS office here?"

"Ah, no. No office that I know of."

He saw the disappointment register on Schutz's face and realized that for all the obvious unpleasantness of this fellow, he possessed a genuine desire to see his little town prosper. Bennett felt obliged to offer some ray of hope. "Kasselbronn is a lovely town and central to all DISS offices. It might be a good location for my base of operations."

Schutz dropped the spoon and offered Bennett his hand. As Bennett shook it he found it was still slightly sticky from the frosting.

"I can help you. I am Kurt Schutz, town councilman and local group leader of the NSDAP. I have very good connections, and even though housing is short, I can help you find very good apartments. I must go to the council meeting now, but do see me if you need anything, Herr Sizemore. This is a wonderful town with good German volk values, and in the next year you will see wonderful things happening here. Good morning, Herr Dobler. Otto."

When Schutz was gone, Dobler picked up the almost empty cake plate, asked Otto and Bennett to wait one moment, and took the plate to the back room. When he returned he helped Bennett out of his jacket and replaced it with a leather one. "Herr Sizemore, you may borrow this jacket until I have your coat ready. Would you come with me please?"

With Otto trailing them, Dobler led Bennett through the curtain, past the dressing room, and to a door at the back of the shop. He took a set of keys from his pocket, unlocked and opened the door. Inside was a storeroom with bolts of fabric, neatly stacked boxes of supplies, and three individuals looking tired and terrified. The family group consisted of a husband, wife, and daughter who looked slightly younger than Otto. They were sitting on makeshift pallets, wrapped in blankets. Three sets of dark eyes looked up. Their gaze went quickly from Dobler to Otto, then settled with fear on the tall, blond, blue-eyed stranger.

"Herr Sizemore, I would like you to meet Herr Davidson, his wife, Frau Davidson, and daughter, Juliane. Nazis vandalized their shop and home last night. They took refuge here."

Bennett wondered why they would trust their lives to this Nazi tailor.

"Herr Davidson and his wife would like for their daughter to leave Germany for a while, until the anti-Semitic hatred stirred up by the elections has settled down. I have arranged for Juliane to attend school in England, and we have transportation for her from Berlin through Holland to England. The one leg of the journey we had not worked out is getting her from here to Berlin. It would not be safe for her to travel alone, and we are hoping we might impose upon you to let her travel as your companion as far as Berlin. There you will be met by someone who can take her on to Holland. Her travel papers are in order. You can do this, yes?"

Bennett took a moment to consider this. He now understood Anna's cryptic parting remark about going to Berlin first, but he was wondering how his simple little weekend had gone so wrong? How had he been ensnared so quickly into this town's intrigue? How could he have been so completely deceived by the detached manner of the tailor?

Five people looked expectantly to him for an answer. Oh, hell, he thought. I ran booze for years without getting caught. How much harder could it be to take one little girl on a train ride?

"Sure," he said, "no problem."

Diana

29

Breakfast had long since grown cold. I sat for several moments, absently wiping the few dust particles from the glass top of the patio table, trying to process what Sam and Robert James had told me. Finally I understood what Uncle Bennett had been hiding down there in his cave for fifty years. I could see why he never married, why he never visited Dad and me. Poor Uncle Bennett! Like Prometheus, he had stolen forbidden knowledge, and as Prometheus was bound to his rock, Bennett was bound, for the rest of his days, to his rock-walled cave.

If Bennett had actually tried to stop or even thwart in a minor way the all-powerful institutions of black operations, I wondered that he had survived to such a ripe old age. Those who challenge the powerful seldom live to tell the tale. He must have been much smarter and much more capable than I could ever be. How could he possibly believe I would know what to do with all of this . . . this deadly information? How did Hedgemen fit into this mix?

Sam was sipping his now cold coffee and looking at the trees down the hill. He knew me, knew where my mind was going, and was giving me time. Robert James was staring intently into my face, trying to read a response, trying to determine if he should have told me Bennett's secrets.

I felt pushed by the intensity of his stare and asked defensively, "How could Bennett possibly believe I would know what to do with this? I'm not up to it."

Robert James looked at Sam and gestured with both hands palms up. His expression and gesture said clearly that this was what he had expected of me all along. That expectation really jerked my chain. It was one thing for me to feel inadequate. It was quite something else for Robert James to expect me to be inadequate.

Sam, on the other hand, was matter of fact. "Yeah, it's a tad overwhelming when you first try to wrap you mind around the whole thing. But, Diana, there's no need to tackle this thing whole."

I was tempted to say, "I don't need to tackle it at all," but I bit my tongue.

"Right now, you have just one little problem. Somebody who knows Bennett had something on him is trying to use Bennett's death as a time to retrieve it. Whoever that someone is, he's just another single case." He paused to let me absorb that one.

"And keep in mind, Beautiful, you aren't alone. Yeabot was created to someday assist you with your uncle's files. That has always been his true purpose. All you have to do is give him the input data and he will help you find that needle in this haystack. In addition to Yeabot, you have me, if you want me, and RJ gets thrown in with the deal."

"Is that right? If Yeabot can search the files, why has Robert James had me reading Bennett's journals and playing cryptic word games?"

"RJ doesn't know you, Diana. He was stalling until I got back here. As for Yeabot, he can do searches just like he does for you on the Internet, but you still have to tell him what to search for. If he comes up with ten thousand hits, you have to redefine the search terms for him. In Bennett's files you will have to give him a search term *and* a code type. He can then search thousands of permutations of that code in minutes instead of the months it would take with paper and pencil. But you're going to have to know enough about Bennett's codes to guide him."

Reasonable and calm as always, Sam had dampened the panic and offered me an approach I could deal with. A single case. I knew how to work a case. As to all the possibilities in the cave . . . I could feel myself close to tears, but I wasn't about to let them fall. I couldn't look at Sam or Robert James. I looked out on the tree-covered hills, closed my mind to all I had just learned, and thought about the case. Several minutes passed. Finally I said, "Okay." My voice was a little husky. I cleared my throat and turned toward my companions. "Let's get to work."

Robert James mouth opened slightly and his eyes widened. He looked first to me and then to Sam for confirmation. Sam gave me a smile.

I took a swig of cold coffee and pushed the food plate aside. "Robert James, when you were in town this morning, had the SICC boys tried to clean up the murder scene?"

"No, they just taped it off and concentrated on searching for you."

"Good. If we're going to handle this like any other case, this is the obvious place to start. There is hard evidence of an unlawful search of Otto's office and of his murder on the third floor, evidence that can clear me and nail them. We need a full crime scene investigation."

Robert James shook his head doubtfully. "Well, normally, yes but . . . for one thing, the sheriff doesn't have a forensic investigator or crime lab. He would have to get someone at state level to process the scene. More importantly, SICC agents claim federal jurisdiction because it is a national security case."

A look passed between them and I knew they had some other bad news for me, but I really didn't want to hear it.

"Okay, Sam, do you still have that contact in the FBI lab?"

He nodded.

"Could we get him to process the scene quickly and quietly?"

Increasingly agitated, Robert James stood and began pacing the patio. "Diana, I see where you're going with this, but keep in mind, there's law and there's power. Hedgeman has power behind him."

I was working the case logically. His obstruction was beginning to annoy me. "We are still a country under law!"

He whirled on me. "Are we? Think about the example of Watergate. Deep Throat, the number two man in the FBI had to go to the press because he knew he couldn't go to the Justice Department. Consider the condition of the current Justice Department. Who in Washington is behind Hedgeman? We don't have a clue, but if we try to process that scene Hedgeman could make one phone call and it would all be over."

"Not if he's out of town."

While Sam and I began discussing various ways to get the SICC boys out of town and collect the evidence, Robert James began stacking the dishes and carrying things in the house. At first Sam pointed out problems with our various strategies. Robert James was in and out of the house, listening, but making no comment. Through process of elimination Sam and I narrowed the possibilities to one plan and began making refinements. When we had the basic outline in place we went into the house looking for Robert James to get his input. He was in the living room reading. He took off his glasses and listened stoically as we told him our idea.

When we finished, he put his glasses back on and opened his book. As he looked down at the pages he said, "If you're both determined to pursue this course, I will offer whatever assistance I can, but . . . I still feel that we should simply leave this matter alone for the moment."

"What is it, RJ? What's worrying you?"

RJ studied his veined and liver-spotted hands. "Perhaps I'm just growing old. Perhaps memories, of other times, other places ,are crowding in upon me."

We waited to see what he would add, but he simply stood and said, "I better phone the sheriff and feel him out on cooperating with your FBI crime scene investigator. From what Ned told me, he already knows the accusations against Diana are nonsense. He's just stymied as to how to get around SICC. He may be open to some assistance. Sam, let me know when you and Diana have completed your discussions and have a finished plan. I leave it to your wisdom."

After Robert James left, Sam and I debated the significance of his reluctance, then gradually worked our way back to enthusiasm for our plan. The three of us used the rest of the day to make our own individual preparations.

When I started to call Richard, Sam suggested, a little too casually, that I should use the house phone, not my cell and that I have Richard take my call away from his salon. Some member of my internal board warned me I should ask Sam why, but I really didn't want to know. I had been told all I could deal with.

I dialed Rick's Coiffures Americain in Beverly Hills. The owner, Richard Barton, is the world's greatest fan of the movie *Casablanca*. He designed the salon to look like Rick's Café Americain, and he regularly hires impersonators to appear at Rick's as the characters played by Humphrey Bogart and Ingrid Bergman, Claude Rains and Sydney Greenstreet. Not only has Richard been my trusted friend and hair stylist for years, but he secretly performs another service. He is my disguise artist.

My call was answered by Sophia, whom I had met recently. Her natural voice and accent were almost identical to Ingrid Bergman's, and Richard's mastery of makeup did the rest. Not only was she his full-time Bergman impersonator, but the last I saw, he was also desperately in love with her, and why not? Shades of Pygmalion. Rick had finally found, or created, his Ilsa.

"Hello, Sophia," I said without identifying myself. "Would you please tell Richard someone needs a 'special' and ask him to pick up the phone in the office."

"Of course, I would be happy to," she answered in her sweet, gentle Bergman voice.

A few moments later Richard picked up. "Hello, Sweetheart." Richard, as he sometimes tried to do, was using his Bogart imitation, but he was very bad at it. His normal voice, with its pleasant British accent, was closer to Tom Conte.

I followed Sam's suggestion and didn't talk openly on Richard's phone. Richard and I had worked together long enough that coded conversation was an established part of our vocabulary.

"Good morning, Mr. Barton, this is Mrs. Dietrich. I have a very special event tomorrow, and I do hope you will be available for one of your specials."

"My dear Mrs. Dietrich, I can always make room for you, however, I shall have to move things around a bit. Call me back in about thirty minutes will you?"

Thirty minutes later I called a different number and knew Richard would be waiting by a pay phone we used. He picked up before the first ring ended.

"Okay, *Dietrich*, you drop off the face of the planet, and the first call I get you're using the trouble number? But then, why should that surprise me? What are you up to this time?"

"I'm in a bit of trouble, Richard, and I'm just taking precautions so I don't bring that trouble to your door."

"And?"

"And . . . I need a favor."

"Hmm, surprise, surprise. What do you need?"

"Can you fly to Tennessee tomorrow?"

There was a very long silence. Then, "Do you know what tomorrow is? It's the first day that Sophia has finally agreed to take a holiday with me."

"Oh, I'm sorry, Richard. Never mind. I'll come up with something else."

"You're damn right you will. You can come up with two tickets to Tennessee. I'll bring Sophia with me. It's not far from Kentucky. The Derby, horse racing, green pastures with white rail fences, mint juleps. Sounds even better than Acapulco. Would you need me for very long?"

"No. Just meet me at the airport with Aunt Tilly, and switch suitcases."

"Which airport, what time?"

"Tri-Cities, eight a.m. local time. The e-ticket is already on your computer.

Companion ticket coming up."

"But as I remember, Aunt Tilly required a lot of makeup."

"Not this time. She won't be searched and just needs to make a very fast change. She also needs to borrow the body suit that the Norwegian woman used."

"Oh, Aunt Tilly has put on a bit of weight has she? I assume she will need her gray wig, frumpy polyester suit, support hose, and sensible shoes?"

"Wig and shoes, yes, but this time have her wear a jersey house dress. Be sure she has a cane and a suitcase just like mine. We'll do a silent swap at the coffee shop just outside the waiting area where you get off the plane. There will be a very big bonus for you in the suitcase. And thanks, Richard."

Diana

30

The alarm was set for five a.m., but I awoke before it went off. I showered, dressed, and strapped on the fanny pack, leaving the Walther on the bedside table. I couldn't have the gun on me at the airport, and if this thing went bad, the gun wouldn't be enough to help me.

We ate a cold breakfast of cereal and fruit and walked to the car barn. I took the red sports car, which Robert James said was an older, highly modified Ferrari, and he assured me would be the fastest car on the road. Sam took the Chevrolet Lumina, and Robert James took the gray van he used for surveillance. The license plates on each car had been switched to nonexisting numbers, and Sam even had a rental car sticker for his. We drove to town, splitting up and converging on the hotel from different directions. Sam found street parking a half a block away, I parked directly in front of the hotel, and Robert James pulled into the parking lot in back.

Robert James had gotten us each a communicator that worked as a satellite cell phone, a pager, and a radio phone, all wireless, voice responsive, and hands free, with tiny bluetooth earpiece receivers. We set them on the same radio frequency for constant communication.

Robert James had gone to town yesterday to set things up with Sheriff Tumey and learn what car the SICC boys were driving and where they parked it. This morning he parked next to it, got out of his car, and walked around the back of Hedgeman's rental. I heard the clatter as he dropped a large key ring to the ground. As he picked it up, he stuck a homing device to the underside of the car. "Done," he said quietly, and his voice registered perfectly in my ear.

Sam walked to the hotel, bought a newspaper from the vending machine, and went inside. After he checked the hotel, his voice came over the radio. "Okay."

At that signal, Robert James pulled out and parked a block down the side street. With his laptop online via satellite, he hacked into the airline computer and entered my early check-in at the airport. "You're there and ready to board," he said.

I walked into the hotel and saw Sam sitting in the lobby reading his paper. A tall lean man dressed in a gray business suit came down the stairs with his newspaper and took a chair across from Sam. That would be the FBI man, Jim Sanchez. Their eyes met briefly, then both studiously read the paper. Quickly I climbed the stairs and entered my old room. I had never checked out and still had the key. I slipped in and looked around. It was obvious that the room had been searched but my suitcase and other belongings were still there. I took only the empty case and left quickly. At the front desk I was greeted by a bored young desk clerk.

"I'm Diana Hunter," I announced. "I would like to check out."

There was not even the smallest spark of interest from the desk clerk as he prepared my handwritten bill.

Behind the desk was the alcove that housed the switchboard operator. She did take notice of my name and was anything but subtle as she turned sharply and looked at me open mouthed. She started to plug in a phone, hesitated and looked back at me. Should she call the SICC guys or should she wait until I was gone?

Jim Sanchez stood, folded his paper, and strolled out the front door.

Finally the operator plugged in the phone, turned her back to me, held her hand to her mouth, and whispered into the mouthpiece. She glanced at me and saw I was almost finished checking out, then tried again in a slightly louder whisper.

"Thank you much," I said, letting Sam and Robert James know I was done and leaving the hotel.

As I went out the door I heard the switchboard operator hit full volume, "I said she's right here, right now, and she's leaving! You guys better hurry."

I stifled a laugh. As I climbed into the Ferrari I saw Jim leaning against a tree in the park across the street. I took time to arrange my belongings and give the SICC boys time to put on their pants. As I did, I saw the switchboard operator peeking through the curtained window of the hotel and Sam standing at the front door. I pulled out and drove slowly down Commerce Street.

Sam stepped through the door to the sidewalk and reported quietly, "They're out the back door." A few seconds later I heard Robert James. "Got them," he said. "Papa Bear and both Mutt and Jeff, heading for their car. Bloody hell. It's the Keystone Cops. They're dressing on the run. Mutt dropped his Glock in the parking lot, and Jeff kicked the thing as he ran by. Mutt's on his knees trying to retrieve it from under the car. Oh for . . . Hedgeman damn near ran him over. Okay, they're on their way. I'll be right behind them."

By this time I was four blocks down the street, almost to the highway and picking up speed. I watched my rearview mirror and waited a minute for them to turn onto Commerce Street and see me. Then I pushed down on the accelerator. Though I was already traveling at forty-five miles per hour, the car bolted forward like I had been standing still. The engine roared, the fence posts at the side of the road became a blur, and the speed sent a thrill through me that erupted in a war whoop. Immediately I heard from both Sam and Robert James.

"What's wrong?"

" Are you okay?"

"Sorry, fellas. Just enjoying Uncle Bennett's little red car."

"Do be careful, will you? That's a powerful machine," said Robert James.

There was no way Hedgeman would catch me in a straight-out race for the airport, but he could call for road blocks. We had therefore settled on an alternate route. About three miles out of town the highway made a sharp right turn. Around that bend, I slowed quickly and turned onto a farm road that lead to a large dilapidated barn. It was hard to miss the weathered old barn because it still had the remains of a Chesterfield ad painted on the great slanting roof. I pulled off and parked around back of the barn. "Stopped for a cigarette."

"Right," replied Robert James. A few moments later Hedgeman's car raced by, followed shortly by Robert James. He stuck with Hedgeman for a mile to make sure he didn't turn around, then he headed back to my hiding place, slowed but never stopped. I pulled out and began following him over back country roads. Though we had to travel more slowly than on the highway, we would still get to the airport ahead of Hedgeman because Robert James knew these back roads and could cut off many miles of the trip.

As we headed for the airport, Sam began his tasks. We listened in as Sam dialed the cell phone number that Hedgeman had given out to the sheriff.

Answering on the fourth ring, Hedgeman barked, "What?"

"Ah, sir, is this the right number to report on that Diana Hunter person?"

"Yeah, who's this?"

"Well, sir, this is James Joyce over at the Tri-Cities airport. I read a bulletin that came in yesterday, and this morning I happened to notice something you might be interested in."

"What the hell is it?"

"Well, sir, I see that a Diana Hunter called in yesterday and made a reservation for a 9:03 to New York. My computer shows that she is due to board soon. Would you like me to take a security contingent and detain her?"

"No, don't go near her, just process her through. We are on our way to Johnson City right now. We will take care of her. Now is that clear? Do not detain her or in any way alarm her."

"Yes, sir, and I understand. Thank you, sir."

I heard another voice over Sam's radio and assumed it was Jim Sanchez.

"James Joyce? One of these days you're going to get hold of a mark who reads."

Sam laughed. "I doubt it. Jim, good to see you. How the hell are you? It's been a while."

"Well, I'd be better if you hadn't insisted I catch the red eye from D.C. last night. I thought you were retired. What's up?"

Sam clicked off his radio, but I knew what they would be doing. He and Jim would check in with the sheriff then go to Otto's office building to photograph, fingerprint, measure, mark, bag, and tag every piece of evidence in both Otto's office and the third-story room where Otto had been murdered. When done, they would box it all up and Jim would hand carry it to the crime lab. Sam had generated documents on Bennett's computer that established orders for this investigation that would be found in the FBI files. Finding out who generated the order would be another matter.

At the airport Robert James and I parked the cars and I headed for the terminal. I was running a bit late and found that Richard and Sophia were already there waiting for me. Catching sight of them, I was horrified. Sophia, who was drop dead gorgeous anyway, was made up as Ilsa, complete with that famous suit and hat from the airport scene in *Casablanca*. Needless to say, every eye in the terminal was on her. What on earth was Richard thinking? Wasn't the fact that she was a perfect double for Bergman bad enough? Did he have to put her in costume? He had worked with me too long to be so stupid. Was he so taken with this woman that he had lost all judgment? There was no way I could contact them like this and attract that much attention. Richard saw the look on my face. At first he was surprised, then, reading my thoughts, he rolled his eyes at me.

I walked the other direction, stopped at the coffee bar, ordered a latte and wondered what I would do now. Hedgeman would arrive at any moment, and I had timed this thing with no room for error. A minute later I heard Richard's voice ordering a chai tea. I looked out the corner of my eye. It was Richard only, standing next to me with Aunt Tilly's suitcase set next to my case. Tilly's cane protruded from the outside pocket. He was dressed in casual slacks and a polo shirt, blending in with the crowd quite well. His only distinguishing feature was the hair. His full head of curly dark brown hair had that sculpted perfection that screams Hollywood.

Sophia was standing alone in the waiting room signing autographs, smiling, and talking to the growing crowd around her. Every eye in the room was still on her.

"She makes quite a beautiful diversion, wouldn't you say?"

I laughed. "Yes, she does. Thanks, Richard. Sorry I doubted you."

"Oh Ye of little faith. You're welcome."

Robert James's voice came over the radio. "They're here."

"Bye, Richard. Have a great date." I left my coffee on the bar, grabbed Aunt Tilly's suitcase, leaving mine for Richard, and headed for my plane. Boarding had already taken place, and the empty jetway to the plane was guarded by one young man, who checked my forged boarding pass and welcomed me aboard.

As I walked up the jetway, Robert James said, "They're out and running for the door. I'm right behind them."

I went into the nearest restroom in the first-class section and set Aunt Tilly's small suitcase on top of the toilet seat. Quickly, I stripped, took the body suit from the suitcase, and pulled it on, instantly adding three dress sizes. I dressed in cotton slip, jersey house dress, opaque support hose that rolled to just above the knee, and clunky walking shoes. Topping the outfit with a gray wig, I noticed that Richard had supplied me with a set of colored contacts that turned my eyes brown. There was also a small bottle of silver-gray liquid with the instructions "apply to face at the corners of mouth, eyes, and cheek hollow." Too trusting, I did as instructed. To my horror, the places where I had applied the liquid immediately shriveled into deep wrinkles, transforming my face until I looked like the apple doll I had bought at Ned and Emma's shop. "Damn it, Richard. This better wash off."

"They've checked the boarding manifest and are up the jetway and must be to the plane by now," reported Robert James in my ear. I could hear the click of the keys on his laptop and knew that all ticket and boarding information on Diana Hunter was disappearing from the airline manifest.

"Confirmed," I answered. "I hear angry voices coming from the front."

Richard had finished Aunt Tilly's outfit with a pair of yellow-tinted, reading glasses, with thick lenses that magnified the brown eyes. I stuffed my clothes into the case, zipped it up, and reported, "Aunt Tilly's ready."

"Well, get her ass moving!"

Pulling the suitcase and leaning on the cane, I left the restroom and headed toward the front exit. A tall, sturdy flight attendant stood with her arms blocking the hatch. Hedgeman, one fist clenched and the other holding his SICC badge before the woman's face, was quite literally foaming at the mouth as spittle frothed on his snarling lips. She was saying, "I've never seen that badge. You could have gotten it out of a Cracker Jack box for all I know, and you do not board this airplane without a boarding pass."

Hedgeman started to yell back at her, but I interrupted. In my best local drawl and my old lady voice, I said, "Scuse me, please."

Hedgeman and the flight attendant both looked at me briefly. Hedgeman growled, "Just hold onto your skivvies, Grandma."

I raised Tilly's cane, aimed the tip at Hedgeman's arch, and came down with as much force as I could muster. He let out a howl and a string of cuss words that turned the air blue. The flight attendant drew back, uncertain which of us she should restrain.

I shook the crook of the cane in Hedgeman's face. "Let that teach you, boy, to have a mite of respect for your elders. Now I said, 'scuse me, please."

Inside every bullying man is a little boy who was once bullied by some woman in his life—a mother, teacher, nun. Catch him off guard and you can access the fear and response of that little boy. It doesn't last long, however, and the second response can be vicious.

"Sorry, ma'am." Holding his arch and hopping on one foot, Hedgeman moved to one side of the hatch, allowing me to exit.

Mutt and Jeff still blocked my exit. I raised the cane and looked at Hedgeman, who yelled, "Well, let her through for Christ's sake!"

As I slipped past them, it occurred to the flight attendant that one of her passengers was disembarking. "Wait," she called. "You can't leave the plane now."

With her attention thus divided, Mutt and Jeff seized the moment to enter the plane. As she tried to stop them, Hedgeman backed her into the flight attendants' area. All the way down the jetway I could hear his voice yelling, "Look, lady, this is a fucking federal warrant for one of your passengers. We've checked, and we know she's already on board. A peace officer in hot pursuit of a felon doesn't need your permission or a goddamn boarding pass. Now sit in your little jump seat and shut up while we find her."

When I reached the bottom of the ramp, the young man stopped me. "Uh, ma'am, uh, are you . . . You really can't get off the plane now. You'll miss your flight."

I turned to him and used the crook of Aunt Tilly's cane to tap his shoulder. "Young man, if 'n you're smart, you will get everybody off that there plane. There's three men with guns just forced their way on."

He was momentarily startled then realized I was referring to the three federal officers he had allowed up the ramp. With a patronizing pat on my shoulder and that voice people use with those they consider senile, he assured me, "Oh, no, ma'am, those fellows were just law officers. It's all right."

I leaned in close. "You sure of that? You ever hear of law officers from something called SICC?"

The condescending smile left his face and his brows furrowed. Sucking on his upper teeth, his eyes darted from me to the ramp.

"If I was you, son, I'd get as many security officers as I could, as fast as I could."

Diana

31

By the time Robert James and I had finished our little scam at the Tri-Cities airport, the diversion had allowed Sam and Jim to complete their investigation, and Jim had left for Washington, D.C.

We returned to the Bennett compound for an early light supper and a mutual debriefing on our various adventures of the day. I arrived at dinner with my face wrapped in a towel. My shower had diminished but not removed the effects of Richard's wrinkle cream.

The first words out of Sam's mouth were, "What's with the towel?"

I showed him my face and told him the source of my prune look. He laughed.

"Richard's note on the bottle assured me that all I had to do was wrap my face with a hot damp towel and I'd be back to normal within a couple hours."

Sam laughed even harder. "So Richard told you to go soak your head." I noted his amusement in my mental black book and vowed to even the score.

On the patio table, Robert James set out some tuna and chicken salads along with bread and a large bowl of mixed greens. We each made our own dinner of either sandwich or salad, washing it down with ice cold beer. As we ate sitting in the shade of the umbrella, we were cooled by a pleasant breeze whispering through the woods and serenaded by the chatter of birds and the rush of the waterfall.

Sam and I were in high spirits and only gradually coming down off the adrenaline of the day. We were confident that our activities would result in the arrest of the SICC agents and would clear my name. Our conversation was filled with mutual congratulations on a successful operation. In short, we were full of ourselves.

Robert James, however, ate in stony silence, speaking only when directly asked a question, and then giving monosyllabic answers. In an attempt to improve his humor, I told the story of pounding Hedgeman's foot with Aunt Tilly's cane. I thought I was at my comic best in presenting what I considered to be a classic Diana Hunter operation, disguises and all. Sam laughed, but Robert James was not amused. In fact, his normally impassive face revealed at least disapproval and perhaps something close to repugnance.

"Not funny, huh?"

He set down his fork, drew a deep breath, and replied, "Yes, quite amusing."

Like errant children before a disdainful parent, Sam and I exchanged "What's wrong" looks. Robert James's morose and disapproving countenance was like the proverbial elephant in the room. Sam took the direct approach. "What's the matter, RJ?"

My uncle's faithful Sancho Panza replied laconically "One would hope nothing is wrong. I just have a terrible foreboding. I am very much . . . You two treat Hedgeman like the buffoon villain in a farcical play. but what I see in Hedgeman and his fellows is an arrogance of power, a sense of being above the law. You see, I am old enough to have seen that before, and I find it truly frightening."

"So do I. That's why we have to do something to help the law out."

Robert James shook his head. "Perhaps I've just lived too long and fill my senile fantasies with Ben's old phantoms."

Neither Sam nor I knew what to say in response. We both knew that despite his years, Robert James was far from senile. If he was worried, there was good reason to be. He rose, put his napkin on the table and said, "If you'll excuse me, I'm feeling rather tired."

The mood of celebration evaporated. With very little conversation, Sam and I cleared away the food and dishes, loaded the dishwasher, and both agreed that we too were tired and went to our own rooms.

I pulled on some pajamas and clicked the TV remote through the dozens of channels the satellite beamed to the house. Finding nothing that could hold my attention, I turned it off. Upstairs in Bennett's room, I picked up the next diary in the series, and took it back to bed thinking I would only read a couple pages before falling asleep. His experience, however, was too fascinating to put down. About midnight I fell asleep with the diary on my chest.

Bennett

32

His holiday weekend in Kasselbronn had not started exactly as expected. In full retreat, Bennett headed for his hotel. When the desk clerk handed him a message from Margo saying that she and Carolyn had joined a group of hikers for a picnic lunch, Bennett was relieved. His morning had left him feeling less than social.

A bellman retrieved his coat and suitcase and led Bennett up the steps at one side of the large atrium lobby to an open balcony that circled the lobby like the mezzanine of a grand theater. Small cocktail tables were arranged around the balcony and a few guests sat sipping drinks. Looking over the balcony railing, Bennett was surprised to see a small stage at the back of the room.

He changed into comfortable clothes and set out to explore the rest of the walled town. That didn't take long. It was an oval about six or seven hundred yards long with all businesses on one central street that ran uphill from the gate to a large city park. Ruins around the edges of the park suggested that once a castle had stood on this panicle, but now the area housed a market square, a memorial to the Great War, and a bandstand. Nice half-timbered buildings formed a semicircle at the top with a small town hall at the center of them.

Bennett stopped at Zimmerman's book shop. The bookman was behind the counter, and the only other person there was an old man who sat at the back table reading a newspaper. His crutches leaned against the table and the left leg of his trousers hung limp from the thigh down.

"Good morning. Like to get a newspaper."

Zimmerman smiled and pointed to three stacks of papers at the end of the counter. "I can offer you a choice. This one gives you the world according to the NSDAP; this one the perspective of the SPD; and this third one is a true business enterprise. It is the most factual, unbiased, and fastest with current news."

Bennett had not expected such a balanced appraisal from the man Otto said was the first Nazi in town. No one he had met this morning was turning out to be a simple equation. Understanding Germans was going to be harder than anticipated.

"Guess I better take all three," Bennett replied.

"Ah! A curious intellect. This is good. In Germany today it is hard to find anyone who reads all sides of an issue."

Bennett smiled, realizing how closely the bookman's words mirrored his thoughts. "Well, I'm new here, from America, and trying to learn a bit about—"

"But this is wonderful. You are here at a good time for learning. The second presidential election is April 10, and April 24 will be the Prussian parliament election; so we are having many entertainments and events. Unfortunately the police have forbidden any more parades or pageants because of the large fight that occurred last week, but we will have a speaker and discussion here in my shop this afternoon. Join us if you like."

Zimmerman picked up a leaflet from the counter and added it to Bennett's papers. "Also, tonight in Remembrance Hall, the NSDAP will have two speakers. They will explain how Marxism and the SPD are the same thing and both are anti-nationalist. Then for the fun they will end with band music and a dance."

"Well, thank you but I . . ."

The bookman added another leaflet. "Then tomorrow afternoon at the bandstand, they will hold a four-act play and athletic demonstration. The acts are: The Traitorous Surrender of Germany, the Shame of the Weimar, the Victory of Nazism, and the Glory of the German Volkish Reich."

Bennett tried again to get in a polite refusal but Zimmerman continued.

"Then if you want to examine the other side, this evening the Reichsbanner band will play at the bandstand and will hold a close drill demonstration, followed by speeches and German songs sung by the SPD men's chorus club. Also, tomorrow the SPD will have a program with Martin Meylin, one of our town councilmen and leader of Kasselbronn's SPD. I'm sure Martin will tell us that all are Nazi lies." Zimmerman laughed. "He usually does, anyhow. Then the SPD will also hold a dinner and dance. Admission is very low for all events. Hard times, you know."

Unable to stop him, Bennett watched as Zimmerman piled up eighteen flyers, more than two events every day for the next week. How could the citizens of this small town even attend that many events, much less find the money and energy to put them on.

"My, you folks really take your elections seriously, don't you?"

"Of course. It is time for change. Our poor Germany has suffered long and unjustly. We didn't cause that war, you know, no matter what the French wrote at Versailles. If your American President Wilson had prevailed at Versailles, things would have been far different. If you read an unbiased history—I have a good one here in the store—you will see the truth. All the countries were in a great arms race. All plotted and made secret war pacts. France, England, Russia, even Japan and Italy, all of them."

Bennett picked up his papers and flyers and tried to find an exit line, but the bookman leaned over the counter and spoke urgently.

"The truth is, all the countries of Europe wanted war before 1914. The hard fact is, they just didn't want the war they got. And when they saw the horror they had unleashed, they had to blame someone. That someone was little Germany."

"Well," said Bennett, "I can see that. But I'll be here only today and tomorrow, so I'll take these four flyers and leave you the ones for the rest of the week. Thank you much, now."

He turned to leave but the old man sitting in the back of the store said, "Hey, young man. You from America?"

Reluctantly, Bennett turned to face him. "Ah, yes, sir. I am."

"You know where I was when those traitors surrendered Germany?"

"No sir. I couldn't guess." That was a polite lie. Bennett assumed from the amputated leg that the old man was a veteran and must have been in the war.

"I was in France, deep in France, with much of the German army. You didn't find any French soldiers on German soil. None. How could they say Germany lost that war?"

Bennett nodded politely, but was backing slowly toward the door hoping he would escape before hostilities broke out in a rematch of the Great War.

"We didn't retreat,"said the old man angrily. "We marched home under orders after the traitors in our government surrendered. I may have lost my leg and my son. We Germans lost many sons. But we never lost that war. We were betrayed by the November Criminals."

Bennett knew he should keep his mouth shut but curiosity forced the words out before he could stop himself. "November Criminals? Who are they?"

"Jews and Communists who sold out the Kaiser and set up the Weimar Republic for their own gain, that's who. Well, I didn't lose this for nothing." He hit the stump with his hand. "Their turn's coming."

Bennett's eyes widened as he heard the hatred in the old man's voice. Reaching the door, he nodded, tipped his hat politely and escaped into the warm spring sunshine. Had he guessed that buying a newspaper would provoke all this, he would have waited until he returned to Berlin.

The day was getting weirder and weirder, and Bennett decided he'd had enough. The whole idea of getting away from the business community and meeting "real" Germans had totally lost its appeal. He would find somewhere he could quietly read his newspapers, eat his lunch, and not talk to anyone. Remembering the beer garden that his train companions had told him about, he stopped in the tobacco shop to buy a pack of cigarettes and ask directions to the place.

Seated behind the counter, reading the newspaper and smoking a cigar, was Martin Meylin, the sandy-haired leader of the SPD whom Bennett had seen at Anna's. He looked up when the door chime rang. Holding the cigar in his teeth he walked out from behind the counter. He had a smooth, self-confident manner, was well groomed, and wore a fine suit that fit his powerful body well.

"Good morning, Herr Sizemore. How can I help you?"

"How did you know my name?"

The shopkeeper removed the cigar. He maintained a hint of a smile on his wide mouth and his deep blue eyes never wavered in their frank and somewhat amused appraisal of Bennett. "Small town. Strangers here are noticed. Ones that buy breakfast for out-of-work Germans get special notice." Shaking Bennett's hand, he said, "I am Martin Meylin. Happy to meet you. I hear you may be looking for a room in our town."

Bennett laughed and shook his head. "You know, Herr Meylin, I only thought of that possibility myself about two hours ago. News does travel fast."

"Yes, especially if there might be business opportunities. For instance, I myself have a room to let. I own a large house, newly remodeled, close by, convenient to everything. The room even has its own bath." He laughed. "See why knowledge is important?"

His polished, friendly manner and gentle sense of humor made Bennett warm to him immediately; and yet, there was something hidden beneath that congenial exterior that conveyed an aura of power, an underlying sense of "Don't mess with me."

"I see you have my flyer. Will you be attending our evening entertainment?"

"Uh, not sure yet. Perhaps."

Martin's knowing look left no doubt that he saw through the equivocation but took no offense. "Well, if you do, my SPD boys will welcome and watch over you. But if you go to the Nazi meeting, sit by the door and be alert for trouble. These are dangerous times, and a lot of people are carrying sidearms." He motioned toward his tobacco stock and said, "Now what can I get for you?"

Bennett selected some cigarettes and asked Martin if he could give him directions to the beer garden above town. Martin's answer dashed Bennett's plans for a quiet lunch by himself.

"The beer garden. Good idea. I will take lunch there myself, so I can show you the way. You don't mind company, do you?"

Good manners demanded he answer, "That would be great, thanks."

He and Martin followed a footpath that left the walled section of town above the park and climbed to a hill above the town. They sat outside on the tavern lawn at wooden tables and looked out over the entire valley.

The beer and the view were every bit as good as the girls had told him. He could see the central town, the outlying residential districts, the river, the farm lands, and the tree-covered hills that surrounded the valley. It looked so peaceful and bucolic, like a sanctuary from the problems of the outside world. This morning Bennett had learned that appearance was deceptive.

As they ate, Martin pointed out landmarks and provided a thumbnail history of Kasselbronn, and Bennett found that his reticence to have company at lunch had ebbed away.

Several of the SPD men came by to satisfy their curiosity and be introduced to Bennett. The respect and warmth these men felt for Martin was obvious, but none ventured to sit at his table without an invitation. Instead, they filled two nearby tables, and after lunch began to sing.

In Bennett's experience singing had been limited to the church choir or singers in cabarets and Broadway shows. The singing of the SPD men was like nothing he had ever heard before. The songs were traditional German folk songs, some ballads, some love songs, many strongly patriotic. They were tunes which managed to convey both sentiment and manliness and sounded as if they were sung for the sheer joy of making music.

Lighting up the cigar Martin had given him, Bennett drew deeply and exhaled in a sigh of content. A beautiful view, cooling breeze, the scent of the nearby pines, good food, good beer, good companions, and music that delighted the soul. These were the types of adventures he'd dreamed of when he'd first learned he was to travel to Germany.

Then like a warped record, the music seemed to go out of tune. Two other tables of men on the far side of the lawn had begun to sing. Kurt Schutz, arms raised, led them in song and cast a challenging look at Martin. The voices of the nearby tables of SPD men trailed off.

The Nazis under Kurt's direction took over. The tune they sang was almost dirge-like as it began, yet each verse ended with a hopeful uplifting ring, like a call to battle. The combination of hymn and call to arms reminded Bennett of the "Battle Hymn of the Republic." He tried to catch the meaning in the lyrics.

Raise high the flag,
The ranks are closed and tight,
Stormtroopers march,
With firm and steady step.
Souls of the comrades
Shot by Reds and countermight
Are in our ranks
And march along in step.

"What is this song?" asked Bennett.

Martin chewed on his cigar, he eyes looked from Schutz to the SPD men and back. "The 'Horst Wessel Song.' It's the Nazi's hymn to their young poster boy, a perfect Aryan youth, cut down in a cowardly manner by the Communists. Shops are filled with his picture postcards. A good-looking young man. It's just too bad he was in reality a pimp and a thug who died in a street brawl. On second thought, perhaps that is appropriate for the Nazis. Excuse me."

Martin stood and walked to the tables of waiting SPD men. He said something to them quietly, then raised his arms to lead them in song. As the Nazis took up the second chorus to the "Horst Wessel Song" the SPD began a rousing song of their own. The vocal challenge between the two groups changed the music tempo subtly from anthem to march. Then with drumming beat, it became a splendid and fearsome round: the harmony of the singing, glorious; the disharmony of the divided Germans, frightening. Men in each group rose from their seats, drawing deeper breaths for greater volume, gesturing angrily at significant points in the lyrics. Bennett tried to sort out the words. Nazis sang of the brown battalion and swastikas and the SPD called for democracy and freedom.

The music pulled at Bennett's emotions, luring him in with its rousing, patriotic siren call, but his mind recoiled on seeing the violence and hatred that boiled just beneath the noble sentiment.

With such passion unleashed, the expression of it could not remain benign. A beer mug sailed through the air, hitting Martin on the back, below his right shoulder. Yells erupted from the SPD. The Nazis responded in suit, and the pent-up anger of both groups erupted into a general melee that excluded no one.

Since Bennett was sitting at Martin's table, his allegiance was assumed, and he was fair game. He was not exactly a stranger to barroom brawls, but if he'd had a choice, he would have preferred to remain neutral. If ISS found he had been fighting in a beer garden, he would be fired and sent home. But with someone's fist on its way to connecting with his face, that was not his first consideration. He blocked the blow and got in one of his own. He shook his head, let out a North Carolina war whoop and joined the fray with gusto.

The owner of the beer garden appeared at the door and ran, dodging the brawlers, to a post at the front of the garden. With a worried eye for breakage of his steins and furniture, he pulled on a rope that rang an alarm bell.

At the ringing of the bell, Martin looked around. He saw Kurt running around the side of the beer house and Bennett in the thick of the fight, giving a good account of himself. Martin ran to Bennett and tried to pull him away. Thinking he was being attacked, Bennett swung around, right fist in motion. Martin ducked just as Bennett realized who it was and pulled the punch.

"Come on," shouted Martin. "That bell will bring the police. I can't have my prospective tenant being arrested."

He led Bennett through the trees, over the crest of a hill and down to a walking trail on the other side. As he slowed to a walk, Martin turned to Bennett, an unspoken inquiry in his eyes. They searched one another's faces for a reaction. Then at the same moment, their serious expressions dissolved, and both men broke into laughter. "Well, Herr Sizemore, welcome to Kasselbronn."

Bennett

33

With its central location and excellent train transportation, Kasselbronn
might make a good home base. Before he could decide on that, however, there was
one thing Bennett needed to check out. A silly idea had lodged in his mind the day
he had spotted a piece of copper for sale, and as foolish as the idea was, it took up
permanent residence in his plans. Sunday afternoon he bought a large rucksack,
packed a lunch, water, beer, and a few tools; and headed for the mountains above
town.

By late afternoon he had left the groomed public trails and Sunday hikers
and followed a small river into a high mountain canyon. Weaving and picking his
way through dense underbrush, he traced a small tributary to a spring that arose
beneath a great granite outcropping. It was far from the beaten track, had cold pure
water and a natural shelter that could be enlarged. It was perfect for his hill country
plans. He took the tools and copper out of the rucksack and set to work.

It was full dark by the time Bennett found his way down the mountain and
back to his hotel. He was physically tired but emotionally rested. The day of
solitude had provided the break he needed from both work and the disturbing
conflicts of the citizens of Kasselbronn. Monday morning he awoke ready to face
the challenges of the new week.

Luther Gugler, the train conductor who took their tickets that morning was
from Kasselbronn. He was an older man and greeted them in a stern and morose
tone. Juliane was crying softly and her puffy face revealed she had been crying for a
long time. Luther looked at the child, then looked at the stranger she was with. He
knelt down and spoke quietly to Juliane, with a gentleness that belied his initial
gruff manner.

"What's the matter, Juliane?"

In a barely audible whisper she answered, "I have to go to school in

England."

Luther nodded. "And who is this gentleman you are traveling with, a teacher?"

Juliane looked at Bennett and back to Luther and shrugged. Luther straightened up turned to Bennett, his eyes narrowed in suspicion. Bennett couldn't let this escalate. He offered his hand to the conductor. "I'm Bennett Sizemore. I'm a friend of the family and was traveling to Berlin this morning. They asked me to escort Juliane that far so she could meet up with her school group."

The conductor held his hand long as he considered him. Finally he said, "Are you the American?"

"Yes," answered Bennett, wondering what that would mean to the conductor.

"It's an honor to meet you, Herr Sizemore. I'm Luther Gugler." Looking from Bennett to the tickets, he said quietly, "I believe you need move to the next car." He led them through the coach car and took them to a private compartment in the next car. "I think Juliane might be more . . . more comfortable in here. I am sorry, but there will be a bit more charge."

Gratefully, Bennett dug out the added fare and thanked the conductor for his consideration.

As Luther leaned down again to speak to Juliane his lapel fell forward and under the lapel Bennett caught the glint of a small pin with the red flag of the Communist Party. No wonder he had compassion for someone persecuted by the Nazis. If what Bennett had learned in town was true, this man might soon be without a job.

Luther said, "I hear England is a wonderful place. I'm sure you will have a grand time there and be home before you know it."

Since Juliane was leaving legally Bennett's only worry about the trip was hostile or harassing actions by anti-Semite Nazis. That he could have dealt with. He was totally unprepared however for the real problem. Juliane cried all the way to Berlin, except for a brief time when she slept. Bennett had never felt so helpless. Nothing he said had helped allay her fears or console her sadness in being parted from her parents and the only home she had ever known.

At the Berlin train station Bennett was greatly relieved to deliver his charge to the woman who was taking forty-one youngsters with her to England on a study program. He marveled at her courage in the face of what seemed a daunting task.

Hailing a taxi, he headed for the office, actually looking forward to returning to the relatively sterile and regimented business environment. How quickly he had been drawn into the vortex of the town, how easily the problems of those people had become his. He reflected on how he had gotten himself into this mess and chuckled as he thought about that large plate of strudel and sausage that Aunt Anna had set in front of him. He'd been bought and paid for with a blue plate special. When he did go back to Kasselbronn, he would view that canny old gal with greater respect and a bit more skepticism.

Back in Berlin, he dived into his work, seven days a week, and let the plans for a home base simmer on the back burner.

Bennett

34

August 14, 1932

Dear Daddy,

I am writing today from a little country inn on the Danube River, picture
postcard enclosed. It is very pretty, and I am enjoying a rare day off work. These
Germans are nuts about records and statistics, and there's nothing else like our
punch card machines to organize all that information. I just thank my lucky stars I'm
working and making good money. You'll be happy to hear that I don't have time to
spend much, so am actually saving for the first time. Depression looks really bad
here. How are things looking back home?

To answer some of your questions, no, don't think the Communists will
take over here. The Nazi fascists might though. Traveling as much as I do, I hear the
Nazis speak out of both sides of their mouth. They tell workers that the bosses are
mistreating them and they need to join the Nazis to free themselves from the
capitalists. Then they tell the industrialist how the Communists, Democrats, and
Socialists are all in a big plot to ruin them and they should give lots of money to
Hitler to defeat the rascals.

Last week I heard Hitler talking to a bunch of industrial big wigs and he
said that democracy was just replacing genius with a majority, and all you got was
the rule of stupidity and weakness. He said if you applied democracy to economics
it was just communism. Those industrial bosses ate it up, cheered when he promised
to get rid of the trade unions, and filled his coffers with money. Guess there's
always some folks who'll buy snake oil.

The working folk love their democracy, gives them a real say-so in things
for the first time. It could really be in trouble, though. This summer this guy named
von Papen used some emergency decree and said Communists and the SPD were
about to revolt or something. Von Papen simply took over the state government of

Prussia, kicked out the folks elected by the people, and put in his own choices, like any old common despot.

Here's the scary part. No one tried to stop him, no army, no police, no courts, nobody. Back home I figure they'd lynch anybody who tried that.

Well, enough of that. Think I'll see if I can line up a fishing pole and some bait and try to forget work and politics for a while.

Ben

Dear Ben

The picture postcard of that Danube River looks mighty fine. I am happy for you, working and good pay and all. I hear the Depression is bad here too, specially in the cities. Course it don't make much nevermind to me. The good Lord hasn't stopped the rain and they haven't figured out how to tax me for it, so my crops grow and my goats give milk.

I found your news on the politics in Germany very interesting. Papers here don't have none of that stuff. I do worry some though about what you told me. Puts me in mind of that story about the old boy trying to cook him a bullfrog. When he stick that frog in a pot of boiling water, that frog, he feels the heat and jumps right out. But the old boy got smart and put that frog in a pot of cold water. He brung up the heat slow like, and that frog sit there happy as could be, not taking no notice that he's in hot water til he finds his self clear cooked to death.

If that's the way things are going there, I'm thinking you might be better off here without that good paying job. Depression can't last forever, and I could use your help with next year's crops. We sure won't starve to death back here in our hills. You might give some thought to jumping out of that pot before you get yourself cooked.

Your daddy, Zeb

Bennett

35

Bennett walked out of the early movie matinee and immediately heard the rattle of the can. In the city the Brown Shirts now traveled in groups of two or more, making it more dangerous to refuse a contribution. This evening he was blocked on the street by three of them.

"Contribution to the Nazi cause, mein Herr."

"Sorry, fellows, but your mates in the theater lobby just cleaned me out."

The leader of the group angrily demanded, "Who's in there?"

"How should I know? Two guys with brown shirts and swastika arm bands."

Angrily the three went to the theater box office and demanded entrance without a ticket, a demand that could not be denied. While they were distracted looking for who was poaching in their territory, Bennett grabbed a cab and headed for his hotel. It was only a few blocks, but he didn't dare walk. One never knew when or where the Nazis, might hold "demonstrations" attacking persons they believed to be Communists, Jews, Social Democrats, or trade unionists.

On his afternoon off, he had finally gotten to see *Grand Hotel*. It was supposed to be set in Berlin, but the film didn't show the Berlin he knew. There wasn't a word about the Depression, the politics, the homeless, or the increasing aggressiveness of the Nazis. Was that ignorance because the movie was made in America or was it just intended to be a diversion and distract people from thinking too much about real problems. Whatever the reason, the movie had made him aware of how tired he was of living in a hotel and living in the city.

Berlin offered few diversions that appealed to Bennett. On the occasions when some fellow worker dragged him to a cabaret for some "fun," he found that what passed for entertainment was in its own way as violent as the roving bands of thugs. Bennett was far from puritanical, and Lord knew he'd seen enough girly shows in New York, but this was different. There was no real joy in it. Just the bizarre and debased. The audience laughed and cheered the hardest at the scenes that seemed to Bennett to be the cruelest. He concluded that the laughter was some sort of charm to ward off any real feeling, a way of saying, "This won't touch me."

As he paid off the taxi driver he realized he had made a decision that he hadn't even been consciously considering. He walked into the lobby, stopped at the hotel desk, and slapped it with his hand hard enough to make the clerk jump.

"Hi there, fella. Herr Sizemore in room 321. I'm checking out. Holler down to your storage room and tell them to retrieve my extra suitcase and steamer trunk, will you please. I'll be back in fifteen minutes to check out."

"Ah, yes sir, Herr Sizemore, but . . ."

The clerk continued to mumble something but Bennett didn't wait to hear it. He headed to his room, taking the stairs two at a time instead of waiting for the elevator. Once the decision was made, it invigorated him. He threw his clothing and toiletries into the single suitcase he had lugged all over Germany and, good to his word, he was at the desk within fifteen minutes.

The clerk could not meet his eyes and studiously examined some papers he was sorting. "I'm sorry, Herr Sizemore, but there has been a slight delay. The . . . the bellman for the storage was busy, but he will have your trunk up soon."

His stammering mumble made Bennett sure there was something the clerk wasn't telling him, and after months in this country Bennett's mind could manufacture all sorts of scenarios. Nothing in his imagination however came close to the real reason for the delay.

He smoked a cigarette and cooled his heels. Five minutes, ten, fifteen. He went back to the desk and was going to demand to see the manager, but before he could, the clerk turned from the telephone and said, "Herr Sizemore, you have a call. You may take it on the house phone by that lounge chair if you like."

Bennett sat in the designated chair and picked up the receiver. "This is Bennett Sizemore."

"Mr. Sizemore, this is the friend you met at the cafe, when you first arrived in Berlin."

Bennett was so surprised, he made no response.

"You remember, we had a pleasant walk in the park and you told me that story about your voyage on the *Bremen*."

"Yes. I remember.

"I hear you're checking out of the hotel. I hope you've found a nice apartment."

Bennett was stunned. He had made the decision to leave less than an hour before and had told no one but the clerk. He was being watched! With that realization, he had an almost queasy feeling. He had played hide and seek with the law most of his life, but this was different. For the first time in his life he was totally legal, yet someone was watching and reporting on him.

Jordan's voice pulled him back. "Will you be living here in Berlin, then?"

"Uh, no."

Bennett looked around the lobby. The slight paranoia that he had felt since arriving in Germany was suddenly verified. How many of the other small things he had noticed were real? How many of the friendly and polite inquiries about his trips and return times had actually been ways of mining him for information? How naive he had been!

"Well, what's your new address to be then?"

"I don't have one yet."

He looked around the lobby with new perceptiveness. Each person he saw was now a question. Are you what you appear to be? His eyes came back to the desk clerk, and he now consciously realized what he had seen but not registered. A small metal pin on the clerk's lapel glittered, reflecting the light of the desk lamp. The pin was a swastika. Bennett wondered who, besides Jordan, this clerk reported to.

Jordan laughed. "I hope you don't plan on lugging that steamer trunk all around Germany with you. Come, Mr. Sizemore. I think there may come a day when you will value my friendship, and your keen observations have already been most valuable to me. We must keep in touch."

There was a long silence as Bennett considered his answer. Though Jordan seemed to think that his coy conversation was sufficiently discreet, Bennett thought about how much he was giving away to whoever might be listening in the telephone switchboard room. Jordan was an American, connected with the embassy, paying a Nazi desk clerk to watch him. The clerk would undoubtedly report that to his superiors, calling Nazi attention to Bennett's activities. A listener would now know that Bennett was a keen observer, had met and talked to Jordan in a park, and had reported something valuable that had happened on the *Bremen*.

Bennett replied, "Look, I'm glad you and that blond hit it off, but I don't normally travel with that set, and meeting her and her friend aboard ship was just the luck of a shipboard romance. I won't even be here in Berlin much anymore, so probably won't see you again, but good hunting, old buddy."

"I see. Well, maybe next time I'll be the one with two voluptuous blonds."

"Sure thing." Bennett hung up the phone, counted to ten, watched the desk clerk receive a phone call and signal a bellman. Within three minutes the fellow returned with Bennett's steamer trunk and extra suitcase. A little voice in Bennett's head often warned him against rash actions. Sometimes he listened, sometimes he didn't. His little voice had tried to warn him against reporting the incident on the *Bremen*, but at that time it had seemed like something right out of a spy novel and was far too romantic for him to resist. This wasn't the first time he regretted ignoring his little voice and he doubted it would it be the last.

Within a half hour he and all his worldly possessions were deposited at the central Bahnhof. His baggage now included the large rucksack he used for secret hikes to his mountain hideaway. He bought a ticket for Kasselbronn, checked all baggage except the rucksack, and enjoyed a late lunch while he waited for his train. The Bennett who got on that train, however, was a man of changed perceptions. He now noticed that a young man who had been sitting in the lobby of his hotel was boarding the train with him. This, he realized, was part and parcel of his new life.

He bought a copy of Dashiell Hammett's new novel *The Thin Man*. Nick and Nora Charles made very good company all the way to Kasselbronn, but like the dramas of the *Grand Hotel*, their adventures were so far from reality that they might have lived on another planet. At that moment, that was exactly what Bennett liked about them.

Bennett had made several visits to Kasselbronn over the last few months, always finding time to sneak off to his mountain hideaway to disgorge supplies from his rucksack or to work on his little project. Now, tired of city life, he was returning to find a quiet room in this little town.

Leaving his bags at the station, he took a taxi directly to Martin Meylin's tobacco shop. Martin sat reading the paper and smoking a cigar but his bored expression changed when he recognized Bennett. He gave Bennett the lopsided grin that came from holding the cigar with his teeth. "Well, well, Herr Sizemore returns. Another holiday?" In a mock conspiratorial tone he added, "Or perhaps you would like to hear another of our choir concerts?"

Bennett laughed. "No, but I did want to buy a pack of cigarettes and see if you still had that room to let."

Otto

36

The Falcons were the youngest of the Socialist workers' groups, and by now Otto should have gone on to an older organization, but with the increased violence of the last year, and no adult leader available, he felt a responsibility to the younger boys. Today however was his sixteenth birthday, and it would be his last day as a Red Falcon.

He walked along the outside of the city wall to the spot his young Falcons would congregate for their weekly distribution of leaflets to the homeless. As he skirted one of the tents, a tall boy in a Hitler Youth uniform turned quickly, averting his face from Otto.

"Leonard?" Leonard Altman had been a Red Falcon and was about Otto's age.

The boy turned back, embarrassment clearly showing on his face. "Hello, Otto."

Otto tried not to let the disgust show as he asked, "So, you're Hitler Youth now?"

"It's not what you think, Otto. It's not for political reasons. They just have the best activities, camping, hiking, and interesting group meetings."

"How could you? You're not stupid. You know what they stand for."

Leonard flushed angrily and his response immediately belied his stated reasons. "Yes, I do. Do you? They believe in Germans and Germany. They're doing something about the future instead of just complaining, and they don't always have to harp on class differences like the Socialists and Communists."

"No, just racial differences."

"You know, Otto, I never figured why you were a Falcon anyway, you and your left wing intellectual parents. Did it make you feel better to be a class above the rest of us."

Shocked at the anger and hatred in his friend's voice, Otto could find no answer.

"Well," Leonard continued, "with the Hitler Youth I'm not a lower class boy whose dad is out of work. I'm a German." He started to walk away then turned back for one final warning. "You better wake up, Otto. The future belongs to us." Leonard turned and ran back to a small group of Hitler Youth by the wall.

The Falcons had been lining up behind Otto and many had heard some of Leonard's words.

"Hey," said an eleven-year-old, "what are they doing in those uniforms? I thought the government had banned uniforms."

"Guess they're feeling cocky after von Papen calling for Reichstag elections. Line up now and I'll give you your flyers."

Intent on the flyers, Otto looked up to see the wide-eye fear on two boys' faces. "What?" He turned to see what they were looking at.

It was fortunate that the Falcons had not yet dispersed among the homeless when the Hitler Youth appeared and formed a line blocking their path. Otto put his arm out protectively.

"All younger boys to the rear. Older boys with me in front." Four eleven and twelve-year-olds lined up with Otto while the rest fell in behind.

Though the Hitler Youth were older and larger, the Falcons were eager to defend themselves and said so in defiant undertones. Otto was afraid that this time they would have to fight the Nazis, and was sizing up the group, deciding which one he should single out for the first blow. Leonard was among them, though hanging back toward the rear.

Then two SA men joined the group of Hitler Youth. One carried a horse whip. He cracked the whip once, and at this signal, weapons appeared from the uniform pockets of the Hitler Youth: brass knuckles, bludgeons, and a leather-covered chain with a steel ball bouncing from the end.

As much as he wanted to use his fist to remove the smirk from the face of the Nazi youth leader, Otto knew that many, if not all, the boys with him were about to be seriously hurt.

"Hold," he said. "Younger boys, go to your school right now. Older boys hold the line." Sight of the weapons as well as Otto's tone of voice conveyed the seriousness of the situation. Without argument the youngest of the Falcons turned and ran for the gate as the older boys spread out their defensive line on both sides of Otto.

Quietly to his comrades he said, "We are weaponless and outnumbered three to one. We hold only long enough for the younger boys to get away, then we get the hell out of here." They nodded and braced for the onslaught.

From the corner of his eye Otto saw movement from the wall. With one eye on the Nazis, he glanced quickly to see what new menace was coming toward them. At least a dozen of the homeless men were running from the wall to where the two groups faced off. They lined up in front of the Red Falcons, facing the Nazis. Luther Gugler, a Communist who had recently lost his job on the railroad, turned to Otto. "You boys better get to school. Don't want to be late for class."

Otto nodded his thanks, and without words he and the other Falcons turned and ran for the gate. One of the boys running in step with Otto said, "That does it. We have to arm ourselves."

Otto shook his head, not in denial, but in quandary. "I don't know. Maybe, but then we become thugs, just like the Nazis."

This balance between living lawfully and self-defense was the very question Otto had heard debated last night by men of the Reichsbanner. This group was sworn to uphold the constitution and the democracy, but they also believed in the rule of law. Civil war was not an option. So they drilled secretly up in the hills, and waited for the Nazis to step so far over the legal line that the national government and the national Reichsbanner would call for legal action against them. Some warned that moment would never come.

Once in town the boys separated, Otto heading for the boy's gymnasium, which was a secondary university-preparatory school, and the rest off to Burgerschule, which was a primary Lutheran school. He was still running, head down, deep in thought, when he ran into someone.

"Whoa there," said the man in English.

Otto looked up startled and ready to defend himself. To his delight he saw it was the American. "Oh, Herr Sizemore. You are back. Are you here to stay?"

"Well, if I don't get run over. Are you late for school or is the Devil chasing you?"

"I am sorry to run into you. It's a little of both, I guess. My Red Falcons just had a run-in with the Hitler Youth. If it hadn't been for some of the out-of-work men at the wall, I am afraid some of the boys might have been seriously hurt. The Nazis were armed with brass knuckles and such. And, I must get to school also."

Bennett tried to smile. "Sorry to hear about the trouble. Guess there isn't any place in the country you don't run into it these days. I've rented a room in Herr Meylin's house. How about we try to have breakfast at your aunt's again?"

"That is good. Herr Meylin is an honorable man—tough, not one to cross—but honorable. His home will be a good place for you. Oh, you must come to our home tonight. We are having a party for my birthday. Please say you can come."

"I don't want to intrude on—"

"Please! Aunt Anna will be there, and my grandparents have come from Berlin, and my parents really want to meet you. Believe me they have heard much about you."

Bennett laughed. "I'll just bet they have. Okay, thank you, Otto. I'll be there. What time, and where is your house?"

"Good. Come at six o'clock and—here, I'll write it out for you." Otto quickly scribbled directions to his home on the back of a Red Falcon's flyer and handed it to Bennett. "I am so glad you will be living here," he said, shaking his hand. "See you tonight."

Otto took off at a run for school. He was pulled up short, however, when he entered the school grounds and saw both students and faculty standing in the yard looking up at the roof. A swastika flag flew from the turret atop the schoolhouse, and Nazis in both SA and Hitler Youth uniforms stood around the yard. Looking around for someone to take charge, he spotted the janitor and demanded, "You must take that thing down! That's a disgrace."

The janitor turned toward him, a gold swastika pin gleaming from his collar. "I don't know if I want to do that. After the new elections, von Hindenburg will have to appoint Hitler chancellor."

Otto ran toward the school building and stopped in front of the principal, who was looking up at the roof.

"Sir, please let me climb up there and take that thing down."

Arms folded across his chest, almost impassive, the principal said quietly,

"It appears someone is taking care of that."

Otto looked up to see a man climb out of the dormer window, make his way across the roof and onto the fire ladder, accomplishing all of this with only one arm. Otto recognized professor Morganstein, a Jew who had fought for Germany and lost his arm in the Great War. Clapping and cheering arose from the schoolyard as this man ripped down the swastika and tossed it to the ground.

On a campus with over two hundred students, not more than thirty were Nazis. But now that minority made their voices heard above the rest as they booed and jeered and fell into a chant of "Jew swine, Jew swine."

Otto told the principal, "You should call the police and report these men."

"For what, yelling?"

"Well, . . . they're in uniform. The government has forbidden paramilitary uniforms."

The principal looked at Otto with disapproval but said nothing. Two of the older students with SA uniforms ran up to the principal, who seemed to cringe in front of the Nazis. It was one of the SA men who seemed to be in authority, not the principal.

"You must stop him. He is a filthy Jew and has no right interfering in German concerns."

This was the final straw for Otto. He rounded on the storm trooper and landed the first punch in his solar plexus, knocking all the wind out of him and doubling him over. Then pounding him with his fists, he knocked him to the ground.

"You asshole!" shouted Otto. "He lost his arm fighting for this country and is more of a true German than you will ever be."

Three other Nazis came running toward Otto. At first he battled them alone and was taking a beating, but seeing what was happening, a large group of SPD students ran to aid him. At that point no amount of shouting by the principal could prevent a general melee. Order was restored only when the city police arrived.

Bennett

37

Otto opened the door and Bennett got his first look at him since they'd met in the street that morning. Otto's right eye was swollen almost shut, his cheek was turning blue-black, and he moved stiffly as if it hurt to breathe. His knuckles were bruised and raw.

In addition to an almost parental anxiety for Otto, Bennett realized with shock that the general violence of this country had suddenly touched him personally. He was so unprepared that he could not control his facial expression.

Otto said, "It's not as bad as it looks, and you should see what we did to them." He started to laugh but had to stifle it or the cut on his lip would open again and bleed. "We had a little disagreement over a flag raising this morning. I'll tell you about it later. Now I want you to meet my family."

Despite his beating, Otto was extremely cheerful and proudly announced, "He's here, everyone," as if Bennett were the guest of honor. Proudly, Otto introduced Bennett to his father. Georg Brehm got up from his chair, removed a carved meerschaum pipe from his mouth and shook hands."We're very happy you could join us tonight, Herr Bennett."

Georg was tall and slender and his dark eyes conveyed both warmth and intelligence. Even if Otto hadn't told him, Bennett might have guessed from the man's dress and bearing that Georg was an academic and writer. "Thank you, Herr Brehm. I'm honored that Otto invited me. He's a fine young man."

With fascination, Bennett's eyes were drawn to the pipe. It was sculpted like the head of a fully bearded cavalier. The white stone was delicately stained a rich auburn on the brim of the cavalier's floppy hat and the curls of his beard. No painter could have improved on the colorful highlights created by the natural darkening created by heat and smoke. "That's the handsomest pipe bowl I've seen."

George looked pleased and Otto said, "That was a present from my grandparents. Come and meet them." Otto's grandparents were a tiny little couple, much smaller than their son. Grandma Sara was less than five feet and Grandpa Franklin no more than five foot two. His neat white beard was trimmed to about an inch around his face giving him a natty air of distinction. Bennett would not have guessed that this man rose from the poor and humble beginning that Otto had described, but he could easily see him as the master furniture maker and antique expert he had become. Grandma Sara remained seated like the reigning family regent she was, but Grandpa Franklin rose formally and shook Bennett's hand as they exchanged greetings.

Otto's mother, Katharina, was in the process of setting out plates on the dining room table, but she wiped her hands on her apron and came into the living room to meet Bennett. To his surprise, Katharina and Aunt Anna both gave him a hug like he was a member of family, and Anna also introduced him to her husband, Willie, who pumped his hand warmly.

A little overwhelmed by his reception, Bennett was grateful when Georg handed him a stein of beer and offered him a comfortable chair. That chair quickly became the hot seat, however, as Grandma Sara endeavored to draw Bennett into the discussion that had been in progress before he entered.

"Herr Bennett, our subject just now is Aldous Huxley's new book, *Brave New World,* and the question at hand is: Can social conditioning and mind control truly make an individual content with his lot, or does the attempt at control breed the seeds of revolution?"

Bennett stared blankly at her.

She tried again. "Now I know that in the book he created some sort of mind numbing drug as well as genetic engineering, but stripping away those fictional devices, the question becomes, do most men truly need freedom and individuality or is that only a need of the more intellectual minority. Are the masses satisfied with slavery if they have enough food, wine and games?"

Totally at a loss, Bennett flushed as he confessed, "I'm sorry, Frau Brehm, but I'm not familiar with that book."

Otto jumped in with a comment, "Well, if you conclude they are so easily satisfied, you're concluding that democracy is untenable."

Uncle Willie took exception to this view, and so the conversation went.

The book was only the central theme, a jumping-off place for general discussion of literature, philosophy, and politics.

Bennett had expected to be a fifth wheel at this party because he wasn't family, but what he was finding was that he felt out of place because everyone in the room, including Otto, was so much better educated and better read than he. Not only did they discuss in detail writers he had hardly heard of, but they also engaged in a crackling exchange of puns and other witticism, each playing off the other one so quickly that Bennett felt like a total dunce. There was no way he could join in this rapid-fire dialogue. In fact he would just barely figure out the meaning of one pun or double entendre when another was built upon it. All he could do is laugh when everyone else did.

One thing became obvious. Grandma Sara, the smallest person in the room, was the greatest intellect. She was a walking encyclopedia of literature: European, American, and classic. No one disputed her facts, but everyone could and did differ on interpretation and analysis. When the subject shifted to art, the recognized expert was Grandpa Franklin.

When dinner was ready, Katharina announced, "We have three more guests yet to arrive: my sister, Greta, cousin Eva and her fiancé, Hans, but they are as always late."

"Why did you invite them?" asked Otto. "I told you they're Nazis now, and they've never been my favorite people."

"Otto! They're family! And . . . I didn't invite them. I ran into Eva at the co-op, and she saw the large roast I was buying and sort of assumed they were invited."

Grandma Sara jumped in before Otto got himself in trouble by saying more. "Invite themselves and then be late? Katharina you didn't go to all this work just to have dinner ruined. I say we eat and they can take what's left when they get here."

Grandpa Franklin offered a compromise. "I have something to show you, Katharina. We can give Eva five more minutes to get here, and if she doesn't, then we can eat."

With that the little man rose and went to his car. When he returned, he handed Katharina an antique mantle clock, carved of many woods and scenes representing the four seasons. It stood on four feet shaped like snow-covered pines, carved from bleached ash. On the top was a nesting bird carved from gray-brown chestnut; on the left, a cascade of fall leaves in a variegated red and gold Brazilian tulipwood. On the right were spring flowers carved in deep red-brown cherry. Katharina almost cried.

"Oh, Papa, you have restored it so beautifully. I couldn't even guess where the damage was. How did you ever find the woods to match the broken pieces? Thank you so much. I so love this piece."

"Well, the wood working I could do for you. The innards, I fear, were beyond my skills to repair. You must still find a clockmaker to see if it can be made to run."

Bennett cleared his throat. Finally, something he knew about. "Uh, back home I learned my first trade working for my cousin, who was a clockmaker. Perhaps I could help."

The whole family quieted and looked at him, then Katharina said, "Oh, Herr Sizemore, I wouldn't want to impose . . . " Her polite assurance was in comic contrast to how quickly she put it in his hands.

Otto mimicked her words, "But she really doesn't want to impose." They all laughed.

"Well, I don't have the proper tools to do the work right now," Bennett said, "but, Otto, if you have a small screwdriver, I could at least take the back off and see what kind of works we got and if it looks like something I could help with."

A knock at the door announced their tardy guests, and Georg rose to let them in. Eva, a tall, big-boned woman with a broad face and pig-like nose, pushed past Georg without as much as a hello, announcing, "All right, we've arrived," as if the party had awaited them breathlessly.

Her fiancé followed, his erect posture and marching step revealing military training, his haughty expression evincing his claim to aristocracy. Without any acknowledgment or apology for being late, they strode into the living room, dropping their coats in a heap on the sofa. Georg politely introduced them to Bennett.

Eva didn't greet him but looked him up and down, saying "Ah, the American." Hans Bubenhofen responded by clicking his heels and offering an ever-so-slight Junker bow.

Katharina looked past Eva. "Isn't my sister coming?"

"No, she didn't feel up to it."

"Oh, my, is she ill?"

"No, Mother's fine, she just couldn't figure out what you two could say to each other. You know, you really should quit badgering Momma about her politics. You two used to be the closest sisters in town. Now she thinks you're just telling her she's stupid to belong to the NSDAP."

Katharina's mouth came open but she found nothing to answer to this.

Eva turned to her next victim. Taking Otto's chin roughly in her fingers, she turned his face from side to side. Shaking her head she said, "You stupid boy. I hope this has taught you a lesson. It's all over town what you did. What a disgrace you are to our family. If you must pick fights, at least fight for a good German cause, not a filthy Jew." There was utter silence as Otto reddened and the rest of the family stared at Eva.

Grandma Sara's short torso straightened as she sat taller in her chair. Her expression did not change, but her face blanched.

Katharina was normally the peacemaker in the family, but this time her anger and embarrassment were too great. "Eva! How dare you speak such obscenity in my house, let alone in front of Grandmother Sara. You apologize this instant."

"Oh, nonsense, Aunt Kat. Grandma Sara knows I didn't mean any insult to her, don't you, Grandma?" With that she walked to Sara, bent over, and kissed her on the cheek. Sara sat rigidly, flinching slightly at Eva's touch.

"Why, no, Eva. What else should I expect from someone of your mental stature?"

Sara's response sailed right over Eva's head but was fully understood by Hans. The look he gave Sara was lethal.

Eva continued blithely, "See, Sara understands. Katharina, still in your apron? You are quite the old domestic, aren't you? I hope dinner's not late, I'm starved."

Enunciating each word slowly and angrily, Katharina said, "No, Eva. Actually, dinner has been waiting on you. Would you like to help me set it out?"

"No, wouldn't dream of getting in your way. Now, Herr Sizemore, tell me what you are doing here in Germany."

Bennett looked at the couple thoughtfully a moment. Then he stood, set the clock on the mantle and replied, "If you'll excuse me, I think Frau Brehm has some heavy plates of food she could use some help with." Then to Otto's delight, Bennett turned his back on Eva and Hans and went into the kitchen.

Hans glared at Bennett's retreating back. One eyebrow rose as he fingered his thin blond mustache. Eva mumbled, "How rude!"

Otto barely suppressed a smile. Looking past Eva, he caught his father's eyes. The look they exchanged was too much. Otto couldn't hide his smile anymore, so he turned away and followed Bennett to the kitchen. Bennett was just returning with a large platter laden with a huge roast beef. As he set the meat on the table he marveled at this luxury which must have taken much sacrifice, even for this middle class family.

Otto's broad smile as he entered the kitchen changed abruptly to concern when he saw his mother leaning over the sink and heard her quiet sobs. He put his arms around her.

"Momma, don't let them get to you."

She turned, clinging to her son. "My own sister's child, to say something like that in my home."

"They're Nazis. They're stupid. Please don't cry. It's my birthday and I don't want them to spoil it."

She straighten and wiped her tears, then patted his cheek as she often did. This time, however, he winced. "Oh, I'm sorry," she said, giving him a gentle kiss on his bruised face. She turned to the counter. "Here, put these bowls on the table."

During dinner all the gaiety, wit, and intellectual exchange vanished from the conversation. Few words were spoken, and the subject matter was kept "safe."

Hans had taken twice as much as he ate, and while the rest were still finishing, he sat smoking a cigarette and dropping the ashes onto the huge slice of beef left on his plate. He fingered his thin blond mustache and studied Bennett. Finally he asked, "Herr Sizemore, I understand you are here working for DISS. What is it you do for them? I mean, with so many Germans out of work, why would they import an American?"

Bennett smiled at Hans. "Well, since they came looking for me, I guess they figured an American was the best man for the job."

Hans returned a smile, just as phony as Bennett's had been. "Perhaps. However, perhaps one must also consider that while DISS appears to be German owned, it is the minority shareholder in an American capitalist firm. It might be that you shouldn't get too comfortable here. When Herr Hitler comes to power, things will change. We will have a Germany for Germans. We will put every man to work, get rid of the parasitic unions, hire real Germans, and banish all the international capitalists."

Georg pushed back in his chair. Katharina put a restraining hand on his arm, but he shook it off, stood and leaned over so he could address Hans nose to nose. "What you have said, Herr Bubenhofen, is correct. If Hitler comes to power, things will change. The Nazis will destroy everything, law, order, civilization, everything we value. They will be a more dreadful plague than we can imagine, an unparalleled terror. As soon as Hitler has power, he will first make war on his own people, on anyone who dares to challenge him. Then he will prepare for a new war, worse than the Great War, one that will leave our poor country totally smashed. But you know what, if that crushing defeat rids us of you hate-mongering Nazis, it will be a small price to pay. I may not be able to get rid of Hitler, but I can get rid of you. Leave my house, both of you. Now!"

Hans rose slowly and put his cigarette out in the beef. "It was not necessary to make an enemy of me, Herr Brehm, nor was it wise. Come Eva."

In total silence the two gathered up their coats and left.

There was an effort to retrieve as much joy as possible during the remainder of the evening. Uncle Willie cut the three layered cake he had baked and decorated, and Aunt Anna served it. Then Otto opened his gifts.

Bennett was almost apologetic when Otto opened the walnut burl pipe he had given him. "It doesn't hold a candle to your daddy's meerschaum, but it does come all the way from North Carolina, and I knew the old boy who made it."

Otto fingered the smooth bowl of mottled light and dark brown wood and the rough black bark ruff on the top edge.

"That pipe's well broke in. I could of gotten you a new one here, but I wanted you to have something from my home. I did go over to Herr Meylin's smoke shop and get you a new pipe stem to and a new holder to keep it in."

"It's beautiful, and very special because it was yours. Thank you."

Soon after Otto opened his gifts, Georg's attorney, Walter, arrived with briefcase in hand. It was obvious he was there for more than a piece of cake, so Bennett took his leave with sincere gratitude for his being included in the family celebration.

Otto

38

Otto said goodnight to Bennett, Aunt Anna, and Uncle Willie then started to help his mother and grandmother clear up the dinner dishes. His father stopped him. "Otto, would you join Walter and Grandfather and me in the study, please."

Otto was nervously wondering what Walter was doing here and was afraid it concerned the consequences of his behavior this morning. His parents had used the few contacts they still had to prevent him from being expelled and arrested, which would have been a life-altering catastrophe. He knew the incident could focus unwanted attention on them. Since his grandmother was from a well known Jewish family, that could result in disastrous consequences for his whole family.

In the study Georg offered everyone an after-dinner drink and tobacco for their pipes. Otto was delighted to fill his new pipe and, for the first time, be included with the men for this traditional after-dinner session. He dreaded the discussion, however, and watched his father and Walter for some indication of the topic.

With pipes lit and drinks sipped, Georg began. "I'm sorry, Otto, that we had to have such an unpleasant intrusion into your birthday dinner."

"Father, I've had a wonderful evening. They didn't—"

His father held up his hand. "I know, I know. But all in all, it's been a dismal day for you, and I'm afraid I have more unpleasantness to discuss with you.

"I've brought trouble on the family, haven't I?"

"No, Otto." He gave a slight laugh. "At least no more than I have by telling off Hans. Our family problems go far beyond that. What I am trying to say is that we, your grandfather and I, believe things are only going to get much worse from here on. The only chance we might have against the Nazis would be for all other factions in the country to join together to fight them, but that won't happen as far as I can see. The Nazi threat is obvious to me, and the inability to make other people see surpasses frustration. Even family. The break between your mother and her sister has broken her heart."

Otto looked down at his pipe, afraid his eyes might reveal his emotions, afraid he might not remain in control.

"But, the fact is, the Nazis are already in power in many important positions. Von Papen's seizure of power in Prussia shows us that no one will defend our democracy. It's now only a matter of time before Hitler becomes Chancellor."

In his heart Otto knew this, but it was still alarming to hear his father state it as fact.

Georg took a draw on his pipe and found it needed relighting. Grandpa Franklin said, "The terror has already started. In Berlin roving bands of storm troopers are vandalizing, beating, and murdering their opponents, especially Jews. My shops have not only been vandalized, but Storm Troopers stand at the entrance telling everyone not to shop there."

Georg took over again. "The question is, what shall we, our family, do for our own protection? Your grandfather and I have considered this for some time, and Walter has been good enough to work out the legal details for us."

Franklin said, "Otto, I have sold all three stores: Berlin, Munich, and Dusseldorf."

Otto sucked in a quick breath and started to say something, but his grandfather continued.

"I could only get about half of what they are worth, but if I wait until Hitler is in power, I will get less or nothing. The laws prevent me from taking my money out of the country except in small amounts and under strict conditions; so when Sara and I leave tomorrow for England, we leave with little."

"When you leave? Grandfather, certainly you're not going to leave Germany. Our family has been here for—"

"Otto, let him finish," said Georg.

"I have been fortunate enough to arrange for a sale of the best of my furniture and antiques to a British shop. It's a paper sale, which we slipped past the export laws with the help of a hefty bribe. The collection will be waiting for us when we get to London and will provide a start there.

"I was going to put my German assets in your father's name, but he and Walter have cautioned me against that. The Nazis are still fighting amongst themselves as to how much blood makes a Jew, but it looks like they are settling on one-fourth. Since Sara is a half Jew, that would make your father a fourth Jew. We can't be sure at this point whether you will be safe, but we think you will. Therefore we have asked Walter to have you declared legally of age at sixteen."

Otto sat silent, looking from his grandfather to his father.

"Your father and I have placed all of our family possessions, homes, bank accounts, everything, in your name. Georg will stay in Germany as long as it is safe and help manage things. You will immediately begin your higher education in finance and law and be tutored in the management of family affairs. I know it's a terrible burden to put on the shoulders of one so young, but it is our only chance. I know you will do well."

Then the old man raised his gray eyebrows and looked at Otto over the top of his reading glasses. "But, Otto, you can't beat the Nazis with your fists. I know I am the one who told you to join the Red Falcons, but now I'm telling you from here on out you must become very German, even when that makes you duplicitous. Drop the Red Falcons and don't join any other socialist group. Excel at your studies. Avoid politics. You are now the head and the hope of the family."

Diana

39

Sam knocked, then opened the door and looked in, saying, "Diana, you better wake up."

His voice was low and controlled, as if he didn't dare let the emotion inside him escape. Hearing his tone brought me out of bed and wide awake. I checked the digital alarm: 2:37 a.m. I searched his face for an explanation. His expression changed him subtly, and he became someone I had seen only once before. My gentle companion had reverted to the old Sam, the one who had run high-tech operations for U.S. military intelligence. This Sam was cold, hard, and dangerous.

"RJ and I are down in the cave. Join us as soon as you can dress." With no more explanation, he withdrew and shut the door.

I threw on some jeans and a sweatshirt, stuck my feet in my slippers, and ran through the house, down the path to the car barn. As the elevator door opened at cave level, I saw the two of them hunched over their respective desks. Robert James was using a computer, and Sam was on the phone. Even Yeabot was there, waiting patiently beside Sam. My gut was clenching. What had gone wrong?

Sam said into the phone, "Can you at least find out who issued the orders or who Hedgeman called? . . . I see. No, no, I understand. Any chance of finding out where they are taking him?"

As Sam listened, he looked up and acknowledged my presence with a nod. To the phone he said, "Okay, Jim, I understand. Thanks. I know you and the senator will do what you can." He turned his chair toward me, ran his fingers through his curly gray locks and looked up at my face. In a voice devoid of emotion he said, "Hedgeman and his agents were able to slip the charges at the airport with one phone call to the Justice Department. Who they called is unknown, but whoever it was had all the juice needed to send commands down the line and make heads roll with both airport security and local law enforcement. Hedgeman and his agents were back in Thomasville almost as soon as we were able to return to the house.

"The SICC boys saw the signs of investigation at Otto's building and went to see Sheriff Tumey, who confirmed that an FBI agent had come to process the crime scene. Hedgeman flew into a rage, and within an hour Jim was being pressured to turn the evidence over to the Justice Department. He's got it buried and is stalling but doesn't know if the Bureau will be able to hang onto it."

With a sinking feeling I remembered Robert James's warning: "There's law and there's power . . ."

"Next Hedgeman and his goons went to Ned and Emma's house." Sam paused a moment, put his head back and turned it, popping his neck with several loud cracking noises. When he continued, he used the same dispassionate tone, but he spoke in a lower volume as if even he didn't want to hear what he had to say.

"From what Emma was able to tell Sheriff Tumey, Hedgeman questioned Ned about the crime scene investigator, then more broadly about Otto and his management of Bennett's affairs."

When Sam paused this time, even he was not able to hide the anguish in his eyes. I pulled a chair up next to his desk because I knew I would need to be seated to hear the rest.

"When Hedgeman felt he was not getting full cooperation . . ." Sam's voice failed, and he had to clear his throat to be able to continue. "He had his goons beat Ned almost senseless and use some crude ad hoc tortures. When that didn't work, they started on Emma. Emma's screams alerted neighbors who called the sheriff.

"Sheriff Tumey arrived alone and tried to arrest them. I guess it was three to one. Hedgeman arrested Sheriff Tumey and sent one of his men back to lock the sheriff in his own jail. Hedgeman and his other agent took Ned with them, leaving Emma lying on the floor, semiconscious. Emma managed to call the sheriff's deputy and tell him what had happened. They got an ambulance out to Emma, and she's in the hospital over at Johnson City. The deputy set up a reception party at the jail for Hedgeman's agent. They freed the sheriff, but the agent managed to escape."

Sam shrugged, not knowing what else to say. We both looked at Robert James, who was working at the computer. He felt our stare and turned toward us.

Robert James was professorial and matter of fact, attacking the problem as if we were trying to solve an algebra equation. There was no hint of "I told you so" in his voice.

"Our first problem in finding and obtaining Ned's release is that he has evidently been taken by an agency which has considerable power but is unknown and unaccountable because they are working under a cover of national security. With statutes of the Patriot Act voiding constitutional guarantees of due process of law, trying to rescue him through any legal action by us quite useless."

He looked directly at me. "Our other problem is that while Ned knows nothing about Bennett's operations or financial matters, he does know about the cave. If they get that out of him, it will be necessary to destroy everything in the house and the cave. Of course, Bennett has . . . had planned on that for a very long time, and it can be accomplished quickly."

I thought about the explosive charges waiting and ready in the tunnel and realized the rest of this place must be rigged also.

"The third problem is how to find Ned. Since they didn't get the information out of him through methods at hand, they will be heading for someplace where they will have more options—and less legal scrutiny. I've learned that a small military plane will set down at the airstrip just outside Thomasville at 2:46 tomorrow afternoon. I'm sure that's how they intend to get him out of here. They might be heading for a military brig or an INS holding facility or maybe taking him out of the country."

"But they can't do that. It's not legal."

He slammed his fist down on the desk. "Damn it, Diana, will you please grow up? Face reality! Since Nine-Eleven, well over a thousand people have been seized under the Patriot Act. We don't know the real total because the government began getting so much criticism that they simply quit reporting the numbers. These 'detainees' are neither charged nor released; they have no right to an attorney nor even the right to let their families know what happened to them. They haven't been to a court. Forget habeas corpus. They are just locked away."

"But Ned's not a terrorist. He's not even Arab or an immigrant. He was born and raised in America. He's done nothing wrong or illegal."

"God, Diana! Don't you understand even the basics here? *The legal precedent has been set.* Once you have created and used a bad law against a supposed 'bad guy,' once you have deprived anyone of his basic constitutional rights, the precedent is set. You can then use that bad law against everyone. And what you'd better come to realize, Diana, is that you are in grave danger of it being used against you."

Bennett

40

*By naming Hitler as Reichschancellor, you have delivered up our holy Fatherland
to one of the greatest demagogues of all time. I solemnly prophesy to you that this
accursed man will plunge our Reich into the abyss and bring our nation into
inconceivable misery. Because of what you have done, coming generations will
curse you in your grave.*
—General Erich Ludendorff, February 1, 1933

Bennett paid off the taxi driver and stepped out of the car. He would have
to get to the hotel on foot. He mentally cursed Don Janeway's choice of hotels and
his timing. Why did he have to come to Berlin this week? But he realized that was
unreasonable. No one could have foreseen this.

In August President Paul von Hindenburg had said he would never appoint
Hitler as Chancellor. Then this morning the news had hit. At 11:15 a.m. Hindenburg
had administered the oath of office, and Hitler was sworn in as Reichschancellor.
Why? Nazi popularity had dropped rapidly since the Potempa murder.

On August tenth, nine SA men had broken into the home of Konrad
Pietrzuch, a Communist mine worker in Potempa. They had bludgeoned his brother;
then, in front of his mother, had kicked and stomped Konrad for half an hour until
he died. In past incidents of Nazi brutality and murder, there had always been
charges and countercharges to confuse the issue, but in this case the evidence was
clear. It was a vicious, brutal murder for nothing more than political ideology.
Justice had been swift, and a court rapidly condemned five of the nine to death.
When Hitler sent the condemned men a telegram with his congratulations, support,
and encouragement, the nation responded in horror. The next election revealed their
disapproval in a dramatic drop in Nazi votes. That, thought Bennett, would be the
beginning of the end for Mr. Hitler.

The pandemonium in the streets of Berlin made clear how wrong he had

been. The Nazis' response to Hitler's appointment that afternoon had stunned
Bennett. There was a passionate upheaval, the "*sturm und drang*," as the paper
termed it. The pent-up storm was breaking, the force of the throng unleashed. And
Janeway's expensive suite was of course at the center of the storm. He was staying
at the Kaiserhof on Wilhelmplaz, the hotel where Hitler used the entire top floor as
his headquarters. Nearby was the Reichschancellory, where Hitler and Hindenburg
would appear to review the troops in a torchlight parade that night.

Bennett saw the *sturm und drang* before he even got back to the city. In
every town the train rumbled through he saw the celebration preparations, and in his
train compartment two school-aged boys enthused for miles, until Bennett wanted to
yell at them to shut up.

In Berlin the street was solid humanity, auto traffic was at a standstill and
even walking became a contact sport. Those who were Nazis rushed to join the
throng; those who weren't hurried off the street to a place of safety.

When he finally fought his way through the crowd to his hotel, Bennett
was greeted by the doorman with "Heil Hitler!" The doorman was an almost poster-
perfect Aryan, in his early twenties, blond, blue eyed, strong cheek bones, and the
teeth—why did they all seem to have such large teeth? He wore the swastika
armband over his uniform and had the same manner about him as one of Hitler's
praetorian guards.

When Bennett failed to return the greeting, the doorman straight-armed him
and told him no one was admitted to the Kaiserhof without a "Heil Hitler." There
was no way in hell Bennett was going to speak those words. His temper was already
at a low boil and he seriously considered grabbing the doorman's arm and doing his
dead-level best to yank it out of the socket. But he was angry, not suicidal. This
crowd would pound him into the pavement. He forced a smile and reached inside
his coat for his wallet. Flashing his Dehomeg credentials and a North Carolina
driver's license, he mimicked American tourists he had seen. He spoke in English,
very slowly and very loudly, as if that would make his words understandable even to
this idiot who couldn't speak English.

"I am sorry. I do not speak German. I am meeting someone here on
business."

The doorman took his wallet and examined the license.

Bennett continued, "See, I American. No speak German."

Not only did the doorman understand English, he also understood the implications of Bennett's tone and pidgin English. He glared angrily at Bennett, but he handed back the wallet and opened the door to admit him.

After a bellboy escorted him to Janeway's two-bedroom suite and let him in, Bennett literally dropped his briefcase on the floor and, without even removing his coat, went right to the luxury suite's well-stocked bar. He poured himself half a glass of whiskey and collapsed into an overstuffed chair. As he did, the newspapers inside his coat pocket crushed into his ribs. He pulled out the treasures. English and American papers or uncensored German papers were becoming harder and harder to find. These he had bought at a little newsstand near his own hotel, where he was known. Only the Nazi *Völkischer Beobachter* was kept in plain sight. The vendor kept other papers hidden below the counter and sold them only to customers he knew personally.

Bennett took three gulps of whiskey without taking a breath, downing half the dark amber liquid. Then he sighed deeply and opened the papers to try to understand how this had happened. How had old man Hindenburg been coerced or convinced to appoint Hitler as Chancellor? Hitler was obviously a demagogue. He wasn't even born a German, but an Austrian. He had been a failure as a student and as an artist, was a down-and-out tramp in Vienna, a derelict of the Great War. He had been convicted as a violent revolutionary and had served time for his beer hall putsch. Now he was Chancellor of Germany.

Bennett was already certain the weasel von Papen would be involved, and papers hinted at backroom political conspiracies. Von Papen didn't have the power to organize a government without the Nazis and had been trying to forge a union between the right wing and the Nazis that would allow him to maintain power. He had even offered to share power with Hitler, each of them being a Co-Chancellor, but Hitler had turned him down cold.

Hitler in power! Did von Papen really believe he could control Hitler? If he did he was an even greater fool than his miserable record indicated.

A knock at the door interrupted his reading. "Who is it?"

"Room service."

Bennett hesitated then grimaced, walked over and opened the door. He was again greeted with a Roman salute and a loud "Heil Hitler."

The waiter paused, expecting a response. Bennett was fed up enough to give him one. He drew himself erect, pulled a snappy American army salute, and answered in English, "All hail Franklin Delano Roosevelt."

The waiter looked nonplused. Bennett changed the subject. "I didn't order room service."

"Herr Janeway did. He called and said to have dinner here by six p.m."

Janeway was behind the waiter, and he'd watched the exchange from the hall. He walked into the room, giving a casual "Heil Hitler" to the waiter and telling him to set out the food. As the waiter set the table, Janeway spoke quietly to Bennett. "We are in their country, old man. When in Rome, you know."

Bennett said nothing and sat back down with his newspaper. The whiskey bottle and Bennett's glass were in plain sight. In his months in Germany he had become so accustomed to the freedom of having a drink that he never even thought about Janeway. "Oh well," he thought as he raised his glass, "at least when I'm fired they'll have to ship me out of the hell hole." He downed the last of his drink.

After the waiter left, Janeway took a long hard look at Bennett's glass. Then he walked to the bar, poured himself a small shot, and brought the bottle over to pour Bennett another.

Bennett's eyes widened as he stared up at his ISS boss. Janeway smiled and shrugged. "When in Rome and all that." They drank in silence, then Janeway suggested they eat dinner before it got cold. To Bennett's further astonishment, dinner included a chilled bottle of French wine, which Janeway poured for them.

"I thank you for meeting me tonight. Didn't know it would be quite such a momentous occasion or would take such effort to get here. Speaking of which, it's getting pretty ugly out there. I think you had better spend the night in the extra bedroom in my suite."

"Thanks, but I can make it back to my hotel after the crowd dies down."

"I don't believe this crowd will die down. The later it gets, the drunker and nastier it will get. And for someone who chokes on the words 'Heil Hitler,' it will not be a good night to be out in the street. You will stay here."

It was an order. Bennett shrugged. In the silence that followed he tried to think of some appropriate small talk but ended up opening the conversation with the question that dominated his thoughts. "How do you suppose they forced old Hindenburg to appoint Hitler chancellor?"

"Obvious, don't you think?"

"How so?"

Janeway waved toward the masses filling the street below their hotel window. "Why, man, the Germans love this guy. Look at this. With the majority of the people behind him, there wasn't much of anything else the old boy could have done, was there? They'd have had a revolution on their hands."

"But no, the Nazis *aren't* a majority. The highest percentage vote they ever got was a little over 37 percent. Last election they were down to 33 percent. They're dropping like a—"

"Step to that window and tell me the Germans don't love him. There is a sea of humanity out there worshiping at his feet. And Bennett, he is now in power and must be reckoned with. Frankly, we like some of his ideas and we think he is going to be very good for us, businesswise. So get a grip on it. Leave whatever personal political qualms you have right here in this room. Don't antagonize these guys. A sense of humor is not one of their virtues."

That laid it out clearly. Hitler was good for business. As casually as possible, Bennett asked, "How is business back home? You think Roosevelt will get things moving too?"

Janeway paused, a fork full of food halfway to his mouth. He shook his head. "Don't even think it, Sizemore. You are our man in Germany, trained in the latest technology and fluent in German. And by the way, you are quite the *wunderkind.* Every place you have worked has the highest praise for your technical expertise. We need you, right here, not back in the States. Look, things are really going to be popping here and very soon. Now this is highly confidential, doesn't leave this room."

Janeway leaned in close. "We are bidding to do the new Prussian census. We're pulling out all the stops to get this contract. There are 41 million Prussians, and the Nazis want them counted and indexed, and they want fast answers. Past census data has taken three to five years of hand sorting. They want detailed results of this one in four months. The Prussian government couldn't begin to do that. But we can. A DISS man, Alfred Kordt, is going to be negotiating the contract. You met him. He was one of the Germans who had been training in New York and took the boat back with us. You remember?"

Bennett recalled Alfred, the one who didn't know Bennett spoke German, who made fun of Janeway. "Yes, I remember him."

"You are to provide any and every kind of assistance he might need. That is the main thing I wanted to talk with you about this trip. This is your top priority from now on. You're going to get rich on this one, son."

Bennett gave him the required smile and nod. As Janeway talked on, Bennett was only half listening. Part of his mind toyed with a mental picture of a bullfrog happily snoozing in a pan of water while the fire gradually brought the pot to a boil.

When they finished eating, Bennett took his chair to the small balcony overlooking the marchers on the street. They had begun about dusk, tens of thousands, in disciplined columns that formed somewhere in the Tiergarten, prepared to march under the triumphal arch of the Brandenburg Gate and down the Wilhelmstrasse. Interspersed among the troops were dozens of bands and fife and drum corps, which provided traditional military marches and kept the jackboots in time with the thunderous beating of the drums.

Crowds packed the sidewalks. Joyous Nazis sang "Deutschland über Alles" and the "Horst Wessel Song." Torches they carried lit the night, creating a river of flame that glowed down the street. Soon they would march past the reviewing windows where Hitler and Von Hindenburg would be standing. The whole scene—sight, sound, and fury—was intoxicating and terrifying.

How did they all get here so quickly? There was no prior announcement to allow time for organization and travel. With that thought Bennett put his finger on something that had been troubling him for the past year. The Nazis didn't just happen. Their demonstrations were never the spontaneous events they appeared to be. How did they do it? What was the secret order and discipline behind this movement that gave it success? He knew that there were no more than fifty Nazi organizers in Kasselbronn; yet, just as Janeway had observed about the crowd in the streets, they were so active and so effective that they made it appear the majority of people were Nazis. That was brilliant organization and propaganda.

From what Bennett had read, Hindenburg was an honorable old gentleman who had not wanted the presidency. He was a monarchist and had no love for the democracy. He wished only to retire comfortably on his Neudeck family estate. He had taken this job because others had told him he was the only man so loved by the people that he could hold his beloved Germany together. He had sacrificed his final years out of an absolute loyalty and duty to the Fatherland. He hated Hitler. He understood his nature. How did they force him to appoint that man?

Paul von Hindenburg

41

Behind a lighted window, beyond public view, Paul von Hindenburg sat alone in his room trying to remember exactly what it was he came there to do. The door opened and he started at the sudden sound. He was much more easily startled these days. A stranger entered the room and came over to him, too close, too familiar. Hindenburg pulled back, apprehensive of the stranger's approach.

"Herr President, it is only I, Heinrich Brüning. Brüning. I was your Reichschancellor last year. Please, don't be alarmed. I just wanted—"

The door opened again and Oskar von Hindenburg entered. "Here, Herr Brüning, what are you doing disturbing my father? You are not to be here."

"I didn't mean to disturb him. I just wanted to wish him well tonight, but I see it is not one of his good days. He doesn't seem to recognize me."

"Nonsense! You've just said something to upset him. Please leave."

Brüning left and Oskar sat with his father until it was time to review the troops. Every few minutes Paul would ask Oskar, "What is it we are doing here?"

With increasing impatience Oskar would give him the same answer he had just supplied a few moments before. "We are going to review the troops who are marching in honor of your appointment of Herr Hitler as Reichschancellor."

"Oh, oh, yes. That's right," his father would say.

When Hitler occupied one window in the Reichschancellory, Oskar led Hindenburg to his window, where the old soldier stood with dignity.

Hitler, constantly giving the Nazi salute, seemed almost unable to contain his excitement and joy. The Nazis below in the street, delirious with celebration, watched, cheered, and sang as the Storm Troopers paraded by.

Seeing the thousands of brown-shirted, goose-stepping Nazis pass in review, Paul von Hindenburg turned to his son in confusion and said, "I didn't realize we had captured so many Russian prisoners."

Diana

42

Robert James turned from me and spoke directly to Sam as if I wasn't there. "I've checked motel and hotel registrations and not been able to locate where they are holding Ned; so the only time we know they'll appear is just before boarding the military plane. Stopping them must be your job, Sam. I must stay here to detonate Bennett's failsafe devices . . . should that become necessary."

In the silence that followed I asked, "What about the car?"

"What car?" Sam asked.

"Robert James tagged Hedgeman's car so we could monitor their progress to the airport yesterday. Why can't we find them with that?"

Robert James slapped his head with his hand. "The car! Lord, I am getting old." He headed across the cave to a table where yesterday's equipment had been dropped and forgotten. Bringing a device over to the computer, he plugged in, and in a less than a minute a little blinking light revealed the GPS location of Hedgeman's car. A quick cross-reference with the Thomasville map gave us an address, and a reverse directory gave us the name of the Fox Motel and Restaurant.

"Got them," said Sam.

Again Robert James spoke to Sam as if I didn't exist. "You and I know the minimum-risk option . . . but we don't have that authority here, that . . . clarity. The decision must be yours. If you try the high-risk option, you could have a reception committee of more than the three we know about."

He rose stiffly and as he picked up a few belongings from around the cave I looked to Sam for a translation. "What's the high-risk option?"

"Attempt to rescue Ned."

"And the minimum-risk option?"

I could see the debate in his eyes. Should he remain my kind friend or give me the truth? The hard, dangerous Sam prevailed. "Prevent Ned talking. Most often a sniper rifle from a discreet but effective distance."

With that incredible statement, Sam turned to walk Robert James to the elevator.

The words welled up from somewhere down around my toes, and propelled by all the emotion I had been feeling for the last hour, erupted in a bellow that surprised even me.

"Sam! Robert James! You two get back here, right now!"

With startled expressions both men turned and, somewhat to my surprise, obediently returned and stood in front of me like chastised schoolboys.

"Okay, I have listened to you, and I got the message. We don't have a snowball's chance in hell of retrieving Ned *legally*. We can't go to the authorities because some of them are the bad guys. People with a Nazi mentality are on my trail and if I don't watch out I could become one of the disappeared ones. It's a hell of a problem. Now you're going to listen to me because there's something you two don't get. You don't see what the real problem is. To paraphrase Peachy, the problem is how to divide one Ned from three bad guys and have one Diana Hunter left over."

Robert James turned to Sam and asked, "Who's Peachy?"

Sam shrugged.

"Aaargh." My anguished yell took the place of words which were insufficient to express my exasperation. "It's a movie reference, Peachy—Michael Caine—*The Man Who Would Be King*. It doesn't matter! It doesn't matter! What matters is they don't want Ned. They don't even want me. What they want is whatever the hell Bennett had. You get it? What did they think would be in my uncle's will? What is it they are trying to pull out of his grave?"

Sam and Robert James thought that one out, exchanged looks of enlightenment, and Robert James had the nerve to say, "You know, I think we're onto something here."

Now I am not one who normally bristles at male chauvinism, because frankly, I've always felt pretty capable of doing just about whatever I wanted to do and have not found it a handicap to be a woman. This, however, was too much. "Oh, *we're* onto something, are *we*? A minute ago *we* were going to go running off, blowing up Bennett's fifty-year collection of Hunter hooch and Hitler memorabilia, and shooting Ned in the head!"

They looked at each other. They looked at me, and Robert James began, "You, uh, you are quite right, Diana. I do apologize for my, uh, my . . ."

For some reason all this struck Sam as funny and a stifled laugh escaped him. Robert James was first startled, and looked sideways at Sam. Then a smile appeared on his face. As he tried to finish his lame apology, the two of them broke down in uncontrollable laugher.

"Would you tell me please what you can find to laugh at?" But it was contagious and cathartic. I too began to laugh.

I walked to the nearest liquor cabinet, pulled out a dusty bottle of aged Hunter whiskey, collected coffee mugs from the desks, and poured us each a substantial shot.

"Okay, fellas. Let's work it out. Let's figure out what they want and how we can use its lure to retrieve what they got. Time for action, Robert James. No arguments, no delays. We need the Hedgeman dossier now."

"Yes, of course." He sat at his computer and began punching keys.

"Yeabot, please read the files Robert James has accessed and search for associated files."

Almost immediately the printer spit out one cross-referenced page. Reading it, I found no mention of Hedgeman, only a cryptic note. I read it aloud.

"I found DPMO NRZPOY, but the bastard beat me by dying in nineteen seventy-seven. If there is any justice he'll burn in Hell, but it looks like he did just fine here in the U.S. However, his son and grandson are alive, active, and dangerous. Them, I'll destroy."

Sam studied the printout. "That note raises more questions than answers."

"Look at the date on it," I said. "It looks as if Bennett had been working on it just days before he died. Perhaps it wasn't just Bennett's death that activated Hedgeman and his unknown masters. Bennett may have fomented this attack with actions of his own. Robert James, do you know who DPMO NRZPOY is?"

He looked up but didn't meet my eyes. "So Bennett finally found him, did he? Strange, such a momentous event and he didn't confide it to me." He gazed across the cave. Then continued, still looking away at nothing in particular.

"DPMO NRZPOY was someone from Bennett's days of espionage. He never told me who, and at times I wondered if he was a real individual or a sort of

Moriarty phantom born of everything evil Bennett had witnessed among the Nazis in Germany. No matter what else he was working on, any time he got the mildest whiff of this DPMO NRZPOY, he would drop everything to go chase him. When he was working on that case, he would become morose and even more secretive than normal."

Sam said, "Yeabot, adjust your search. Search for any file on DPMO NRZPOY."

"You won't find any. I've tried."

Yeabot whirred and clicked as he searched. "File not found."

"Any suggestions, RJ?"

"There's just too small a piece of it to decode. The most common letter in English is *E;* the second most common is *T.* There are two letters used twice in that name, *O* and *P.* If he used a simple substitution code with monoalphabetic encoding, those should stand for *E* and *T.* I have tried every permutation I can think of but found nothing. He either encrypted the whole thing in a much more complex computer-aided code or he hid it someplace else."

"Like where?"

He shrugged. "He always had stuff squirreled away in places all around the world where he felt they would be safe."

"Safer than this cave?"

Again he shrugged. "I never fully understood how his mind worked. All I can tell you is what his methods were. If he had been working on this DPMO NRZPOY in say Bogota, he might very well have left documents hidden there rather than smuggle them back to the cave. For instance, he once sent me off to Cairo to meet with a fellow who knew where there was a particularly damning bit of information on a high ranking politician here in the States."

"Is there any memo or file to let us know what he had where?"

"Not that I know of. I was without doubt his closest confidant, and even I was not trusted with such information."

"Sam, you said Yeabot was built to help me with the database. How can we use him to find this file?"

"He can do multiple searches in minutes that would take you a year to work out on paper, but he has to have something to go on. You would have to know what kind of code and what key was needed to begin his search. If we had lots of time to work at it, we could break it. We simply don't have time for all this. We need to retrieve Ned."

"Wait, There's got to be something here. So far we know Bennett was searching for someone from the war years. We know that just before he died he found him, learned he was dead, and learned he had a son and grandson active, probably here in the U.S. He was going after those descendants. We know the Hedgeman file was in some way connected to this search. We can even guess that Bennett might have done something that alerted the son or grandson and triggered—Robert James, do we know for sure how Bennett died?"

"What? Oh. Yes, of course. He was right here at home with me. It was his heart . . . There are, of course, drugs that could trigger a heart attack, but. . . . Oh dear. I never considered such a thing. He was ninety-six you know. He had been away for a few days . . . I didn't ask for an autopsy. I took him to the hospital and he died there. Heart attack. Doctor present. No autopsy done."

He was obviously so distressed by the suggestion that I wished I hadn't asked the question. It would have made no difference anyway, and it was an unnecessary burden to lay on Robert James.

"Let's consider something else. How about where or how he might have found this DPMO? Which computer did Bennett use?"

"That one that I logged you in on."

I sat down to search his Internet history, but found the system automatically wiped out its tracks each time you shut down..

Sam said, "Diana, we don't know for sure this is the file they're after, and we know where they are. Let's just work on a plan to grab Ned and worry about the file later."

"But if we dangle the file they want in front of them, they won't need Ned," I replied.

We all sat silent for a moment. Then I asked, "Sam, when I was making calls you warned me not to use my own cell phone. Do you think they have it bugged?"

"I . . . think it's highly likely."A brief look passed between them and I was absolutely positive they were keeping something from me. Whatever it was, it would have to wait.

"Could they tell where I am?"

"If they can triangulate your signal," said Sam. "What are you thinking?"

"We don't have time to decode the DPMO file, but if it's what they want, we don't have to. They already know what it is. If this is what they want, the mention of it could lure them away from Ned or at least divide them up and make rescue possible."

Sam looked worried. "I'm not crazy about you playing the role of rabbit, and . . ."

"With the three of us playing them, Hedgeman will end up being the rabbit, and we can follow him to find out who's behind this, maybe even to the DPMO son and grandson. At least that's my thought. Robert James, you were right about the disaster we unleashed last time. If you have reservations about this, please voice them. I'm ready to listen this time."

"They're not comic buffoons, Diana. If you're planning on getting them to chase you to the airport, they'll not fall for that one again."

"I know Robert James. I won't underestimate them again. Besides if we did name a distant place their boss would leave them with Ned and pull in a new team for me. This must be a local operation and it must be subtle."

He held me in his gaze for several seconds then said softly, "Perhaps I had better not underestimate you again either." Then he added, "Now that we all understand what these men are capable of, we can plan our actions accordingly. What do you have in mind?"

First they came for the communists, and I did not speak out—
because I was not a communist;
Then they came for the socialists, and I did not speak out—
because I was not a socialist;
Then they came for the trade unionists, and I did not speak out—
because I was not a trade unionist;
Then they came for the Jews, and I did not speak out—
because I was not a Jew;
Then they came for me—
and there was no one left to speak out.

Pastor Martin Niemöller
Protestant Evangelical Church, Germany

Bennett

43

First they came for the Communists.

The news stand near his Berlin hotel, where Bennett had bought
newspapers just two days ago, had disappeared. It had been one of those wooden
structures tacked onto the outer wall of a building like a lean-to and extended a short
way onto the broad sidewalk. The newsman had paid a small rent to the owner of
the drugstore within the building. This morning, nothing but a few wood chips
remained on the sidewalk. Bennett went into the drugstore.

"Good morning."

Fritz, the balding, round little pharmacist, looked up from the pharmacy
window, returned Bennett's greeting with just a nod, and continued counting pills.

"I was wondering what happened to the news stand out front."

"I know nothing. Do you want to buy something? If not, I am busy."

"But that news stand was attached to your store. There's nothing left but
wood chips. Certainly you must have some idea what happened to it."

The little man pointed to his new swastika armband and spoke loudly, as if
he wanted all the world to hear. "I am a German. This is a good German business. I
had no idea he was a Communist, that he carried those revolutionary publications."

The woman who usually waited on Bennett when he bought his cigarettes
and sundries came out from the back room. She looked to see who was there, went
over and spoke quietly to the old pharmacist, then turned her attention to Bennett.
"Good morning, Herr Sizemore. What can I help you with this morning?"

"A pack of cigarettes, please. My usual."

As she rang up the sale, she spoke quietly. "They came for him as soon as
he opened the news stand yesterday. Beat him until he was unconscious and his face
looked like raw meat, took the papers he carried under the counter and knocked
down the news stand. Then they came in here. They ransacked our store looking for

Communist material. Fortunately there was none. But it took me all the rest of the day to put the place back together. We'll be months making up the loss in breakage."

"That's terrible. Did you call the police?"

She gave him an incredulous look. "It *was* the police, Herr Sizemore. Poor old Fritz was dragged down to police headquarters and spent hours being questioned about the 'dangerous revolutionary newsman.' His back has welts where they whipped him. He had to join the NSDAP before they would release him."

Where do you turn when the thugs who attack you are the police? All Bennett could get out was "I see."

"Be careful, Herr Sizemore. Don't admit you ever bought papers there."

As Bennett continued his business rounds that week, he found that was the way things were all over Berlin and beyond. The terror started before Hitler had been in office forty-eight hours. Orders were issued to the police to confiscate all Communist newspapers and other publications. This became an excuse for breaking into homes, beating and arresting anyone suspected of being a Communist.

When the Prussian police forces weren't sufficiently brutal or deadly, Goering, who was Minister of the Interior for Prussia, issued orders that any officer not using a firearm would be punished. Still dissatisfied with the results, Goering created an auxiliary police force for the state of Prussia, fifty thousand of them. Forty thousand were the worst of the SA and SS ruffians, already seasoned by street fights and other "demonstrations." The other ten thousand were the same sort from the Stahlhelm.

They made no secret of their brutality and terrorism; in fact, they made every effort to broadcast and publicize it. Beatings, arrests, and inhumane behavior of all sorts were undertaken in loud attention-demanding actions. All was reported proudly in the *Völkischer Beobachter*. If everyone knew the consequences of disobedience, the population would be far easier to control. But Bennett thought he saw more to it than that. There was a provocation, a taunting, an active invitation for the Communists to begin the much-prophesied revolution. But no attempt at revolt was in evidence. Known Communists went underground or fled to Russia. Everyone else kept their heads down, hoping this plague would pass their house.

On February 6 it was announced that new Reichstag elections would be held on March 5, and the tremendously energetic machine of Nazi propaganda began all over again. By Bennett's count there had been eight or nine elections of various sorts this year. How could these people stand another one? Everywhere he traveled there were Nazi programs, parades, and pageants. Far from resting on the success of Hitler becoming Chancellor, they redoubled their efforts. It had all the appearance of a do-or-die effort. This time, that effort included denying the Communists the right to hold meetings, and using SA and SS rowdies to break up meetings of the SPD and the Catholic Center Party.

On February 27 Bennett was compelled to attend a lavish luncheon at the Kaiserhof Hotel, which was by now solid Nazi. Wilhelm Hartzman and other DISS officers were present as well as representatives of almost every major industry and financial institution in Germany. Even Janeway was in from Paris.

The purpose of the shindig was obvious. Hitler was requesting, no, demanding contributions to his election campaign. This was not the first of these types of dinners Bennett had attended, but it was certainly one of the most enthusiastic. This group of business leaders obviously felt their ship had come in, and they were ready to give Hitler anything he wanted.

The enthusiastic millionaires at the lunch reminded Bennett of the bit of country wisdom that Zeb had offered a year ago. "What some old millionaire does is always gonna bring about some bump in your road; so you best pay attention to what they's doing and why."

Hitler had obviously learned that same lesson, for he had lead the National Socialists away from working-class socialist views and replaced them with monied-class fascism. He had promised to destroy Communism, socialism, and unionism, and restore the Rhineland. His *wehrwirtschaft*, his promise to rearm the *Wehrmacht*, would pump profits into the defense economy. The word on the grapevine was that Hitler had already met with a few business leaders, such as Krupp von Bohlen, Bosch and von Schnitzler of IG Farben, and Voegler of United Steel Works, and had promised them this would be the last election for at least a hundred years. In short, he had promised an end to democracy.

Bennett, a small fry on the fringe of all this power, sat quietly at a table far in the back of the grand ballroom. At the table with Bennett were four men from munitions and armaments divisions of Krupp and IG Farben. They spoke only among themselves, mostly about the increased business their companies would receive for rearming Germany. The fifth man was a statistician from DISS by the name of Wilhelm Myer. Myer was a young collegiate *wunderkind*, who had displayed such genius in his field that he had been employed at a level and a salary much higher than most twenty-three-year-olds. He was quite full of himself, and with Bennett as his audience of one, he poured forth an endless monologue intended to educate this foreigner in the fine *German* science of statistics. Bennett's end of the conversation consisted of an occasional nod or a responding "umhum." Once in a while he ventured an, "Is that right?" When the program began and the official speeches took over from the mind-numbing statistics monologue, Bennett escaped into his own thoughts.

As the program was ending, one of Goering's policemen arrived with a copy of an official communique. It seemed that his police had that day raided the Karl-Liebknecht-Haus, the Communist headquarters in Berlin. Of course, it had long been abandoned because the leaders of the Communist Party of Germany, the KPD, had quietly disappeared. The police nevertheless found piles of abandoned propaganda. Goering's communique announced that the Communists were about to launch a revolution. This announcement was obviously intended to energize this group of right-wing Commie haters, but as Bennett listened to the conversation around the room, it became obvious that even these conservatives greeted the announcement with skepticism.

Wilhelm, however, responded as Goering intended and was stampeded into a new tirade on the evil of the Bolsheviks and the need to wipe them out to the very last man and cleanse the earth of their foul presence. His enthusiasm for this mayhem gushed forth in the bloodthirsty blather Bennett had heard from Nazis all over the country. As the young man waxed eloquent on the superiority of the Germans unfettered by the debilitating effects of bolshevism, Bennett reached the end of his patience and his tolerance. He thought about the poor old newspaperman, beaten and dragged away for the crime of selling an uncensored version of the news. Anger overwhelmed him and every fiber of his being screamed at him to respond.

Bennett's little inner voice told him it was a mistake, but at that moment he had no idea how great a mistake or how it would again alter the course of his life. He knew his boss had told him to keep his mouth shut. He knew that recently Germans who didn't keep their mouths shut tended to disappear. He understood that his American citizenship would not necessarily protect him from the same fate. He even knew that trying to reason with this young Nazi parrot was futile. Despite all that, there was just something deep-down American about the right to stand up and be counted. Freedom and principle made the foolish act of standing up irresistible. He interrupted Myer's diatribe.

"Doesn't it bother you just a little bit that your police, the people sworn to protect you and serve the law, have been using the methods of thugs, gangsters, and murderers?"

Myer quit speaking, mouth open. His eyes, magnified behind thick glasses, opened to wide round circles. Bennett waited for an answer.

When Myer finally found words, he sounded incredulous. "But they're Communists, traitors, sworn to overthrow the state, terrorists. They deserve whatever methods it takes."

Bennett waited for it. He knew what would come next. There it was, the *Deutscher blick*: the furtive rotation of the head and eyes, checking to see who is close by, who might have heard, who might report the forbidden conversation. Myer now turned pale. Next would be the swift denial, the save-your-own-ass statement.

"How dare you speak such treasonous words! You are an American, a foreigner, a guest in our country. You have no right to criticize German affairs." Then the young man poked Bennett in the chest and said, "You had better be much more careful of your words or someone might take you for a Communist spy. We shoot spies, you know."

Bennett was aware that the weapon manufacturers from Krupp and IG Farben had now ceased their own conversation and were listening,, but he didn't care. He poked Myer in the chest.

"Well, friend, just think about this. What if those police get tired of chasing commies and decide to use those same methods on statisticians? Hmm? If the police are above the law, who you got left to protect you from the police?"

Bennett

44

In a conference with the Fuhrer we lay down the line for the fight against the Red terror. For the moment we shall abstain from direct countermeasures. The bolshevik attempt at revolutions must first burst into flame. At the proper moment we shall strike.
—Goebbels' diary, January 31, 1932
"The burning of the Reichstag was to be the signal for a bloody insurrection and civil war. . . ." Prussian government announcements

Before the Kaiserhof luncheon was officially ended, Bennett's DISS superior, Gunter Epp, walked to his table, placed a hand on his shoulder, and whispered, "Come with me, Sizemore." He walked Bennett out to the street and turned to look up into his face. Epp was a short man of middle age and slight build. His face was normally placid and his thoughts focused on technical problems. At this moment, however, he looked furious.

"How can a man as smart as you be such a fool? Did you truly think you could make such comments, here, God forbid, in the middle of Nazi headquarters? Fool, fool, fool!"

Bennett considered playing dumb, but the situation was obviously beyond that. "Well, in America, we call—"

"Don't! Stop! Don't say another word. You are to go to your hotel. Do not come into the office tomorrow. Keep quiet. Talk to no one . . . and pray. You will be contacted when we have further instructions for you." With that, Epp turned and went back into the Kaiserhof.

Bennett stood on the sidewalk for a few moments, hands in his pockets, looking around him. Was he about to be arrested? There were SS and SA all around, but none seemed to be paying any attention to him. Then he spotted one he recognized. It was the doorman who had tried to make him say "Heil Hitler" on the day Hitler was made Chancellor.

His name was Karl Ernst. Bennett had met him more formally the following day in a humiliating experience. The memory was vivid. The day after he'd pretended he couldn't speak German, Ernst had caught him chatting with the hotel desk clerk in German. He had stopped and demanded Bennett's name, then had written it down in a small notebook he carried. In a loud voice he had said, "Well, Herr Sizemore, it seems the only two words of German you cannot speak are 'Heil Hitler.' If you are going to live here and profit off the sweat of good Germans, these are two words you had better learn. Let me help you. Repeat after me: 'Heil Hitler.'"

Ernst's voice carried throughout the large lobby. Every SA and SS officer in the place turned to see if his assistance was needed. There and then Bennett learned how helpless an individual was under the Third Reich. If he was to avoid arrest or worse, there was nothing he could do but answer, "Heil Hitler."

"What was that? I didn't quite hear you. Say again, louder."

"Heil Hitler."

"I think you are beginning to get it, but it is still not quite right. Try it with a salute and much louder."

"Heil Hitler."

Karl had definitely taken his pound of flesh that day. He had kept Bennett standing in the middle of the Kaiserhof shouting "Heil Hitler" for a full fifteen minutes, and let him go only after giving him dire warnings of what would happen if he failed to give the proper German greeting again. Bennett left the Kaiserhof knowing that if he had been a German rather than an American citizen, the pound levied might have been real flesh.

Ernst was a doorman no more. He now wore the uniform of an SA officer and commanded a squad of Storm Troopers. Well, Hitler's chancellorship hadn't harmed his career.

Bennett turned and flagged down the nearest taxi. He was in the middle of giving the driver directions when he noticed something strange. Ernst and his troopers were carrying large cans of gasoline and boxes of something from a military vehicle to a limousine. An odd means of transportation for gas.

"Tell you what, driver. I'm a tourist here and I'm not sure exactly what I want to see. How about we sit here for a few minutes while I think about it. That okay with you?"

The driver shrugged and answered in Polish-accented German. "You pay, I go or sit, whatever you want."

"You got a map of the city?"

"Of course." He handed Bennett a well-worn map.

Bennett studied the map, looking around the edge of it, watching Ernst and his boys finish the loading. Ernst pointed up the street, and his troopers headed off at a brisk run while he climbed into the limo. Bennett waited until the limo was a short distance down the street, then instructed the driver to go slowly so he could observe the fine German state buildings. When the limo stopped in front of Goering's Reichstag President's palace, the troops were already waiting to unload. Bennett figured he had solved the mystery. If Goering was getting supplies of fuel free from the Stahlhelm, it would look better if those supplies arrived by limo rather than being directly off-loaded from a military vehicle. He dismissed the incident and headed for his hotel.

On the way to his hotel Bennett began giving serious consideration to the idea of hopping out of this pan of hot water. Job or no job, maybe it was time to get the hell out of Germany and head home. Once the idea was born, it matured rapidly, and by the time the taxi dropped him off at his hotel, he had decided to do it immediately. As soon as he got to his room, he would call for the first flight to Paris or Lisbon. From there he could find some way to get home. He could arrange for his steamer trunk and extra suitcase to be shipped from Kasselbronn later.

That plan was scratched, however, the minute he entered his room. It had been searched and all of his belongings tossed in heaps around the room. He hadn't taken that long to return to his hotel. This must have been done by Gestapo already in place. He sat down on the bed for a moment and considered the ramifications of this search and his situation.

His thoughts focused, and he began frantically searching through the mess for his passport. It was missing, as well as a small stash of deutschmarks and his copy of *All Quiet on the Western Front*. None of his DISS paperwork had been disturbed. It had, in fact, been neatly stacked on the dresser. This included some notes he had made for his diary. When Hitler took power Bennett knew that many of the observations he made in his diary would be dangerous if discovered, so he stashed the diary in his mountain hideaway outside Kasselbronn, and wrote only coded notes in his business log. He dearly wished now that he had left his passport with the diary, but he had been afraid not to have it handy in case he needed it for identification.

He began carefully sorting his tossed belongings, but instead of putting them back in the closet and dresser, he threw some things in the trash and arranged the rest neatly in his suitcase. This methodical organization allowed him not only to prepare for leaving but also to keep his hands busy with mindless work and his mind busy analyzing his situation and alternatives. He had almost finished the reorganization when there was a loud knock at the door. The muscles of his gut constricted.

"Who is it?"

"Janeway."

With relief, Bennett opened the door. The look Janeway gave him as he entered made it clear that he had already heard about the luncheon comment.

"I want to get out of here and go back to the States. I don't give a damn about the job. I can't live with Hitler. But they've taken my passport. I need help to get it back."

"I warned you the last time we met to keep your mouth shut. What's the matter with you? You have a death wish?"

"No, I have a freedom wish, and I can't live under a tyrant. Now, can you help me leave or not?"

"Not, I'm afraid. At least not tonight, so you might as well quit packing. You're gestapo meat now, Sizemore. That removes it from ISS hands."

"Then drive me to a border area where I can slip out of Germany and get to an American embassy in France or Holland."

"Don't be a fool. I told you, it's a Gestapo matter. You go anywhere near a German border, you'll be killed. Your every move is being watched, every phone call, every visitor. I put myself at risk to even come here. And I'll tell you, if it wasn't for a request from Hartzman himself, I wouldn't be here."

Bennett sat down heavily on the bed with a sigh of resignation.

Janeway nodded. "That's more like it. You ready to listen now? Now don't be too alarmed. If they were ready to arrest you, it would have happened at the Kaiserhof. It's not hopeless, but your situation does need to be handled properly."

Bennett looked up, waiting to hear "properly" defined.

"You're a key person to something the Nazis want badly, namely the Prussian census. I had a talk with Alfred Kordt. Both he and Wilhelm Hartzman are deep into the Nazi movement, and they have excellent contacts. They know you're needed to get this job done. They're going to vouch for your future behavior and try to convince those in power that you're worth keeping . . . ah, in Germany."

Bennett knew that Janeway had almost said, "worth keeping alive," but he wasn't going to call him on it. It was clear where he stood and what the company would or would not do on his behalf. All he answered was "I see."

"Now here's what you need to do. Lay low, stay away from the Nazis and the Kaiserhof, and for God's sake, keep your mouth shut."

"Right."

As soon as Janeway left, Bennett found a phone number in his business log and picked up the phone. Then he remembered Janeway's words: "It's a Gestapo matter." He gently replaced the receiver.

Bennett

45

Bennett made his preparations and waited for night. He had dinner in the
hotel's small dining room, then beer in the bar. In the process he managed to
identify the two Nazis who were hanging around the hotel keeping tabs on him. One
was the little man had followed him off and on ever since that day he had decided to
move to Kasselbronn. The man wasn't a very good shadow, always easily spotted.
But then, maybe he didn't really care if Bennett saw him.

Around ten p.m. Bennett made his way from the bar to the men's room.
The hall to the restroom T-ed into a short hall to the kitchen. As Bennett reached
that hallway, he looked back toward the bar and lobby and verified that neither of
his shadows were in position to see him. They had simply noted his trip to the *die
toilette* and not followed.

Bennett slipped quickly down the hall and into the kitchen. He walked
through the kitchen to the back door without a word to anyone. As expected, no one
paid the least attention to him. In his years of playing hide and seek with Prohibition
enforcers, Bennett had learned that if you simply act like you know what you're
doing, most people believe you do.

Once outside he made his way down the narrow alley to the end of the
hotel building. Stepping onto the sidewalk at the side of the hotel, he strolled
casually to the shrubs growing directly below his third-story window. The dark blue
rucksack with his jacket tied to it lay undisturbed where he had dropped it earlier.
He lit a cigarette and waited until there was no one near to observe, then reached
over the shrubs and pulled up his rucksack. He untied the jacket and put it on, then
took a soft newsboy cap from one of the pockets and pulled it low over his face. He
shrugged into the shoulder straps of the rucksack, settled it comfortably on his back,
and took off at a brisk walk toward the American Embassy.

He had gone only a short way before he began to hear the alarm bells. He felt a momentary chill as he pictured the police chasing him, but dismissed that as nerves. These were fire engine bells and, from the sound, lots of them. There must be a major blaze somewhere. As he rounded the next corner, he saw where.

The Reichstag, the German Parliament building, was ablaze; flames and smoke funneled up through the great central glass dome while separate fires raged throughout the huge building. A crowd was gathering, while more fire engines were arriving, and a mixed collection of authorities tried to establish a police cordon to keep spectators safely back from the fire. He could see Goering at the entrance to the Reichstag, identifiable in his massive camel hair coat. Bennett spotted a few other Nazi officials, but not Hitler, Goebbels, or von Papen.

He listened to the crowd as police, reporters, and onlookers exchanged information. An eager policeman reported excitedly to a foreign reporter that Goering had already arrested one man and announced that the fire had been set by a gang of Communist terrorists. Another assured the reporter that the police were currently searching the building for other suspects.

From there, the rumors grew wilder. It was said that Communist members of the Reichstag had been in the building within the hour soaking rags with gasoline and distributing them all over, then setting them ablaze. Terrified citizens repeated the rumor that this was the signal for the Communists to begin the revolution and to murder Germans in their beds. Gangs of Communists were said to be, at that moment, attacking every public building in the city. Special police were being deputized and sent to guard the city from the murder and mayhem.

Bennett's mind raced. How much was rumor and how much was fact? Was there a Communist revolution in process? He had never seen any real indication that the Communists were either strong enough to foment a revolution or interested in doing so. The main thrust of the Communist actions had not been against the government or even against the Nazis, but against the Social Democrats, because the KPD and the SPD fought for the same votes, those of the working people. But he had to admit that the provocative actions of the Nazis in the last two or three weeks might have been enough to make the Communists realize that the Nazis were intent on wiping them out. Maybe they had decided to fight back.

As he listened to the growing panic of the people on the street, he suddenly became aware of a strong smell of gasoline. With the fire raging in the Reichstag and fear being kindled around him, the smell of gasoline was alarming. Looking around he realized he was standing at the entrance to Goering's Presidential palace across from the Reichstag. Was the palace to be one of the buildings attacked? Would it too be consumed by fire? Certainly not, for all around the steps to the palace was a large contingent of Storm Troopers.

Then with shock Bennett realized two things: One, the strong gasoline smell he detected was coming from the damp stains on the uniforms of the nearest SA men; and two, the leader of this squad was none other than Karl Ernst, the doorman cum Storm Trooper commander who had kept him shouting "Heil Hitler." It was the same Karl Ernst and the same troopers he had watched carry cans of gasoline and boxes of something from an army truck to a limousine and into Goering's palace.

The calculations and conclusions were instantaneous and incontrovertible. Karl Ernst and his merry band of Nazis were the real pyromaniacs who had set fire to the Reichstag. After Bennett saw them bringing the incendiary material into the palace earlier that day, they must have somehow gotten it into the Reichstag, probably through the underground tunnels after the building was closed for the day. If they had used Goering's Presidential palace, he of course had to know what they had done. If Goering knew, Hitler knew. Of course! What better tool could Hitler have? If he was putting down a terrorist insurrection, who in the land would stay his hand? This fire would mean an unhindered hunting license for all Communists.

"Oh, holy hell," muttered Bennett.

The shock of full realization showed clearly on his face. Unfortunately for Bennett, it was at that moment Karl chose to look his way. It was not a casual or accidental look. It was one of those sharp looks that people sometimes give in response to some unknown and unseen power. Bennett didn't understand it, but he knew that if he stared and concentrated on someone, it often made them look around quickly, and when they did, they often had a look of fear or anger as if they sensed danger. Whatever this inexplicable response was, Bennett knew it existed and had learned long ago to avoid such mental concentration on another person. This time his thoughts had been so concentrated on the sudden realization of the truth that he forgot caution.

Recognition showed on Karl's face, and he called out and started toward

Bennett. Not waiting around, Bennett pulled down his cap, hitched up his rucksack, and headed for a knot of people. He pushed and shoved his way through the crowd, trying to put people and distance between him and the Nazi, but he wasn't fast enough. A strong hand grabbed him by the upper arm and spun him around.

Pleased with himself, Karl had something that approximated a smile on his face. "Heil Hitler," he said in a taunting tone.

Bennett took a deep breath. As he did he breathed in gas fumes from Karl's uniform. He replied, "Heil Hitler." That seemed to please Karl, and Bennett felt a momentary hope that this was the only reason Karl had come after him.

"What are you doing here, American?"

Bennett shrugged. "Just trying to find out what's going on, like everybody else."

"Really? I think you will come with me and we will talk more about—"

At that moment two black Mercedes pulled up. Bennett and Karl had to move as the cars were allowed past the police cordon and drove up to the steps of the Reichstag. Hitler, wearing a trench coat and floppy black beret, jumped out of one of the cars and dashed up the steps two at a time, trailed by Goebbels and the bodyguard.

Bennett side-stepped away from Karl. Two of Karl's men came running up to give him some papers and tell him that the Fuhrer had arrived and that Goering had orders for them. When Karl turned to talk with them, Bennett slipped under the police rope, ran to the far side of the Reichstag and into the trees of the Tiergarten.

Bennett

47

At the gate to the American Embassy Bennett was told that the offices were closed and to come back later that morning. No amount of argument could persuade the Marine to let him in. Bennett considered taking a room at another hotel, but the clerk would ask him for his passport. Neither could he stay on the street. Berlin citizens had locked themselves in their homes while gangs of Nazis were out arresting and beating people, throwing them in large trucks, and hauling them off to God knows where. At every sound of a truck, Bennett hid in the shadows.

He returned to the dark of the Tiergarten, where he could hide among the trees and think. A childhood spent hunting in the North Carolina hills made this a natural sanctuary and one where Bennett's experience and skills gave him the advantage over jackbooted Nazis. At two in the morning, after sorting out his options, he went to the nearest public phone and dialed a number he had not wanted to call. The phone picked up on the third ring, but it was not the distinctive voice of the man who called himself Jordan. It was the sleepy voice of a woman.

"Yes."

"Let me speak to Jordan please."

"Who's calling?"

Bennett hesitated. He didn't know who was on the other end of the phone. "Tell him it's the friend with the amusing story about the ship, *Bremen*."

Almost immediately Jordan came to the phone. "Well, well, long time since I've heard from you. You have another amusing story for me?"

"Yeah, it's a real doozy." Both fatigue and annoyance registered in his voice. He would have to check that. His dislike of dealing with Jordan was showing.

"Does it involve another ravishing blond?"

Bennett's mind was going in too many directions at once, and he failed to understand the almost playful code Jordan was throwing at him. He hesitated.

"Like the last one, I mean," explained Jordan.

"Yes, only more . . . more . . . "

"Where are you?"

"A public phone outside a drugstore, at the edge of the Tiergarten."

"Good, go get a cup of coffee, same place we met last time." He hung up.

The Tiergarten was a huge park in the center of Berlin, rather like Central Park in New York, and the cafe was on the far side of it. No taxis were in sight. Bennett walked, keeping to the darkness of the park until he could emerge across from the cafe. By the time he got there, Jordan was standing in the shadow of the building, which was closed and dark. As Bennett approached, Jordan beckoned with a head motion and Bennett fell into step with him.

"So, what's up?"

Bennett looked around, the *Deutscher blick*. It's contagious, he thought. I've caught the German glance. But that furtive look around confirmed that with the late hour, police activity and February cold, no one was around to overhear him.

"I've got some information for you, but I want some help in return."

Jordan gave a noncommittal nod which Bennett accepted too trustingly.

"I was at a meeting today at the Kaiserhof, and I shot my mouth off about the police acting like thugs. Before I could get back to my hotel, the Gestapo had been through my room, and they got my passport. I need a duplicate passport and help to get out of the country."

"They searched your room and took your passport, but they didn't arrest you?"

Bennett shook his head. "Not yet. My boss at DISS is trying to convince them I'm indispensable to the Prussian census. But I really don't want to wait around to see what the decision is. I need you to help me get into the embassy before they arrest me.

Now it was Jordan's turn for the Deutscher blick. "Were you followed?"

"No, I was being watched at the hotel, but they were amateurs, and I got out without them even knowing I'd left."

"What's your information?"

"I know who burned down the Reichstag. It wasn't the Communists. It was the Nazis themselves." Bennett thought this would be earth-shattering news and waited expectantly for Jordan's amazed response. But the man's face took on that blank look people get when they are trying not to reveal their thoughts. He simply nodded again and waited for more.

"I even know the name of the storm trooper who lead the group that did it, and I know how they did it."

"Uh huh."

"Don't you get it? This is a put-up job. The goddamn Nazis are running all over the city beating and arresting and shooting people, claiming there is some Communist uprising, when actually they burned the fucking place down themselves. Don't you see what's happening?"

"Lower your voice. Let's not get too excited here. Now tell me, what is it you will be doing for this Prussian census that is so important to the Nazis?"

Bennett almost asked Jordan to repeat, but he had heard just fine. He simply couldn't believe Jordan had changed the topic from something so important to something so mundane. Bennett considered him for a long moment and realized that this man was going to be as unhelpful as Janeway had been. Slowly wrapping his mind around that fact, he decided to answer the question in order to see what this embassy spy's agenda was going to be.

"The Nazis want a census that would normally take three or four years to do to be finished in four months. The ISS machines are the only things in the world that could give the kind of detailed results they want in that time period. Programming those machines is a technology ISS hangs onto pretty tightly, so there aren't too many of us who can do the work."

"I see. So that would keep you working very closely with Hitler's government."

"No, I would be a peon working down in the trenches, and what's more, I have no intention of doing anything that would help Hitler's government. Don't you get it? He's a thug, and he's well on his way to being a bloody dictator. Doesn't our government care about that?"

Bennett saw a new look on Jordan's face. He didn't know the man well enough to interpret the look, but he did have enough sense of him to distrust him. Jordan stopped walking next to a Mercedes. He put one hand in his pants pocket and pulled out the car keys.

"Exactly. We understand precisely what kind of man Hitler is, and that's why we are working so hard at getting information on him. That information may someday be very valuable to America. That's why we need men like you and me keeping an eye on him."

It was very neat. Jordan had identified Bennett's motive and braided that motive into reins to ride this horse. But it wasn't going to work. Bennett was more mule than horse.

"Forget it. I'm not going to play spy for you guys. I gave you some information. Now you come through with your part of the deal. I want a replacement passport and help to get out of the country."

"Right." He unlocked the car. "Climb in."

Once in the car Jordan headed away from Embassy Row and got on a main boulevard headed south. "Where are you going? I thought you were going to take me to the embassy."

"No, that's no good. They're too busy and have no room. But don't worry, you're not in any danger of arrest unless you get accidentally caught up in the mass arrests tonight. I'm going to take you south of town to a train station the Gestapo won't be watching. Get on the train for Kasselbronn. Go home to that room you rent and lie low. DISS will get your passport back. You'll be fine."

Bennett had no reason to believe Jordan's reassurance, but there was little point in calling him on it. The bottom line was, Jordan would not help him get into the embassy. Getting out of Berlin sounded like the next best thing. There was something else that bothered him, however. "How do you know about my room in Kasselbronn? I never gave you my address."

Jordan looked over at him with a smile. "That's my job. Knowing things."

Diana

47

As Robert James and I set up our end, Sam loaded equipment into the van and we all headed for Thomasville. Sam parked and sat in the back of the van with a good view of the area around Fox Motel and Restaurant.

At 9:05 our earphones cracked to life as he reported in. "The motel and restaurant is an L-shaped complex and open to view from a street parking place. Hedgeman and the tall, thin agent came out of 103 and are over eating breakfast at the restaurant now. The short muscular guy come out of 104, bought two breakfasts at the restaurant, and carried them back to the room; so Ned must be in there and be at least well enough to eat. You ready to rock and roll?"

Once again I waited in the hot little red car just out of town. Robert James was in one of the sedans across the hills in Cranberry "Let's do it," I answered.

I dialed a throw-away cell number. Robert James answered in a very good North Carolina accent. "Who's callin'?"

I hesitated then answered, "It's me."

"You secure?"

"For the moment."

"Did ya get it?"

"Hell no! The place is nothing but ashes. SICC must have torched it. Maybe they found the file already."

"No, I know for a fact they're still looking. Try the law office."

"They tossed it before I even got here. Besides if I go back there I'm liable to be seen and caught."

"So they must have missed it. Look that DPMO file is worth two million to my client. Search the office!" He hung up and we all waited in silence to see if this call drew any reaction. We were baiting our line with guess and assumption.

Minutes passed in silence. At 10:16 I heard Sam's voice in my ear. "Okay, they're moving out. I never heard them receive a message on Hedgeman's cell. Must have gotten the call on the motel phone. I'll be a little busy on this end. Muscles is in with Ned. Leave the com on so we're in touch. Be careful."

Like sticking my tongue out, I roared past the motel headed for Otto's office.

"Oh yeah," said Sam, "they saw that." I listened to keys clicking as Sam dialed. The phone was answered by a woman's voice saying, "Office."

Sam let out a cry like a stomped cat and yelled into the phone. "Help! I fell! I'm in room 104 and I fell and I can't walk. I think my back's broke."

"Holy smoke!" said the woman. "I'll be right there."

"Uh oh! The motel owner is heading for the room. I better get over there and make sure she doesn't get hurt. Stay in your car. Back to you later."

Robert James dialed a number and said, "Jason, please bring the ambulance around to the motel, room 104. Pick up the injured man and take him to the Beaumont Private Hospital in Coreville."

Pulling up in the alley behind Otto's office, I knew I should stay put but there was something I had been wanting to do ever since I read about Otto's sixteenth birthday party. Jumping out of the car I ran around to the front entrance and up to Otto's office. What I wanted was still lying there where Hedgeman's goons had tossed it. Emptying a waste basket, I scooped up all the springs, wheels and broken wood of the once beautiful clock and deposited them in the basket.

Car doors slammed out front. Damn! They got here too soon. I looked frantically for the old meerschaum pipe. The front door banged open. Spotting the pipe, I tossed it into the basket and ran for the back door to the building. Footsteps pounded up the front stairs. I pulled on the back door. Locked. Damn! I tried turning the knob on the lock. Thankfully no key was needed. I went out to the landing and pulled the door shut just as they reached the second floor and headed for Otto's office. Robert James was yelling in my ear as I leaped over the door into the driver's seat of the red convertible. I shoved the waste can on the floor of the passenger's side, and hit the ignition.

"Diana, are you clear of the office? Answer me!"

"I'm clear, I'm clear and heading your way." I tromped the gas and squealed tires all the way down the alley. Hedgeman would be on me in a heartbeat.

Diana

49

As I raced out of town Sam reported in. "I've good news and bad. When that woman from the motel office walked into 104 looking for a fall victim she saw Ned beaten and bloody and started to scream. Muscles tried to shut her up but just made her scream louder. Good old boys ran to her rescue from the rooms and the restaurant, and Muscles had to take off on foot with a couple big fellows in hot pursuit. In the confusion, the ambulance team managed to spirit Ned away."

He paused as he checked the equipment in the van. "Diana, those guys are right on your heals. You better kick that car in gear."

"What do you think I'm doing?"

He was silent a moment. "Ok, now that you hit the highway you are pulling away from them."

"Now for the bad news. I am afraid the two breakfasts that Muscles bought must have been for him. Ned is unconscious, and the paramedics don't have much hope for him. The things that were done to this man . . . No one who could commit such acts can be said to be human."

"Diana, they're catching up again. What are you doing?"

"They have to see where I'm turning or this won't work."

I made a sharp right off the highway onto a narrow paved road and clicked on the car's navigation system. I had tried to memorize the route but since all the directions were in landmarks like "bent tree on the right" Robert James knew I would get lost. So he programed the route and the system guided my every turn with both verbal directions and visual map. It soon guided me off the paved road, and with Hedgeman skidding around every turn behind me, I wound my way up into the hills. After twenty minutes of ever-narrowing roads and tightly wound turns the nav system said, "Destination ahead. Slow down now."

As I slowed Hedgeman came roaring up on me and hit the breaks to keep from ramming me. As he slowed two pick-up trucks pulled out from behind some brush and across the one-lane road. One truck was between my car and Hedgeman's and the other was behind him. Hedgeman slammed on the brakes, skidded sideways and came to a stop inches from the pick-up. Jumping out of the car, he pulled his pistol. As he did men stepped out from behind every bush and tree, all armed with rifles and shotguns. All that could be heard in the quiet woods was the sound of multiple rounds being chambered. Whatever Hedgeman had planned to say, died on his lips. He dropped his pistol and put up his hands.

"Okay," said Robert James. "Get the hell out of there, Diana."

I quit gawking and hit the gas. "Wow! Robert James, how did you round up so many so fast?"

"It only took one word. 'Feds.' These old boys have been dealing with 'revenuers' for over two hundred years, since the Whiskey Rebellion."

"Will they . . . will they hurt them?"

"No, just legally detain them for trespassing and eventually turn them over to the local sheriff. They're not stupid."

Bennett

49

"We come to the Reichstag not as friends, not as neutrals, but as enemies. The National Socialists plan to use this arsenal of democracy to bring it down . . . we are committed to the legality of means, not of ends."

Paul Joseph Goebels

On the train south to Kasselbronn, Bennett dozed on and off and climbed off at his stop groggy and hungry. It was still dark, that quiet hour just before dawn. The station was empty and no taxis were around, so he began the cold walk home.

At first the only sound he heard was the crunch of his feet on the snowy shoulder of the road. Then he thought he heard another sound but wasn't sure. He stopped and listened: nothing. He walked on a few steps, more alert now. There it was again, a human sound, a moaning sound. He reached into his rucksack, pulled out a flashlight, and with the light walked toward the sound. It led him to a mound of railroad ties piled in a clearing to his right. There, lying against the ties, was what was left of a human, his bloody face swollen almost past recognition.

"Jesus Christ!"

The man at his feet was barely conscious but enough aware of Bennett's approach to raise his arm and beg, "No, no more. Please."

As he spoke, Bennett recognized Luther Gugler, the old conductor who had given him a private compartment the day he had taken the little Jewish girl to Berlin. Bennett stooped and said, "I'm not going to hurt you, friend. Can you walk?"

His answer came out with a sob. "No!"

"Okay, hang in there. I'll be back in a minute." Bennett walked to the rail yard, where he knew there were hand trucks used for loading cargo and baggage. He quickly found one, turned off the flashlight and returned pulling the flat-bottomed hand truck, which rumbled alarmingly in the quiet morning.

The poor man screamed when Bennett lifted him from the ground to the cart, but in a way that was a blessing because he passed out from the pain and would suffer less as Bennett towed him to town.

Bennett didn't like to hate. If someone pushed him past tolerance he simply wrote them off, and had nothing more to do with them. But as he thought about what the Nazis had done to Luther, what they were doing all across Germany, hate took over. Luther's crime had been that he refused to join the Nazi Party. That act of defiance had cost him his job and his pension after twenty-seven years with the railroad. Luther had protested his firing, but the union was helpless to do anything because all the hierarchy of the railroad had already been taken over by Nazis.

There was no hospital in Kasselbronn. There was a day clinic and several doctors, but none would be open at this hour. The only thing Bennett could think of was to take Luther home with him and nurse him there until he could find a doctor who would treat him. The cart rumbled and bumped over the cobblestones, and now and then a light went on in a house as the noise awakened the residents. No one, however, offered any assistance. They peeked from their windows, retreated, and turned off the light.

Bennett had his own entrance to his room on the side of Martin's house. He pulled the cart off the road, over the walkway, and up to the steps at his door. He opened the door, set his rucksack inside, and returned to carry Luther in. As he reached down to pick up the man, a light beamed in his eyes. Martin stood there with a flashlight in one hand and a club in the other. Bennett was relieved to see it was his landlord and not the Nazis.

"Martin, thank God. Give me a hand here, will you? This guy is really in bad shape."

Martin walked over without a word and shined the light on the victim. "Luther Gugler. You will not bring this man into my house."

"But . . . I don't have anyplace else to take him. There isn't a doctor's office or clinic open."

"He's a Communist. He won't come into my house. Get him out of here."

"The Nazis did this, Martin. They're doing the same thing all over the country. Are you afraid to help him? Is that it?"

"If the Communists had helped the SPD instead of fighting us, the Nazis wouldn't be in power. I won't have a Communist in my house. Get him out of here."

The sun had not yet appeared over the rim of the mountains, but the sky was becoming lighter. In that early predawn light, Bennett could see from Martin's face and that it was useless to argue. He bit back the angry words he wanted to say, turned and pulled the hand truck away toward the street. To his back Martin said, "Take him to the Jewish doctor down behind the Union Hall. He's the only one who will treat him."

The Union Hall was back out the gate and into the flat land where most of the workers' homes were. Bennett made the return trip, the cart bumping and Luther moaning because he was conscious again. More folks were awake now, but no one came out their door.

The doctor's office was a small room on the front of a family residence. It wasn't necessary for Bennett to awaken the doctor. He was already busy treating several other patients. Luther was in the worst shape, and the doctor with his wife's assistance took charge of him immediately. Bennett waited a while to get the word that Luther would live, and then walked slowly back to his room, climbed into bed, and slept until late afternoon.

He was awakened by a booming voice. Startled and disoriented he pulled on his robe, stepped into his slippers, and walked out to the front yard to find out what was going on. Loudspeakers were blasting the Nazis' radio message from the Market Square and at least two other locations on Main Street, one of them right in front of Martin's house. As he stood there groggy and confused, two Storm Troopers came running up to him.

Surveying his dress critically, one young man handed him a flyer. The other said, "I hope you aren't ill, sir, but even if you are, you will be able to hear the Fuhrer this evening and every evening until the election. His speech will be broadcast by radio so that every German in the country can hear his voice, and local group leader Kurt Schutz has placed speakers so that everyone can listen whether he has a radio or not."

"Oh, wonderful!" said Bennett, hoping the sarcasm wasn't too evident.

The enthusiastic young Storm Trooper beamed. "Yes, and I hope you will be well enough by tomorrow night to come to Remembrance Hall. We have the great honor of having Elisabeth Zander, national leader of the Nazi Women's

Auxiliary, to speak. Tell your wife to attend. Frau Zander will instruct our women to buy only German goods and to instill religion, morality, discipline, and love of the Fatherland in our children. It will be a wonderful speech."

He rattled a collection can, but Bennett indicated his empty robe pockets, and the troopers headed off down the street.

Bennett wandered back into the house. By the time he had showered, shaved, and walked to Zimmerman's bookstore, it was already four o'clock, and the late addition of the *Völkischer Beobachter* was in. Bennett picked it up and looked around for the other two papers. No other paper was in the store. Zimmerman had been watching, but when Bennett looked up and met his eyes, the bookman quickly looked away. Bennett had gotten fairly well acquainted with Zimmerman and had attended a few of the discussion groups held at his shop. He knew the man to be an intelligent idealist who would carry the other papers if he could. Bennett picked up an airmail letter form, paid for it and the *Beobachter,* and asked no questions.

Folding the paper and letter form and slipping them into his coat pocket, he headed to Anna's to get something to eat. She greeted him in the same matter-of-fact way she greeted everyone, but seated him at her special table, saying, "Otto will be here soon. You two can share this table."

Bennett was early for supper and late for lunch, and the place was empty; so he knew she had some reason to want him to sit with Otto. She served him coffee and bread without being asked and said his dinner would be a few minutes. Menus were not used at Anna's. She fed you what she and Willie had cooked that day. Bennett slathered a thick layer of creamery butter on the home-baked bread, took a huge bite and washed it down with hot coffee. He hadn't eaten since dinner the night before, and he was starved.

He pulled out the airmail letter and newspaper, laid the folded paper aside, and began writing to his Dad. He knew he had witnessed a secret so momentous, so monstrous, it could, and appeared it would, change history. And who could he tell? There was no way he could tell the police in Germany. The only newspaper now allowed was the Nazi paper, so there was no way he could go to the press. Neither his company nor his embassy seemed to give a damn. He had to tell someone. His letter to his Dad would have to suffice.

Otto arrived as Bennett was finishing his letter and beginning his second cup of coffee. Though he greeted Bennett warmly, it was immediately obvious that something was very wrong. The overall distress Bennett had felt for the last two days was suddenly focused on his young friend. "What's wrong, Otto? Is your family okay?"

Otto shrugged. "Yes, they are okay so far. I must leave soon however for the university."

"Don't you want to go? You seem . . . upset."

Otto looked at him for a moment and then around the café. They were still the only ones there. He said in almost a whisper, "I was forced to be a coward today and failed to support a close friend."

"Oh, I doubt that. What happened?"

"We were having lunch at school. My friend was at the next table and was talking far too loudly, saying he was sure the Nazis burned down the Reichstag themselves and just blamed it on the Communists." Otto sipped his coffee. "It is, of course, what many of us were thinking, but not a wise thing to say. I tried to signal a warning to him, but he kept it up until they came for him."

With moist eyes Otto confessed, "I did nothing! I just sat there and watched the SA drag him off. I didn't dare get into it because I have the responsibility of my family to think of now."

"That wasn't cowardliness, Otto. Nothing you could have done would have helped your friend. You couldn't have stopped the consequences he brought on himself. You could only have hurt yourself and your family. You used judgment and did your duty, and it was painful. That's as good a definition of bravery as I can think of."

"Is this what we are all coming to? Is this what life for us Germans is to be under the Nazis? Are we to become cowards for secret purposes, and betrayers for self-preservation?"

Bennett feared that Otto saw the future quite accurately, but he tried to find some way around that answer. With a wicked grin he said, "Now if you want to talk about cowardly acts, let me tell you about the little show I put on right smack dab in the middle of the lobby at the Kaiserhof." He then launched into a self-deprecating version of his humiliating fifteen minutes of yelling "Heil Hitler" in the lobby of the Kaiserhof. Telling the tale with humor and exaggeration, he accomplished his goal of getting Otto to laugh.

Anna served their dinner, then as she stood behind Otto she gave Bennett a nod and a warm smile. He noticed she had heaped their plates again. He hoped that making Otto laugh was all she wanted.

As they began to eat, Bennett said, "Your friend was right about the Reichstag. I know it. I even know who did it, how they did it, and who commanded them to do it."

Otto stopped eating. Even though he knew the cafe was empty, he looked around again to be sure no one could have heard what Bennett said.

"There doesn't seem to be a damn thing I can do about it," Bennett continued. "The only person I could think of to tell was this guy at the U.S. Embassy, because it's for damn certain that telling the German police would only get me dead. So last night I got hold of this guy and told him. You know what? He didn't give a damn. He put me on a train here and told me to keep my mouth shut."

Otto nodded and said nothing. There seemed to be nothing to say. As they ate, an old couple came in and sat at a small table in the front corner of the cafe.

"The only thing I could do to take out my frustration was write my dad a letter." Bennett patted the letter, which lay on the table with the newspaper. "At least that way I'll know that one person in this world will know the truth."

The boy grabbed the letter and shoved it into Bennett's pocket. With his eyes, he indicated the other diners. They seemed like a harmless old couple, but these day, one never knew.

Under his breath, Otto said, "I wouldn't mail that letter if I were you. Haven't you heard about Hitler's emergency decree? The post is no longer safe."

Otto picked up Bennett's newspaper, which was still lying folded on the table, and opened it up. Bennett looked at the huge headlines for the first time. He'd known it would be full of the Reichstag fire and the phony Communist uprising, but he was unprepared for the real story of the day.

Hitler and von Papen had gone to Hindenburg and gotten the old man to sign an emergency decree "for the Protection of the People and the State." With a sinking feeling, Bennett read that this decree suspended seven sections of the democratic constitution, wiping out all civil rights in Germany. There could now be no freedom of opinion or speech; no freedom of assembly and association; no right to privacy of postal, telegraphic, or telephonic communications; no need for legal warrants for the search of persons or their homes or businesses; no need for legal authority to confiscate property. In addition the decree authorized the Reich government to take over all the state governments when deemed necessary. It imposed the death sentence for a number of crimes, including "serious disturbances of the peace."

Bennett looked up at Otto, not daring to say a word, for the cafe was now beginning to fill up. He looked back down at the paper and read further details.

In one stroke, Hitler had wiped out constitutional freedoms, given himself dictatorial powers, and had done it all on the pretext of protecting the people from terrorism. How long had he been in power? Twenty-nine days. What weapons had he used to establish a dictatorship? Not a military coup. He used an alleged act of terrorism and a constitutionally legal emergency decree.

With a sick feeling in the pit of his stomach, Bennett realized that the Nazis had done just what they'd said they would do. Goebbels had always claimed they would use the instruments of democracy itself to bring down the republic.

When Bennett had first read Goebbels' words, he couldn't imagine that the Germans would allow this to happen. Certainly the leaders in the Reichstag or a judge or court, someone would do something. People would demonstrate in the streets or bring a complaint or suit. Raised in the United States, where his people cherished their democracy and civil rights, where generations had fought and died for freedom, he couldn't imagine that a free, democratic people could so easily surrender their freedom in the name of security from terrorism.

Diana

50

I slept in late and when I went down for coffee I found Sam and Robert James already up and looking grim. They let me get coffee then insisted I join them in the living room for a serious heart to heart. They spread the various newspaper stories out in front of me.

Sam explained, his voice as gentle as possible to soften the news. "I think we got our answer. The mention of the DPMO file definitely got someone's attention, someone very powerful. The stakes have just been raised. You have now been *publicly named* in connection with a terrorist investigation. We believe they had named you in an investigation that put you under the provisions of the Patriot Act before you ever left Bluff Beach. Now, however, every law enforcement agency, national security agency, as well as private security officers will be looking for you. The rules have changed."

I read the headlines but really wasn't up to reading more and sat for a long time trying to figure out what I could have done that would in any way implicate me with terrorism. They waited patiently for my response. Finally, shaking my head I said, "I can't think of a single case or contact that has in any way . . . what on earth did they cite as probable cause?"

"Under the Patriot Act, they don't need probable cause."

"But, but that's guaranteed by the Bill of Rights. Certainly the Patriot Act couldn't shred the legal rights our founders—"

In his instructional voice, Robert James interrupted. "All they need is the agent's say-so that a warrant involves an ongoing national security investigation. The courts and judges no longer have any discretion. They cannot demand evidence proving the allegation has any probable cause. The court must simply produce the requested warrant without reviewing any evidence."

Sam picked up there. "RJ and I have been digging into this ever since you and I talked to the postmaster. We have a few facts we have to lay on you. I'm sorry, but with these headlines, you have to understand what you're facing.

"Your usual expectation of privacy and civil rights are gone. Federal agents can enter with no warning and no warrant, search your home or business without specifying what they are looking for or why. They can seize anything they want without even telling you and without due process of law.

"The Patriot Act has overthrown laws against domestic spying. Everyone you have ever known can be under surveillance and investigation without probable cause and without a specific court order. Every phone number you call, every email you send can be intercepted, and the person receiving it can be added to the investigation without ever knowing it."

I interrupted him as I remembered something. "Is that why you told me not to call Richard at this salon? His lines might be bugged?"

Sam nodded and continued. "They can set up a trap on AOL or Earthlink and the ISP must simply *trust* the agent to take only information on bad guys. In case you decide to avoid using your own computer or phone, they can issue a roving warrant and can put traps on any place you use for communication, or any place they even think you *might* use, an Internet cafe, a library, or a university campus. People receiving such an 'assistance' demand not only can't object, they're forbidden to even disclose that it has been issued."

"That's why the postmaster couldn't tell us what happened to my mail."

"Right. Your mail was taken with a National Security Letter demanding obedience and silence. They can also demand your health records, your financial records, your school records, your library borrowing records; and again, no one can even tell that such a demand has been presented."

At first I was angry that Sam and Robert James had been "digging into this" since before I left Bluff Beach, and hadn't bothered to tell me. Considering the terror and hopelessness I felt at this moment, however, I decided they had been both wise and kind. Finally I asked, "I can't believe that Congress would shred the Bill of Rights. How did this happen?"

"That is a good question," said Robert James. "The short answer is they didn't know they had, because not one member of Congress had read the bill they passed."

"What?"

"The committee studying what to do after 9/11 wrestled with the balance of security versus civil rights and freedom for weeks. Finally they voted unanimously on a version and sent it to Congress for a vote. According to the ACLU, the bill was rewritten late that night by the Justice Department. The revised version, more in line with the Bush administration views, was printed after three in the morning and was still warm from the presses when it was presented to the Congress the next morning. Not one member of Congress had read the revised version they voted into law."

"Why haven't they corrected their mistake?"

"I wish I had a hopeful answer for you, but I am afraid the facts do no offer much hope." He clicked the computer keys and pulled up a newspaper headline dated August 6, 2007 that read: *House and Senate Quickly Approve Expanded Surveillance Powers.*

Bennett

51

The damned loudspeaker was booming incessantly, spewing Nazi propaganda. As Bennett walked down to Anna's, the subject was that Hitler was serious about eradicating Bolshevism. A feeling of hopelessness overwhelmed Bennett. They had come for Luther Gugler, yanked him from the cot at the Jewish doctor's, and dragged him off along with every other Communist in town. They had come armed with a list of names. No one knew where the list had come from, because the local leader of the KPD had burned the membership records. A few were taken to the local jail, but most were taken to a concentration camp that had been set up at Dachau for political enemies of the state. Some were just taken to empty buildings used by the SA and were beaten and tortured. All who were later released were under penalty of death if they discussed what had happened to them while they were held. For good measure, the Nazis who grabbed Luther also tore up the doctor's office.

While Bennett was dressing, he overheard Martin and two other SPD leaders in the living room raging about the slanderous attacks on them in the local section of the Nazi press. Since both of the other papers in town had been shut down and the Nazi paper would not take their response or their political ads, they were helpless to defend themselves or to campaign for their seats on the town council. They had been refused use of Remembrance Hall for a political rally and thus were relegated to organizing a march from the city gate to the town hall with all the SPD members plus the Reichsbanner marching band. They planned to hold their rally in Market Square in front of City Hall.

Bennett's thoughts were confused. Part of him wondered why they even bothered. It was so obvious that their cause was lost. But another part of him wondered why in the hell they hadn't tried a lot harder, a lot sooner. Why hadn't all the parties of Germany put aside their rivalries in order to stop the Nazis? That brought up the anger he'd felt when Martin had refused to let him bring Luther into his house. Then he thought about the beating the SA had given the Jewish doctor and the damage they had done to his house and office. If the SA had found Luther in Martin's house . . . What was it Otto had said, something about becoming cowards for self-preservation?

How long would it be before the Nazis finished with the Communists and came after the Social Democrats? Hell, for that matter, how long before they came for him? It had been days, and he had not heard a word from DISS.

Entering the cafe, he said good morning to Aunt Anna and took a seat in the front corner near the window. This morning he didn't bother with the newspaper or letter writing. For reading he had a novel. Novels were his only escape. He sent his dad a simple tourist postcard with a picture of a local lake. He wrote only the "Hi, how are you, I'm fine" sort of message..

He had buried the letter he had written to his dad about the Reichstag fire in the hiding place where he kept his diary. Hopefully he could take them with him when and if he was able to leave Germany.

Funny how being away made you more aware of what you had in the States: a simple thing like mailing a letter, knowing it would get to the person you were sending it to, knowing it would not be opened, knowing it would not be stolen. Small freedoms he had taken for granted. He would never take them for granted again.

He had finished his late breakfast and was continuing to read and drink coffee, trying to kill the morning, when suddenly the tramp of jackboots reverberated on the cobble stone street. Those few still in the cafe walked over to the window. Anna walked up behind Bennett, and even Willie came out of the kitchen to see what was happening. A huge contingent of SA marched down the street toward the gate. As they marched past the cafe, Bennett heard Anna mumble a quiet prayer. He put an arm around her and gave her a hug.

"I'll go see what's happening and come back and tell you. Stay inside, okay?"

She nodded. "Be careful, Herr Sizemore."

Staying behind and off to the side, Bennett followed the troops to the gate. There he saw the reason for them. At the gate, an SA platoon was blocking the entrance, forbidding the Reichsbanner and the SPD from entering. There was some pushing and shoving taking place, and it looked like a full donnybrook was about to break out. As the reinforcements marched up, however, any consideration of resistance by the SPD dissipated. The SA not only outnumbered them, but its members were fully armed. The Reichsbanner carried only ceremonial weapons, such as swords from the Great War.

Kurt Schutz stepped out from the head of the SA and walked up nose to nose with Martin Meylin. "Herr Meylin, there will be no more violence and disorder in this town. Your parade permit has been rescinded. You are forbidden to enter the town. Turn your men around before someone gets hurt."

"Schutz, this is a peaceful political march. You can't do this. We have as much right to hold a political rally as the Nazis."

"You try to come in this gate and heads will roll. Now, if you want a rally, go back down to the workers' beer garden."

The two stared each other down. Bennett could see no real option for the SPD. They were an unarmed group of citizens against well-armed troops. Even if they had a chance here, resistance locally, without nationwide organization, would be suicide.

Martin must have arrived at the same conclusion. He turned in a smart military about-face, marched through his lines of men, and shouted a command for an about-face and rear march. As the SPD marched to the workers' beer garden, they were followed by a large group of police and SA troops. There, isolated by the high walls of the garden and by the police cordon, Kasselbronn's Social Democrats held their last political meeting, while storm troopers marched freely through the streets of the town.

Bennett walked solemnly back to the cafe to report to Aunt Anna. She took the news silently, then began scrubbing down the already spotless dining room. As Bennett left the cafe, Storm Troopers were moving back up the street in small groups, tearing down all SPD political posters, replacing them with Nazi ones. They placed swastika flags on store fronts, including Anna's cafe and Martin's tobacco shop, and on every other building on Main Street, from the city gate to Market Square. No one was allowed to refuse the flag. Everyone had to pay for the flag. No one dared object. Additional loudspeakers were set up at Remembrance Hall and in

Market Square. In short, the scene was set for the final act before tomorrow's election.

At nightfall the torchlight parade began at the city gate. There were over six hundred uniformed SA, SS, Hitler Youth, and Stahlhelm, three fife and drum corps, and two full bands.

The Treaty of Versailles had forbidden a large standing army, so Germany had many small armies, some secret, some not so secret. Bennett ticked off all the ones he had become familiar with. The Reichswehr was the small regular army allowed by the treaty. The SPD's Reichsbanner, was pledged to defend the democracy, the Stahlhelm was a right-wing group pledged to prevent rebellion. It should have guarded against the Nazis, but it was an association of veterans—old guard, nationalist, right wing—who had no love for democracy and sided instead with Hitler. The SA was a creation of the NSDAP, and the SS was the elite corp created by Hitler. The Black Reichswehr, well, Bennett didn't know too much about them. They were a secret whispered rather than spoken.

The Germans did love a good military parade, and this night the Nazis put on quite a show. In addition to the torches, many units carried flags, both swastika and the imperial black, white, and red. The people, those not hiding in their homes, watched from the roadside, then joined in at the end of the parade. All marched to the Market Square park and gathered around a large bonfire. There the crowd listened to Hitler over the radio loudspeakers. Anyone who couldn't crowd into the square could listen to the speech at the three speakers along Main Street or at the extra speakers that had been set up at the Lutheran church and at Remembrance Hall. In fact, there really wasn't anywhere in town a person could escape it.

Bennett stood in front of the hardware store, halfway between the speakers on Main Street, thus avoiding the crush of the mob but able to watch the spectacle. As he stood there, Otto walked up beside him. They greeted each other with nods. After a quick *Deutscher blick*, Bennett said, "Sort of like watching a train wreck, isn't it? Too fascinating to look away and too horrifying to watch."

Otto smiled and nodded, finding nothing to add.

"I don't get it, Otto. Why do the Nazis work so hard at this farce? They have basically outlawed all other parties, closed down their papers, forbidden them to assemble or speak. Hitler's already in power. Why put on the election show?"

"For the same reason Hitler called for new Reichstag elections. He must have a two-thirds majority to make sure he can dominate the Reichstag."

"The last I heard he only got one third of the vote. Do you think he can really draw another 33 percent in this election?"

Otto smiled, a sad smile. "My father and I discussed that very thing. He will draw some more votes now that he is in power and now that he can use all the government and unlimited amounts of money from the industrialists, but we don't think he will get the full two-thirds majority. He may get no more that forty-five percent, but it won't matter. He's already outlawed the Communists so he can simply refuse to allow the Communists to take their seats, and arrest enough Social Democrats to make sure of his majority."

Bennett nodded. The kid was smart. "But then why doesn't he just say the Communists can't run and get rid of them now?"

"Because every vote they draw, they take from his only strong opposition, the Social Democrats and . . ." Otto paused. Bennett's attention had been drawn in another direction.

Bennett pulled his cigarettes and lighter out of his pocket. Under the guise of shielding the lighter flame, he shielded his mouth as he talked. "Join that crowd, kid, and melt in. I'm about to have company. You don't know me."

"No! If you're in trouble, let me help."

"There's nothing you can do. You have a wonderful family. Take care of them."

Bennett turned away and walked casually down the street, looking in shop windows and smoking his cigarette. He had spotted them because he knew the little guy in plain clothes. This was the fellow who had followed him here to Kassellbronn and was supposed to be watching him when he'd slipped out of his hotel in Berlin. The two Storm Troopers he had in tow were looking for someone, searching faces in the crowd and checking them against photos in their hands. Bennett had no doubt that they were looking for him. The one bright spot was that they hadn't noticed him while he was with Otto.

He considered trying to run, but that seemed like a useless exertion because he hadn't yet completed a plan for safely leaving Germany. Why hadn't he? He had to admit that it was that foolish notion of personal invincibility. After all, he was an American Citizen. It wouldn't happen to him.

A strong hand landed on his shoulder. "Herr Sizemore?"

Bennett turned to look into the stern face of one of the storm troopers. The two arranged themselves on each side of him, taking hold of his arms. The little guy did the talking.

"Heil Hitler, Herr Sizemore."

"Heil Hitler."

"I trust you have made good use of your days off work?"

He was more surprised by the social nicety than he would have been by a punch in the gut. "Ah, yes, so far," he answered.

The apprehension in that answer was not lost on the little man. He smiled and seemed pleased with his personal power to engender fear.

"Good. I am Herr Miller. The Fuhrer sent me to escort you to Berlin."

This too was power. A personal emissary of the Fuhrer himself.

"Since you left clothing and toiletries in your room at your hotel, I trust it will not be too much of an imposition if we simply walk straight to my car without stopping for you to pack."

Not only powerful but all knowing. Perhaps this little man was getting even with Bennett for slipping out of the hotel so easily, a failure Miller must live with. If he hadn't been the one to find and return Bennett, that would probably have been a career-ending failure.

Bennett shrugged. "Sure." Led by Herr Miller and in tight step with the storm troopers, Bennett was marched down the street, out the gate and put into a black Mercedes.

Otto

52

Against Bennett's order to melt into the crowd, Otto had followed and watched them load his friend into the car and drive toward the highway to Berlin. Once again he had to just watch as the SA hauled off a dear friend. Instead of going straight home, Otto waited until he could stop the tears. He was too old for such a childish reaction, but the helplessness and rage had to pour out somehow.

He stood at the outer edges of the crowd in Market Square and stared at the scene. Hitler's speech had ended. The bonfire was burning down and the crowd was singing "Deutschland über Alles." After they finished all choruses, they started the "Horst Wessel Song." For the grand finale, many Roman candles and multicolored rockets were fired. Then Kurt Schutz spoke from the bandstand. His voice, broadcast over the loudspeakers, instructed everyone to go home and sleep and be ready the next morning to vote for a new bright future for Germany. He closed by leading them in three *Sieg Heils*, Hail to Victory. The final cheering of the crowd was almost deafening.

Otto turned and silently made his way home.

Bennett

53

The only thing needed for evil to succeed is for good men to do nothing.

Edmund Burke

They hadn't touched him—yet. On the drive back to Berlin the storm troopers had been silent, and Herr Miller had been formally polite. They answered all his questions with the same response: "The Fuhrer wished it."

They deposited him in his hotel room and posted a twenty-four-hour guard at his door. His room had obviously been searched again. This time the searchers had taken all his books and left him a copy of *Mein Kampf.* With too much time and nothing else to do, he actually read it. Seeing how Hitler's mind worked was both revealing and frightening. Bennett hadn't realized how clearly Hitler had outlined his plans or how much more he planned to accomplish. God help Germany and the world if he was allowed to continue. Had the Germans who joined the NSDAP really read all this stuff?

Bennett had been kept under house arrest, allowed to eat his meals in the dining room but not allowed to leave the hotel. This time they watched his every move and even went with him to the men's room. He had been allowed no phone calls, in or out. He hoped the fact that he had not been roughed up or thrown into a jail or taken to one of the SA torture houses was an indication that his company had successfully pleaded his case and he would soon have his passport returned. The longer they kept him here under guard, however, the less likely that seemed, and his nerves were beginning to fray.

On the third morning he had been ordered to shower, shave, and put on his best suit. His shoes were taken downstairs and returned to him with a fresh shine. No explanation given. As he was finishing dressing, the guard at his door knocked politely, then opened the door, permitting Janeway to enter.

"Good morning, Mr. Sizemore. I trust you are well rested and ready to do the sales presentation of your life."

"Sales presentation? Of what?"

Despite the businesslike demeanor that he was trying to project for the storm troopers' benefit, Janeway's dismay showed on his face. "Haven't you been told?"

"I haven't been told sh—anything. I was grabbed off the street three days ago and brought to the hotel, and I've been kept under guard, with no explanation, ever since. What the hell is going on?"

Janeway nodded. "I see. Well, you remember that I told you that DISS was going to make an all-out effort to get the Prussian census? This morning at ten o'clock, we have an audience to demonstrate the ISS punch card and tabulating system to the Fuhrer himself along with Goebbels and a few others. Wilhelm Hartzman, Alfred Kordt, and your supervisor, Gunter Epp, will be there representing DISS. I'll be there for ISS. You have been chosen to give the demonstration."

"Before Hitler? Why me? I'm not even a salesman; I'm a technician."

Keeping his face averted from the waiting SA, Janeway used an eye motion to remind Bennett that their every word was being heard and noted. "Because I and Gunter Epp put our reputations on the line, saying that you are the best-trained, most knowledgeable technician in the country. Hartzman and Kordt will do all the talking. You have nothing to worry about."

Since Bennett had been in Germany someone else had always done the sales work. Bennett's job started after the machines had been delivered and needed programing to do specific jobs like inventory aircraft parts, track railroad schedules, or in this case, take a population census. Each machine and card had to be designed with proper data fields in proper columns; each sorter and counter had to be programmed to read that card. Now, with a huge company contract and his own freedom riding on it, Bennett was about to make his debut sales presentation in front of Adolf Hitler!

He grunted a short mirthless laugh and answered, "No, nothing to worry about at all."

On the ride through Berlin, Bennett mentally went over all the instructions he had received while in training at ISS's "School for Success." They had been drilled in simulated demonstrations on how to pitch the many models of machines.

Some machines had as many as fifty-five thousand parts and seventy-five miles of wire.

To make sure they were always in control, they were trained to speak calmly and look the customer directly in the eye. Bennett wondered if it was proper to look Hitler in the eye. Well, that would be Kordt's job. But if something went awry with the demonstration, Bennett would have to use slight-of-hand techniques like using his body to shield the machine, or using diversionary tactics to keep the customer's eye off the problem. Bennett prayed nothing would go wrong this morning.

They were taken to the Kaiserhof Hotel and escorted to the top floor. There they were left standing in a hallway until 12:49, over two hours past their appointment time. This extended wait did not add to Bennett's preparation, just to his agitation.

When they were notified that they would be called next, Janeway repeated instructions he had whispered to Bennett before. "Remember, let Hartzman and Kordt do all the talking. You are not to address the Fuhrer other than to salute and say 'Heil Hitler' when we go in. As Kordt explains the function of each machine, you will simply demonstrate that function. Understood?"

"Yes, sir."

Bennett entered the room, greeting others with the "proper German greeting" of "Heil Hitler," but Hitler was nowhere to be seen. Janeway motioned toward the three machines set up on the far side of the large suite, and Bennett walked over to make sure they were ready for the demonstration, as Janeway had assured him they would be. He would have felt much better if he had done the entire setup and wiring himself rather than depending on someone else.

A door behind him opened. Others in the room snapped to attention and cried out "Heil Hitler." Not having seen the man, Bennett almost missed the cue, but seeing others raising their arms in a Roman salute, he was able to join in the greeting only a half second late.

The room was silent as the smallish man made his way to a desk. Bennett was fascinated by the man's walk, which was quite ladylike, with dainty little steps. Also, with every few steps, Hitler would cock his right shoulder nervously, and his left leg would snap up at the same time. His tics gave the appearance of a weird tribal dance step. Recognizing the danger of his thoughts showing on his face, Bennett cleared his mind and tried to think only about the machines.

Looking for his cue to begin the demonstration, Bennett listened attentively as Hartzman told the Fuhrer what an honor it was to serve him, then began telling him how helpful he and DISS could be to the Nazi race scientists.

Bennett wasn't sure he had understood correctly, but as Hartzman continued, there could be no doubt about what he was saying.

He said that their superior German characteristics were deeply rooted in their race and must be cherished and protected like a holy shrine, and that DISS could dissect, cell by cell, the German cultural body and report every individual characteristic on a little card. These cards could then be sorted by characteristics at the rate of twenty-five thousand per hour and could thus help the Fuhrer in eradicating the unhealthy and inferior segments of society.

There it was in a nutshell. Bennett had now read *Mein Kampf* and was well versed in Hitler's views of race. He hadn't understood why the Nazis were so hot for a census, but he really hadn't given it much thought. Now he wondered why the obvious purpose hadn't occurred to him before. Perhaps because the purpose they had in mind was too monstrous to consider. No sane man would think it.

Bennett felt physically sick. He wanted to heave the morning's breakfast, and he felt hot, sweat wetting his hair and armpits. What kind of a nightmare was he involved in? Could he simply carry out a demonstration of a technology that was to be used for genocide?

After Hartzman's emotional introduction, Kordt took up the practical, explaining the function of each machine, pausing for Bennett to demonstrate. Relying on rote memory of his months of work, Bennett forced down his own emotions and functioned as mechanically as the machines. As Bennett demonstrated the power of this technology, Hitler and his staff occasionally asked questions. Most of these were fielded by Kordt, some by Hartzman.

A set of census cards had been prepared, and as a final demonstration Bennett loaded them into the sorter. Kordt asked what characteristics his audience would like to see displayed.

All eyes turned to the Fuhrer. He answered in a word: "Juden."

With shaking hands, Bennett programmed the sorter and turned it on. Like a flurry of oversize confetti, the punch cards flew from the machine, colliding and falling into piles on the floor. He watched the cards fly; then, out of the corner of his eye, he saw the startled and somewhat frightened expression on Janeway's face. Epp stood in the front corner behind Kordt and Hartzman, looking positively terrified. Kordt's face was turning red. Hitler frowned. The only person in the room who had anything approximating a smile was Propaganda Minister Goebbels, and the one-sided smile on his pinched little face contained as much real mirth as a crocodile's.

Bennett turned off the machine, and the last of the cards floated quietly to the floor. Very briefly his mind toyed with the notion that here was his opportunity. If he failed to make the sale of this technology to the Nazis, would it slow their mad plans for its use? Could this moment be a turning point in history, hinged upon his success or failure with this little demonstration? If he unsold them on the technology, would he die but many others live? It was a fleeting thought.

The answer was, yes, if he failed in this demonstration, he would die. If Goering's police didn't kill him, Kordt looked furious enough to throttle him then and there. However, that really wasn't the deciding factor. Bennett knew the djinni had already been let out of the bottle. For evil use or good, the technology existed, and it would be used. What Bennett did or did not do here could not stop it. Only the mass of humanity, awake, aware, and informed, could control this mechanical magic.

Goebbels was the first to break the deadly silence. "I am sure Herr Kordt can explain this little mishap."

Kordt took too long. Three beats passed with no answer.

Salesmen, Bennett had always believed, were just legal con artists. That was an art he had a passing acquaintance with. Against instructions, he spoke.

"Well, sir–no, he really couldn't; because you see, this was no mishap. This was actually part of our little demonstration. Let me show you something here." He turned the machine around, exposing the confusion of wires in the back. "You see this? There're miles of wire here, and it looks so complicated that you might think only DISS's finest customer engineers could manage it. But the truth is, the engineering has already been done, and once you have trained staff to run it, it can do everything but brew your morning coffee. You see this plug board here? Please watch this. You just unplug these and plug them back in there. Would any of you gentlemen like to give it a try?"

It always worked. Men were fascinated with any kind of mechanical contraption and always drew close to examine the machines anytime Bennett gave them an opportunity. Hitler remained seated, but several others around him came forward and examined the innards of the machine like amateur mechanics leaning on the fenders and peering knowingly at the engine of a car. Under cover of this distraction, Bennett quickly picked up the fallen cards and reloaded the machine.

"Now you see these plugs here? I reset these wires like this."

He focused his attention on the proper wiring while trying to appear casual and unconcerned. When he was sure he had it right, he repositioned the sorter so that it again faced Hitler and turned it on. Every eye in the room was fixed on it, waiting to see if it would work properly. Only Janeway and Hartzman looked confident and relaxed. They knew the training salesmen were given and knew they had just witnessed a classic save.

As the machine finished sorting, Bennett pulled out a pile of cards. He almost made the mistake of handing them directly to Hitler but caught himself. In a show of confidence, he didn't even check to see if they had sorted for Jews as Hitler had requested, but simply passed the cards on to Kordt. Kordt did check them before passing them on to Goebbels, who gave them to Hitler.

Hitler looked through the cards briefly, then studied Bennett for several seconds. He handed the cards back and said something quietly for Goebbels' ear only. Then he rose. All in the room clicked to attention and said, "Heil Hitler." Bennett watched, fascinated and horrified, as Hitler left the room with the same odd mincing step.

Bennett

54

The result of his command performance before Hitler had been that Bennett was advanced from wanted by the Gestapo to slave labor for DISS. He had been informed by Epp that the officials needed to hold his passport a little longer while they cleared his case. This explanation had been clarified by Janeway, who had said that Bennett was basically on probation. As long as he did his work well and made no further critical statements, his passport would be returned, eventually.

When Bennett informed him that wasn't good enough, Janeway told him to be patient just a few more weeks because plans had already been made to ship him home for further training. Kordt had promised that they could provide an upgrade, going from a sixty-hole punch card to an eighty-hole card so that greater amounts of information could be gleaned from the census. At that explanation, Bennett felt compelled to ask Janeway a question that had been on his mind since the demonstration. "Did you hear what Hartzman said they wanted to use this census for?"

Janeway's face flushed. "This is business, Sizemore, not philosophy or science or politics. Do your job and keep your mouth shut and soon you can go home."

It was March 27 before Bennett received his passport and a ticket home aboard the *Bremen*. What a year it had been. He got his stuff together in Berlin and caught a late train to Kasselbronn. There he would finish packing his steamer trunk and take a couple days off before heading to Bremerhaven and the ship home. Once again the train arrived after the station had closed, and he found himself walking in the dark from the train station to his room in Martin Meylin's house. Exhausted mentally, emotionally, and physically, he looked forward to sleeping most of his time off. Arriving at his house, however, he was alarmed to see an SA guard posted at the front door. As he walked up the path to the door, the guard greeted him with

"Heil Hitler."

It still grated every time he was forced to say it, but he had long since given up any hope of avoiding it. He replied, "Heil Hitler," and attempted to walk to the side door and let himself in.

The guard barred his way. "Halt. No visitors are allowed in this house, by orders of local group leader Kurt Schutz."

Bennett sighed and explained patiently, "I'm not a visitor. I live here. I rent a room from Herr Meylin."

"I am sorry," replied the guard in a tone the Germans called *schadenfreude*, more gloating than regret. "My orders are that no one may enter this home. Herr Meylin is under orders that he is to hold no meetings of any sort."

Hearing the malicious pleasure in the young hooligan's tone, Bennett discarded both caution and reason. He was long on fatigue, short on patience, and over the past weeks had gotten his snoot full of cocky young bullies clothed in SA uniforms. With one swift motion, he used his suitcase to knock the rifle from the young man's hands, then continued to shove the trooper backwards with the case. His voice rose to a shout.

"Look, you young punk, I am not a guest, I am not here for a political meeting. I'm an American businessman who rents a room here, and I couldn't care less about your fucking politics. All I want is a goddamn bed and a full night's sleep."

Bennett then heard three sounds. One was the locking mechanism on a military rifle as a bullet was chambered. The others were the opening of the front door and running footsteps. Bennett looked up to see another storm trooper with a rifle pointed at him. Coming at a full run, Martin put himself in front of Bennett, shielding him from the weapon. But he spoke calmly.

"Hold, men. This man is my tenant. He has rented a room in my house for many months now and is just back from a business trip."

"Stand aside, Herr Meylin. This man attacked a storm trooper."

"Don't be silly. In this dark he couldn't tell who was accosting him, and he was only trying to enter his own home."

"We have orders to—"

"I know, I know. And we won't violate your orders. Now that Herr

Sizemore understands who you are and what the orders are, he will be happy to go to the hotel, and we can work this out with local group leader Schutz in the morning."

Angry at his rough treatment and embarrassed at being disarmed, the first trooper was not about to let Bennett off that easily.

Before he could speak, however, Martin continued, his voice changing subtly. For over fifteen years Martin Meylin had been one of the two most important and powerful leaders in town, and he was a man accustomed to command. His words now lost their tenor of reasoned argument and took on an unmistakable note of authority.

"Local group leader Schultz will make it quite clear that Herr Sizemore is the representative of DISS, and as such is a man of great importance to the Fuhrer. It would not be wise to detain him longer."

Turning his back on the angry young trooper, he spoke to the one holding his rifle on Bennett.

"Leonard, escort Herr Sizemore to the hotel and see that he has no further mishap in the dark."

"Yes, sir, Herr Meylin. But we will need to make a full report of this incident in the morning."

"Of course, I and Herr Sizemore will be at your service. Till then, good night."

He patted Bennett on the shoulder and with a nod of his head indicated he should leave.

Bennett had by now cooled and realized that he had once again behaved very stupidly. As he walked silently to the hotel, Storm Trooper in tow, he realized two things: He really had to get out of Germany before his temper got him killed, and he had to reappraise Meylin—again. When Meylin had refused to let a Communist into his house, Bennett had put him down as a coward, afraid to stand up to the Nazis. Now Meylin had not only risked himself to defend Bennett against the Storm Troopers, he had actually placed his own body between Bennett and a rifle bullet. Meylin might be a lot of things, but coward wasn't one of them.

Bennett recognized his young escort. Leonard was one of the boys who had been a Red Falcon with Otto but had joined up with the Hitler Youth. He had seen him at several Nazi events and had watched his growth from youth to manhood over the last year. When he had been accepted in the SA, he had quit school and spent all his time in physical training that showed in his muscular body. Bennett wanted to ask the boy what he thought of the SA, but knew better; so he asked in a roundabout manner.

"You're looking mighty fine, Leonard. Muscled out a bit there. The SA training do that?"

Leonard was still unsophisticated enough to beam at the compliment. "With the Nazis in power, we shall all grow strong, Herr Sizemore. We shall recover our pride and make Germany great again."

Bennett showed the hotel clerk his newly returned passport and rented a room for the night. There were many questions on his mind. Why was Martin under guard? What had changed in Kasselbronn while he had been gone? Would his little run-in with the SA be reported to his keepers? Once in a small room on the second floor, however, Bennett closed his mind to all of it. All he could think of was sleep. He didn't even open his suitcase. He simply hung his suit in the closet and climbed into the bed wearing only his boxer shorts. He was asleep in less than thirty seconds.

Bennett

55

*Then they came for the socialists, and I did not speak out—
because I was not a socialist*

"*Sieg Heil*" roared through his mind, totally disrupting his dream and assaulting his thoughts. Bennett rolled across the bed instinctively, like a man avoiding a body blow. Unfortunately, the hotel bed was barely as wide as his body, and the sudden roll landed him off the bed, and onto the floor with a thump. The fall brought him fully awake, but his mind had not had time to adjust. He sat blinking and looking around the room, trying to remember where he was and why. Two more loud "Sieg Heil"s were shouted by a large and enthusiastic crowd, followed by delirious cheering.

He was awake enough now to remember he was in the Imperial Hotel in Kasselbronn, but that in no way explained the shouting and cheering he heard. He walked to the door and opened it enough to look out. He could see only part of the atrium lobby below, but it seemed to be packed with people, some seated and many others standing anyplace they could squeeze in. SA and SS as well as local police were everywhere. Still confused by the noise and groggy from sleep, he opened the door wider and took a step into the hall to get a better look.

There was a startled gasp from a hotel maid who had just come out of the room next to his. He turned to look at her and found that the young woman was blushing. Small cocktail tables with two chairs each lined the edge of the balcony, and a couple at the nearest table also looked at Bennett in shock. He realized with embarrassment that he was standing in the hall, nearly naked and ducked quickly back into the room.

Poking just his face through a small opening, he whispered, "I'm sorry, Fräulein. Could you tell me, please, what's going on down there?"

"Yes, mein herr," she whispered back, "It is the Town Council meeting. Local group leader Schutz ordered it held here so more people could attend the new town council."

Bennett nodded. "Would you bring me up some coffee and strudel, please?"

"Yes, mein herr." Recovered from her initial shock, she couldn't help a small guilty smile as she headed down to the kitchen.

Walking down the hall to the shower room was out of the question. Bennett opened his suitcase on top of the small dresser and quickly pulled out a pair of trousers and a sweater, socks and underwear, and was fully dressed by the time the maid returned with his breakfast.

Normally the chairs along the rail were either empty or occupied by just two or three hotel guests. This morning every person staying in the hotel had garnered these choice seats unavailable to the general public. They sat all around the railing watching the event taking place below. Bennett carried his coffee and strudel and walked the entire length of the semicircular balcony, looking for an empty chair. The only vacant chair was at a table occupied by a dignified older woman. Bennett paused in front of her, and with the hand that held the coffee he pointed politely to the empty chair. With a gracious hand motion she gave him permission to join her.

Down on the small stage, Kurt Schutz was standing at the podium introducing the ten delegates he had handpicked to run on the National Unity list. Though they hadn't all run as Nazis, today every one of them was dressed in the Nazi brown shirt. Behind them were huge pictures of Hitler and Hindenburg, and giant flags, one swastika and one imperial. The flag of the Republic was conspicuously absent. Smaller swastika flags were hung from the balcony in a semicircle around the lobby.

The SPD sat to Kurt's left, but only four of the five who had been elected were there. Where was the all-important fifth Social Democrat? Five was the minimum number to win the controlling positions on city committees.

Martin Meylin sat at apparent ease, his face revealing no emotion. From his jacket pocket, he pulled a cigar and matches. As he puffed to ignite his cigar, a young officious Storm Trooper marched from the side of the stage to inform him he could not smoke at the Council meeting. Martin fixed the young man with a look that would wilt many older and more experienced warriors. Slowly, he exhaled the smoke in the trooper's face.

"Boy," he said, loud enough to be heard over Kurt's speech, "this is a Town Council meeting, and here the Council runs things, not the SA. As long as I am a councilman, I will decide whether I smoke or not."

It was Martin's personal power, not his political power, that convinced the young trooper to acquiesce and return to his post at the side of the stage. It was a momentary victory, and it would be Martin's last.

Kurt Schutz did not bother to introduce the Social Democrats but began his opening speech.

"For fourteen years our glorious Germany has been governed by traitors, Jews, and Communists, and by union *bonzes*, fat union bosses who dupe the working man to feather their own nests. This rule has brought unspeakable unhappiness to Germany, and it is the SPD that has been responsible for this misery. Well, there is a new wind blowing!" Cheering from the audience interrupted his speech.

"Wasteful, inefficient democracy is finished! It was a filthy American export forced upon our Kaiser by President Wilson and was accepted in the futile hope that Wilson would keep the French and English from destroying Germany at Versailles. And did it work?"

His audience responded with a thunderous shout of "No."

"No! With democracy good Germans were sold out by the November Criminals who traitorously surrendered our country and signed the Versailles Treaty which bleeds our people with reparations for all of our lives, our children's lives and our grandchildren's lives. Well no more! No more!" Cheering again.

"No longer hindered by the inefficiency and bickering of one man, one vote, Germany will now grow strong under the Fuhrer's leadership principal. From now on a dictatorship will rule. It will hit every enemy and correct every wrong. We haven't forgotten a single thing and we will pay them back for everything. We will take these seducers of the good German working men, and in locked concentration camps, they will learn how to work for Germany again." Kurt paused once more for applause and cheering.

"Our Fuhrer has pledged that 'The common good goes before that of the individual,' and as National Socialism moves into Kasselbronn, we will see our town and our nation returned to the greatness of Germany's past."

When the cheering subsided, Kurt began the business of the new council by reading two announcements from Goering's Prussian Ministry of the Interior. The first said that the Communist Party had been declared illegal and that none of those elected could be seated.

When Bennett heard that he remembered Otto's prediction. The boy had been correct.

The second instructed that the Social Democrats would not be hindered from doing their duty so long as they were cooperative.

Bennett wondered how "cooperative" would be interpreted. He didn't have long to wait before he found out.

Kurt announced the committee appointments. They were all given to Nazis. Martin Meylin rose even though he was not recognized.

"We Social Democrats have had five members elected to the Council. Just because you arrested one this morning so he could not attend does not change that. By rules of the Council, you must appoint us to committees."

Kurt turned on him. "You have not been recognized, Meylin, sit down." He then turned to one of the other SPD councilmen. "Gregor Moeller, I believe you have a statement for the Council."

Moeller rose stiffly. Since he had taken his place on the stage, he had not said a word, nor had he met the eyes of Martin or the other two SPD councilmen. From his pocket he pulled a small folded paper, opened it, and read in a barely audible voice.

"With this new era dawning in Germany, I can no longer belong to the Social Democratic Party. I declare myself a neutral."

Cheering and applause was almost deafening as Moeller moved to the right side of the stage and joined the Nazis. As the applause died down, Martin rose and asked for the floor. Kurt Schutz turned and shouted, "Sit down, Meylin! For fourteen years you wouldn't listen to the NSDAP. Now we won't listen to you."

Martin shook his head. "You've arrested one of our members, and," he waved toward the turncoat, Moeller, "and bribed or threatened another into desertion. You have a majority on the Council, and now you won't even listen to us?"

"No, I won't. I run things here now. I run things because I am the local group leader of the NSDAP. From here on out you will learn what our Fuhrer means by the leadership principal."

Martin studied Kurt for a moment. "Then I see no further possibility of representing my constituents. There is no point in remaining at this session."

As Martin turned to leave the stage, the two remaining SPD councilmen rose and followed him, forcing their way through the jeering, heckling crowd. As they left, the SA guards at the door showered them with spit.

Bennett

56

Once the crowd cleared, Bennett packed his suitcase and checked out. He expected that he would have to spend the afternoon trying to work things out with Kurt Schutz so that he could get into his room in Meylin's house. He really didn't want to do that. He had plans for his last few days in Germany. His whiskey would be ready by now, and the anticipation of escaping into the mountains to enjoy the product of his still was all that had kept him going these last weeks.

After taking the first piece of copper up there, it had taken weeks to assemble all the materials to build even a very small still. If someone had asked him why he bothered, he really couldn't have explained it. Here he could buy a drink anytime he wanted. But this wasn't about just having a drink. Making good whiskey was an art, enshrouded in secrecy and tradition, and it had been part of his life since he was a boy. Enjoying it included having a hidden place of your own, sipping quality whiskey you made with your own hands, enjoying the woods, the babbling stream, the night stars, and the critter sounds. It was his place of solitude and peace, his escape from the insanity that was happening around him.

The first pleasant surprise of the day was that there were no guards at Martin's house. He went in his little side door, set down his suitcase, and walked through the house looking for Martin. After checking every room, he looked in the backyard and saw a light on in the shed. Bennett crunched down the gravel path and knocked gently on the shed door. As Martin opened the door, his face looked strained and his eyes wary, but on seeing Bennett, he smiled broadly.

"Come in, come in. Good to see you."

Bennett stepped into the shed and found that Martin was working on straightening the tines of a pitchfork and had a small coal brazier lit, which warmed the shed and made it an inviting retreat.

"I am sorry you had to stay in the hotel last night. I shall take it off your rent."

"Hell no, Martin. You don't owe me anything. I came to thank you. If it wasn't for you, I'd of spent the night in jail, or worse–got shot. What you did, running between me and that rifle—"

Martin waved his hand and cut him off. "No, that was nothing. I've known that boy Leonard since he was born. He would never have shot me."

Bennett found Martin's certainty troubling because he was far less sanguine about what Leonard might be capable of. Throughout Germany he had observed packs of young SA recruits like Leonard who were capable of terrible brutality and barbarity. "Well, maybe," he said, "but thanks anyway."

There was an awkward silence as Bennett tired to figure what to say about the Town Council meeting. Instead he asked, "What happened to the guards?"

Martin smiled. "They were just waiting until I wasn't looking so they could toss some rusty old gun into my garden. Then they could 'find a weapon,' and it would give them an excuse to arrest me if I caused any trouble at the Council . . . They don't need that now. Were you at the hotel? Did you see . . . ?"

Bennett looked down at his shoes and nodded. "Yeah, I had a balcony seat for the Nazi show. What happened to your fifth member?"

"They've taken him to Dachau."

Another silence. Those who returned from there were such broken men that the name was already synonymous with torture and inhumanity.

"You are off for the weekend, yes?"

"Yeah, not only the weekend. ISS is shipping me home next week so I can learn some new technology to help DISS with the Prussian census."

"Wonderful! Then with my recent retirement from the Council, we both have some free time, so to speak. I have a young fellow running the smoke shop for me. How would you like to pack a rucksack and take a little hike together, hmm?"

Bennett was caught off guard. A hike was what he had intended, but he certainly hadn't expected company. Giving up his trip to the still would be a hard blow, but how could he refuse Martin's invitation? In the long pause as Bennett struggled with a reply, Martin looked at him with a knowing, almost mocking smile.

"After all," said Martin, "the product of your little distillery should be about good to drink, yes?"

If Bennett had felt at a loss for words before, he was now totally dumbfounded.

Martin began to laugh, a belly-deep laugh. "You should see the look on your face. You don't really think that in these times I would allow someone to live under my roof without keeping a sharp eye on him, do you?"

The first thing he could think of to ask was "Does, uh, does anyone else, anyone like Kurt Schutz know?"

Martin laughed again. "Has he demanded 90 percent of your production for the Nazi cause?"

Bennett shook his head.

"Then I think you can be sure it is our little secret. You have been most discreet, and I believe only I would know, because you live in my house. If my tenant sneaks out in the middle of the night, you can be sure I would have to know where he was going and why. But if you want to keep it all for yourself, I won't tell."

"Oh no, in fact I would truly enjoy your company. It's just that for a minute there, I wasn't sure how much trouble I was in."

This time Bennett could join Martin in laughing.

They timed their trip for late afternoon, with arrival scheduled for dusk. That gave them light for travel and night to cloak their fire smoke. They kept their hushed conversation to a minimum on the way up the mountain, moving in stealth, zig-zagging their way, backtracking to make sure they were not followed.

High up the mountain in a tiny, narrow dell, Bennett carefully moved back the shrubs and brush that concealed the entrance to his little cave. Martin surveyed the roof of natural rock and the large hollow beneath it.

"I've hiked these mountains many times and never seen this cave."

"When I found it, it was just a small shelter excavated by flood waters. I spent many weekends here with a small camp shovel, enlarging what nature provided."

They ducked low and entered the shelter. Nested in the rock-and-clay furnace of the still was a collection of dry wood that Bennett had left during his last visit. More wood was piled against the back of the cave. Bennett lit the tender, and a small fire caught and began to give off light and heat. Smoke rose to the rock roof and followed the upward contour, escaping into the night air.

"Don't know that I'll get back here, so I want to show you, over here's where I buried the body and cap of the still, should you ever have need of such. You got to dig for them."

In the other corner of the shelter, he rolled aside a large rock, lifted a lid of flat wood, and revealed a small hole lined with leaves. Nested in the leaves were two jars of whiskey and the can he kept his diary in. Giving one jar to Martin, he opened the other, took a long appraising sniff, then took a sip.

"Well, a bit young, but drinkable."

Martin took a sip and replied, "Very good. To your voyage home."

As Bennett put his diary in his coat pocket, he told Martin what he had seen happening and why he'd hidden his mail and diary here.

"You mustn't trust my house, either. It's been searched twice so far. Once for something illegal; the second time for mischief, to either break or seize anything valuable. Bring your can and bury it again in the garden until you leave for home"

Martin leaned back against a rock, savoring the whiskey. "The Nazis are searching all SPD property, repeatedly. If they find anything they can call a weapon or propaganda, they haul the man off to jail, beat him, or send him off to the concentration camp for *retraining*. For every one of us they brutalize, ten more will fall in line."

"I really don't understand," said Bennett, "how it could happen so easily. The Nazis wiped out your democracy without a shot being fired. How come no one fought for it?"

"We did. We lost."

Martin took sandwiches out of his pack and handed one to Bennett.

"Thanks.

Munching the sandwiches, they were silent for a while, each with his own thoughts.

"Maybe we were too smart for ourselves," said Martin. "We Democrats spoke to people's minds of freedom, civil rights, legal rights, economic justice, things they had to think about. Nazis played the bands, waved the flags, and spoke to people's hearts of German pride and patriotism, militarism, religion . . ."

Bennett nodded. "And hate. As I travel, I hear them spew a lot of hate."

With sandwiches finished, they settled in for serious whiskey sipping.

"There's still one thing that puzzles me," said Bennett. "In the November election 66 percent of the people voted against Hitler. Where is that majority now? Why aren't they rising up against this tyranny?"

Martin took a longer pull at his jar and stared into the fire. "The only thing left to us is civil war."

"No. That makes no sense. You had a majority."

"Don't you understand? Have you lived here this long and not seen? It doesn't matter that the people were against Hitler. *He didn't need the masses to win. He didn't need a putsch to seize power. He already had the power.*"

"What power? Not the vote, not the law, not the constitution."

"Hitler said it years ago. It's what he learned from his failure in the Munich Beer-Hall Putsch. Any group that hopes to gain power must first make alliances with the existing institutions of power. Do you understand?"

"No. What existing institutions of power?"

"Hitler convinced the church that all SPD were really godless Communists and would destroy the church as they have in Russia. Now the church pushes the Nazi cause. *Alliance with power.*

"Hitler told the Right Wing that he would destroy all the Communist, socialists, taxes and social welfare laws. So Papen and his ilk invited Hitler in, believing they could use him and control him. *Alliance with power.*

"Hitler promised the rich industrialist that he would restore the industrial Rhineland, end reparations, and destroy the unions and socialism. The industrialists gave him money and helped him by firing any employee who refused to join the NSDAP. *Alliance with power.*

"The military was humiliated and largely disarmed at the end of the war. Hitler promised to restore and rearm. They do not attack him when he attacks democracy. *Alliance with power.*

"You get it? No election mattered. No law mattered. Our vote didn't count for a damn. By the time Hitler struck his blow that wiped out our democracy, he had already seized the real power of Germany. It was a silent coup that took place before he was ever named Chancellor. If we 66 percent of the people who voted against him were to rise up and fight his dictatorship, we would also have to fight the church, the wealthy, the aristocrats, the military, and the industrialists."

The truth of Martin's words hit Bennett, replacing his confusion with a feeling of hopelessness. "Jesus! I can see it now."

When Martin spoke again his voice was quiet but urgent. "It is lost for us. There is no appeal, no saving power, no hope. Your position with DISS gives you some safety, but don't trust it too far. When they come for me, and they will come for me soon, don't try to be a hero. Your efforts would be futile. Save yourself. Save your diary. Go home and tell our story."

Bennett

57

Then they came for the trade unionists, and I did not speak out—
because I was not a trade unionist

It was about four in the morning when they returned to Kasselbronn. They wanted to get back while it was still dark and before people were up. Martin had led Bennett to a small opening in the upper wall that allowed them to slip into town unseen and down an alley to Martin's house. A few hundred meters from the house, however, Martin raised his hand to halt them.

Bennett peered around Martin's shoulder and saw why he had stopped. On a street of dark houses, Martin's house shown brightly, with lights on in every room and armed men visible throughout.

Martin muttered, "Shit! Too soon."

He turned and with no explanation ran back to the opening in the wall. Bennett followed. Down a path that led around the walled part of town and out to the lower residences, Martin ran at breakneck speed. Arriving out of breath at Union Hall, he ran to the back door, unlocked it, and went in. Only when he tried to shut the door in Bennett's face did he realize that Bennett had followed him. Martin ran to the file cabinet and began hauling out membership logs and other files with members' names. He handed them to Bennett.

"Hurry, take these over to the stove and start burning them."

Understanding the urgency, Bennett accepted the task, no questions asked.

Martin continued to tear through the union files, trying to find everything that should be burned. He cursed himself under his breath for not having done this before. He just hadn't expected the Nazis to turn on the trade unions so soon.

Bennett tore the pages from the ledger, two or three at a time, making sure the pages burned totally and didn't form unburned clumps that could be retrieved and read. Martin joined him, and silently they fed the pages from ledgers and files to the flames. Before they were finished, however, they heard the sound of trucks coming down the road from the inner town. Martin went to the front window and peeked out, then returned on the run.

"They will soon be here." He took the membership ledger from Bennett's hands, tore out the last few pages and tossed the cover into the flames. Then he spun Bennett around and opened his rucksack. Removing the hiker's gear, he began stuffing the rest of the documents into the sack. When he finished, all that was left on the table by the stove were a few empty file folders.

Martin smiled as he looked at the empty folders. "That should frustrate them nicely. Now go, out the back door. I will open the front and greet them. That will give you time to get away."

"No, Martin, I can't leave you here alone. I'll—"

"Shut up, fool." Martin grabbed Bennett by the arm and began pushing him toward the back door.

"What did I tell you? When they come for me, you cannot save me. No one can. But if you get out of here and burn those papers, you may be able to save a few other men. Do that for me, please. And if you live to get back to the States, maybe you may also save at least my memory. Go, my friend."

With that he shoved Bennett out the door and shut it. Bennett turned back and tried the door but found it locked. He looked up the road and saw a half dozen trucks rolling down the road toward Union Hall. The sun had not yet risen over the mountains, but dawn was not far away. If he didn't run now, the Nazis would get close enough to spot him. Bennett turned and ran toward the shadows.

As the first truck pulled up, Martin opened the front double doors of Union Hall. He greeted Kurt Schutz with a toothy grin. "Well, well, Kurt. I didn't know our local group leader got up so early."

Schutz jumped down out of the truck and pushed past Martin into Union Hall.

"If you are doing what I think you are, you will be very sorry, Meylin."

Schutz searched through the empty folders that lay on the table, then the open file cabinet. Finding it empty also, he cursed and banged his fist on the table. When he turned back to Meylin, his face was red. It was a frightening look that everyone in town knew. When Schutz got this way, he became a madman, capable of anything.

"Seize him!"

At first Bennett worked his way south away from Union Hall and slightly east toward town, without any plan. Once he was safely out of sight of the SA, he stopped to consider where he was going and how he would fulfill Martin's plea that he finish burning the union documents. Meylin's house was out of the question. Burning papers in the great fireplace in the lobby of the Imperial Hotel was also out of the question. Perhaps he would have to hike back up to his hideaway to burn them.

He didn't actually think of the answer; he just saw it and headed for it. In the light of dawn Bennett could see the smoke from the fires of the homeless at the outer wall of the town. The Medieval Fair of his fantasies.

Bennett wasn't much for prayer. He had never found evidence that God answered prayer. Nonetheless, when he was helpless to change fate, he still prayed. He prayed now as he walked toward the homeless camp, prayed that Martin's faith in his fellow townsmen would prove valid.

Rusted fifty-gallon oil drums served the homeless as stoves. Three of them were burning when Bennett approached the enclave. Men were standing by two of them. Bennett walked up to the third, shrugged out of his rucksack, and with a *Deutscher blick*, checked those around him. The two men closest seemed to be asleep. Those farther away had watched him approach without looking directly at him, then looked down at their fire.

Trying to hide his activity with his body, Bennett pulled a few papers from the pack and dropped three pages into the smoldering embers. When they blazed up, showing they would burn thoroughly, Bennett added three more. As he continued to feed pages, the embers roared into a full blaze. Still, he added the pages a few at a time.

As he looked down at his pack to pull out another handful, he noticed that the sleeping man beside him had his eyes open, focused on Bennett. Then Bennett turned to see that two other men who had been standing by the other barrels were now on each side of him, watching him curiously. An explanation seemed in order.

"Had some scrap paper that needed burning. Warm the fire a bit."

The three men exchanged looks, then one acted as spokesman. "Share with us. We will add to the other two fires also."

Bennett hesitated. If he refused, they would think he was selfishly hoarding the fuel. If he gave them all papers, they would see what he was burning. He had no idea how they would react. Would they think he was a vandal or thief? Would they report him to the Nazis?

In the silence as he considered his response, the man added, "You'll never get it done by yourself." With a nod of his head toward Union Hall, he said, "They'll be starting back up the hill soon."

Bennett said, "Thanks," and began passing out handfuls of the documents. Five men fed the pages into the three barrels as fast as the greedy flames could digest them. As Bennett was searching his pack to make sure all the union papers were out and his diary was still safely tucked into a side pocket, he heard the sound of trucks and voices singing the "Horst Wessel Song." The man who had appeared to be asleep beside the oil drum had finished burning his share of the papers, and he tugged at Bennett's sleeve. Then he laid down on his mat and offered Bennett part of his blanket.

"They're coming. Best lie down."

Bennett thanked him and lay down on his side, using his pack as a pillow.

The trucks lumbered up the hill. As the first one came in sight just a few meters away, Bennett was barely able to stifle a cry.

Tied to the hood of the truck like a deer carcass was the naked, bloody body of Martin Meylin. There were multiple wounds from eyes to feet, as if the entire troop had used him for bayonet practice. Nazi training to toughen the troops.

Sitting in the truck with Kurt Schutz was the young storm trooper Leonard. To his small credit, he looked pale and shaken; but he sat tall and, with the rest, mouthed the words to the "Horst Wessel Song."

As the last of the trucks rolled through the town gate, tears began to roll down Bennett's cheeks. He had not cried since age six, when his older brother ran away from home. Hiding his face beneath his arm, he gave in to the overwhelming sorrow he felt for Martin, for Germany, for democracy, and for all humanity.

Diana

58

It was three in the morning by the time I finished reading the second of Bennett's diaries, but there was no chance I could go to sleep. I put on a robe and slippers and made my way through the house. The living room lights had been left on, and a bottle of Hunter whiskey had been emptied. The boys must have had quite a party after I went to my room.

Once down in the cave, I pulled out a sheet of paper and worked with pencil to check my suspicions.

KURT SCHUTZ

DPMO NRZPOY

I knew that Bennett would have witnessed many barbarous acts during his years in Nazi Germany, but the savagery with which Kurt Schutz killed Bennett's friend, Martin Meylin, had hit Bennett so hard that I was convinced that Kurt was the hated DPMO NRZPOY. Even the number of letters in his name was the same as the code name.

To check my theory, I used the name Kurt Schutz as my key and created a substitution alphabet.

A B C D E F G H I J K L M N O P Q R S T U V W X Y Z
K U R T S C H Z A B D E F G I J L M N O P Q V W X Y

Using that alphabet as a code definitely gave me DPMO NRZPOY. I had identified DPMO. He was or had been Kurt Schutz of Kasselbronn, Germany. But where did that leave me? I already knew there was nothing in the database under that code word. Not knowing what else to do, I supplied this information to Yeabot and asked him to search for permutations of this code as well as other possible file names written in the same code. He searched for over an hour but found nothing. I gave up for the night, or rather morning. It was now 4:38 a.m. I went up to Bennett's room and searched the diary for any other clue I might have missed, then returned that volume to the shelf and picked up the next. I stood for a while looking at the pictures Bennett had on the wall, especially the ones of Kasselbronn, wondering whether Martin Meylin and Kurt Schutz were there. There were no captions to tell me.

My eyes drifted to the dresser and the plastic sack with Bennett's personal effects from the hospital. I had seen it earlier but hadn't gone through it. It seemed like prying, almost like grave robbing, to open the man's wallet. Now, however, I had cause. Robert James said that Bennett had gone off on one of his mystery trips just before he died. I now knew that sometime during those days, he had learned where Kurt Schutz had lived and what his assumed identity had been. I hoped there might be something in his wallet, a plane ticket or hotel receipt that might tell me where he went. His wallet was slim, contents kept to the bare minimum: driver's license under the alias of Burton Simons, two credit cards also under Simons, no pictures, business cards or any of the other miscellany most people tend to carry around. There were, however, dollars and a stack of Euros. Had Bennett traveled to Europe on his secret trip? In a small compartment under his driver's license, I found the answer: a Eurorail ticket, and three cash register receipts from Old Town Books, The Meylin's tobacco shop, and Anna's Café. The names registered on my brain in disbelief. Could they still exist?

I went to bed and slept from about 5:20 to 7:55. Questions about Kurt Schutz, his secret identity, and the identity of his son and grandson kept my mind too busy to be able to sleep longer.

Sam and Robert James were still sleeping as I padded into the kitchen. My eyes stung and my stomach hurt, my body's way of telling me I needed more sleep, but by the second cup of coffee, I was feeling somewhat better.

At 8:15 Robert James appeared downstairs in robe and slippers. Both the hour and the attire were out of character. I put a cup of coffee and a glass of V8 juice at his place at the table.

"Thank you," he mumbled as he lowered himself carefully into the chair.

Leaving him holding his head, I went upstairs and knocked on Sam's door. Poking my head in I said, "Sam, time to rise and shine. I need your assistance."

He sat up quickly, then squeezed his eyes tightly closed and rubbed his head. "What? What's up?"

"Come downstairs and have coffee and we'll talk."

"Coffee. Right."

I let them get down the first coffee and insisted they try my V8 hangover cure before I started laying out my information.

"I need to go to Kasselbronn, Germany, Sam; and I need you to fix me up with multiple passports, credit cards, and so forth, like you did when I went to Costa Rica."

"Why?"

"I have two choices. I either clear my name or I hide in Bennett's big hole in the ground for the rest of my life."

"Why Kasselbronn?"

"I know who DPMO is, and I believe his son and grandson are the power behind Otto's murder, Ned and Emma's beating, and this phony charge against me.

"You broke the code?"

"No. Well, yes and no." I smiled sheepishly at Robert James. "I did what Robert James has been telling me to. I read more of Bennett's diary. Have you ever read those, Robert James?"

"No. Bennett made it clear they were for your eyes only. So who is DPMO?"

"The town bully in Kasselbronn, Kurt Schutz. He was the Nazi local group leader and ran the place with tyranny and brutality. Just after Hitler took power, Bennett witnessed the death of his friend and landlord, Martin Meylin, at the hands of Kurt and his SA thugs." I opened the diary to a page and laid it in front of them. "Read this page."

"*For months I have wanted nothing more than to escape Hitler's Germany. But now, as the train carries me north from Kasselbronn to Bremerhaven, to the comfort of first-class passage home and the safety of the United States, I know I will have to return. I owe Martin my life, and I owe Kurt a death as horrific as the one he meted out to Martin. If it takes the rest of my life, I will get that bastard.*"

On the table, I spread out my scribbles, showing how I had decoded the name. "The only problem is we already know there is nothing under DPMO NRZPOY in the database."

"No," said Robert James. "Bennett would never have encoded so important a case with such a simple encryption. Any amateur could break it." He stopped short. "I didn't mean—"

"No offense taken. Continue. What would he have done with it?"

"First, he would change the plain text into this basic ciphertext. That's the part you've decoded here. Then he would use one of the many sophisticated computer encryption programs to further complicate unauthorized decoding. He would also use a secondary key so that even if you used the right encryption program, you would also need to know the key."

"I see. Tell me something. If Bennett uses computer-assisted encryption, why the hell did he leave me all these silly little code games in the diaries?"

"He's teaching you the basics, Diana. You must start somewhere. And might I point out that it was one of these 'silly little games' that allowed you to identify Kurt Schutz."

Sam asked, "Why do you think you have to go to Kasselbronn, Diana? This incident with Martin Meylin happened in 1933, and we know from the one file we did find that Schutz has been living in the U.S."

From Bennett's wallet, I pulled various bits of paper, laying each down on the table. "These receipts show that he was in Kasselbronn just before he died. He either found information or stashed files there. Either way, it's the only lead I have."

Robert James looked worried. "Diana, my dear, that may well be, but your picture is in every major newspaper in the country. Every law enforcement agency is looking for you. You try to fly to Germany and you'll never get out of the airport."

I smiled. "You want to bet on it?"

Diana

59

In my business I have learned that anyone in uniform becomes almost invisible as long as they appear in a place appropriate for the uniform. For this reason I never discard any uniform I get my hands on. They are cleaned and pressed and stored carefully in a self-storage unit near Richard's beauty shop.

My phone call yanked Richard from a sound sleep at about 5:00 a.m. California time, and I gave him our code name, which meant for him to go to the pay phone. He had read the papers, so he didn't question my need. "Right. Fifteen minutes."

When he answered my second call at the phone booth I spoke rapidly. "You remember that flight attendant's uniform I appropriated in Costa Rica? I need you to express it by the fastest same-day service to RJ Westerman at Box 27, 233 Commerce Street, Thomasville, North Carolina. Look up the Zip. Tell the delivery service that it is a private postal and will accept packages. Stick in a couple wigs, one red, one blond, and a make-up kit. Get it?"

"Got it."

I smiled. Richard and I never tired of the old Danny Kaye lines. I added the last line, "Good," and hung up.

Over the next couple of days I put Sam to work making my passports and credit cards, and Robert James provided some untraceable off-shore accounts for those cards to draw from. Surprisingly, I hadn't yet given it much thought, but on receiving the cards I realized that having a fortune at my disposal could be quite useful. Robert James also used his computer skills to log me in as an employee catching a free ride to her home base in Berlin. Sam created all the necessary paperwork and airline identification.

That night I was in bed by seven and asleep within sixty seconds. I awoke before the alarm went off at five, feeling rested and up to the long day ahead.

I put on the flight attendant's uniform and found it fit better than it had in Costa Rica. I must have lost a few pounds. The shoes, however, still hurt my feet. I chose the blond wig, tied it back in a soft bun at the nape of my neck, and topped it off with the uniform hat. Robert James had warned me that they might use computerized face identification at the airport; so I applied a small amount of the wrinkle cream, not enough to look really old, but enough to draw worry lines and add about ten years. I could tell that both Sam and Robert James doubted the effectiveness of this, but it was all I had time for. With the hat and large sunglasses, I hoped I would pass. I was relying on the real trick: entering through the crew entrance rather than the passenger entrance.

There were security cameras all over the international airport in Washington D.C. Head slightly down, hat pulled over my forehead, I hoped none of them were scanning me and checking against my wanted picture.

By eleven I was standing with the flight crew, waiting to board, my extra IDs hidden in the false bottom of my suitcase. With the preparations I had made, I really had not been too concerned, but was relieved to find that security at the crew gate was perfunctory.

The crew understood the needs of a homeward-bound flight attendant, settled me in a secluded seat, and put my hat and jacket up in the hold so I wouldn't be troubled by passengers wanting me to get them a pillow.

Diana

60

Kasselbronn was a village no more. It had become a mid-size city, with a bustling population in the tens of thousands, car-cluttered streets, and air fouled by car, truck, and bus exhaust as well as by factory smokestacks. The entire valley that Bennett had described as farmland with two rivers running through it was now mostly developed suburbs and factories. The surrounding mountains were both higher and more massive than I had imagined. They still had many trees in the upper area, but the lower foothills were scraped, crisscrossed with roads and pocked with upscale housing developments. As I surveyed the hills, I wondered if Bennett's hideaway was now someone's suburban home. Finding any trace of the spot where he had distilled his moonshine seventy years ago looked like an impossible task.

I was so disappointed. I had envisioned a small town in which one could easily glimpse its medieval roots. Somehow I had forgotten to calculate for the growth and modernization that was inevitable. Of course, it never was the fairy tale kingdom of my vision. When Bennett was here, it was suffering from defeat, the Depression, unemployment, and eventually Nazi dictatorship. My failure to grasp this reality made me painfully aware of how unreal my other expectations for this trip had been. What did I think I was going to do, walk up to the nearest friendly face and say, "Could you please tell me where my uncle left his file?"

During the short ride from the airport, I had already considered telling the driver to turn around. This was a fool's errand, but I had nowhere else to go. As we turned the corner and headed up the street leading to the old walled city, I was treated to a view of such beauty that it brushed aside my defeatist thoughts. In my tourist phrase book German, I attempted to ask the driver to stop for a moment. In the rearview mirror, his face revealed his confusion. I tried again, saying the phrase I hoped meant "I would like to see" and waving my arm toward the lovely park and ponds that circled the inner city. With understanding, he pulled into a parking spot.

He stepped out and opened the door for me. I thanked him and walked to where I had a good camera shot. Before me was a beautiful green park filled with willowy trees and lush lawns. Through it ran a series of little swan ponds chained together by a narrow stream. Arched over the stream were three delicate white footbridges. With the camera in my little pocket computer, I snapped a digital picture. It was fairy tale perfect, but Bennett had not written about this, at least not in 1933, so I suspected it must have been constructed later.

Almost instantly I received a message from Robert James on my computer screen. "Playing tourist, are we?"

Well, at least it was reassuring to know he was keeping tabs on me. This was possible because of the almost magical gadget that Sam had made for Bennett. It was not as compact as the new iPhone but then Sam had created it years before. It linked to satellite, provided phone, Internet, GPS, camera, video, and computer, all in one. More importantly, everything on it was encrypted so we could call or email with security.

I put away the computer and began searching frantically through my phrase book to ask my driver when the park was built. He said with some impatience, "I speak English."

"Oh, thank you. I just had never heard about this park and was wondering if it was new."

He smiled. "New is a relative term in Europe. In the Hanseatic times, this was a moat surrounding the city, and that ruin of the wall you can see had great battlements and towers. During the Thirty Years War, however, Kasselbronn was plundered and lost both its population and its splendor, but the moat remained as a place to drain the city sewage. There was an upper moat at the top of the inner city that is filled from the Castle Spring. That is what 'Kasselbronn' means. They would release water from an upper moat once a week and sweep the sewage downhill into this one."

I pictured washing all the city sewage down the streets into the moat, and my thoughts showed on my face. He chuckled at my expression. He had undoubtedly told this story to many tourists and enjoyed its shock value.

He continued, "In the early Nineteen Hundreds, under the Kaiser, we put in a modern sewage system, but still the moat remained, stagnant and full of garbage.

Then under Hit . . . uh, during the Depression, our government set up the *Arbeilsschlacht*, the Battle of Work. It was a government agency that put everyone to work and created wonderful public works like this park."

I heard what he said and what he left out. I decided this was as good a time as any to test how difficult it was going to be to talk to these people about a touchy subject. "You know, I wouldn't be shocked or offended if you said it was done under Hitler."

He thought for a moment before responding. "Most Americans do not want to know that Hitler ever did anything good. They think of him only as a monster. If you say something good about him, you must be a monster too."

"I believe Hitler was a monster. I also believe he put jobless people to work and built this beautiful park. I don't find those facts mutually exclusive."

He gave me a barely perceptible nod and retreated to safer ground. "We should get you to your hotel. I must leave the meter running when I make a stop."

As I climbed back into the car, I noticed that on the other side of the park were tent-like pavilions set up around the outer wall. "What are those pavilions against the wall?"

"Those are little places for the tourists and park users to buy drinks or food or souvenirs."

I smiled. Bennett's mediaeval fair. We drove across a bridge, took a right turn, and circled around the edge of the town to the top of the hill. My driver explained that no cars were allowed in the inner town, but he assured me that my hotel was right at the upper gate and that a porter would meet me there and escort me in. No cars. After the smelly, honking ride from the airport, the promise of no cars sounded wonderful.

The hotel porter carried my one small suitcase in the back door and across the lobby to the registration desk. I tipped him and was looking around the lobby while I waited for the desk clerk to finish with another guest. I had indulged myself by booking a room at the Imperial Hotel, where Bennett had stayed decades before. The lobby was dotted with comfortable chairs, couches, and coffee tables. On the right was a coffee bar, and on the left, a liquor bar. Stairs at each side of the room led up to the semicircular hallway that gave access to the second-floor rooms. I noted the dark polished wood railing that almost circled the great atrium lobby, and in my mind I saw it as Bennett had described it, festooned with Nazi swastika flags. I looked back down to find the stage where Martin Meylin and Kurt Schutz had stood on the day the Nazis took control of the Town Council. There was no stage. That had gone with some postwar remodel. I was so engrossed that the clerk had to clear his throat and repeat, "May I help you, *miene dame*?"

"Yes, sorry." I showed him my false ID. "I have a reservation. Could you give me a room there, on the second floor, please?"

I couldn't know which room Bennett had stayed in, and since all the rooms now had private baths, they must have been remodeled anyway. Nonetheless, it was fun to think that I might be staying where he had stayed.

The bellboy escorted me to my room and set my suitcase on the luggage stand. I tipped him, changed from my flight attendant's uniform to jeans and blouse, and left the room.

Though I planned to get right to work, I found myself distracted the minute I stepped out the front door of the hotel. It was market day. Just above my hotel at the top of the street was a great park with a sign that read, *Marketplatz*. Beautiful half-timbered buildings lined the upper wall, serving as a backdrop for a market square. The place was filled with people and ablaze with flowers, so different from the descriptions I had read. I imagined it at night with a great crowd of Nazis singing and cheering around a bonfire. As I viewed it now, one side of the square was a green lawn that lay like a great quilt folded in soft mounds and embroidered with swaths of flowers. Each ribbon of flowers was a different color and began at the edge of the park in four-foot-wide beds, then narrowed to a small coil at the foot of a war memorial. On the far side of the square was an open cobblestone street where vendors had set up brightly colored canopies under which they sold their wares.

It was too tempting, and I found an excuse to walk through it. My excuse was that I had spotted a building at the back of the square that I believed to be the town hall. It wouldn't hurt to see what records might be available there. A little background on Schutz might be useful.

I walked through the open market, seeing baskets of flowers, both potted and cut, as well as vegetables, fruits, home canned jellies, honey, homemade breads, and arts and handicrafts of all sorts. I didn't dare stop to shop.

The building at the back wall had a plaque confirming my speculation that it had once been the town hall. Unfortunately, the building was now a tourist and visitor bureau. Town hall had been moved to a high-rise down on the valley floor. I picked up a map and brochure in English and headed down the street looking for the businesses Bennett had visited during his last week of life.

All the buildings along Main Street gleamed with fresh paint and sparkled with well-scrubbed windows. Not a bit of trash could be seen anywhere on the street. Most of the shops appeared to be filled with tourist treasures rather than everyday items, and made me feel like I was in a sort of Disney version of a medieval town.

Halfway to the lower gate, I found the first business, the Old Town Bookstore. It was no longer called Zimmerman's, but as nearly as I could tell, it sat in the same location. I entered and exchanged greetings with the proprietor. He was the male version of what my great-aunt would have called "a snippy young girl." I guess I would dub him a "snotty young man." His facial expression, his tone of voice, and his body language all said he was far too good to have to deal with the likes of me. I suspected he was a paid clerk rather than the owner, but he was the only person in the shop. Dismayed by the unlikelihood of a friendly chat, I examined the local history section to see if I could find any opening for a conversation. He appeared at my side, speaking German. I turned and gave him a smile, hoping to warm him a bit. "Do . . . do you speak English?"

"Of course. Don't you speak German?"

"Sorry, no."

"Then why do you look at German books?"

"I was hoping to find a bit of local history in English."

He gave me a condescending look. "This is a German bookstore. We do however have one English newspaper if you would be interested in that."

"Thank you, yes. I'll take one."

As he rang up my newspaper I gave up on congeniality and decided just to ask the question. "An uncle of mine used to live here. He said the owner of the bookstore at that time was a friend of his. I was wondering if it's possible that the store is still in the same family. Would the owner by any chance be named Zimmerman?"

His eyes narrowed. His lips compressed into a tight straight line. While he had been less than friendly before, he was now truly hostile.

"No, *meine dame*. The store is definitely not owned by Zimmerman. I know of no one named Zimmerman. He was long before my time."

I thanked him, paid for my newspaper, and left. He never heard of him but knew he was before his time. Well, what could I expect? A stranger, a foreigner, asking questions likely to evoke memories no one would want to talk about.

Next stop was the Meylin Smoke Shop. This one still bore the same name it had during Bennett's time, which gave me some hope that it remained in the Meylin family. As I entered the store, my eyes had to adjust from the bright sunlight to the darkened interior, but even blind, my nose would have told me where I was. The little shop was redolent with sweet and spicy aromas of fine tobaccos. It was almost enough to make me wish I smoked.

The gray-haired shopkeeper sat on a high stool behind the counter. As the little chime alerted him to my entrance, he looked up with a ready smile. *"Guten Morgen, miene dame."* He then launched right into English without my saying a word.

"What may I help you with?"

I smiled at him and tried to think of someone I knew who still smoked so I could buy some little thing, but there was no one I could think of. Spotting a case of lighters, pens, pocket knives, and nail clippers, I thought perhaps I might find something there for Sam and Robert James. I pointed to the pens and knives, which both had lovely carved wooden handles, and asked, "Are those made locally?"

Blue eyes twinkled out at me from the wrinkled old face, and he thought a moment before answering honestly, "No, I am afraid not. But if you are looking for some local handicrafts, you are in luck. Today is market day and you will find some very nice ones up in the *Marktplatz*."

"Yes, I was up there and saw lovely things. It's just that I was hoping to bring home some little souvenir from this shop."

"This shop? Is it then so famous?"

"In our family it is. You see, my uncle lived here many years ago, and one of his best friends in Germany owned this shop. In fact, I see that it still has the name of my uncle's friend, Meylin. I was hoping that the Meylin family might still own it and that I might meet them."

His smile disappeared but it was not replaced with the hostility I had received from the bookstore owner. His response was more confusion. "This must have been very long ago. This shop is actually owned by a fellow who lives now in America. No Meylin has owned this store since the early 1930s. And, if I may say so, you look quite young."

"It was in the 1930s. Bennett is actually my great-uncle, or was. He passed away."

"Bennett? You are not referring to Herr Sizemore, are you?"

I almost said no until I remembered that Sizemore was Bennett's alias. Now it was my turn for surprise and the stirring of hope. "Yes, do you, or did you know my uncle?"

"Not really. I met him once, when he brought in that pipe up there in the case."

I looked where he pointed and saw a portrait of a man, and read underneath it, "Martin Meylin 1898–1933." Beneath the portrait was a small glass case that held a plain, uncarved meerschaum pipe.

"Martin was only thirty-five when he died. I had no idea."

"You tell me Herr Sizemore is dead?"

"I'm sorry to say, he is. But tell me, wasn't he in here last week to buy some pipe tobacco?"

"No, not that I know of, but then I'm not sure I would recognize him after all these years. What about his partner, Herr Brehm?"

"Otto Brehm? He also died within a week of my uncle's death."

"Oh dear. And who is heir to their company?"

I was taken back by the man's tone of voice and by the question, which seemed to be a bit on the personal side. "I, uh . . . I don't know about Otto, but I am Bennett's heir. Why do you ask?"

I had no idea how to read the expression on his face, but there was no doubt he was very upset. His face flushed, and he looked away from me down at the counter.

"I had not been notified. You realize, of course, that I will need proper verification of this before we can proceed?"

Now I was confused. "Proceed with what?"

"With your receivership of the store, of course. Surely that is the true purpose of your visit. Yes?"

I sputtered and stammered a moment before I managed to get out, "No, I don't have a clue what you're talking about."

"Come, Frau . . . Sizemore, is it? You tell me the owners of the shop are both dead and that you are the heir. My stewardship of this shop has always been—"

"Whoa, whoa, whoa. You're telling me Bennett and Otto owned this shop and you think I'm here to take it back? First, I didn't even know they owned it; and second, I wouldn't dream of changing whatever arrangement you had with them, and third, even if I had known, I wouldn't show up here without all kinds of paperwork. I'm here for a very different reason."

He took this in and looked somewhat less defensive but still suspicious.

"Look, I came to this town, not knowing anyone, just trying to check a few places I . . . I had heard about in the family. I was just trying to find someone who knew Bennett, someone who might know where he had stored some, uh, some papers. I promise you I wouldn't do anything to change the way you run this place."

He was still reserving final judgment but with my assurances he did seem a bit more open. "Otto required three things of me when he made me manager. He said I was to change back the name to Meylin, keep Martin's portrait on the wall, and always be honest to my customers. They tried to find a Meylin heir to give it to, you know, but . . . I have done my best, and the shop has prospered over the years."

"I can see that. It looks great. You're doing a great job. Could I ask your name?"

"I am Herr Thomas."

We shook hands. "I'm happy to meet you, Herr Thomas. Sorry it was under these circumstances. I just have one question. Did Otto or Bennett ever leave anything with you for safe keeping?"

"Martin's picture and pipe."

"Not that, something like a file of papers or maybe film or possibly a CD?"

He shook his head slowly, thoughtfully. "No."

"A lock box, a key, a letter? Did either they ever leave anything in your store safe?"

He continued to shake his head slowly.

When I realized Bennett had owned this shop, I was so certain this was the place I would find the file, I just couldn't let it go. "Have you ever had the back off that portrait?"

His eyes grew wide as he understood my meaning. He walked over, took down the portrait, and without hesitation, opened the back of the frame. There was nothing behind the picture but standard matting.

Diana

61

The sign read "Anna's Cafe" and had a painted wooden cutout of a smiling Anna. Though the style of the sign and Anna's clothing implied a bygone era, the condition of it seemed too good to be original. Bennett's diary had never mentioned a sign, and I wasn't even sure what the cafe was called in the early Thirties. In front of the cafe was an awning-covered patio filled with tables and diners. I was sure the patio was new.

A sign at the front door said "Seat yourself." At least that was my translation. It was a beautiful day and the patio seating was appealing, but I wanted to see the interior; so I found a small table at the very back of the room. Over the years I had formed a habit of sitting with my back to the wall, an occupational necessity.

Three waitresses hustled plates of food, but one of them seemed to be in charge, keeping an eye on the whole place and orchestrating both service and quality. She looked to be in her mid-forties, with curly blond hair that had a few streaks of gray. It was cut in a short, no-fuss, no-nonsense style. My bet was she shampooed, bushed it into place, and let it dry. She was tall, five-foot nine or ten, had a large frame and large bust. She carried quite a bit of weight, but looked muscular and solid, not fat. Her attitude was neither overly friendly nor unpleasant. She was simply serious about seeing that people were efficiently fed.

As one customer was leaving, he said something to her that I couldn't translate with my tourist German. Whatever the comment, her expression changed, and she flashed him a smile that revealed a warmth and sparkle of humor. It was like lifting the mask of her public persona and glimpsing the private person she saved for those close to her.

I was surprised when the customer said, "*Auf wiedersehen*, Anna." Was the cafe named for this Anna instead of the one in my uncle's day? This was my last lead to someone who might have known Bennett. How was I going to break through that efficient public Anna and earn the right to make inquiries of the private one?

I felt the vibration of the small computer in my waist pack, pulled it out, and found a message from Sam.

"Where R U?"

I typed in "Anna's Café. Y?"

"Tailed our friends 2 powerful DC law firm. Might be op front. They bought tickets to Raleigh, not Germany. Find anything?"

"Yes & no. No one near. Let's switch to phone"

Speaking quietly, I gave him a brief report on the smoke shop. Once I had been able to reassure Herr Thomas that I wasn't there to take the store, we'd had a very nice chat. He'd told me a lot about the old days, but none of it helped my search. I told Sam I would send encrypted notes later.

"One thing for now. Bennett and Otto bought the shop after the war. Tried to find a Meylin heir. When they couldn't, they gave it to Herr Thomas, the heir of a burgermeister who was defamed and ruined by the Nazis. Ask RJ to search business files, send Herr Thomas official notice of Bennett's and Otto's death, and assure him that whatever arrangement he had with them is to continue."

"He's already working on such things. Things from the trust fund. Problem is finding all that stuff without Otto."

I was thinking, "What trust fund?" Leaving that for later, I answered, "I see. There was nothing at the bookshop. Don't know yet about the cafe."

"Okay. Watch your back. Hedgeman's not on you, but we don't know who else could be.

"Thanks, talk to you later."

As I finished putting the computer away, Anna walked up and asked in English what I would like. Did I wear a sign on my back or something? How did they all know to use English? I ordered a locally made sausage with sweet and sour cabbage and even indulged in the potatoes and Kasselbronn's own local beer.

I had arrived at the cafe after the main lunch hour and now ate slowly, hoping the place would clear out and I could find a way to speak to Anna privately. I watched her discreetly, trying to find something that would be a logical opening. Finding nothing more brilliant, I had decided that I would use the same bit about my uncle knowing the person who owned the place in the Thirties. By the time the inside room was empty, I had switched from beer to coffee and was on my third cup. When Anna swung by my table again, I was prepared to refuse another refill and try to strike up a conversation with her. However, she arrived at my table sans coffee pot, and instead she carried a cup of coffee for herself. Before I could speak, she said, "You seem to be my last customer. Would you mind if I joined you for coffee?"

I smiled and was gesturing for her to sit down when she added, "Frau Hunter."

My eyes met hers then glanced quickly around to make sure no one was within hearing range. I wonder if you can inherit the *Deutscher blick*. When I looked back, she wore a slight grin, and her green eyes sparkled with humor. As she seated herself she said quietly, "They're all gone. You came at a good time, and yes, I know who you are."

I considered denial but instead asked, "How?"

"Bennett made me memorize your picture and told me to expect you someday. He also said that when you came, he would be dead."

With this last statement, her eyes searched my face for confirmation. I nodded. A flicker of sadness showed in her eyes.

"Do you know the back gate out through the wall at the top of the city?"

Again, I nodded.

"Don't come back to the café again. I will leave at seven o'clock. By seven-fifteen I will pick you up outside the wall. Wear walking shoes. We will have a long hike."

With that she rose and walked to the kitchen.

I returned to my hotel room and, despite the coffee, felt I might get a nap. I took the computer off vibrate, set an alarm, and dozed. I was awakened by the musical tones of an incoming call. I opened the phone to see Sam's face looking out at me and realized he was using the phone webcam feature. I tabbed to web cam and gave him a groggy hello.

"What are you doing sleeping at this time of day?"

"I'm taking a late-night stroll with Anna."

"What do you mean a late-night stroll?"

I described my encounter with Anna and her plans for us to meet.

"You sure she knows you from Bennett?"

"I thought about that. My gut tells me yes; my mind reserves judgement."

"Damn, I wish I was there to back you up. Just talked to RJ. We have more problems here, which is why I called. First, through a contact, RJ has learned that our friends have made you on a face ID at the airport. They now know where your flight took you and what alias you're using. Did you use cash or card to move about in Germany?"

"Cash."

"That will slow them down a bit, but they'll probably find you on the hotel registration; so expect company soon, and hope Anna isn't it."

"Okay, what else?"

"We must've really built a fire under them with that DPMO file thing. Since they learned you went to Germany, they've really changed tactics. Suddenly there's a media blitz.

"Not sure I understand."

"When the powers that be really want people to believe something the propaganda wheels roll and suddenly you hear the exact same sound byte from coast to coast."

"And what does that have to do with me?"

"You're the sound byte of the day. In addition to the terrorist thing, you're wanted for questioning in the murder of Otto Brehm and the disappearance of a kind old couple in Otto's building. Your picture is on TV about every hour. They want you caught or discredited or both. Whatever is in the Kurt Schutz file must really be dynamite."

I have stared down the barrel of a gun and been less frightened. How do you survive against a power that can control and mobilize the media?

"Diana?"

I looked at his image on the screen, not even trying to hide my fear.

"Come on, Beautiful. When this thing clears up, it will mean millions of dollars of free publicity."

"Right. I'll be the most famous dead PI in history. What about the evidence from Otto's office that would clear me?"

Sam looked away from the screen and rubbed his face with his hand. Not a good sign. When he turned back, he said, "Jim, my FBI friend, has disappeared. The Bureau is saying he's on vacation but nobody seems to know what happened to the evidence."

"Oh Sam! What the hell are we into?"

"Not sure. I'm debating talking to Senator Motfeld. His Intelligence Oversight Committee is powerful and may have a lead on this SICC outfit. In the meantime, you better get moving."

"I'll be out of here in ten minutes."

"Like a prairie dog, Diana. Keep a dozen exits available and don't use any German airports. By the way, I expressed a hair dryer to you at the Amex office in town. I put it under the Martinez alias. It ought to be delivered by now. You might pick it up before you meet Anna tonight."

"Thanks, Sam. One thing bothers me. Are you sure it's a good idea for you to be talking to Motfeld? Remember the intelligence community thinks you lost your marbles, and there are phone records and such that connect you and me."

"I'll give that some thought."

"Okay. You and RJ stay below the radar on this one."

I shut down the computer, changed into my cargo pants, a shirt, tennis shoes, and nylon windbreaker. I discarded the blond wig, wadded the red one in a ball and stuffed it, the extra IDs, and other items I needed into the zippered pockets in the pants and windbreaker. Leaving the suitcase and all other clothes in the room, I turned the service sign to "Do not disturb," made my way down the side stairs, and slipped quietly out the back door.

Diana

62

Catching a taxi to the American Express office, I picked up my "hair dryer" and some Euros on my Martinez Amex card. Then wrapping the old ID cards in a couple sheets of paper, I stuffed them in a large padded mailer and expressed them to Robert James.

Using my Martinez ID, I took a room in a boxlike hotel down in the valley. Once locked in my room, I dismantled the hair dryer and put some of the parts of it back together as a small plastic pistol with twelve plastic bullets. When Sam first showed it to me, I was afraid the plastic would melt or break if I fired the thing, but he assured me this plastic was not your average Tupperware variety. It was developed for the space program, but in mankind's perverse way, it was turned into something deadly. This thing was undetectable by a metal scanner, and lethal.

With the alarm set for five-thirty, I stretched out fully clothed on the bed to grab a power nap. The sleep felt good but didn't make up for the past week. When the alarm woke me I splashed cold water on my face, stuffed the gun into the inside pocket of the windbreaker and headed out the door.

The danger of carrying all my worldly belongings stuffed in my pockets was that if I were stopped for as much as jaywalking, it would all be over. The advantage was my hands were free and I could travel rapidly and be ready for any action necessary. I would find someplace to stash the extra paraphernalia tomorrow.

Out on the street I made a short stop to buy a large coffee then caught a taxi up the hill. Arriving at the back gate by six-fifteen, I paid the driver and walked up a footpath to the beer garden that was on the hill above town.

I sat at a table out on the lawn where I not only had a delightful view of the town but also could watch the area where I was supposed to meet Anna. In the twilight, I nursed a beer, ate a sandwich, and wondered if this was the same beer garden where Bennett had watched the Nazis and the SPD go from song to brawl.

Were any Germans were still alive who would remember that? How much of the pain and hatred of those times was still buried in the hearts of Kasselbronn residents? How could anyone continue life as usual with a Nazi neighbor?

At the gate below, several taxis stopped to disgorge passengers, and many cars drove on up the road to the housing developments in the foothills. I saw nothing however to arouse concern, no one lurking near the wall, no one sitting in parked cars. No one like me watching the spot. Anna arrived at seven-ten and parked in the lot outside the wall. I walked down from the beer garden, and while she was inside the wall, looking for me, I slipped into the passenger side of her car and quickly checked for weapons, recording devices, and radios.

When she opened the driver's door and saw me, I saw her hesitate and heard a slight intake of breath. Then she slid into the driver's seat, and in the same matter-of-fact tone she used in her business, she said "Good evening, Diana. Brunette tonight, are we? Though you take your looks from someone else, I can definitely see a resemblance to Bennett in your stealth."

There was just a touch of reproach to her words. I wasn't sure whether to apologize or to thank her for comparing me to Bennett. Over the last few days he had grown into something of a mythical character in my mind. "Really? Did you know him well?"

She smiled, put the car in gear, and started up the foothill road. "I doubt anyone ever knew Bennett *well*; however, I can't remember a time in my life when I didn't know him."

Briefly, I wondered why that statement bothered me. Was it because this stranger, this non–family member, knew my uncle better than I did, or was it because it meant that Bennett's recent visit here might have been for something other than the Schutz file?

"Really? He was here a lot then."

"No . . . not a lot, but throughout my life. He would just appear, sometimes with cousin Otto and sometimes by himself. There would always be a present for me, usually something useful or instructive rather than indulgent, and often something for my parents as well. After dinner, I would be sent off to bed, and the adults would huddle in the living room to discuss great secrets. I grew up during the cold war, so there were, of course, always secrets."

"So was your mother the Anna who owned the cafe when Bennett was here?"

She looked over at me with a quizzical look. With surprise in her voice she asked, "You don't know anything about me, do you? How did you know to come to me in the first place?"

I wasn't quite ready for a full heart to heart, so I said evasively, "Bennett left me some information. I'm filling in the gaps."

"That sounds like Bennett. Always the enigma. Well, it was Grandma Anna and Grandpa Willie who owned the cafe before the war. They lost it when they got caught smuggling a Jewish family out of the country. Otto and Bennett managed to buy the place after the war and gave it back to my parents."

"They gave it to your parents? Not to Anna and Willie?"

She was silent a moment, then answered, "Grandpa Willie was shot on the spot when the Nazis caught them, and if it hadn't been for Bennett and Otto, Anna would have ended her days in a concentration camp."

"What happened with Anna?"

She studied me a moment. "I guess I shouldn't be surprised that Bennett never told you, but somehow, I am. I wasn't born yet, but I've heard the story many times. It's quite an exciting tale. While Bennett, dressed as an SS officer, rescued Anna from the Gestapo, Otto smuggled my mother and father out of the country. They all met up in Holland and made their way through enemy-held territory to go live with Otto's father, who was already in England. Anna was too old to run the cafe by the time they got it back."

"You were careful in setting up this meeting and making sure we weren't seen together. Is that part of Bennett's instructions?"

She laughed a loud, short, barking laugh. "I take it you haven't seen a newspaper today. You're one hot suspect. Murder, kidnaping, terrorism, you've done it all."

"Shit! Here too?" I looked at Anna. If she knew all that, was she delivering me to the police or maybe to American agents? She looked sideways at me and saw me appraising her. She pulled to the side of the road and stopped the car.

"Diana, let's get this over with right now. I grew up in a family that has been involved in clandestine activities for over sixty years. I knew your uncle all my life, and evidently I know a great deal more about you than you do about me. I know you didn't kill cousin Otto, and I know you're not a terrorist. I know a propaganda blitz when I see one. Somebody wants you very badly, and since the search for you is connected to Otto and Bennett, it's not hard to guess at the nature of the people who are after you. Now, when you showed up in the cafe today, I assumed it was because you knew I was a safe contact, but I see now that isn't the case. What can I do to reassure you?"

"How about starting with telling me where we're going?"

She smiled. "Of course. I had planned to take you to a place of safety, a hideaway that belongs to . . . that did belong to Bennett. I guess now it's yours. But I can take you anyplace you want to go."

"This place we're going isn't a lean-to under a cliff with a whiskey still, is it?

She laughed. "Well, I see he did tell you some things. But, no, it's not that den he made under the cliff. It does, however, sit on the same piece of property. It's now quite a comfortable mountain chalet."

I shrugged. "Sounds good, and if my picture is all over the papers here, too, I need it even more than I realized."

She put the car in gear and headed up the mountain. We had driven past the last of the subdivisions and were winding up a dark two-lane road. As we drove, I broke the silence. I had decided to trust my instincts regarding Anna. "Bennett didn't tell me about the place under the cliff," I volunteered. "He didn't tell me anything. I read it in some of his journals. I only met the man twice, once at age five and once at nine."

"No! I can't believe that. He always, every time he visited, had pictures of you and some wondrous story about what you were doing at that time. I was so jealous of you. It seemed like you were his daughter rather than his niece."

"That's an amazing thing to learn and . . . seems so sad. I don't know who I'm more sorry for, me for never knowing him or him for never having a real family of his own."

For the next few miles I asked Anna questions about Bennett, trying to know him through her experience. All too soon, however, she pulled off the main road and drove to a public campsite beside a small stream.

Quietly, she explained, "I'll take my car when I return tonight, but I'll leave some camp gear to hold the place and tomorrow there will be another car here with keys under the driver's seat. You can drive it out of the country or drop it anywhere convenient. She held a small piece of paper low in her lap and used the tiny LED flashlight attached to her keys to light the phone number on the paper. "Memorize this number and call to let me know where you leave the car. When you leave here, pick up our phantom camper so no one will ask questions. The gear might even come in handy. I am afraid you're going to need every bit of help you can get."

Then she beckoned me to follow, and silently we began our hike.

Diana

63

We finished the hike under a thick overcast sky, but no rain fell. Anna led me to the chalet, gave me keys, and assured me the place was stocked with anything I might need. Then she headed home.

The chalet was small, one bedroom with a bath, a tiny kitchen, a large well-stocked pantry and liquor cabinet, and a cozy living room with a fireplace and large windows that looked out upon the surrounding mountains. The wood-paneled ceiling was high and the roof slanted at a steep angle to shed the snow. The wall behind the fireplace was set with natural stone all the way to the ceiling. Double-paned thermal glass doors in the back led to a wood shed that was almost as big as the house. Inside the shed was a large store of firewood, a small motor bike, skis, snow shoes, a small snowmobile, a water pump over a well, and a large generator as well as an array of batteries for solar power storage. Bennett's chalet was quite self-contained.

More for company than heat, I built a small fire, poured myself a glass of port, and sat down on the rug in front of the fireplace. I had kept active most of the day and hadn't had the opportunity to ruminate upon the new threats. Now I was feeling very alone and very vulnerable. Not here, maybe, not in the sanctuary of a home that again was Bennett's, but out there in the real world. I had to go back out there. I had to somehow survive against an amorphous assailant that was obscure, and above the law. Fear tugged at the back of my mind, threatening to drag me into full panic. Powerful people wanted me for what Bennett had hidden from them. I didn't have it, and I couldn't find it.

On the drive up I had quizzed Anna as I had Herr Thomas about anything Bennett might have left in her care. There had been only one thing. The keys to this chalet. I pulled them out of my pocket and studied them a moment. One opened the doors to the house and shed. Anna hadn't been told what the other one was. It didn't fit the bike or the snow mobile.

I put the keys back in my pocket but decided it was time to unload the other stuff. I turned on the desk lamp. Dust coated the shiny wooden desk top. With a damp paper towel from the kitchen, I wiped it down and then began unloading my pockets.

As I set the computer down, my conscience nagged at me to check in with Sam and let him know I was safe, but I felt so discouraged I wished I didn't have to talk to him right now. Dutifully I dialed and was both relieved and alarmed when I couldn't get a signal. Someone on my internal board whispered, "Be careful what you wish for." I turned to the keyboard to type a message. Maybe it was just the cloud cover hiding my satellite and the email would go through later. I typed, "Anna is pure gold. Brought me to a chalet high in the mountains, another Bennett hideaway. Has car for me tomorrow, but I'm all over the news here too. I'm safe for the moment, but tired. Need sleep. Talk to you in the morning." I set the message to send automatically when there was a signal.

I shut down the computer, attached an adapter for German wattage and plugged it in to charge. Idly, I began opening desk drawers to see what was there. The file drawer was empty, and the rest of the drawers contained a few office supplies, clean and untouched. Checking the drawers in the coffee table, I found a few old magazines and fanned through the pages as if I would discover a hidden message stuck there like those annoying advertisements and subscription cards. Next I pulled the drawers completely out of both the coffee table and the desk. Taking the rechargeable flashlight from its wall mount, I searched the drawer spaces and under all the furniture.

The panic I was fighting to hold at bay provided the energy for a search that was growing into a frantic quest. I unzipped the cushion covers, pulled at the edges of the carpet, and knocked on the walls and floors, listening for a hollow sound. I checked the books in the bookcase, knowing that if he had hidden something really well, I wouldn't find it because I would never razor the books apart like the creeps had done in my apartment and Otto's office.

When I had searched everything I could see in the living room, I headed to the kitchen and pantry. I emptied every shelf and every drawer, stacking the contents on the small floor until I couldn't walk, then rotating things back into shelves and drawers so I could empty others. My fatigued body and mind responded to the frenetic activity by suspending reality. My mind zoned and disregarded my body's demands for sleep.

When I finally replaced every item from the pantry shelves, I headed for the bedroom. Again I emptied every drawer from the dresser, the dressing table, the night stand, and the bathroom cupboards, searched the drawer cavities, tore the bedding off the bed, and searched the bed and mattress. A VCR and monitor sat on the dressing table, and above that were three shelves of videos. I opened each one, shook the boxes, and looked to see if the video inside appeared to match the label. They all did. Of course, something else could be on the tape, but for a search like that I would have to ship them home and have Sam check them out.

Only in the closet did I find anything of use. On the upper shelf were three suitcases exactly like the ones I always used, small cases on wheels, each with a specially made hidden compartment in the bottom. I wondered at the coincidence of Bennett using the same bag I did, then I remembered a photo of me with my suitcase and realized it was not a coincidence at all. With rising hope I searched the suitcases and their hidden compartments. Each one contained a thin money belt that could be worn inconspicuously under one's clothing. The suitcases were empty, the money belts filled with a nice stash of ready cash in various currencies.

In addition to men's clothes, which must have been Bennett's, the closet also had women's clothes in my size. Uncle Bennett was meticulous with detail. I looked at the suit jacket, trying to envision Bennett in it. The jacket still bore traces of human scent and aftershave. Again I felt a twinge of sadness at never having known him.

"But Uncle Bennett, you didn't leave me a clue. Where did you hide the Schutz file?"

I gave up, too tired to think. After a hot shower, I climbed into the pajamas and robe I found in the closet, heated a can of soup and poured myself a glass of Bennett's excellent port, the real stuff, from Portugal. Once again I had that strange realization. The port and the whole chalet were no longer Bennett's. They were mine.

Setting my supper on the dressing table, I remade the bed. When I went to pick up the soup, I paused to look at the videos. There are times when favorite old films are the only escape left, and this seemed like one of those times. I picked up *The Secret Life of Walter Mitty,* stuck it into the VCR, and started it playing. Sitting in bed sipping cream of mushroom soup alternately with port, I watched Danny Kaye and Virginia Mayo and tried to forget the outside world.

I first saw this movie at age six in a mining camp high in the Sierra Madres in Mexico. It was a new mine and still primitive, so there was no movie theater or any other entertainment. My dad would order old films by mail. They would arrive on huge old reels, and he would set up a projector in the camp cookhouse and show the films on a makeshift screen. All the miners and any wives and kids in camp were invited to the movies every Friday night, and popcorn and Pepsi Cola were served, on the house. When I first watched Walter Mitty lose himself in his fantasies, my six-year-old mind confused actor with role, and I decided then and there that I wanted to be an actress when I grew up. Actors got paid lots of money to do nothing but pretend, and pretending was my most favorite thing to do. Though I later gave up the acting career idea, I never lost my admiration for the comic genius of Danny Kaye. Though I had watched this movie dozens of times, it was normally able to hold my attention, but not tonight.

Tonight my mind kept wandering . . . or was it my eyes? I would realize that I had just missed a scene because I wasn't looking at the TV. This happened three times before my conscious mind asked why. My eyes were drifting from the monitor to the dresser. With my poor visual memory, I often fail to note or remember my physical surroundings. Sherlockian powers of observation are not among my skills. When I realized that it was the *dresser* that was tugging at my mind, however, I really looked at it, and the reason for my distraction became obvious.

The dresser in the chalet was a highboy. Though it was slightly taller and a different wood, it bore a remarkable likeness to the dresser that had stood in the old Bennett farmhouse from the time I was a little girl. And as I had already concluded, Bennett was meticulous with detail, and nothing he did could be attributed to coincidence. As realization dawned, I held my breath; my eyes followed the shape of the dresser, with its little round knobs, down to the floor.

"Maybe you did leave me a clue after all, Uncle Bennett."

I got up and walked over. I could see no sign of a cut in the carpet. I pulled and pushed the dresser out from the wall and over toward the closet, then reached down and pulled at the carpet. It lifted just a bit, then fell with the weight of the trapdoor beneath. I pulled again, slipped my fingers under the raised edge, and lifted. The hinges squeaked as I raised the trapdoor and laid it back against the wall. Damp musty smells rose from the dark hole below.

I ran into the living room, grabbed the flashlight, and ran back to shine the light down in the hole. It was a very small cellar, no more than five feet deep and about the same wide. It was, however, finished in concrete. I descended the three stairs down to the cellar floor and shined the light around. The shelves around the edges of the cellar were filled with miscellanea, including mason jars filled with home made whiskey. Surprise surprise. But my eyes were drawn to two large water-tight file cases. Locked. I lifted them out one at a time and set them on the bedroom floor. Retrieving the keys from my pants pocket, I tried the mystery key in the first locked box and turned it. The lock clicked, and the lid popped open.

The first file said "Kurt Schutz." The date of the most recent entry was just over two weeks ago. Bennett had put pages into this file just before his death. The only surprise was how thin the file was. There was no way this could contain enough documents to account for all the years Bennett must have spent looking for this man. I searched the rest of the files in the two cases but found no more information on Kurt Schutz. I shined the light back down in the cellar but saw nothing else that looked like files in any form.

Picking up the Schutz file, I pulled out the most recent pages; and as I did, a small envelope fell out. Inside the envelope were identification cards for safe-deposit boxes with both my name and Bennett's. Their locations were all over Europe. Attached to each card was a key.

I set them down and began to read his latest entry. As I learned what Bennett had discovered about the secret identity of Kurt Schutz and his descendants, the panic I had forced down all night rushed through me, and I could no longer control it.

"Oh God, save us. I've got to call Sam before it's too late."

Diana

64

I checked my computer and found that my last email to Sam was still waiting to be sent and still had no signal to send it. If I didn't talk to him quickly, he could do something that would expose all of us, all of Bennett's secrets, and possibly get Sam killed. I had to tell him the name Schutz took when he'd settled in the United States. I couldn't contact him from here. I was assuming it was my location or the cloud cover, but what if something happened to them? What if Hedgeman's people had somehow gotten through Sam's high-tech safeguards and compromised our communications? I shut down that line of thinking. It did no good to waste emotional and mental energy on imponderables.

I looked at the Schutz file and debated what to do. If I left it here it would be safe but useless. If I were caught with it on me, it would be all over. Finally I decided to make photocopies with the camera on the computer and protect them the way the rest of the files were protected. The files might be destroyed if someone other than me tried to access them, but at least no one else could read them. I could upload them to Robert James later when I had signal.

After making copies of the entire file, I put all extraneous material back in the case and replaced it in the cellar. I kept two things out of the file, the original documents that supplied Schutz's new identity and the safe-deposit cards and keys. The original documents were the problem. If we were ever to use them, the best-evidence-law demanded we present the originals at court. That meant that no matter what the risk, they had to go with me. I finally decided to stash them in one of the money belts, wear it under my blouse, and pray they would be safe. I removed the keys from the cards and added those to the chalet key ring, marking each key with the first letter of the city the box was in. The ID cards themselves I put in the money belt. After pushing the dresser back over the trapdoor, I brushed the marks from the carpet.

Dressed again in the same unwashed cargo pants, I took down one of the suitcases, stuffed the extra credit cards and passports into the hidden compartment, and put a couple changes of clothes into the bag. The gun, computer, and Martinez ID I kept in my pockets. I made a quick check through the chalet for anything left or not done, turned off all the lights, and closed the damper on the fireplace. The small fire had burned down to ash. There was no point in trying to wipe my prints. I had touched every can and package in the pantry, every book, and every surface in the place. I didn't really think anyone would find the chalet, anyway. I borrowed Bennett's, no, my flashlight, for the dark hike down the mountain, locked the door, and headed downhill.

Going down the mountain in the dark I could get lost or fall and break my neck, but the need to reach Sam overrode the risk. I considered using the bike, but on steep, rough hiking trail I would have to walk it and it would only slow me down. On the way up the bubbling music of the little river was always just to my left; so as I came down, I chose paths that hugged the river on my right.

There were no people sounds, but occasionally I heard a rustle or a twig crack as some critter hastened away through the underbrush. I walked with nothing but a whisper of sound, a talent learned at my father's side. My childhood play did not lean toward dolls and tea parties. Hunting and prospecting were the primary activities I shared with my dad. In the interest of silence, I carried the little suitcase rather than pulling it on its wheels. The farther I carried it, the larger and heavier it became. I wondered if I really needed it this badly.

Eventually I left the crisscrossing, forking game trails that led to Bennett's and hit the improved walking trails, complete with trail markers.

When I was a couple kilometers above the campsite, I paused to try again to call Sam and Robert James. Still no signal. Quickly I wrote a second email to both and set it to automatically send. I said simply, "Need to contact. Urgent!" I changed from rings to vibration in case Sam got back to me when others were near.

I kept the flashlight off from there to the campsite. Anna had said that Germans are nuts for hiking and camping, and even though it was past the high season and was a weeknight, there were sure to be at least a few other people there. The dark, silent walk across the campground to my waiting bedroll seemed like a good idea until I stumbled over someone's campfire, knocking over pots and pans and falling right on top of a slumbering camper. I might as well have blown reveille. Flashlights and lanterns came on all over camp, and people called out either to say "be quiet" or ask what was going on. The gentleman I landed on came out of his bedroll ready to fight. While he held me down, his wife shined a light in my face.

Looking up into the light I mumbled, "*Yo siento, Señor, Señora.*" I continued to mumble in Spanish, spitting out a few phrases in tourist German indicating that I had a call of nature. After abject apologies in Spanish and broken German, the woman finally turned off the flashlight and mumbled something inaudible. The man let go of me with a few choice words of his own. Though I couldn't translate it, I understood perfectly.

Since stealth was no longer an option, I flipped on the flashlight. I found the sleeping bag and backpack where Anna had left them, but no car. Too early, I guessed. A quick check of the computer told me there was still no signal. I looked down the road and considered walking out. Not only was I exhausted, but if I waited a couple more hours, I would have a car to get clear of this place. Despite my anxiety, I decided that waiting for the car was my best hope, and I really needed sleep. I put my suitcase with the backpack and pulled both close to me, wrapping the strap of the suitcase around my arm. It was four in the morning. I tucked the computer into the large square pocket below my right knee so that the vibration would wake me if Sam called.

Confident that I would awaken when the car arrived, I didn't bother setting an alarm. Very dumb. My body had been abused too long and took full control. I slept like the dead.

When I opened my eyes again, the sky was partly clearing and the sun shown directly down on me from mid sky. In all directions I saw legs and feet. I was surrounded. Murphy's corollary: "Anything that does go wrong will go wrong at the worst possible time." I sat up, and everyone began talking at once. I mumbled, "*Yo no entiendo.*" and began rolling up the sleeping bag and trying to ignore them, but that wasn't to be.

An old gray-haired fellow called out to a woman named Greta. He wore a uniform, and I assumed him to be an equivalent to our park rangers. Greta was summoned because she spoke Spanish and, I was to learn, spoke it quite well. As the German ranger asked me questions, she translated. I learned that I had aroused concern long before I fell on top of a fellow camper. The other campers had noticed that though my gear was there, I had not returned to camp. By about midnight they decided to notify the ranger that there must be a hiker lost in the mountains. A search was to be organized in the morning. So, the ranger asked, who was I and where had I been? Had I been lost?

I was about to answer when I felt a vibration against my leg. Thank God I hadn't left it on ring. With the sky clearing, Sam must have gotten my messages and was calling me. Of course, the timing couldn't have been worse. I sat on the edge of the brick fire enclosure so that I could reach the pocket without being obvious. From the outside I felt for the buttons and hoped I was shutting off the computer, not answering the phone. A man's voice emanating from my pocket at this moment would not be convenient.

Then I looked at the ranger and lied. Yes, I had gotten lost and returned to camp very late. Sorry to have troubled everyone.

Then he asked for my ID, which I supplied. Gloria Martinez of Costa Rica, here as a tourist.

Then he pointed to the car behind me and asked if I knew I was supposed to have a pass displayed, showing I had paid my camping and parking fee.

I looked dumbly at the car parked at my campsite and realized I had slept right through the delivery. Then I did a double take. Lounging against the trunk was a young blond man with a buzzed haircut. He remained aloof from the rest of the curious crowd and watched the show through half-closed eyes. Despite the nonchalance of his body language and the lack of eye contact, I felt he was taking in every detail. A small piece of newsprint poked out of the breast pocket of his jacket. I suspected that it was ripped from one of the papers running my picture.

As Greta repeated the ranger's question, I pulled my attention from the young man and the car. Pleading ignorance of the need for a pass, I immediately pulled out some Euros and offered to pay the fee and any fine there might be for this infraction. In some cultures the offer of a fine is understood as a bribe and is accepted as a matter of course. Not so here. He took the fee, the precise fee only, made change and supplied a receipt written on a pad in duplicate. Damn the German compulsion for records! That made a paper trail, complete with the car license plate. With a terrifying certainty that Blondie had made me, I said a little prayer that this car could not be traced to Anna.

Then the ranger asked his gotcha question. The other campers had also noticed that my car wasn't here all night either. If I had been lost in the woods, was my car lost with me, and how did it get here at seven this morning?

To be caught in such a lie told me how stupid and inept I had been. I could feel the money belt under my blouse, almost burning my skin. If I was taken now, the key piece of information on Schutz and the reason for Otto's murder would be taken with me. Feeling my face blaze hot with embarrassment, I silently cursed my lack of emotional control. Oh well, the secret of life is not to mourn what you lack, but to use what you got.

Building on the blush, I smiled sheepishly. In Spanish I explained, "I didn't exactly get lost in the mountains. Yesterday evening I went out looking for a place to eat and found this great place with food and music and dancing and, . . ." I stood, leaned close to Greta, and in an embarrassed and confidential tone, I told her, "I had a little too much to drink to find my way back so I . . . waited for a while with this guy I was dancing with. . . . then he gave me a ride here and said he would bring the car to me this morning when he had a friend to drive him home."

After Greta translated my answer, the old ranger asked, "Who was this fellow?"

I shrugged. With a slight gleam in my eye I said, "Ernst something or other. He was a gorgeous German with beautiful eyes and a spectacular body."

That did it for the old fellow and for most of those with an ear to our conversation. All the inconsistencies were explained. Another tourist getting her thrills. He gave me a fatherly warning, saying young women tourists should be more careful or they could end up in real trouble. I thanked him and began loading everything into my car as rapidly as possible.

The young fellow with the buzz haircut had moved off a few yards and sat in the driver's seat of a black Fiat, a cell phone to his ear. That reminded me of Sam, but I still couldn't turn the computer back on and talk to him. I had to get out of here. As I shoved the suitcase in the trunk, I wondered why Blondie didn't try to tell the ranger who I was. The answer was easy. Instead he made his phone call and told . . . who? He was still on the cell phone when I bailed out of there and took a left on the highway, heading east. I was sure he would be on my tail.

I checked the rearview mirror frequently until I saw his car behind me. He wasn't trying to catch me but was maintaining a loose tail. Was he waiting for backup? I had to lose him before that could happen. Fortunately, it's easier to lose a single car tail than it is to maintain one. I looked for an opportunity. When we hit a stretch of road that ran through a small town, I found my spot. The two-lane main street was lined with two and three-story masonry buildings. Tourists milled along the sidewalks.

My tail was out of sight, far behind and around a bend in the road. I made a sharp right turn on a side street, then a quick left into a parking lot behind the row of businesses. Parking so I could see the main street, I watched as Blondie drove right past. I waited a few moments then headed back to the highway, this time traveling west.

I checked the road atlas Anna had thoughtfully left in the car. In case my friend wised up and backtracked, I took the first road north that was a through road. I followed it until I hit the main highway to Dusseldorf, then headed west. Among the safety-deposit keys that Bennett had stashed in the Schutz file was one for a box in Dusseldorf. It was the closest one, and I decided to head there first and discover what Bennett had squirreled away. I now had documents that told me Schutz's identity, and I had Bennett's diary describing how Schutz had barbarously killed Martin Meylin. That was bad enough, but I was sure Bennett had much more information or our search for the file would not have caused such a huge response.

Twenty miles down the highway, I spotted a large resort with a parking lot full of cars. The marquee announced a local festival with a contest of folk singers and dancers. The grass-covered park behind the hotel had blossomed with multicolored pavilions and was filled with tourists and performers in colorful folk costumes. This was just the kind of mob scene I wanted. Hiding my car in the middle of the parking lot, I went to the trunk and opened the suitcase. Martinez had been identified at the campground, and Blondie would be looking for her. I dropped that set of ID into the case and retrieved Margaret Atwater from Devonshire, England. Shutting the trunk and climbing back into the front seat, I pulled out the computer and turned it on. I was about to call Sam when the thing started to vibrate in my hands and startled me so much I almost dropped it.

Answering in webcam mode, I could see Sam staring at me from what looked to be a motel room. I started to tell him how relieved I was to see him, but he shouted me down with questions.

"Where are you? Why didn't you answer my calls? What's wrong? Why the urgent message?

When he finally paused long enough for me to answer I said, "I'm fine. How are you. Having a wonderful time. Wish you were here."

That enraged him. "Diana, for Christ's sake. Don't be a smart ass. We've been worried sick here."

Anger at his tone coupled with my experience of the last couple days made me just a bit testy. "Damn it, Sam. Did you get my email?"

"Yes, and your last one said urgent, and when I did get through, you turned me off."

"Did you notice there was a time difference between when I wrote them and when you got them?" I could tell by his expression that he hadn't checked. "I didn't have any signal, Sam. And I had to turn you off because I was being questioned by a park guard."

"Why? What park? What was happening with the guard?"

"We don't have time now. I'll send you a picture postcard. Now shut up and listen because I have information you've got to have."

"Bennett left the secret of Kurt Schutz's new identity at the Chalet. Sam, did you speak to Senator Motfeld?"

His expression told me he had, and my stomach contracted in fear.

"Why?" he asked but looked as if he had guessed.

"When the CIA relocated Schutz in the United States, he was given the name of Motfeld. His son is Christopher Motfeld, president and CEO of the petrochemical conglomerate HICHEMCO, and his grandson is Senator Motfeld.

"Oh my god!"

"What did you tell Motfeld?"

"I only got as far as saying I was an old friend and trying to find Jim, and his secretary had suggested he might be at the senator's office. There was something in his attitude, an eagerness, that put me off, so I didn't take it further."

"Thank God for your instincts."

"Yeah! No wonder our little file raised such hell. A few Nazis in the closet might be enough to derail Motfeld's train to the White House."

"Maybe. But I've been thinking about this, and I'm not sure that a Nazi ancestor is all that important politically. Schwarzenegger's father was a Storm Trooper, and it didn't hurt his run for California governor. And I am learning that a shocking number of American individuals and American corporations had business connections with the Nazis both before and during the war. There must be something more in this file, something that scared Motfeld and his people enough to commit murder."

"Maybe. You got the file?"

"Not exactly. Our secretive Bennett was careful, didn't put all his eggs in one basket. At the chalet I found the *original* documents showing the name and location the CIA gave Schutz. That information Bennett had only just found before he died. I have those original documents on me and will express them to you as soon as I get to Dusseldorf.

"I also found some summaries of other documents that Bennett has hidden throughout Europe with references to Schutz war crimes and something I don't understand about the CIA. But I haven't had time to read any of it. As soon as I saw Motfeld's name I concentrated on getting to where I could call you. I have photocopied all of that and am sending to the compound as we speak. To find the rest of the file, Bennett left me an elaborate scavenger hunt that looks like it may take me all over Europe. I'm going to need . . .Shit! . . . How did he find me?"

I was certain I had lost him, but Blondie had just pulled into the resort and was driving slowly through the parking lot. For a moment, I was dumbfounded. Then I remembered he had been leaning against the trunk of the car. He must have tagged the car.

"I got to get out of here, Sam. Later."

I shut off the computer despite the loud demands from Sam. I ducked down out of sight and tucked the computer in my pocket. Opening the passenger door, I crawled out onto parking lot. Crouching beneath window height, I ran away from the car.

Diana

65

I made my way toward the crowd attending the festival. Blondie circled the parking lot, zeroed in on my car, and parked just a few spaces away. As I entered the festival grounds I looked back to see Blondie was joined by a dark-haired older man in a second car. The two of them got out and converged on my car. Only then did it occur to me that in my rush to get away, I had left the old Martinez ID and my last three good passports and credit cards in the suitcase in the trunk. Damn! This prairie dog just lost three back doors.

I joined the crowds milling around the pavilions and tried to think. There were three calls I needed to make at once. First I called the number Anna had given me. As she answered I could hear the clatter of dishes and the din of conversation. She was at the cafe.

In guarded words I told her, "The missing car has been found by unknown authorities. Do you think they will find the owner?"

There was a pause, then she answered, "Not a problem. The car was a rental. Was the driver injured?"

"Uh, no. Walked away from it." I wasn't sure if "rental" was meant literally or was also coded, but the important thing was she knew someone had it and she wasn't concerned. Her family had been at this game for three generations. She knew what she was doing.

"That's good. Have a nice trip." She clicked off.

I put through the second call to Sam. When he answered I gave him no time for questions. "Sam, just listen. I have a problem. My car was bugged. I had to bail out and left all ID and cards except the Margaret Atwater. The others will soon be found. Can they trace them to bank accounts that will—"

"No. That goes to a dead end. Are you secure?"

"For the moment, but I have to keep moving. Call you from Dusseldorf."

I shut down before he could stop me and started to dial my third call to Richard's salon.

"Coiffeurs Americain," answered Sophia.

"Sorry, wrong number." Even if he expressed something to Dusseldorf, I wouldn't have time to get a new makeup kit from him. I was on my own and would have to ad-lib something.

For my immediate need I entered a booth where they were selling lederhosen shorts and other folk costumes and wasted no time buying a long, elaborately embroidered dress, a hat, and some hair combs. I stepped into the dressing room in back of the booth and slipped the dress on over my clothing. Pinning my shoulder-length brown hair up with the combs, I pulled on the hat and tilted the brim down to hide as much of my face as possible, then added a pair of large sunglasses.

The car would keep them busy for only a short time. Then they would begin to look for me. I had no idea what kind of backup they might call in. I didn't know if they wanted to grab me or just follow me until I led them to the Schutz file. I didn't know if they were with the police or were freelance. I just knew I had to get away quickly and unseen.

To leave I needed to get to the front of the hotel where there were taxis, but to get to the hotel I had to walk right past them on a walkway that ran through the parking lot. Even with my costume, I didn't want to parade right in front of them. As I was debating a longer route to the far side of the park, a performance group walked past me, wearing costumes not too dissimilar from mine. Impulsively I latched onto the group and walked with them to the hotel.

As Blondie worked on opening the trunk of my car, the older fellow turned and walked right toward us. Looking up from something in his hand, he saw our group and picked up his pace. In a moment of panic I considered making a run for it, but as I debated that move, he cut into the sidewalk ahead of us and beat us through the door. As we walked through the lobby, I saw him talking to the concierge, showing the man a scrap of newsprint that I was sure displayed my face. I looked away and followed the folk troop right through the lobby and out the front door. When they climbed aboard a tour van, so did I.

A heavy woman had taken two thirds of the seat behind the driver. I slid in and sat on the remaining one third. As our hips bumped together, she turned and looked at me questioningly. I smiled, then looked away, hoping she wouldn't strike up a conversation. The driver put the van in gear and we were off. I was relieved to be away from the hotel but hadn't the foggiest notion where we were going.

As we rolled down the highway and into the heart of the nearby town, I could feel the heavy woman's eyes on me. With peripheral vision I could see her scanning the embroidery of my dress, which was not the same as the rest of the group's. She peeked around the brim of my hat to look directly into my face. From this close perspective, she asked me a question in German. I hadn't a clue what she was asking. I gave her another smile and looked away. I noticed then that the driver was signaling for a turn into the parking lot at a large restaurant.

With determination, she pulled at my sleeve and spoke the same words again. Once more I smiled and this time answered, "Ya."

With question and disbelief in her voice she said, "Ya?" As the van pulled to a stop, she turned to the couple in back of us. I couldn't translate, but I was certain she had made me as an interloper and was ratting me out to the folks in the next seat. That might make me more memorable to this group than I wanted to be.

In my best Devonshire accent I said, "I say, what are we stopping here for? I thought this was the bus to the Hilton."

Though my seat companion answered in German, it was apparent she understood English and was explaining to this dummy that I'd gotten on a private group van.

I apologized and was the first one to get off the bus the moment the door opened. As the group went into the restaurant, I headed for the taxi stand. When I asked the driver to take me to the train station, he gave me a doubtful look and explained that the nearest station was thirty miles away. That, I thought, was perfect. The farther, the better.

My first stop after he dropped me at the station was the ladies room, where I slipped out of my costume. I folded it in a tight roll and decided I would hang onto it until I found a safe place to leave it. If it was found in a place that raised questions someone might connect the dots and that might lead my pursuers my direction.

Then I bought a ticket for the train to Dusseldorf. Though I used cash, I was still required to produce an ID because I wanted to reserve a private compartment. Weighing the odds, I could think of no reason Margaret Atwater should be known, and felt it was more important that I not be seen.

During the wait for my train I bought a meal, my first of the day, and wolfed it down. When I was finally able to slip into my train compartment and shut the door and draw the curtains, I drew three deep relaxing breaths and tried to calm both body and mind. At first I just sat there, my mind refusing to chill out, darting in many directions. I picked up a German magazine that had been left on the seat and tried to decipher enough of the language to get the gist of a story, but I didn't really have the concentration for such a task.

I decided to put the time and the busy brain cells to better use. First I used the computer to check the location of the American Express office and book Margaret Atwater into a small hotel within two blocks of it. Then I opened the copies I had made of Bennett's file. Now in the quiet and relative safety of my private train compartment, I would see what I might learn about Herr Schutz and his descendants that could be of use to me.

Diana

66

The first document was a chronological index of everything Bennett had done to find Kurt Schutz, and the results of his efforts. The original documents of this lifelong search, however, were not in the file.

I skimmed through the first section, which told the sad fate of Kasselbronn after the Nazi seizure of power in 1933. Schutz became the local dictator, eliminating both city and county government, and carrying out the orders of the Nazi hierarchy. Bennett wrote that this happened all across Germany with other little dictators like Schutz in each town, enforcing Hitler's will with terror, beatings, imprisonment, and death.

The people didn't lose just their democratic political structure. All clubs and social groups were outlawed, disbanded, and replaced by Nazi counterparts. The Nazis called this *gleichschaltung,* which Bennett translated as "bringing in line." Whether a club enjoyed paramilitary exercises, card playing, singing, or needlework, whether it was for young or old, it ceased to exist by Nazi order. Even those church leaders who had welcomed the Nazis and damned the Social Democrats found they too would either be brought into line or end up in a concentration camp. *Gleichschaltung* had the effect of bleaching every form of social structure out of the fabric of German life, replacing it with the one unifying structure of Nazism.

What a tool for a dictatorship! I tried to imagine what that must have been like for a town that had enjoyed such a rich club life. What was it that Otto had told Bennett? Two Germans talking, a conversation. Three Germans talking, a club.

All public money and all social welfare programs were run by Schutz. The homeless disappeared from the streets: Some were killed, some imprisoned, some put to work on projects like the swan ponds and park I had seen. Political opponents of the Nazis were either worked to death in rock quarries or starved to death with no job. If you wanted decent work and food, you became a Nazi. Jews, Social Democrats, Communists were all denied any assistance. Even the elderly and sick were thrown out of nursing homes and refused food.

Despite the overwhelming power of the regime, a few brave people continued to resist. A secret conspiracy provided intelligence on who was in danger, and through the efforts of the Resistance, many people were rescued and moved to safety. Active in the Resistance were Otto, Anna, Dobler, and Bennett.

Bennett had also been working on a way to kill Kurt that would not reflect on the town. He had witnessed Nazi revenge, and knew that the murder of a group leader would bring retaliation too horrific to imagine. He had finally worked out a plan he felt would eliminate Kurt while placing blame on another Nazi. Before he could carry it out, however, the party announced that Kurt had been promoted, and he disappeared from Kasselbronn. That was 1936. It was 1946 before Bennett was to learn what happened to Schutz.

My train was a local and was beginning to make stops in some of the towns surrounding Dusseldorf. As we would stop, I would peer through the slit at the side of the window shade and read the name of the station to check our progress. About the third stop I realized that I had seen police uniforms at each stop. I took particular notice at this stop because I saw one of the officers checking each passenger against a photo he held.

"Oh, Hell." Slipping onto the train in a burg in central Germany was one thing. Getting off in a major city where the train passengers were being screened for my bright little face was something else. Now what was I to do? Pull out my plastic pistol and shoot my way out?

In town I could buy some makeup, hair dye, and a costume, but for now I had nothing but my wits and whatever I could scrounge on this train. I looked around. In my compartment were two seats that made down into a bed at night, a mirror, a small basin, and a couple of hooks for clothing. I looked in the mirror at my shoulder-length hair and sighed. I had no choice. The hair had to go, and there could be no tell-tale evidence left behind.

I had no sacks, bag, suitcase, or purse. This was really traveling light. The German magazine would have to do. I set it in the basin and opened it to about the third page.

The process of downsizing from a house to a suitcase to a purse to a fanny pack to pockets is a common exercise for most women, and experience creates a sort of short list of indispensable items. I emptied my pockets onto the seat until I finally found the little Swiss pocket knife with the tiny pair of scissors. I took one last look at my hair, then picked up the first strand, chopped it off, and put it in the pages of the magazine. Turning the page, I cut another, put it in between the pages, and turned. I continued the process until my shoulder-length hair was earlobe-length and I had worked my way to the end of the magazine. What next?

I loaded my few possessions back into my pockets, and taking the magazine and folk dress with me, I left the sanctuary of my compartment. A risk, but I had no choice. Somehow, before I got off the train, I had to have a change of clothing.

As I walked through the train I looked for any opportunity: an open, unattended cabin, a coat left on an empty seat, a luggage area unlocked and unattended. I saw a few possibilities but none I felt certain I could get away with. This was not a time to take chances. In the dining car I took a seat, ordered coffee, and tried to think. Even if I did snag someone's coat and hat, the haircut would hardly be sufficient disguise. It was getting dark. That would help a little, but there were lights at the stations.

Perhaps I could find the conductor and buy an additional fare to some small town where I could get off in the middle of the night. When the waitress set down my coffee, I asked her in English how far this train went. She told me the last stop was in Dusseldorf. With a smile she added, "Then I get to go home and see my children for a night." I took a close look at her uniform: white hat, jacket, and apron over white pants. Not bad.

"Do you have to clean up after the passengers leave?"

"Oh no. As soon as we pull in, I'm through. Another crew comes in for the cleanup."

"That's good. I'm sure your family will be happy to see you. Have a good evening."

Fortunately the coffee was tepid, because I drank it down as rapidly as possible and walked up the car toward the galley. The service bar with coffee and water was at the opening to the galley. I stood at the bar looking around for any sign of a uniform closet or peg, but everything was shipshape. A steward saw me and did a double take. As I lifted the coffee pot to refill my cup he came toward me, wagging a finger and admonishing me in German.

I smiled and said, "I'm sorry, but I don't understand a word you're saying."

He took the pot from my hand and switched to heavily accented English. "You must sit, please. You could have a terrible accident here and get very hurt."

That, I thought, sounded like a good idea. At the next lunge the train took, I lost my balance and fell into him, spilling my cup of coffee on his jacket.

"Oh no! Have I burned you? I am so sorry."

"No, the coffee is not so hot, not to worry; but see, this is why you must sit. I will bring the coffee."

Continuing my apologies I took the seat nearest to the galley. When he brought me the coffee I took a napkin and tried to blot the coffee stain on his jacket, saying, "Oh dear, I made such a mess of your coat. Please let me pay for the cleaning."

"No, that is not necessary."

Despite his politeness to me, he had some words for the woman who served me that didn't sound so understanding. I was sorry I had gotten her in trouble but was rewarded when the steward pushed on one side of the panel behind the coffee stand and it swung open, revealing the clean uniforms.

By the time the train slowed for the last stop, everything had been cleared from the dining car, all the window blinds had been closed and the lights dimmed. I had moved to the other end of the car and the service people were sitting at the table where I had been. They had not changed into civvies. That was good news. Now I just needed to see what door they left by.

I rested my head on my arms on the table and pretended to sleep. When the train stopped and the crew rose to leave, they of course roused me and ushered me out of the car and through the passage to the next car. There, just inside the next car, was an exit to the platform. As they headed down the steps, they told me I needed to go out at the passenger exit two cars down. I thanked them and went into the toilet. I waited for them to leave, then hurried back into the dim dining room. In the galley, I pushed on the panel and grabbed a uniform and hat.

Slipping the uniform on over my clothes, I walked back to the staff exit and down the steps. I could see police standing at both passenger exits, checking everyone against my picture. No one, however, took any note of one more uniform leaving by way of the employee exit.

I grabbed a taxi in front of the station and gave the driver an address two streets south of the hotel. I went into a small cafe, walked directly to the ladies' room and took off the uniform I had borrowed. Now I had three things I needed to dispose of: hair, uniform, and folk dress. I would worry about that tomorrow. At the cafe I bought a sandwich to-go and walked by a circuitous route to my hotel. At each turn I checked for a tail but saw nothing suspicious. Finally, tired and stressed, I got to my hotel, checked in, and crashed.

Diana

67

I was asleep by nine-thirty and didn't wake up until nine a.m., when the housekeeper knocked on the door. I sent her away. Once conscious, my first act was to pick up the computer and dial Sam. I reached a tense-sounding Robert James.

"Yes?"

"I need to talk with Sam."

"He's not here, Diana, and may be in a position that would be inconvenient to receive a call. May I help you?"

Briefly, my mind hovered on what Sam might be doing, but I decided not to waste time trying to pull information out of the reticent Robert James. "Okay, here's my problem. They are really hunting me here, and I need to disguise myself, but Bennett put the safe-deposit boxes in his name and mine. I don't know what ID I will need to access the box, but if I leave here as Margaret Atwater I won't—"

"I don't believe you will have a problem. Most likely you will need to present only the box number, the key, and your thumb print, no ID."

"Most likely? How sure are you?"

"Reasonably certain. Bennett was also fond of disguise and false identification. I don't know about the Dusseldorf box specifically, but I do know that the reason Sam put in that thumb print doorbell on your California apartment was so he could digitize your thumb print for Bennett to use as ID on numbered bank accounts and so forth."

"Ah, more secrets. Okay, I'll go ahead with the Atwater look. At least if it fails I won't have used the Hunter name and exposed myself. Now the next problem. Once I get Margaret groomed, she will no longer fit the picture in the passport."

"Email me a picture as soon as you're 'groomed,' and I will take care of the new passport and express it to you."

"Good. I'll need it ASAP because next I'll need to go to Italy and then—"

"No, Diana, you mustn't do that. Call back when you see what you have in the Dusseldorf box. Sam may be back by then or be where he can talk. We have not exactly been idle here, and there are several things . . . things we will need to coordinate with you. We may need to bring you home right away."

I didn't know what to say to that and so for a moment said nothing.

"You still there, Diana?

"Yes. Why the mystery? Why not get all the files while I'm at it?"

"Even though we have a secure line, I would rather not say more on the phone. Sam will explain it all to you when he picks you up. Let's ring off for now."

With that, he hung up on me. Momentarily I indulged in a bit of anger. Evidently Robert James still didn't trust me and wanted Sam to "handle" me. What were they doing and what "things" did we have to coordinate? What did he mean, when Sam "picks me up"? Damn I was getting tired of being treated like a mushroom. I considered calling him back and demanding more information but decided I didn't have the time or emotional energy to argue with him. I squashed the bubbling emotions, cleared my mind, and returned to the project at hand.

By the time I had showered and dressed, my stomach was growling, but before breakfast I had a couple things to check. With the help of the German phrase book on my computer and the local phonebook, I found the address of a specialty shop that sounded as if it would handle the type of clothing and accessories I had in mind. My first stop was at a Fed Ex office, where I picked up a box large enough to hold my growing collection and some package tape. Then I headed for breakfast.

At the cafe where I had gotten the sandwich the previous night, I seated myself at a rear corner table. As I downed the coffee, eggs, and pastry, I studied all the other patrons who came in after me and watched for anyone hanging around outside. I saw nothing that caused concern. Nonetheless, when I left, I went to the ladies' room in back and then out the back door to the alley behind the shops. I jogged down the alley for two blocks, then onto the sidewalk at the second cross street. There I caught a taxi and had the driver take me to the specialty store.

Though the shop was small, it served my needs, and I began assembling Margaret's outfit. This shop catered to rock musicians, wannabes, and those simply seeking a rock party costume. I began to think of Margaret as Magz. I selected a pair of bile yellow tights, a hot pink miniskirt, a black wife-beater undershirt, with a torn off-the-shoulder sweatshirt and the highest platform shoes I could find. I added some body tattoos that you apply with water, and some false teeth that would fit over my own teeth and give Magz crooked, slightly protruding teeth. I also found an amazing little appliance that attaches to your back molars and makes your cheeks puff out, totally changing the shape of your face. I selected some skin toner to darken me to a nut brown, black hair dye, and hair goo to spike my hair. Magz's jewelry was stunning: gems and charms for nose, tongue, and ears. They would appear to be body piercing but were either glued on or applied like a clamp earring. Magz would be over the top. I felt certain she could walk the streets unrecognized as Diana Hunter. I just wasn't sure the security guard at the bank would let her in the door.

Loaded with packages I took another taxi back to the hotel, locked myself in and began the creation of Magz. It took over two hours to get her hair dyed and spiked and her skin tanned and tattooed. Then I added brown contacts and reluctantly started stuffing my mouth with false teeth and cheek puffers. The cheek things took several tries before I figured out how to make them stay put. Then, with all this stuff in my mouth, I had to practice speaking without sounding like I had a mouth full of marbles. For my manicure I glued on long plastic nails, painted them black, and added tiny skulls and crossbones to the tips.

Examining my creation in the mirror, I was both satisfied and horrified with the results. I added heavy black eye shadow and applied the jewelry. It wasn't as good a job as Richard would have done, but years of watching him had taught me a good deal.

With the computer I snapped a picture and zapped it off to Robert James.

I transferred my belongings from the pockets of my filthy cargo pants to the backpack-style purse that Magz carried. My dirty clothes, the uniform I had borrowed from the train galley, the folk dress, and the magazine with my shorn locks were all packed into the Fed Ex box along with the original documents in the money belt. I addressed the box to Robert James but didn't seal it. The box and the package tape went into the large sack I had gotten at the rock costume store, along with the items left over from my makeup. Then dressed, coifed, made up, and packed, I took one last look around the hotel to make sure I had left nothing. I was ready to go to the bank.

The security guard was short, fat, past retirement age, and looked like he was suffering from both boredom and sore feet. Nonetheless, when Magz walked through the door, he came to attention. For those of a certain age, the BP, or Before Punk age, tattoos and body piercing have two possible effects. The people are either so astonished they stare or so repulsed they can't look. The guard was one who stared. Though he was now probably working on his second career to stretch his retirement income, I suspected he had been a policeman in his younger years. He had that "presence" I had learned to recognize in my cop friends. He would be a trained observer, so the trick here would be to get past him quickly while he was still startled by Magz's appearance and before he had time to notice too much detail.

I couldn't translate his words, but it was obvious as he stepped into my path that he was asking what the hell I wanted in the bank.

Like a snake tasting the air, I gave him a quick attention-grabbing look at the jewel on my tongue, but not a long enough look for him to notice the flesh colored clasp that held it on. Then, like the magician distracting the audience's attention, I raised my hand with its black manicured nails. In my fingertips I held the safe-deposit box key.

"Got to check my box, ducks." The Devonshire accent I had planned for Margaret had been changed to a light cockney for Magz.

The guard took the key, examined it, and handed it back. Still in German he gave me a response I couldn't understand, but he pointed to the appropriate window across the room.

"Thanks, love."

I laid the key on the counter. The clerk looked up, caught sight of my multiple nose and tongue jewels, and quickly looked down again.

"I need to check my box."

Avoiding looking at me, he mumbled in the direction of the key, "Yes, *mein dame*. One moment please."

When he first checked safe-deposit box number 627 against bank records, he appeared at a loss as to how to proceed and excused himself to seek advice of a senior bank officer.

Damn! What did this mean? Could Bennett have left a photo or something? I watched their whispered conversation and sidelong glances in my direction. Maybe I should have just chanced coming in as Diana, but so far no one had even asked for identification. What would I do if they did? What if Robert James was wrong about my only needing a thumb print?

When a third bank officer was called, I went to high alert. That third officer took over assisting me. Perhaps forewarned, he didn't react to my appearance in any way.

In a pleasant, accommodating tone and lightly accented English he said, "Good afternoon, madam. I am Herr Marx and will be happy to assist you in accessing your security box."

Then holding open a polished wooden half-door next to the window, he said, "Won't you please come to my office?"

Briefly I wondered if this was so he could hold me until the police arrived, but I smiled and followed him. In his office, he shut the door and offered me a chair. I sat uneasily.

Herr Marx was polite and apologetic as he explained the problem. "I am sorry our clerk could not accommodate your request more quickly but, as you probably know, the person setting up this account specified unusual instructions to the bank. He required a thumb print ID, and that is not routine."

Then from his office safe, he took an envelope labeled "box 627," and pulled out a small square box, which he attached to the USB port on his computer.

"Now if you would be so kind as to place your thumb on the little lighted box, I shall be able to verify your ownership and escort you to box 627."

I touched my thumb to the lighted box and began to breathe normally again.

After the danger of getting here and the elaborate disguise, the actual act of obtaining access to the safe-deposit box turned out to be surprisingly easy. Again, Bennett left little to chance. As I considered my short spiked hair, I wondered if creating Magz had really been necessary. Then I thought about my face being in all the newspapers and the watchers checking passengers at airports and train depots and decided it was. Diana Hunter would never have made it this far. Oh well, the hair would grow.

Once we had both turned our keys and unlocked box 627, I was provided with a small private room to open it. As I removed the lid, musty odors were released into the air: damp old money, mildewed books, decaying leather, and gun oil. I sneezed and looked inside. It was the largest box the bank provided and held a huge amount of pounds, franks, and marks, useless now, but there were also dollars and euros. There were also gold coins and a small velvet bag of precious stones. A Luger pistol with ammunition was sealed in a small case and protected with packets designed to prevent humidity from rusting the pistol. There were also several passports with Bennett's picture and different names and nationalities. There were two small leather bound books that showed much use, filled with notations that I was at a loss to understand or decode.

Standing up at the edge of the box was an expandable reddish brown file tied with a yellowed ribbon. As I lifted it out, my breathing once again became short, shallow, fast. Would this finally explain Otto's murder, Ned and Emma's beating, and the worldwide manhunt for me?

I untied the ribbon and opened the flap. Inside, I found two packets of original documents on Kurt Schutz. All of the papers were yellowed and brittle, and I had to handle them with great care. At last I could read the secrets that Senator Motfeld would murder to keep concealed.

The first set contained reports written in German that dated from 1936 to 1945. Well, maybe I couldn't read them. On top of this file, however, was an introduction by Bennett:

The following files are reports sent to __SS RSHA Amt VI__— (Department Six) Nazi Germany's main security headquarters. Department Six combined foreign intelligence, sabotage, and propaganda (a mission similar to the CIA). By war's end, it had consolidated foreign sections of Nazi police intelligence, military intelligence (Abwehr), Gehlen's FHO, and much of foreign espionage networks as well. Both Gehlen and the U.S. took their most valuable recruits from this unit.

I reread that sentence to make sure I read it right. The U.S. took recruits from the Nazi Department Six?

These particular reports cover the activities of the __Einsatzgruppen,__ or murder commando unit, under the command of Kurt Schutz. They were made by a team that followed behind the Einsatzgruppen to verify the numbers killed and other claims of the units. The Germans love to document everything, and thanks to Gehlen, who stashed records as a bargaining tool for his own protection and freedom, many records have been preserved.

  Even though KS hadn't the physical stature to be SS (too short and squat), he had proven himself in Kasselbronn as a leader of a murder squad and a man who knew how to train men to become mass murderers. He understood the propaganda base necessary to convince the men under his command that the victims were either subhuman or were guilty of causing harm to good Germans, and therefore deserved what they got. He became one of the first commissioned for "special operations," including terror, extermination, genocide, mass murder. His troops served in Germany, France, Czechoslovakia, Austria, and the USSR. At most locations all the able-bodied men were shipped out as slaves, all women, children, and old were murdered.

  No wonder the Senator came after Bennett's files. This gruesome record was not exactly the closet skeleton one would want to find in a Presidential candidate. There followed an index to the file's contents. I knew I would express these to Sam and Robert James, but as a caution, I also used my little computer to photocopy each original document. The introductory page to the second file read:

  Once I had been able to gain his release from Dachau and prove his record as a member of the resistance, Otto Brehm and I were both put to work with the staff of the CROWCASS, the Central Registry of War Crimes and Security Suspects. There we helped in identifying and capturing those who were to be tried as Nazi war criminals. This was at first very satisfying and rewarding work. Then we became suspicious that the information we were supplying was being used by some elements for a different purpose. This suspicion was confirmed on a day when I was given the assignment to find and <u>recruit</u> *Kurt Schutz as a "valued asset" for the new Cold War against Russia. At that time I was given his record from Nazi files and told that he was to be recruited by the U.S. I decided I had to do a little checking of my own to learn who could be issuing such orders.*

  This was when I first discovered the deal made by Reinhard Gehlen, Hitler's most senior military intelligence officer on the Eastern front. This man, responsible for the torture, murder, and starvation of millions, had buried all his microfilmed intelligence on the USSR and made a deal to give it to the U.S., in exchange for his freedom and employment. With the help of American military commanders, as well as clandestine assistance at the highest levels of the CIA, a deal was struck. Gehlen set up operations and hired many of his Nazi associates to run the Gehlen Organization, all secretly paid for by the U.S.

I reread the entire last paragraph, wondering how I missed this in the history books.

By the time I was told to find and hire Kurt, the hiring and importation of Nazis was well under way. Two American officials, Herbert Cummings and Samuel Klaus, had tried to stop this program; but the Dulles brothers, and others had simply set up operations such as Project Overcast and Operation Paperclip, which whitewashed Nazi records or supplied false identities. Only a handful of Americans knew what was happening. Elected senators and representatives knew nothing of the secret government within the government. I considered trying to take this information home and expose it. Having lived under the Nazis, however, I recognized the hidden power at work and knew how futile that would be, and how fatal. Disclosure would have been in violation of the secrecy oath I had signed and would be in defiance of a power too great for one man to challenge. I would have been silenced, one way or another.

With clarity, I now understood the origin of Uncle Bennett's secret files.

Those orders to hire Kurt Schutz, however, altered the course of the rest of my life. Realizing that I could only work secretly for the disclosure, I set up my own organization of two, Otto and I. There were some small successes for us but our efforts did not bear much fruit for <u>forty</u> years. Only with the Watergate affair did Congressional investigations finally begin to unravel the secret world of covert operations. The attempts at coverup at that time were not really to hide the third-rate burglary of the Watergate Hotel but primarily to protect the extensive covert operations, the secret government. I am inordinately proud of my small part in this disclosure, but that story is for another file.

If I had been successful in finding Kurt, I would have slit his throat. Far too fast a death for any true justice, but expedient in preventing him from being employed by my country. Unfortunately, he turned himself in to Gehlen Org and was put to work secretly. It was years later before I gained files showing what that work had been.

Kurt was put to work on CCPs, Clandestine Containment Programs, to influence and control foreign governments. In Italy in 1948, the Communists were heavily favored by the people, which caused such alarm in Washington that some were calling for the U.S. military occupation of the Foggia oilfields. A CIA program was quickly put together to manipulate this election. It included a multi pronged attack, including money given to support candidates, creation of publicity campaigns including Radio Free Europe, and much more. At Kurt's level it meant paramilitary gangs funded by the CIA whose job it was to beat left-wing candidates and activists, break up political meetings, and intimidate voters. In other words it was the same job Storm Troopers had done for Hitler in the early years. Funds for these early black ops came from "black currency," Nazi German assets, often blood money, that had been seized by the U.S. under the War Powers Act. Kurt was by this time a seasoned professional and a trainer of such groups. His talents were used in Italy, Greece, and Turkey, and perhaps other countries I have not yet documented.

There followed an index of the original documents he had managed to obtain. My mind darted in several directions at once and I wondered if the current attempt at coverup was triggered by fear of the first packet or of the second. I didn't have time to think about it. I copied it all, then replaced everything in the expandable file and packed it in the Fed Ex box with the clothes. I used the package tape to seal it securely and put the Fed Ex box back in the sack. Replacing the lid to box 627, I called the attendant to make sure it was safely locked up again, and then I quietly left the bank.

I was in a taxi headed for the Fed Ex office when the computer phone rang in Magz's purse. I pulled it out and answered, "Call you back in five," and turned it off again. When the taxi dropped me off, I found a quiet doorway and returned the call.

Sam's face appeared on my screen. I toggled on the webcam. "What's up?"

"Got the package?"

"Just did. Headed for Fed Ex to express it when you called."

"Don't. I'm coming for you tomorrow by private jet I'll have Margaret Atwater's new passport and will bring you and the package home."

"Why, Sam? Margaret is perfectly safe. I put a lot into this, and I want to finish collecting the rest of Bennett's stash."

"I'm sorry. I'll explain everything on the ride home. It has to be this way if we're going to clear your name. Otherwise you might have to be Margaret the rest of your life." He laughed and added, "From what I see on this screen, I doubt you would want that. I emailed you the airport location and all instructions for the pickup. See you tomorrow, Beautiful."

With that, he signed off. More secrets. I checked the email and found that Sam would be picking me up at a private aviation terminal at Dusseldorf International. A new hotel, near the airport, seemed to be the next order of business.

I settled for dinner in my room but treated myself to an excellent bottle of German wine and an early bedtime. Tomorrow I could show Sam what I had learned about Motfeld and find out what the hell Sam and Robert James had been up to.

Diana

68

Sam and I met in the terminal, and he slipped me Margaret Atwater's passport with the new photo. I had changed to jeans and a blouse but kept the teeth, cheeks, spiked hair, and jewels until after I cleared the terminal.

He led me aboard a Gulfstream G-V and with a smile told me to make myself comfortable. He went into the gleaming galley and began mixing us some drinks and watching me as I surveyed the luxurious private jet. All the chairs were softly upholstered, all the tables highly polished hard woods. It was like entering someone's home rather than a plane.

"Nice ride," I said. "Who did you con out of this?"

"You."

"What do you mean?"

"It's yours, or rather it belongs to one of your corporations. It was the way Bennett got around the world quickly and quietly. RJ finally coughed up the secret when we figured we needed to get you home quickly."

Shaking my head, I looked around the jet. "I've got corporations? Do I have to know how to run them?"

He laughed. "Worry about that later. We're fueled, cleared, and ready for take off. Here's a little something to help you relax." He handed me a Perfect Rob Roy, up with a lemon twist, my favorite drink; the glass was chilled, the proportions perfect. I knew then that I wasn't going to like the news he had for me.

He made himself a Manhattan, sat down across from me and made small talk as the plane taxied down the runway. After take-off he asked questions and I filled him in on the details of my trip to Germany and the lowdown on Kurt Schutz. We opened the express box and pulled out the Schutz file. He read the two notes written by Bennett and looked briefly at the various reports. He asked more about the chalet and about Anna. Then he gave me the first news from home.

"By the way, I've got some very good news. Ned will make it. He was in intensive care, and we didn't have much hope. Then Emma got well enough to be moved, and we sneaked her out of Johnson City Hospital and into the private hospital where Ned was. He turned around as soon as she was there beside him."

"Thank God. The last I heard, he wasn't expected to make it."

The plane reached cruising altitude and leveled out. Still we chatted. It was like two cousins who didn't really know each other trying to make polite conversation at a family reunion. What was he waiting for? I decided I couldn't stand it any longer. "Okay, Sam. Spit it out. No matter how bad it might be, it can't be worse than the anxiety of waiting for you to tell me."

"Oh sure," he said, as if he hadn't been holding out on me at all. He pointed at my empty glass and jumped up to mix me a second drink. He knew very well that two was my limit. If he felt he had to get me thoroughly anaesthetized to tell me the news, I really was worried. As he mixed the Rob Roy, he continued his small talk. "Ya know, I'm really glad I saw that passport picture before I saw you. I wouldn't have known you. That's really good makeup."

I had removed the teeth and cheeks in order to have my first Rob Roy. With that reminder I started to remove the jewels, but Sam stopped me.

"Better keep Magz until we clear customs at home."

He handed me the glass. Pointedly, I set it down on the table. "Cut the bullshit, Sam. Give it to me straight."

He set his glass down too. "Okay. There's a lot to catch you up on so . . . Look, you've done a great job getting this file, but you know our first priority is to clear you of the allegations of that federal warrant. Second is what to do about Hedgeman and Blain, and third is how we can use this file. You said it yourself the other day when you called. Who's going to care about the material in this file? It was his grandfather, not Motfeld, and the senator has an excellent record, bending over backward to never take any anti-Semitic stance and making sizable contributions to the Simon Wiesenthal Center, et cetera."

"So this whole trip was just a waste of time? What about the crime scene evidence?"

He smiled. "We've got it. However, when Jim realized that these guys were the killers, he went to Senator Motfeld, who is chair of the Senate committee investigating unauthorized black ops, to tell him that SICC had some rogue agents. And, as you figured out, that was the wrong person to talk to. Jim must have known he was in trouble after he spoke to Motfeld. He disappeared from home and work, and the bureau gave out the story he was on vacation.

"The report that Jim sent to Sheriff Tumey gave him the evidence he needed; so he went to the judge and got a warrant for Hedgeman, Blain, and the third man, whose name was MacIntire. I was tailing Hedgman and Blain who were cooling their heels in Raleigh at that time, but it looked to me like they were making plans to leave the country. Tumey brought the warrant and two deputies to the motel where I had them under surveillance and arrested them."

"Well, that sounds like all good news. I thought you had something terrible to tell me. So they're in jail now?"

"Two are. The third one was killed."

"Killed? Did Robert James—"

Sam shook his head. "No. He would like to have taken the bastard out, but once the passion cooled, he knew that if we were ever going to get you cleared, we needed these guys alive. He just followed MacIntire long enough to see he was flying back to D.C., called to let me know, and then went back to the compound. We don't know for sure what happened to MacIntire. He was driving out of Washington and was found dead, his car wrapped around a power pole. Accident or Motfeld cleaning up his mess—we don't know."

"Does Hedgeman know about MacIntire?"

"Yes, and he's no dummy. He may have figured out by now that he has become expendable. When he first called back to Hannover, Doppler, and Peggler, that D.C. law firm, for someone to represent them, they wouldn't even talk to him. He had to get an attorney here in North Carolina. Whether that will encourage him to deal or just make him loyally bite the bullet for his boss, I can't guess. He may be a cutout and not even know Motfeld is involved."

"So? What happens now?"

"Sheriff Tumey and the county Solicitor had all the skids greased before we got back from Raleigh. He ran Hedgeman and Blain through the preliminary hearing in district court before they or their local attorney had much time to think. The attorney was way out of his league, and all he tried to do was get bail set. Not only is it a murder case, but when Tumey arrested them, they had false passports and tickets for Argentina on them. Needless to say, the judge considered them a flight risk and denied bail. He asked the solicitor to draw up the indictment and bind them over to the grand jury.

The grand jury will hear the witnesses and examine the documentary evidence. This is where you and your little file come in my dear. We have very good evidence from the crime scene, Ned, Emma and Jim to testify, but you are the only eyewitness who can put Hedgeman and Blain at the scene at the time Otto came out of that window."

"Then what happens?"

"If twelve out of eighteen find a true bill, Hedgeman and Blain will be tried in superior court for the murder of Otto Brehm and the beatings of Ned and Emma."

I picked up the Schutz file and smiled. "So we will get this out there by entering it in the court record. That all sounds . . . good, so what's the problem you haven't told me about yet?"

"There's still a federal warrant out on you. They didn't need probable cause to get the warrant, and they won't need it to grab you. So if someone at the federal level grabs you before we get these guys indicted and the evidence safely documented in the public record, we might have a tough time getting you back and getting these assholes convicted."

"Oh, I see."

"You are lucky though. When Congress renewed the Patriot Act they inserted the right for persons like you named in some National Security matter to have a hearing before a judge. If they hadn't we would have no way to get the warrant voided."

"I still don't see . . ."

"We think that since the preliminary hearing, Senator Motfeld has secretly taken more interest in Hedgeman and Blain. They have somehow obtained the services of some high-powered criminal lawyers. Now the grand jury hearings are secret. Not even the Solicitor or the defendant are allowed at them. So that's not a problem. But if Motfeld's people get hold of the indictment before the grand jury meets, all the witness names and a list of all the evidence, including the Schutz file, will be in it. We're concerned not only about your safety, but also Ned and Emma's.

Obviously the Bureau is taking the threat seriously too. because they have Jim stashed somewhere, but have assured us he will be available for the grand jury."

"The judge and solicitor are working from the photocopies you sent on the stipulation that the originals show up in time for the grand jury." Sam reached into a cabinet and pulled out a mailer that was addressed to me at my old apartment in Bluff Beach. The return address was Otto's law office. It was the envelope that the courier had delivered, notifying me about Bennett's will. There was nothing inside the envelope. I looked at him questioningly. He picked up the Schutz file and put it into the envelope. "At some point you will be asked why you think Otto's office was being searched. Then there will be a reason to introduce this as evidence. You won't want to explain how you really came up with it, so I retrieved that envelope for you."

"You guys have been busy, haven't you?"

"Yep. Now put your teeth in, Magz. We will have to land in New York to clear customs. We have another private aviation terminal. An agent will come aboard. Should be no problem. Once we take off again, I need you to get rid of Margaret Atwater and become Diana Hunter again as fast as possible."

"Why?"

Sam hesitated a long time, looking into my eyes with a plea for me to accept and trust him. "We're going to land at a private field outside Thomasville. The plane will be met by Sheriff Tumey. He'll be there to place you in custody."

"Why?"

"It's protective custody. He's putting you in the care of the Attorney General of the State of North Carolina. It will be legal but keep you completely away from Tumey's jail or anywhere else Motfeld's people might hunt for you."

"Then why get rid of Margaret? She's perfect. I would be completely safe in this getup. Hell, for that matter, I would be safe at Bennett's house. Why do I have to be in custody?"

"The solicitor will not include you as a witness in the indictment unless he and the judge see you and talk to you personally. Likewise, they need to see the original Schutz file. Our compromise agreement is that you and the file remain in the custody of the AG. We gotta do things legal, Diana, if we're going to get these guys."

I slammed the file down on the shiny wood table between us, rattling the drink glasses.

"Damn it! Damn it all to Hell! No wonder you made me Rob Roys. Senator Motfeld's above the law and he goes his merry way while I have to be locked up? It's not fair, Sam."

He picked up his Manhattan, which I had narrowly missed with the file, sipped the drink and looked at the glass, not at me.

"No," he said "it's not fair, and as power and wealth are consolidated into fewer and fewer hands, it becomes easier to manipulate the government to even less fairness. The very fact that Motfeld *is* above the law is the precise reason we must use the law. Because, Diana, if we are not a people under law we cannot be a free people."

I could feel the tears well up in my eyes. Looking away from Sam I swigged down half of my drink, then took three deep breaths and reined in the emotion.

"How long?"

Sam didn't smile, but his face relaxed. "The grand jury meets in just five days. That's why we had to get you back to talk with the Solicitor so he can complete the indictment. If we don't catch this meeting, it would be weeks. Besides, You're not going to be doing hard time, you know. You will be stashed in a very comfortable safe house. Give you a chance to catch up on your reading."

Diana

69

When our plane landed at Thomasville, Sheriff Tumey formally took me into custody then turned me over to the State Attorney General of North Carolina. The AG made a few polite words, then placed me in the hands of Mr. James Jenson from his office. Mr. Jenson and his partner, Michael Lester, were to take me to the safe house until the grand jury hearing.

The first stop, however, was at an office where they literally snuck me in the back door. I hadn't a clue where it was. There I was introduced to the solicitor charged with writing the indictment. He carefully examined the Schutz file, compared it to the copies Sam had printed from the computer file, and agreed to work from the copies as long as the originals were filed in court before the grand jury hearing. I was sworn in, right there in the office, and gave my account of events the night Otto was killed.

Before we left for my safe house, the AG took charge of the originals of the Schutz file. He said he would return them before the grand jury met, but he needed them for something urgent. He implied that it was something on my behalf but declined to give me any more information. I looked to Sam, who gave me a nod, and I reluctantly parted with the file I had risked my life to obtain.

I must admit that when Sam first said Sheriff Tumey was putting me in custody, I pictured handcuffs and a small smelly cell surrounded by scary people. Instead I found myself living in an antebellum mansion in a rural part of North Carolina. It was the kind of digs I'd only seen in movies, a gorgeous cage, but a cage nonetheless. I wasn't even allowed to go for a walk on the extensive grounds surrounding the place.

I was very well cared for. My meals were prepared to my specifications by a cook named Sylvester, and my clothes were washed, my bed made, and all my personal needs seen to by a housekeeper named Mary Jane. Of course, I had only three changes of clothing: the blue jeans and blouse I had been wearing when I was taken into custody; the cargo pants, blouse, and windbreaker I had packed up in Germany; and the steward's pants and coat I had borrowed from the train in Dusseldorf. I gave the folk dress to Mary Jane, who thought it was wonderful. I did have the outfit I bought for Magz, but I wasn't about to put it on. The steward's outfit made pretty good pajamas, and by day, I traded off between the jeans and cargo pants. When this whole affair was over, I was sure I would burn all these clothes.

My guardians were polite enough but too professional to say anything about the case and in fact they had little to say on any subject. As the first day rolled into the second, I gave up all attempts at conversation and resigned myself to some well-earned quiet and solitude. I had trouble concentrating on a book; so by the third day I was spending much of my day and night watching *Turner Classic Movies* on TV. I took my meals in my room in front of the television, and when there was a movie I didn't like, I turned on my little computer and played solitaire. By the fourth day I was really bored.

Mid-morning on the fourth day, we had company. I was playing cards on the computer when I heard the car coming down the long gravel driveway. Looking out my second-story window, I watched a black town car pull to a stop in the circle drive in front of the mansion's colonnade entrance. Mr. Jenson met the car, opened the passenger door, and held it while the Attorney General stepped out. I saw a briefcase in the AG's hand and wondered if he was returning my file. He and Mr. Jenson spoke quietly for a moment and headed toward the house.

I shut down the computer and considered setting it on the window sill to let its solar battery charge, but it was too late in the day, so I just tucked it into a large cargo pocket below the knee of my pants.

Mary Jane offered tea, but the AG declined and ask me to join him in the study. He asked a few polite questions as to my well being, but I got the impression he really wasn't hearing my answers. It was a giveaway when I mentioned having only two wearable outfits and his response was "Good, Good."

Changing the subject, I asked him if the file had been useful.

His eyes seemed to focus as if we had touched on a subject that tapped into the part of his brain that was engaged. "Yes. Quite." He patted his briefcase but made no offer to return the file to me. "As well as the rest of the evidence in this case. I didn't mention before what I needed it for because I didn't want to get your hopes up in case our efforts failed. What we have done is taken the evidence of this case to court in Washington, D.C., and we have gotten your federal subpoena vacated." At that pronouncement, he actually smiled, ever so slightly, but a smile. "You're no longer a wanted woman, Ms. Hunter."

As this sunk in I felt a tremendous relief and also a realization that despite all the abuse of power I had seen in this case, the law can still work.

"Thank you, sir. I can't tell you what a relief that is. I really didn't know you could do that. Can . . . can I leave here now?"

"We really want to keep you under protection until after you have spoken to the grand jury. It's only one more day. Think you can manage that?"

I was so grateful for his efforts on my behalf, I readily agreed. We exchanged mutual appreciation, and he rose to leave.

"I'm headed back to Thomasville and will place all this material in the hands of the Solicitor, and he will see it is properly handled with the court."

It was just as we were opening the door to leave the study that all hell broke loose.

The sound of yelling, glass shattering, wood splitting came from every corner of the house. Men armed with automatic rifles, wearing military-type uniforms, heavy boots, and gas masks broke into the lovely old home through every door and window in the place. I didn't see Michael Lester, but I saw Jenson try to draw a weapon and get hit hard with the butt of a rifle and go down. I heard the AG say, "Oh my god! They must have followed me." I was gasping for breath. Gas canisters were all around us. Whether they were thrown in before the men or after they were inside, I didn't know. It all happened too fast. Two men threw the AG to the floor then grabbed me. I don't even know if they threw me down on the floor too or just carried me out, because by the time they took hold of my arms, I was already losing consciousness.

My nightmares were like a surreal Busby Berkeley review as brown-suited Storm Troopers with Nazi armbands marched quick time though ranks of white-armored *Star Wars* storm troopers. Every time I tried to escape them by coming to, the waking reality sent me back to the dreams. My nose and eyes burned, I was nauseated and my clothing reeked with the smell of vomit. Once or twice I woke just enough to see the lights of the instrument panel and hear the thwat, thwat sound of the chopper blades.

I don't remember landing or being moved to a car, but sometime during the car ride, I became fully conscious and stayed that way for a while. I was lying on my side in the backseat of a sedan. Two seatbelts held me, under my arms and around my hips. Somehow I doubted this was done out of concern for my safety.

I thought about the Schutz file. The AG had been holding his briefcase when they broke in. Was it overlooked or . . . then I thought about the others who had been at the house when these guys broke in. What happened to them? I know at least Jenson suffered a head injury. I had no idea about the rest.

My head was aching so badly, I wondered if they had used a rifle butt on me too. I tried to raise my hand to touch my head and both hands rose. The metal handcuffs bit into my skin, and some of my fingers were numb. Gingerly I felt around my head but found no lumps or cuts. Must be from the gas. I wished dearly for two Excedrin, and drifted back to sleep.

When I woke again the car was stopped and I was being dragged roughly out of the backseat by my arms. They stood me on my feet, but my legs folded under me and I crashed to the ground. A deep commanding voice barked, "Damn it. Carry her to the basement."

One man picked me up, threw me roughly over his shoulder, and carried me into a house. I rewarded his roughness by vomiting down his back and onto a lovely bird's-egg blue carpet. This was not the first time I had thrown up, so there was very little left in my stomach but a caustic bile that burned my throat and nose and dripped in a slimy string from my mouth. Nonetheless, it brought a vicious string of curses from the man with the deep voice.

My porter tossed me on a cement floor, banging my head against the wall so hard I saw stars. I hadn't realized that expression described a real phenomenon. This brought a string of curses from me, but my voice sounded weak and far away, nothing like the deep-voiced man who cursed with such authority. They left me alone on the cement floor and climbed back up the short stairway to a door.

I sat for some time rubbing my head with my cuffed hands while my brain tried to clear and begin to think. I must have been taken by the Senator's people.

Did he not know that the warrant had been vacated? Or did he know and decide to move before I could testify? Oh God, what I'd give for some Excedrin.

If I had been arrested under a legal warrant, wouldn't he have taken me to a jail or some official holding cell somewhere? I had been taken to a house, a private home with nice furnishings. That didn't seem like good news. If he was working that far out of the box, he would have to make me disappear. Without a witness, Hedgeman and Blain could claim they came into the office after Otto was killed. No witness, no conviction. I would go down in history as Otto's murderer. End of story. No rat line climbing up to tie the senator to any of this. And the file? If he had the file, there would be no motive for him to have been involved. The file and I would both disappear.

I looked around the basement. Some basements have little windows at ground level. This one was solid cement. I stood, wobbly at first, but I didn't fall; and made my way up the stairs to try the door handle. Yes, it was locked. What had I expected?

I was beginning to shiver. Back down the stairs I looked around for anything to keep me warm. The only thing I could find was a piece of gray tarp, moldy and already the home to a couple of spiders. I brushed them out, appropriated the tarp, and with that meager comfort nested myself on a some boxes. Pulling my knees to my chest, I wrapped the tarp around me and slipped my cuffed hands over my knees. As I wrapped my arms around my legs, and hugged myself for warmth, my forearm came to rest on something hard, something in the lower pocket of my pants. *Holy shit! They didn't search me.*

My computer was still in the pocket of these dear old cargo pants. Bless them. Even if I never wore them again, I would save them forever in a place of honor. Whether it was caution or paranoia, I considered the possibility that there was hidden surveillance equipment in this basement. I would not take a chance. I thought back to what happened before they came. I had been playing cards on the computer and when the AG came I shut it down.

Raising my cuffed hands off my knees but making sure the tarp stayed in place, I felt along the pocket. Unzipping it carefully I pulled the computer out of the pocket. Carefully I felt the surface, locating and identifying all the buttons before pushing any of them. First muting the speaker so no incoming sound would give me away, I turned on the computer. Almost immediately it began to vibrate with an incoming call that had to be Sam. I switched on the phone so he could hear me and also hit the button that activated the GPS signal. I didn't dare talk to him and just slipped the little computer back and zipped the pocket.

I yelled in the direction of the door. "Hey, out there, it's getting damn cold down here. How about letting me up in the house? My head is splitting. Hey, whoever's got me! Can you see me down here in this basement? Have a heart. If you got a video down here, you can see I'm not nauseated anymore. I won't barf on your carpet again. At least give me some water, Excedrin, and a blanket."

No one answered. No one came to the door. But it didn't matter. That was enough to let Sam know my condition, and hopefully that GPS was telling him where to come and get me.

I considered shutting down the phone and putting the computer on sleep to conserve batteries, but I was afraid I wouldn't have the opportunity to turn it on again unseen, or a new call from Sam would cause a vibration that would be noticed. So I left it on and waited and hoped.

It was forty-five minutes before one of the modern-day storm troopers came to get me. He yanked the tarp off, grabbed me roughly by the arm and removed my handcuffs. Then without a word he marched me up stairs and into a dark study, paneled in mahogany. The only light on in the room was a green-shaded banker's lamp. A man in an expensive three-piece suit sat at the desk, the light coming through the green shade reflected up onto his face, creating a grotesque image. That was appropriate. This was a grotesque man. Senator Kurt Motfeld, grandson of Kurt Schutz, bearing not only the name, but evidently also carrying on Grandpa's murderous tradition.

Another trooper brought the AG's briefcase in and placed it on the desk, in the spotlight thrown by the lamp.

Motfeld stood, towering over me at a good six foot four inches. Where did he get his height? Kurt had been too short to qualify for the SS. Motfeld, on the other hand, was broad shouldered, muscular, and trim. His blond hair was graying at the temples but wasn't showing any sign of receding. He stared at me for several seconds.

Finally he spoke. "Well, little Diana Hunter. You are a disappointment. I expected much more of someone with your mythical namesake and legendary uncle." His was the deep powerful voice I had heard upon arrival.

I could understand why he might not be too impressed at the moment. I was weak and bedraggled, and I reeked. But in truth, I had to admit it was more than that.

There is an aura that radiates from powerful people. I can't explain it. I can point to the obvious physical expressions of it, the way they hold themselves, the voice tone and quality, the expense of their clothing and other outward trappings of wealth and power. But if you strip that all away, there is still a clear distinction between them and ordinary mortals. Power, along with love, hate, fear, evil, and good, emanates not from the clothing or the voice or the eyes or stature, but from the soul itself. If a person has a good sixth sense about people, it is this expression of the soul that they sense.

It was power, unfettered by any restraint of morality, that I sensed as I stood looking up at Senator Motfeld.

He, on the other hand, could readily see that I am not a person of power. I don't like wielding power, and I don't like having someone wield it over me. I don't even like being part of a society in which power is a common aphrodisiac. He would sense this in me, and it would make me insignificant by his standards.

Neither, however, am I intimidated by power. I live my life in a way that allows me to simply fly solo, not depending on the pack, not kowtowing to the leader, not finding my position by dominating others. This he would not understand.

"Well, Senator, you are exactly what I expected, and that too is disappointing."

"God, you stink. Sit on the floor."

I sat on the nicest overstuffed chair in the room. "As to my perfume of the day, I can thank you and your *sturmabteilung* for that."

He glowered at my use of the German word for "Storm Trooper." His eyes contracted in anger, but he controlled it, not allowing an insignificant thing like me to bait him.

"Now I'll have to dispose of that chair when I dispose of your body," he said. "You're going to find, little girl, that it wasn't wise to play with big boys." He sat down at his desk and put on a pair of reading glasses. "Let's see now what Uncle

Bennett's famous file has in it."

He pulled the files from the envelope and studied the address a moment. Then he began to read the first Schutz file. He didn't just scan. He carefully read each page, both English and German. He read rapidly, using his finger to lead his eyes quickly down the page, as if he had taken and mastered a speed-reading course. He finished the first file and turned to the second. Again he read every page.

I studied his face, looking for reactions. Which file would hit him hardest? What did he think of his grandfather? Through the reading, he gave away nothing. It was when he reached the final page that he registered confusion, even disappointment. He turned over the pages and looked on the backs of the sheets for more. He went back to the first file and searched it for anything missed. Then he looked inside the envelope and the briefcase.

"This is all?" He had mumbled it, talking to himself as if I was not there.

"All? Jesus, your grandfather was the leader of murder squads. He killed thousands. Isn't that enough?"

He put the file down on the desk and looked at me with something almost approaching a smile. There was no doubt in my mind: He was relieved with what he had found or, rather, with what he hadn't found. Son of a gun. He thought I had something much worse. What the hell could have been worse? What else would I have found if I had continued on Bennett's European scavenger hunt?

"Yes," he answered almost joyfully. "Terrible old Nazi that he was." He pulled open a door in the credenza behind his desk and pulled out a paper shredder. "But of course no one will ever read this file."

"I wouldn't do that if I were you."

"You're not me."

"Senator, I'm warning you, that file has already been read, not just by me." With a sneer, he picked up the first page and turned on the shredder.

Raising my voice to be heard over the noise of the shredder, I said, "You know who your men knocked out at the safe house today, Senator? The tall man in the gray suit wasn't a court clerk or guard. That was the Attorney General of the State of North Carolina."

That got his attention. The page hovered over the shredder as he considered my statement. "You're lying."

I shook my head. "Nope. You want to know what he was doing there?"

He looked at me without answering, so I took that for a yes.

"He was returning the file after using it in Washington D.C. You see, the Attorney General has been privy to that file and to all the evidence in the case against Hedgeman and Blain. He has used that evidence to have the federal warrant against me vacated. By the time you and your boys grabbed me, that warrant you had in your pocket was a worthless piece of paper."

He didn't turn off the shredder but replaced the piece of paper on top of the pile and studied me.

"If you still think I'm lying, make a call. Check the status of the warrant. Hedgeman is claiming that you sent him to Otto Brehm's office to retrieve that file on your grandfather so you could spare yourself bad political publicity. If you destroy that file, it will verify his story."

"But if you're dead and the file's gone, I'm afraid no one will ever know."

"Oh, I'm afraid they will." I unzipped the pocket of my pants and pulled out my computer. "Technology is amazing. Take this little gadget here, for instance. It's a computer, a phone, a camera, and even makes videos. You've been on the air live all the time we've been talking." As I held it up a red LED light winked at me mockingly, telling me I was lying. With each wink it whispered, "dead battery, dead battery." If the Senator saw that, it would mean dead Diana.

For the first time Motfeld looked shaken. Then his face began to change. His skin became bright red, the flesh around his eyes and cheeks puffed as the blood rushed to his face. The anger inside this man had transformed him from handsome and debonair to frightening and monstrous. He may have gotten his build from someone else, but he must have taken his temper from Kurt Schutz. He stood, knocking over the shredder then kicking it halfway across the room. As the electric cord yanked out of the socket, the machine sputtered to a stop and the room was utterly silent. Motfeld let out a guttural, primal yell, then as he lunged toward me, he screamed, "You fucking bitch!"

I jumped from the chair and got behind it. He swung at me over the chair. I ducked and the blow swept above my head, throwing him off balance. He half fell and half reached for the arms of the chair, picking it up and tossing it across the room with such power and fury that it flew into a curio cabinet, shattering the glass and knocking the cabinet to the floor with a thunderous crash. As rewards, plaques, and pictures spewed across the floor, I moved to put a heavy oak work table between me and Motfeld. I was no match for his physical strength if he was sane, and in this rage, if he got his hands on me he could break me in pieces.

I had dropped the computer when I took refuge behind the chair. There it lay on the floor at his feet, its little red LED winking up at him. As he looked down at it, I grasped at a straw.

"That computer has one other neat little feature: a GPS and a homing device. See that little red light? It's been on ever since you tossed me down in that basement, letting people know where I am."

In fury he stomped on the computer, smashing it in pieces like a child throwing a temper tantrum. Then he turned his rage back toward me. I circled the table, trying to keep him at arm's length but knowing the odds were against me. Suddenly he tired of the ring around the rosy game and lunged himself across the table top, grabbing me around the waist as I tried unsuccessfully to dodge him. His body continued to slide, carrying him across the table top, knocking me off balance and backward into the bookcase behind me. As I looked up for something to catch myself on, I spotted a massive bronze bust. Grabbing it as I fell, I brought it down with all my strength on the back of his head. As he slid completely off the table we both fell to the floor, with him landing on top of me crushing my chest and leaving me pinned and breathless. The blow I had landed on his head had incapacitated him long enough for me to shove his two-hundred-pound carcass off and wiggle out from under him but as I tried to crawl away he grabbed my ankles. I landed a solid kick to his nose and pulled away again. As I reached the center of the room he tackled me and brought me to the floor. His large hands reached for my throat as I fought with all my strength to keep him from choking me. I picked up a piece of broken glass from the curio cabinet and stabbed it into his hand. He yelled and took his hands from my neck trying to grab my wrist. In the struggle he grabbed my blouse and ripped it open.

At that moment the door to the study burst open, and one of Motfeld's Storm Troopers stood there, his rifle in hand. He started to speak, but the expression on his face made it clear that he was stunned to silence as he tried to make sense of the scene in front of him.

Blood from the back of Motfeld's head and from his nose ran down his face, which his soldier must have read as battle. Yet I lay with my blouse open, and Motfeld sat straddling me, suggesting another kind of struggle. The soldier stared for a moment, then he regained his purpose and reported, "Senator, we've got intruders. The house is surrounded."

Motfeld sat, mouth open trying to evaluate the situation as the sound of helicopters and men yelling invaded the room.

With a weak and hoarse voice I said, "That will be the Marines to my rescue, Senator. What's it going to be? A firefight and go out in a blaze of glory, or you going to use your mighty power of spin to make yourself the hero of the tale?"

He looked from the soldier to me, then stared into a dark corner of the room as his mind debated the odds. I knew before he did that I had struck the right note to harness his rage. The only weakness in this man of power was arrogance. Arrogance would assure him that he could manipulate this situation and, with guile and spin, control it.

He stood and said to his trooper, "Stand down. They're ours. Pass the word. Stand down."

Epilogue

Fall was threatening to turn into winter, and it was quite cool, but we had been determined to enjoy one last meal outdoors. Bundled in sweaters we sat around the outdoor fire pit sipping our after-dinner brandies and enjoying the soothing music of the waterfall. It was wonderful to be home again, and even more wonderful to really feel that this was home.

The Grand Jury had come in with an indictment, and the Solicitor believed he had a solid case against Blain and Hedgeman. Neither man, however, was talking. They both were going down without implicating Motfeld. If luck was with us they would be in for life, if not, they would be out in a few years with book deals and TV shows.

The good Senator had, unfortunately, done exactly as I suggested and spun this thing so he looked like John Wayne saving America from the bad guys. His treatment of me and the AG was spun as collateral damage in the war on terrorism.

We had managed to get the Kurt Schutz file into the court record, but so far it had gotten surprisingly little play in the press and media. For something that damning to be ignored really made me wonder about freedom of the press.

"What is it, Diana?" Sam was studying my face, and he read me pretty well. "Did that news report upset you? Hedgeman and Blain are going down, and don't give up on the senator yet. The press is beginning to wise up."

I laughed sardonically. "I think two newspapers and NPR are carrying the story. The rest of them are running stories that say 66 percent of the people still think Motfeld is a good and admirable man. Hitler outlawed all opposition papers. Motfeld just has a friendly corporation buy them up."

"Give it time. Just think of what Woodward and Bernstein did with a little hotel burglary. The reporters have only run the first of a series of stories on Motfeld, his father, and his grandfather. With our anonymous help, they've dug up much more, even the questionable sources his father used to finance HICHEMCO. Once they get start following the money, it will lead them to the power."

"Doesn't it bother you just a bit that we have to depend on the press, that Motfeld has so much influence that . . ." I looked at both Sam and Robert James, wondering if they would admit what they knew, wondering if they would reveal one more Bennett secret?

"When I was having my little tête-à-tête with Motfeld, he took time to speed read through the Kurt Schutz file. When he finished, he searched through the file and the envelope looking for something more. There is no doubt in my mind that he was greatly relieved by what he found, or rather didn't find. He expected . . . expected something else to be there. I think you two know what it was. I want you to tell me."

Robert James said, "I don't know with certainty what Motfeld was expecting, but I can make a guess as to the most likely possibility. The material he read is basically ancient history, all that old Nazi stuff."

"Actually I thought it was pretty horrifying myself.

"Yes, it is," said Sam, "but not so secret anymore. It may not be common knowledge, but there have now been Congressional hearings on it and every *gate* since *Watergate* has exposed more of this hidden government.

"The hidden government?"

Sam asked, "Do you remember that I told you the most dangerous part of Bennett's files concerned the use of covert means to control power within our own country?"

"Yes."

"Illegal means in the seizure of power began with black operations in foreign countries in the name of anti-communism, tactics learned from and perfected by the Nazis. Very quickly people began applying the same tactics at home. The first victim we know of was a U.S Senator who had dared to try to regulate oil and finance corporations. A secret meeting of powerful individuals was held, a successor for the Senator was chosen and a campaign planned and financed. The Senator was accused of being a communist. That was in 1946 and was the beginning of the whole McCarthy era. It was a totally successful campaign and completely ruined the Senator. They've had sixty years since then to whittle down our freedoms and consolidate power."

Robert James added., "Motfeld most likely feared the exposure of his and others' covert operations in domestic politics. He was being groomed for the presidency. He was probably relieved to see the file only contained his grandfather's sins, not his own."

That gave me hope. "Maybe some of the other safety deposit boxes would reveal that. I would so love to nail that bastard."

Quietly, Robert James said, "I doubt that you will ever 'nail' him, not in terms of seeing him led away in handcuffs. All you can hope to accomplish is rendering him politically impotent and that you have already done. You should be quite proud of what you have accomplished."

That wasn't what I wanted to hear and I sat glumly staring into the fire place.

Robert James saw my mood and continued. "You know, Diana, you really haven't had the experience yet to clearly see the bigger picture. You're thinking of one man as a villain. Before you can really understand the dynamics of this movement you will need . . .

Sam and I both knew what was coming and we said in unison with Robert James, "to read Bennett's diaries."

I was afraid he would take offence but when Sam and I laughed, he joined us. Then he shrugged and sipped his brandy. For a while the only sound in the night air was the crackling of the fire. Then I said, "So, it sounds like you're telling me there's some major conspiracy going on here."

"Conspiracy is also too limited a way of looking at things," said Robert James. It gives you the idea that there is a finite number of people all with the same plan. It's far more complex and far more dynamic than that. But, yes, there is more to it than Senator Motfeld and our democracy is very much in danger. Your recent experience under the Patriot Act should have alerted you to how fragile our freedoms are. And you, my girl, are not in any position to ride out on a white charger and tilt this windmill. Your uncle gave his whole life to that cause and . . . despite all his efforts, those who would concentrate power in the hands of the few have grown frighteningly strong."

I had gotten my wish. They had told me another Bennett secret. All I could think was, be careful what you wish for. It was frightening and overwhelming.

Sam read my reaction and said. "Well, we don't have to try to solve all the problems of the world tonight or even tomorrow or the next day. Be happy you stopped Motfeld. You're a wealthy woman now. You could chose any life you want. You don't have to lock yourself into your uncle's cave."

Robert James shivered and pulled his sweater tighter around him. "It's getting cold out here. Think I'll clear away the dishes and tuck myself into a warm bed."

Sam rose with Robert James and looked back at me. "Come on kiddo, let's hit the hay."

"I'll join you in a just a little bit. Guess I need a little think time."

Sitting on the terrace looking at the stars, listening to the night sounds, I took deep breaths of cold night air, trying to clear my mind of the chaotic thoughts and fears. I tried to visualize my future, both what it was likely to be and what I wanted it to be. From the many paths open to me now with Bennett's fortune I tried to chose one, but no matter where else I tried to look, my thoughts and my eyes were constantly drawn to the dark little path, lighted only by Bennett's solar lights, leading past the waterfall, down into Bennett's Cave.

The End

Joan Francis is a licensed private investigator and owner of Francis Pacific Investigations. She has also worked as a newspaper reporter and is the author of a previous Diana Hunter mystery, *Old Poison*. She spent her childhood in small mining towns and camps in the western United States and in South America with her family and mining engineer father. Moving from place to place as her father opened up new mine sites, she attended fifteen schools before graduating with a B.A. in history from the University of Washington in Seattle. Married with three grown children, she and her husband now live in a secluded valley of the Tehachapi Mountains.

www.ingramcontent.com/pod-product-compliance
Lightning Source LLC
Chambersburg PA
CBHW020332180626
46812CB00001B/163